Silver Guard

Silver Guard

Master of Games Saga
Book I

R. A. Hayden

Cover Design by Alexandrea Abbott

Library of Congress Control Number:		2015914841
ISBN:	Hardcover	978-1-5144-0637-3
	Softcover	978-1-5144-0636-6
	eBook	978-1-5144-0635-9

Print information available on the last page.

Rev. date: 11/10/2015

To order additional copies of this book, contact:
Xlibris
1-888-795-4274
www.Xlibris.com
Orders@Xlibris.com
724527

CONTENTS

Part III—Battle

Ages

1st Age: Age of Dragons—0 to 3023 A.D.

The often referred to known ages of the continent of Drilain on the planet Unarhi begins with an era marked largely by oppression for most races under the rule of chromatic dragons. The largest and strongest of the dragon lords, known as the Ancient Dragon Kings, ruled for over three thousand years. There were three chromatic cousins who ruled without reprisal or fear from one another as they collaborated with one another, which helped to maintain their positions as rulers for so long a period. Largest and strongest of the three chromatics, was Junraz the Red. His lands extended from the very northern most reaches of the Ashen Mountains to Prurst Peaks in the south and the east coast of Drilain to the Sranihn Mountains. West of his lands and ruling the northwest corner of the continent was Baltus the Black. His lands consisted of the entirety of the northwest corner of Drilain to the shores of the Strymn Sea. There his reign ended for Ariadne the Blue ruled the Strymn Sea and the Broken Grasslands to the south and as far west as the Qoros Ocean. The Age of Dragons came to an end with the killing of Junraz the Red. As he was the strongest of the three chromatic ancients it was he who was the last to fall at the talons of Talroomat the Gold, the gold metallic dragon general who lead the charge against his chromatic cousins. A great battle that lasted for weeks erupted over and in the mountains of what is now referred to as the Ashen Fields. Once a fertile land in the center of what is now dead forests, covered in the constant flow of soot and ash that has been falling from Primordial Peaks in the lands center. The end of their great battle came with the two dragon leaders falling to their deaths above the Primordial Peaks, each crash landing on an opposing peak. Their falls ended with the eruption of the peaks and ever since that time a continuous flow of lava and ash has been spewing forth, mixing with the circular air currents above the surrounding mountains thus keeping the entire area covered in perpetual darkness. Legend says that the souls of the mighty combatants wage war to this day beneath the mountains; forever locked in combat hence the reason the Primordial Peaks still flow to this day.

2nd Age: Age of Enlightenment—0 to 1575 A.E.

The end of the Age of Dragons did not see an end to war on the continent of Drilain but instead marked the beginning of centuries more of wars between the various races fighting for supremacy. It was however in this time that wise elven scholars were able to make the current calendar system, still used to this day, even dating it back, through arduous work, to mark the beginning of the first age. It was also during this time that great wizards and clerics rose up and expanded their powers beyond that which they held in the past. Great schools of learning were erected to aid wizards and clerics in surmounting their considerable power. Throughout the many centuries of war that waged on, it was humans who became perhaps the most dominant race. Several kingdoms under the rule of humans sprang up, including Casta, which would become the most dominant kingdom. To do so the humans, aided considerably by the many wizards and clerics among them, put down kingdoms controlled by orcs, goblins, liches, and even the metallic dragons that came to the aid of all races to end the Age of Dragons. At the very height of their power, Casta was thrust into a war with a new enemy. The first vampire, Braden Aranor, appeared amidst the ranks of wizards that called Casta home. In Hareth Academy, the school of wizards on Creet Island just off of the coast of their capital, Braden Aranor discovered vampirism. His discovery of a new form of undead was seen as a betrayal to mankind and the many races that despised necromancy. After trying unsuccessfully to end the existence of Braden Aranor, he thrust a war upon Casta and most of the continent. It was the biggest war seen since the Age of Dragons. This war would come to be known as The Hundred Year War. For one hundred years to the day, Braden Aranor's forces ransacked, murdered, and destroyed all human kingdoms east of The Talt Mountains. Even aided by the mountain dwarves and their considerable forces, Casta fell, castle-by-castle, city-by-city, until there was nothing left except for Creet Island. When all seemed lost and the defenders at Hareth Academy stood against the ranks of Braden Aranor appearing on their shores, Braden Aranor declared and end to the war and dismissed himself from the battlefield, leaving the many lords and generals he had put in place to fend for themselves. It was on this day that the scholars decided to mark the end of the Age of Enlightenment.

3rd Age: Age of Kingdoms - 0 to present A.K.

The end of the Hundred Year War fostered knew hope for the many races fighting against Braden Aranor's former forces. With the vampires he had created taking leave of the many fronts to the war, slowly the humans and their allies took back their territories and the old kingdoms saw new light and hope for their futures. Despite this new hope the many kingdoms on Drilain still war with one another to this day but Casta has emerged as the powerhouse it once was and the kings that have followed in line and control Casta have vowed to never take up arms against Braden Aranor and the Vampire Nation in the form of open battle at least, under threat of a return of his forces. That was over a thousand years ago.

Map of the Continent
Drilain on Unarhi

PROLOGUE

To my successor,

Inevitably, as an immortal you are going to feel like the passage of time is perhaps your most devastating enemy. The simple task of watching history pass you by like a historian flipping the page of his latest tome, as you watch from the shadows has brought the end to more of our race than many other threats. This of course makes us not truly immortal for we are capable of a true death. While time alone will never kill us, since we do not age, it is the precursor to which we may find our end. Whether it is by your own hand or as a direct result from the flagrant disregard for our laws concerning how one should conduct oneself for the preservation of our race as a whole.

Perhaps it is the fact that we were all once human. Humans are often self-destructive which is odd concerning they are not on this world for a long time as it is. As humans go they are not even close to being among the long-lived races of Unarhi. The normal lifespan of a human on Unarhi is between sixty and seventy years. Few humans reach past these years although there are many exceptions, as you will find for magic has aided many in extending their lifespans. Sadly if you were able to calculate the typical lifespan of our race you would probably also find that our average lifespan, once making the turn, is probably the same as a humans. An interesting conundrum for sure and one I have thought on many times.

In regard to humans being self-destructive I have personally witnessed humans over the centuries that have brought more destruction on their own race than any other race in comparison. This may give some insight as to why so many of our kind find their end so early. However, do not despair, for they are also capable of the most honorable deeds I have ever witnessed as well. This is perhaps why I've chosen to share my thoughts of a particular group of humans who I have watched for many centuries but let me not get ahead of myself.

Time, as I was saying, can be devastating for a vampire. How to pass the time when you know it is virtually without limits is the ultimate question. Even the thought of something so vast has brought many of our brothers and sisters to an early end, as they do not have the will to contemplate something so much larger than themselves. That could be something engrained into us from our human past but as the very first vampire and founder of our race I have found many ways to deal with the boredom and tediousness of day-to-day life.

Once you pass into your new life as a vampire, which I assure you is not a sure thing for many human vessels are not capable of handling the magic contained within our blood that grants us our existence, your first task will be to undergo the arduous task of being able to control your thirst for human blood. Mind you I said control and not lack there of. It is essential that you feed regularly and the most exhilarating and wonderful of experiences. I will never forget my first feeding and the power I felt that came along with it. It must however, be done discreetly if you are not within the lands of our nation or likewise safe location. Drawing attention to our kind puts us all at risk and the penalty for doing so can be severe, even death. If you are at war such things can be disregarded but we can talk about that some other time.

Once you have regained conscious control over all of your actions once more your worldview will change entirely. At first you will become consumed with the powers granted to us by our blood. It is not always the same for all vampires but most of us are granted strength easily equal to ten human men, increased reflexes, the ability to see in pure darkness, control over particular animals as well as the undead, and most share the ability of mind control over weak willed individuals. This is perhaps your most formidable tool as to being discreet while hunting for your next meal. Leaving a trail of bodies in your wake is unwise and despite our many strengths, a good hunter can take you down if you are unaware of their pursuit. Feeding on a willing victim, while not always the most fun, is easier and one not need to be killed if left with no memory of the incident. This will also provide ample opportunity for more than one meal with each victim.

After those skills are mastered you will have to find what truly makes you happy. This is where it gets tricky. While we have always been the sorts to fully enjoy the ecstasy that comes along with our powers and the advantages we share over the mortals, it does become tiresome and simply living for your next meal will not be enough.

Many vampires turn to the interests they had while still human especially those capable of wielding magic. As a sorcerer myself I retained that gift once turning to vampirism. With my long years and increased capacity for stamina and intelligence I have broken most all barriers that stand in the way of other

R. A. HAYDEN

races in my search for new magic and ultimate dominance over the spells I use. That is not to say I don't have rivals or that I've mastered everything. We are not the only immortals in the world or even on the continent of Drilain and many of the long-lived races such as elves and dragons wield incredible power. Surprisingly human wizards and sorcerers, even with their short years, count themselves among the most powerful magic wielders in the world as well.

There is of course personal conquest, which many vampires have taken a liking to. Controlling your own territory or kingdom can be enlightening. Wars have been waged over the simple need of our kind to not be bored. I have to admit that I have taken up this course early in my life. Like many things though it loses its appeal, at least for me. The constant governing of your own lands can become tiresome, not to mention you draw great attention to yourself in the form of enemies. Vampires are not tolerated by the so-called good races of Unarhi and other enemies such as liches, who we have a longstanding battle for supremacy over title of the ultimate undead beings, can be drawn to you for confrontation.

Alas I have found that the most rewarding way to pass the time is taking pride in the accomplishments of others. This may sound ridiculous to you at first but I surely don't mean just sitting idly by watching the world from afar. I certainly don't mean just watching the accomplishments of our brothers and sisters either.

We live on the continent of Drilain, perhaps the most diverse continent in terms of other races, in all of Unarhi, and rife with confrontation. While the other continents have distractions worth watching and managing, as well as the lower planes, I have found that I am most content watching over the concerns and battles right here in our own back yard. After all this is the birthplace of our race.

For more than a millennium I have watched the destruction and rebirth of many nations on Drilain. Many under my own terms and wars I have brought to bear upon opposing forces. Most of those were happening simultaneously. I refer to these events and others as my own personal games. At any given time I personally manage a dozen or so games. Sometimes I'm in the forefront of the confrontation but mostly from behind the scenes while other times, I am merely an observer.

Being able to veer a situation one way or another without anyone being the wiser takes a lot of practice. Even as practiced as I am, sometimes things arise that are unforeseen. This is when it becomes most exciting. A player of any particular game might surprise you or unforeseen players may emerge and insert themselves in a game, unraveling everything your quarry has worked towards.

One such game I wish to share with you regards perhaps one of my most formidable enemies. We have fought many times but I wish to share with you a certain transition in their outlook of the world and a change in their ranks. While I am still at odds with this pair of humans and the mercenary band they control, we have come to somewhat of an understanding of live and let live. More on their part than mine for I have found entertainment in watching them from their beginning and would indeed feel a sense of loss if these valuable players were no longer of this world. They however refuse to see themselves as players in a wider game and concentrate solely on their own ambitions.

Many times I have even offered them to join my ranks and join me in being an even bigger player of the endless games throughout our world. However, they do not share my philosophies or outlook on the world and past confrontations with them have led to them wishing for my true death at the hands of any capable since they were not up to the task. Perhaps it will be different with their newest members.

In hearing this turn in their story and keep in mind I was not there for all of it, for I manage many games, I hope you will come to appreciate the delight that can come from watching others in their endless struggles. I hope as well that you can even take pleasure in your enemies, whether past or present, glories. Especially those who hold some code of honor, even if this code is not your own, in their dealings with the world.

—Braden Aranor

R. A. HAYDEN

PART I

Tribulations

CHAPTER ONE

The Widow—Selmeril, 1014

S ITTING AT HER dining table, Cecilia Alio, wiped another tear from her eye as she sat in the lowlight of the kitchen area looking across the table to the empty seat across from her, that she so wished was occupied. It was well after midnight and Cecilia had come to the kitchen to boil some water for tea, hoping it would calm her sore throat and ease her unstill nerves. It had been a week since the passing of her husband and not a night has passed that she has not found herself doing the same. Sleep would not come to the widow for more than a couple hours at a time since his passing. Constantly waking with a start from dreaming of the day when she found her husbands' body lying blood soaked and warm under the midday sun, some two hundred yards away from their house. Despite her own sadness at his loss she also imagined the horror he must have been feeling at the time of his brutal end. She played it over and over in her head each day and was doing so again as she drifted of to sleep:

Jon Alio had gone about his business of starting the days' work on their small farm like he had been doing ever since Cecilia and he had bought this land and settled in Lanos, a small but prosperous town located at the northern most part of territory in the Castan Kingdom. Jon had previously been a soldier and served in the Lanos Outpost where he met Cecilia who was working as a serving girl in one of the local taverns. After his tour of duty in the Castan Infantry he opted to not re-sign for another tour of duty and instead used every bit of coin he had saved and bought a small piece of farmland on the outskirts of Lanos. He took Cecilia as his wife and together they had started their new lives on their small farm.

Jon worked arduously on their little speck of land. Being that it was just the two of them, most of the hard labor fell to Jon, which he enjoyed. A tireless worker, Jon was proud of himself for having tilled most of their land before the first week of Selmeril. Selmeril marks the first month of spring and other farm, even those with hired hands, usually didn't start tilling until the first week. Having had a mild winter, Jon took advantage and had a great start to the season. He brimmed with excitement as he thought about how he would brag to all the naysayers, mostly his old infantry pals who were still stationed at Lanos Outpost, when he was the first to have his ground seeded.

Shortly before he was to take his midday meal with his wife, Jon came across a patch of ground that look disturbed. He pulled the reigns to stop his mule alongside the ground and leaned down to take a closer look. Suddenly the mule snorted and tried to pull away. Jon tugged hard on the reigns and yelled, "Whoa, easy girl!" The ground next to Jon seemed to come alive as a bulette punched through the soft surface sending dirt and debris every which way.

Jon would surely have died right there and then as the bulette reached it's massive jaw toward him, had the mule not pulled with all of her might trying to run from the vicious predator. Jon having the reigns wrapped around his writs and hands lurched forward landing face down in the dirt and was dragged but not for any great distance. The mule was pulling as hard and fast as she could and was initially gaining ground on the bulette that now followed. That is until the plow began digging into harder ground. She pulled with everything she had but that was not enough and within seconds the bulette had its jaws clamped around the back of her neck and pushed her down to the ground.

Jon rubbed the dirt and mud from his face to clear his vision so he could survey the scene. He had heard his mule's horrible death throws and the horrific sound of bones crunching under the bite delivered from the bulette. He lifted his head and looked over the plough. There on top of his barely wining mule was the bulette, still clamped around her neck and using the weight of its entire body to hold her down.

This beast was massive, easily twice the size of his poor mule. It looked to Jon as though a walking piece of armored rock had slaughtered his mule with no real effort. Jon was desperate to get away from the scene. He began extricating his left hand, which was still caught in the taught reigns. He was desperate to get help. To rally men to kill this creature that didn't belong *here. He had heard of bulettes before and had heard first hand accounts of men who had fought them. They had often called them landsharks and had detailed encounters with them, describing them as the most brutal of fights that the seasoned soldiers had ever been through. But what was one doing here? They were known to frequent the Broken Grasslands but that was hundreds of miles away.*

The bulette loosed his grip and lifted his head. Jon could see a massive row of teeth dripping with blood and pieces of torn flesh and hair. Still looking down at its kill it seemed to have forgotten about him. He finally slipped his hand of the now knotted leather strap that had hung on so tightly to his wrist. Careful not to make a sound and draw attention to himself he began to turn and rise. He planned to make a full out sprint back to the safety of his house so he could grab his darling wife and keep running straight for town.

Behind him now he heard movement. He chanced a glance only to see the bulette move off of the mule and move towards him slowly with its front shoulders hunched down and eyes intent on its next victim. Before a second thought Jon jumped to his feet and began running, or tried to. His right leg would not take his full weight and he only then realized that there was aching coming from his right knee where it had skipped off of a rock during his drag through the field. Adrenaline, fear and a longing to get away had him miss that now obvious pain that was hindering his escape.

No looking back now as he pushed on with the bulette on his heels. He thought to scream, to warn Cecilia, to make any desperate attempt for help and that fleeting thought was trampled under the weight of a massive bite encompassing his face, throat, and shoulder.

Cecilia woke with a start as the kettle whistled its high pitch scream signaling that it was ready. She had dozed off while sitting at the table staring at the orange embers emanating from the hearth across the living area, behind the empty chair opposite her. Fresh memories of the short dream she had filled her with a deep sadness as she recalled them and berated herself for not having gone out in the field with her beloved husband that day. The kettle's sound eventually took her from her reverie and she screamed at it, "Alright, I'm coming! Can't I get a moments peace?"

She rose from her seat and pulled her shawl around her shoulders more tightly. The house had grown cold despite the heat from the stove and the fireplace across the way. There was a storm approaching and she could just hear the resounding sound of thunder in the distance. She reminded herself to throw some more logs on the fire after she had set her cup to cool. Grabbing her favorite tea cup set in the open cubby hung on the wall she stretched out her pointer finger to touch the larger mug reserved for her husband, sitting next to hers.

The feel of rough ceramic was comforting and for the briefest of time she was having a thought of happier days sitting around the table. After setting her cup on the hot stove and retrieving some tea leaves from the jar on the counter and placing them in her cup, did she finally lift the kettle and stop the horrendous noise it was making and pour the hot water into her cup. The aroma was settling and she wafted it towards her nose as she turned to walk to the table but a sudden voice filled the air, startling her. The cup fell from her grasp and crashed on the ground. She gave out a brief scream as she cupped her mouth. Scanning the room she saw nothing but the orange embers in the fire. The only other light was a candle she had lit earlier and was now sitting on the counter behind her, casting her shadow into the already dark living area beyond the kitchen.

Breaths could not come fast enough. She thought she might have imagined it. Perhaps it was the thunder or wind pushing open a window in her bedroom.

"I said where is mine?" A dark robed figure said as he stepped in front of the orange glow coming from the fire. His voice like none other she had heard before.

Cecilia screamed again, this time without any delusions of where the sound was coming from. Looking at this dark figure she was suddenly awash with the most awful feeling of hopelessness and fear she had ever experienced. She stepped backwards into the stove burning her right hand. Reflexively turning she dislodged several items from the counter onto the floor. The jar containing the tealeaves among them fell and broke, spilling its contents onto the floor.

"I surely hope that was not all the tea you had." The dark robed figure said with the slightest chuckle deep in his voice. He was obviously enjoying the scene.

R. A. HAYDEN

Cecilia tried to go for the window to her left though it would not have done her any good unless she crashed through it for it did not open but she never even made it that far for the option. Though only a few steps for her and more than twice that distance for the intruder, he was on her in a flash. Grabbing her by the throat and lifting her with one arm well above his head then casually walking back to the table where he slammed her down, taking the wind from her and all notions of screaming again or of making any sounds other than those of someone trying to regain their breath.

Cecilia looked up, finally able to see the face of whomever this was for his hood had pulled back slightly in the brief struggle and the candles' light illuminated most of his face. What she saw confused and scared her all at once. Her eyes had never beheld such a creature before. It wasn't human though it had the same facial structure. Its skin was pale and white hair could be seen under his hood. Whiter hair than she had ever seen before but nothing was more confounding than this ones' eyes. Even with only the flickering light from her candle she could see they were black as night. Set against his pale white skin and whiter hair they appeared darker than even the hood covering the top of his head.

"One more time, my little beauty. Do you have any more tea?" He said while pulling her by the throat back to a seated position and putting her face within an inch of his.

The casual yet obviously forceful way in which he did this perplexed Cecilia even more. That along with his strange appearance and horrid breath now hot upon her nose had her reeling and dumbfounded with how to respond. She was grabbing at his hand around her throat though any try at prying it loose soon fell away as he squeezed a little tighter when she tried and a slight smirk rose on his right cheek. Finally she squeaked out a short, "Yes."

Without warning he released her and she fell from the table to the floor among the broken glassware. She grabbed for her throat and took in huge gasps of air while the intruder walked to the other end of the table, pulled out her husbands' chair, sat, put his elbows on the table and crisscrossed his fingers in front of his chin.

With a satisfied grin he began, "Now lets begin again. I require a cup of that delicious smelling tea you were brewing. And it had better not be from what remains on the ground. Any more delay and I will have to get serious." With that last sentence his voice seemed even stranger as it became inexplicably louder and more grating.

"What do you want?"

"I told you little beauty. I want a cup of tea. Do make it quick. My patience grows thin."

Sobbing and attempting to extricate herself from the broken glass on the ground without cutting herself further, she could think of no other action. She crawled on hands and knees to the cupboard, opened it and pulled forth a larger jar matching in color and shape to the broken one strewed upon the ground and placed it on the counter top. Then pulled herself to her feet and grabbed a cup.

"Not that one my dear. I'm rather thirsty. Do grab the larger mug there." He said while pointing out his right pointer finger though Cecilia could not see the move.

Hands trembling she grabbed for her husbands' mug hesitantly. Tears flowing and sobs emanating from her little body, she suddenly stiffened and took in a deep breath to steady herself. She must have courage. What would Jon do she thought? He would fight. An idea came to mind. She finished putting in the tealeaves and went for the kettle albeit slowly, all the while keeping focus on the task and avoiding the penetrating gaze coming from her attacker. She filled the mug with the steaming hot water. She planned to throw it right in his face and bolt for the door. It would work. She could get away. Taking in another deep breath she turned towards the table and all hopes dashed away. Startled again and almost dropping the mug she gave out a little shriek.

"Please my dear, do not drop my tea." The intruder said while glancing over his shoulder to his companion who now stood back and to his left. "I do not believe my companion wants any. He hasn't the taste for such human luxuries. Besides you are quickly running out of cups."

Now standing in the archway between the kitchen and the living area was another of this one's ilk. She thought he matches the description of an elf although she had never heard of them having white hair and pale skin. This one was slightly shorter than the first but had the same white flowing hair. He was not wearing a cloak or hood of any kind like the other but instead was wearing some fabulous looking armor the likes of which Cecilia had never seen before either. On his right hip he wore a sword. The plan to get away was dashed to pieces. Even though this newcomers hand was heavily bandaged as well as the right side of his face she doubted she could simply run past him after heaving the mug at her attacker. One slash of the sword is all it would take. The unending stare coming from this ones' dark eyes trimmed in red told her immediately that he was not to be trifled with.

"Do bring that to me." He pointed at the table where she was to put the mug and from the look on his face that had better be exactly what she does with it.

Cecilia couldn't help but wonder if he somehow read her every thought. She slowly walked over and placed it on the table. Her hands still trembled and fresh tears were starting to form. The intruder grabbed the mug and hoisted it to his lips. Without even letting it cool he took a long drink, smiled and placed it back on the table.

Turning his head to the other he said in drow, which Cecilia did not recognize, *"Beautiful and can make a good cup of tea."* Turning back to Cecilia he added in the common tongue, "Sit down little beauty."

Cecilia walked around the table and pulled her chair back to the seated position in which it normally sat and took a seat. She wanted to be as far from them as possible. She wanted to run. She wanted to scream. She wanted her husband most of all.

The latest intruder began speaking again in the language Cecilia could not understand, *"Why do we waste time? This accomplishes nothing."*

"This accomplishes plenty my friend. It's not often I'm away."

"We need to attack now. Our forces are in place and I want my vengeance."

As if not fully listening to his companion the intruder stared long and hard at Cecilia while taking another sip of his tea then added, *"Have you ever seen a more beautiful human? Small for a human woman wouldn't you say? Yet full figured, not slight like most starving slaves we so often see."*

"I'm not interested in your new pet."

With that came the most horrific sounding low growl that Cecilia had ever heard emanating from her attacker. Without even turning his head or making any vocal comment the second intruder backed up a step. Obviously he had said something to anger this one. There conversation started again while Cecilia rocked uncomfortably in her seat. She could only hope they would come to blows.

"We would not be here young Brosa of Drae if it were not for your incompetence. Still I enjoy the distraction. However, raise that tone with me again and you will no longer be my favorite assassin. You will be a dead one." He said in an even tone as far as Cecilia could tell.

"He was Silver Guard and his father, your old friend Josef Righe was there to help him." Brosa protested.

Righe. Now there was a word Cecilia recognized. Josef and Oran Righe ran The Silver Guard. Although she knew those two were not at their Keep at the present time because they were away with other members of The Silver Guard when the townsfolk and soldiers stationed there went to them to ask for assistance in slaying the bulette which had come to stake out territory in their land. Other members were there though and did indeed slay the bulette who had so savagely taken her husband away from her. The Silver Guard Keep was not far from her house. A slight glimmer of hope returned. Perhaps these two meant to engage The Silver Guard. Despite her obvious perilous situation she could hope that The Silver Guard could be near. They are after all the finest warriors in all these lands and watch over the entire area. The conversation started again bringing her from her thoughts.

"That perhaps is the only redeeming part of this entire situation. I do owe this Silver Guard a debt of gratitude for past transgressions. They have long been a thorn in the side of many for centuries."

Turning the conversation back to Cecilia her attacker asked, "Tell me little beauty, what can you tell me about The Silver Guard?"

Cecilia as defiant as she could said, "Nothing."

"Now, now lets not make this difficult."

"I don't know anything."

With that the attacker put out and outstretched hand and uttered a word Cecilia didn't know and she flew backwards out of the chair and into the hot stove. The stove burned her skin through her clothing even though she was only against it for an instant. Then with a wave of his hand to the left, she slammed against the adjacent wall and crumpled to the floor.

The attacker got up from his seated position and slowly advanced around the left side of the table towards Cecilia. He grabbed her by the back of the neck and with ease lifted her off the ground only to slam her once again back onto the table, knocking his mug over in the process.

R. A. HAYDEN

Gasping for breath and lying on her back his words came again sounding unpleased, "Look at that. You made me spill my tea. After all that effort to get a cup I won't be able to enjoy the last of it."

When he finished his sentence he grabbed her by the throat and lifted her to a seated position on the table again. Desperation for breath had her attacking his grip but he squeezed even harder. She went slack in his arm and he released enough for her to breath.

"Now it seems I will have to find something else to enjoy."

With his other hand he slipped it between her thighs and spread her legs out wide positioning himself in-between them.

"No. Please."

He moved his right hand from her throat to her chin squeezing ever so hard while grabbing her right wrist with his left hand and pinning it to her side. He moved his face right next to hers again, closed his eyes, took a long smell of her, opened his mouth and out came his tongue. His tongue was not what was to be expected. Reptilian like and longer than what should have been possible. He gently licked her face starting on her right cheek and slowly moving upwards. Not seconds later Cecilia began a muffled scream, as she couldn't open her mouth with his hand so forcefully holding it closed but still she tried to. The pain was unbearable. Along the same line of her face that he licked, her skin began to burn like nothing she had ever felt. She thought her face was on fire. A small amount of acrid smoke lifted from her flesh. Smacking at his forearm with her free arm was futile. She began mumbling through pursed lips, "I'll tell you, I'll tell you."

With a satisfied grin he eased his grip on her mouth but did not fully release. The burning sensation subsided slowly. She reached under his arm and tried to touch her cheek but pulled her hand away quickly as the tips of her fingers touched it and began to likewise burn.

"Little beauty, tell me, how many Silver Guard are present in this quaint town of yours?" He asked.

Through mottled cries she answered, "Four I think." As far as the actual Silver Guard she was telling the truth. She neglected to tell him of their servants, Georgette and Harold Lindsey, who prior to taking on the job of housekeeper and groundskeeper ran a small shop in Lanos that unfortunately ran into money issues. It was while they ran this shop that Cecilia had first met the couple for they occasionally frequented the tavern in which she used to work. The two had become friends and Georgette made it a point to keep in touch and visited her on the farm when she had a free afternoon.

"And are the Righes present?"

"No. They haven't been in town for some time."

"And how do you know this?"

"Because they weren't at my husbands' funeral."

"Ah, the reason you are so sad and alone." He said as he pulled away from her and laughed ever so softly. Looking over to his companion he stated in the drow language, "*There you see, they aren't even back yet.*"

Growing impatient Brosa of Drae was not pleased at the news. "*What then?*"

"*You can still have your fun Brosa. Go and kill all at the Keep. Even if there are more than what little beauty claims our forces can handle Righe's little minions. Leave a clear message as to who is responsible. We will wait for a reply, or not. It matters little in the grand scheme of things.*"

"*What about you master?*" Brosa asked as he walked towards the front door.

"*My presence will not be needed. Act quickly. No need to arouse and engage the guards in Lanos. Meet me here when it is done for the return journey. I will leave a message here as well.*"

Brosa of Drae knew exactly what that meant. His master's appetites were insatiable. He gave a crooked smile as he exited the front door for his right side of his face still stung from his previous encounter with the Righes. Behind him, his master, Deathmar the Black slapped Cecilia across the face knocking her to her back once more. Her head spun with an onset of dizziness. Deathmar reached out his right hand and his fingernails elongated into wicked black claws. He tore at her blouse revealing the alluring flesh beneath and pulled himself closer into her thighs.

Cecilia screamed, "No!"

CHAPTER TWO

Silver Guard Keep—Selmeril, 1014

RAIN HAD JUST begun to fall as Brosa of Drae exited the small cottage. The thunder and lightning was not far behind. Flashes from the not so distant lightning intermittently lit up the area providing a brief glimpse of the landscape to most but not so for Brosa of Drae. Being drow he hated light of that magnitude. Although brief he preferred the darkness provided by the clouds that now blocked out the light of the moon and even the small amount shimmering from the stars. The ever-increasing flashes did not deter him from his mission though as he closed the expanse to the small barn situated some thirty yards or so away from the house. As he rounded the corner of the far side of the barn he could hear the sound of a horse inside stamping its feet and neighing, perhaps nervous from the approaching thunder and lightning but it could have been his proximity to the now present drow. On the backside of the barn awaited his fellow drow. Brosa could see a handful of them. Most were dressed like him, in fine armor, although one stood out in flowing black robes with silver inlet on the hems, which even in the dark of night stood out to Brosa and his keen sight in the dark. It was this drow he approached directly to report on the task at hand.

"*Jhaeros, we can now continue without delay.*" Brosa said as he finished his approach.

"*Your familiarity still astonishes me Brosa of Drae.*" Jhaeros Drae replied putting great emphasis on the "of" between the surname and family name.

Brosa squinted his eyes and stared hard at Jhaeros. He knew, all too well the edict concerning the use of the family name when confronting nobility handed down in drow society. Jhaeros, being a direct descendant of the Drae family did not augment his family name with "of" as all soldiers or the like did in service to their house. Actual members of the Drae family were to be treated at all times with the utmost respect and full use of their name or the accompaniment of lord before the name was required. Jhaeros loved to remind him of this, which irritated Brosa to no end. Jhaeros was after all only a nephew of their matron mother. He thought it high time he put a sword through this one's gut, however Brosa was injured and Jhaeros is an accomplished wizard in his own right. Now was not the time for confrontation. Especially considering five other Drae soldiers stood behind Jhaeros and would undoubtedly not take his side.

Instead Brosa thought better of his next action and bowed to the young mage. He added, *"Apologies Jhaeros Drae. My thoughts were elsewhere as I am anxious for battle and thirst for blood."*

"What of our host?" Jhaeros questioned, referring to Deathmar the Black whose employ they were currently serving under.

"He has interrogated the women. Apparently the Righes are not present at their little hovel. He bids us to annihilate the others and return upon completion."

"What of our resistance then?"

"Apparently only a handful." Brosa said as he looked down at his hand fully engulfed in bandages and utterly useless for the impending fight due to his fight with Oran Righe, who only days prior to this night cut off the two small fingers of his right hand while disarming him with his own sword.

"Such a pity. I had hoped to engage this mere human mage with such an ominous reputation." Jhaeros bragged as he slightly raised his voice so the other drow in attendance could clearly hear.

That thought brought a smile to Brosa' face which he quickly removed before Jhaeros could see. He knew well the reputation surrounding Josef Righe and having recently seen the old wizard in action and the quick work he made of his now dead drow cohorts, left him with no doubt that he would make short work of Jhaeros.

Jhaeros Drae added, *"No matter. Let's be off. Our other forces are likely nearing their destination. We don't want to miss all of the fun."*

Brosa protested a bit too loudly for the like of Jhaeros, *"You sent them off?"*

"Mind your tongue. They are not to engage. They are merely positioning. Not all of us are as incompetent as you in your dealings with humans. They are to await final instruction outside of the perimeter. Now shut your mouth." Jhaeros berated then turned and headed out in the darkness, his drow soldiers following close behind.

Brosa let his stare linger after Jhaeros' back once he had turned and began walking. He would have liked nothing more than to end Jhaeros' life. Simply walk up and stab him through the back with his one good arm remaining. Oh how he detested the nobility of drow society. He much preferred to be out in the wilds of the underdark or on errands from his true master, Deathmar the Black, dealing punishment out as he saw fit to whomever he wished.

As he began his trek through the tall grass heading in the direction the others had taken he lamented on how long it would take him to come under good standing with his brethren. No, not good standing he realized but feared as he most often was. He was after all the unnamed champion of the Drae House. He had only to challenge the first sword of House Drae if he so wished to take the title, which most assumed he would. Brosa had delayed such action, not sure if he wanted the responsibility of such a position, not to mention the politics he would have to endure always being within Veszdor, the drow capital located in the underdark under the mountains surrounding the Ashen Fields. Alas, he could not make that challenge now being so handicapped. He would at least have to wait until he was fully healed to weigh the outcome of the use of his now injured hand would allow him. A loud crash of thunder brought him out of those thoughts and he cleared his head. He turned his attention back thinking of the task at hand. Blood would surely flow this night.

The team of drow assassins made quick time to where The Silver Guard Keep was located. It sat about a mile away from the farmhouse they had left, situated a couple hundred yards away from and in sight of the town of Lanos. As they approached a small copse of trees another drow exited the cover of the trees and surrounding brush and approached the group. This one was clad in robes similar to that which Jhaeros was wearing. Brosa recognized him as another of the house mages of Drae though couldn't recall his name. House Drae had many young mages and this one had only recently joined the crew that was under service to Deathmar. He was part of the reinforcements sent after the loss of some of their comrades to Josef and Oran Righe. As he neared, Brosa couldn't help but notice the uneasiness in this ones features. He winced noticeably as another bolt of lightning arched across the dark sky. This was probably his first trip to the surface and he looked absolutely miserable in his rain soaked robes. This was as well his first time experiencing weather conditions on the surface such as rain. Such inconveniences are not present in the underdark.

Jhaeros began questioning him when the young drow stopped in front of the group, not bothering with keeping his voice low or switching to the silent hand gestures that drow often used to communicate when silence was a necessity, which it wasn't now still being far enough away and with the noise of the storm to drown out their voices. *"Report."* Jhaeros ordered as he casually stepped around the young mage to get a better view of their intended target.

"As you see Jhaeros Drae. No defenses save a little fence surrounding the main building. The scouts report no guards posted as well. There are only two entrances to the main building. A set of large double doors in the front entrance and a single door in the rear."

Jhaeros Drae looked on in happy surprise at The Silver Guard Keep. He turned to Brosa, *"This is what we are to attack? This is the home of the supposedly dangerous and infamous Josef Righe? It's not even a Keep. It's just a large house surrounded by a fence."* He turned away from Brosa and added, *"What a pity."*

Brosa tightened the grip he had on his sword hilt still in its scabbard. He looked around to those in attendance and took note of the sly grins worn by a couple of the drow soldiers. That last remark meant to shame him had surely hit the mark but he would remember all who took that note to heart and silently vowed to repay in kind those who thought it funny that he was bested by a couple of humans.

The young mage then added relieving the tension in the air, *"However my lord, it is heavily warded. Attempts at scrying produce no results."*

"Fool." Jhaeros said as he turned back to the young mage and slapped him across the face.

"My lord?" The young mage asked as he took a step back.

R. A. HAYDEN

"*You were not to engage. Merely position. If the proper wards were in place then you in your infinite stupidity could have warned them of our approach.*"

"*No movement has been noted.*" He said trying to sound positive.

"*No matter. We face only a few. You take ten of our brethren and position in the front of the building. I will take our remaining forces and the orcs and begin the assault from the rear. Once that has begun you may begin your attack from the front.*"

Brosa interrupted, "*We are to go in force?*"

"*Something to add Brosa of Drae?*" Jhaeros shot back.

"*Our master discussed discretion. Quick and quite as to not alert the town guard.*"

"*He is not our master Brosa of Drae. You would do well to remember that. He does not speak for the nobility of House Drae. Deathmar should not have even bothered us with the taking down of this shack.*" Jhaeros took in a breath to steady his rising anger and continued; "*Now we do as I say. We will be in and out faster than any pathetic human guards from the town can come to their aid and if not then we will slaughter them as well.*"

With that Jhaeros Drae waved his fellow mage off in the direction towards the front of The Silver Guard Keep while he turned and began walking with men in tow towards the back of the compound. Brosa could not help but smile at the incompetence of Jhaeros and his unimaginable inexperience with surface dwellers. While Brosa believed that drow soldiers were undoubtedly the best fighters in the entire world they would be hard pressed with only twenty in number and a handful of orcs for fodder if the entirety of the Castan soldiers stationed in Lanos descended upon them before they were away. Brosa knew this area well enough to know that the Lanos Outpost boasted at least a hundred men. His true master, Deathmar the Black, would indeed have to descend if that outcome came to pass.

"What is it dear?" Georgette asked as she rolled towards her husbands' side of the bed, awakened by him clamoring about the racket going on outside while trying to locate his second boot in the near complete darkness of their room.

Harold replied, "Damn dogs are on about something."

"Oh its just the storm. You know Lady always makes a racket with thunder about."

"Aye but Walker is making a fuss too. You know that old boy doesn't get excited about anything except food or when something is amiss. Probably just the horses making a fuss from the storm but you never know. I'll go check on 'em and let the dogs in for the night before they wake up the whole house. Go back to sleep my dear. I'll only be a minute."

Harold finished putting on his second boot, turned and leaned down to kiss his wife on the forehead, then walked towards the light coming from under the door jam. He fumbled for the door latch in the dark. Cursing, he finally got the door open and he stepped out into the main hall of Silver Guard Keep.

The scene before him was at it should be. Set in the center of the large room that made up the majority of this level of the Keep, the fire burned brightly not having burnt through the majority of the wood that had been placed into it before he had went to bed. Even if it had the light would still emanate from the central fireplace since at its four corners were small brass braziers that were enchanted with faerie fire, a spell cast by Josef Righe that he had made permanent so that the central living area of their great house was always lit up and the need for a fire in the hot summer months would not be required for a source of light. Harold walked around the perimeter of the central room avoiding the steps that surrounded the room as he walked towards the back door where he could hear the dogs barking.

The main floor was built a couple steps down from the perimeter of the room so that you had to step down to be in the most central part of the Keep. In the very large central chamber were comfortable arm chairs at the corners closest to Harold and Georgettes' room, where the occupants of the Keep could relax and socialize after a days work, hunting some local criminal down or after returning from some campaign or the other which was the usual calling for the Silver Guard. Surrounding the central fireplace was a set of tables placed in a horseshoe pattern, though not rounded but were squared off, around the beautiful stonework of the large hearth. The opening of that horseshoe faced the front double doors leading to the large deck that ran the entire length of the front of the Keep. Opposite those doors was a large door centered on the opposite wall and lead to the back of the Keep and was the most used door for it lead to the back of the property where the Silver Guard had a small training area so as not to get rusty in their skills as well as the most direct route to the stables and the small garden that Georgette attended to and provided much of the sustenance of her very well made meals.

Harold reached the back door and was about to lift the large metal swing latch securing the door and step out to retrieve the dogs when he stopped himself short. Just beyond the door he could still hear Lady barking but he could also hear their other dog, Walker, growling low. He knew Walker never growled at anything that did not mean him harm.

Harold silently worded to himself, "Something's wrong."

Releasing the latch, Harold instead went for the latch on the porthole centered in the door at eye level. Before he could open it, suddenly the dogs, one after the other let out loud yelps. After, he could hear them wining and thrashing about on the deck. The square porthole swung open violently as Harold threw it open. There at the edge of the deck, Walker lay very still without a sound while Lady a few feet away still scampered about trying to bite at the arrow lodged in her rear flank. A second later Harold could see a small flame approaching from the courtyard. It was growing larger as it neared. Having lived among wizards long enough he realized what was happening and grabbed for the porthole door trying to slam it shut. The door heaved as a great explosion sounded just on the opposite side of it sending Harold backwards a couple steps as flames shot through the porthole singing the hair on his hands. Flames also licked at the seams of the door but soon subsided for this door would not cave in so easily. At that very instant torches set along the inner walls flared to life with orange faerie fire. Something Harold had never seen before but knew of, having been told by Josef Righe that their lighting meant danger was near.

Adrenaline took over now. No time for rattled nerves. Harold yelled at the top of his lungs, "Georgette! Georgette! Hurry!"

Already on the move after hearing the explosion Georgette burst into the room. She knew her husband was in trouble. "Harold, are you alright?" She screamed.

"No time wife. Wake the boys now." He said and pointed towards the stairs.

She instantly ran for the stairs in the opposite corner of the room leading downwards to the rooms below while Harold leaped back toward the door. He slammed and latched the porthole closed. Leaning against the stonewall was the doors' heavy bar. He began lifting the solid piece of oak with runes engraved into its surface lengthwise. He knew he had to get it into place. Set and secured into the stone on either side of the door were steel hangers meant to hold the locking bar if he could just lift it into place, which proved difficult. Not because it was overly heavy for Harold was not a slight man nor was he weak as he was constantly working on the grounds of the Keep as well as helping any of the townsfolk who required a bit of help with any kind of physical labor but just as he was sliding the second end into place another blast of energy hit the door and Harold loosed his grip and one end fell to the ground. He backed up a step shielding his eyes from the blue-black light now present at the seams of the door. The barrage lasted for several seconds and upon finishing this strange light show the door still held. The wood and steal seemed to sag a bit as if it were relaxing after taking on whatever it was trying to break its will. Harold again went for the bar.

Gaebald Hogg bolted upright in bed. The explosion upstairs had taken him from his dreams. For a brief time he wondered if it was part of his dream. The old war veteran often had dreams of battlefields from his past and sleep did not always come easy. That notion flew away as muffled screams could be heard coming from upstairs. Not bothering with trying to light a lamp he ran for his door and threw it open to allow light in from the hallway so that he could gather his things. He began shouting orders while he quickly grabbed his pants and sword, "Eric, Rowena, Freemund, upstairs now!"

Gaebald entered the hallway wearing only his pants and nightshirt with sword in hand. Rowena's door, which was opposite his swung open and the half-elf female joined him in the hallway. Somewhat more dressed than he for she managed to adorn her boots and was still wrestling with the studded leather top to her armor set.

Rowena looked at Gaebald and asked, "What's happened?"

Before Gaebald could answer Georgette appeared at the far end of the hall at the bottom of the stairs. She pointed back the way in which she came and yelled, "Harold's in trouble. Something is trying to break in the back door."

They swung into action. The veterans ran towards Georgette. Gaebald began shouting for Freemund and Eric as he went down the hall. As they neared Georgette, Freemund's door opened next to where she stood and the youngster hopped out on one leg while trying to finish putting on his second boot. Without even slowing Gaebald shouted orders to him, "Hurry boy. Grab your weapons."

"What about my armor?"

As the two passed the inexperienced eighteen-year old and took to the stairs Gaebald said, "Forget it. Wake Eric."

Freemund stepped across the hall and pushed open Eric's door. There sitting on the bed rubbing his temples with both hands was Eric Treby. He was still dressed from the night before having arrived back at the Keep late after drinking with many of the Castan soldiers at Willow Bark Tavern. He had raised many of toast the previous night with the soldiers who had accompanied The Silver Guard in the hunt for the bulette which only days prior had slain poor Jon Alio. Having been the one to strike the final blow and drop the beast Eric was drinking free as the other patrons and barkeep bought him many rounds.

Very quietly Eric asked, "What is all the racket?"

Freemund replied. "We are being attacked."

"What? That's ridiculous."

Behind Freemund, Georgette piped in, "No Eric it's true. Harold is in trouble. Please Hurry."

Eric looked to his left and saw the frantic look on Georgette's face. Without another word he reached for his massive warhammer leaning against the small bedside table and stood up hoisting it onto his right shoulder with one arm and headed for the door. He pushed Freemund out of the way with his free hand and stepped into the hall and quickened his pace as he began the ascent up the stairs. If there were any remnants of drink in his system or the onset of an impending hangover the large warrior showed neither. Meanwhile, Freemund ran back into his room and grabbed his longsword and shield and hurried to meet the rest of his companions.

As Freemund reached the top of the stairs, Georgette right behind him, another strong blast struck the back door. The locking bar placed by Harold showed signs of splitting in its center. Harold went to push on the door as though trying to hold it shut. For a brief second the four Silver Guard were taken back and stopped in place but then Gaebald took charge of the scene.

They had to act quick Gaebald knew. Whatever magic could tear at that door had to be powerful indeed. He began shouting orders, "Harold get away from that door now. Take your wife downstairs and lock yourselves away in the safe room."

Harold protested, "I can help."

"You've helped enough. Take your wife and do not open until one of us comes for you. Now get away from that door before you get blasted to bits"

Harold thought to argue but looking beyond Gaebald and seeing his fear stricken wife standing at the top of the stair shook all notions of a reply. He ran to her, took her hand and the two started down the stairs while the four remaining Silver Guard sprung into action. Harold thought, as they descended down the stairs going to the hidden safe room that they could not be in better hands if they meant to survive whatever this was.

Gaebald dropped his sword on the center table surrounding the fireplace and ran towards the weapon rack next to the front double doors where Rowena was already; having slung her quiver of arrows she now picked up her bow. As he got there and reached for one of the crossbows another blast of energy struck. This time the blow was on the front double doors. Gaebald and Rowena dropped their weapons and went for the securing bar next to it. This one much larger than the one for the back seeing how the front doors were twice as wide. The two of them lifted it and slammed it into place. Just as they stepped back another blast sounded on the rear door nearly taking it from its hinges.

"Hurry!" Gaebald shouted.

He went back to the weapon rack and grabbed a bolt quiver and two crossbows then headed back to the center table. He threw them down into a pile next to his sword and picked up the first crossbow and began setting it while giving orders, "Rowena, stay in the northwest corner and cover from there. Freemund get behind me and to my left." He stopped talking and looked over at Eric who was standing at the other end of the table. Eric met his gaze then Gaebald asked, "You still drunk?"

"Yep."

"Good. You do your best fighting that way."

Both smirked at that last remark and Eric slapped his large warhammer down into his left palm. Gaebald was not exaggerating. Indeed he had seen the large man do his best fighting in tavern brawls. The former gladiator often drowned out his sorrows with drink, which eventually led to those fights. Trying to erase the memories of his past and the many lives he took after being forced as a slave into the service of a gladiator training facility. He stood there waiting for his latest opponent. His trusted warhammer in hand, a trinket he kept from his days as a gladiator after winning his freedom. Like the man wielding it, the weapon was most remarkable. On one side was an oversized hammerhead and the opposite was a large spike, which Eric had coated in silver after joining The Silver Guard. It was a symbol for whom he fought for as well as being a formidable weapon against some of their prey such as undead and werewolves.

Just as Gaebald set his second crossbow with a bolt, both doors were hit again. The front double doors held their ground but the back door blew apart sending flaming wood and metal fragments flying in towards the defenders. They tensed not sure what was coming behind it. Gaebald and Rowena leveled their weapons waiting for their first look.

Battle cries erupted through the breach followed by orcs wielding shields and heavy maces or axes. They filed in one after the other or tried to. The first one through was hit square in the forehead by Gaebald's first bolt sending him backwards into the orc behind him. The second pushed him through the doorway then went left to clear way for others behind him. He spotted Eric and ran his direction but was blasted through the throat by an arrow loosed by Rowena. Quickly she had another set and was ready to fire again for she had many more targets now.

Gaebald's second shot hit square against the shield of the third orc that had come through the door and stuck there. He dropped his crossbow and grabbed his sword from the table. That orc rushed towards him and went to bash Gaebald with his shield hoping to send him careening backwards except Gaebald was the quicker and wiser. Recognizing the tactic immediately he feinted accepting the blow then turned rapidly sending the orc past him while simultaneously sticking out his left leg to trip the stupid beast flat onto his face in front of the waiting Freemund who stabbed downwards into the center of the orcs back. His sword pierced right through the orcs armor and severed his spine. Freemund withdrew quickly and sidestepped towards his left wanting to give Gaebald room to swing his bastard sword and to draw them towards him so Gaebald and Eric didn't have to meet all of the on comers.

The fighting was everywhere now. Rowena kept firing trying to score a hit in-between Eric's massive swings with his warhammer. He was keeping them at bay and they were unable to get around him to get at the deadly archer. Even when one accepted a blow on their shield it sent them flying or toppling to the ground under the strength and ferociousness that was Eric Treby.

Out of the corner of her eye Rowena saw the front double doors erupt again in flames at its edges as another explosion hit it. The locking bar splintered in half and the locking bolt broke free. The door swung open slowly. She aimed her next arrow in that direction and waited for another of the orcs to come in and be at Gaebald and Freemund's backs. None came. Instead everything went black.

Rowena was suddenly engulfed in a globe of darkness. She could not see anything. Instinctively she rolled to her right down the two stairs to the floor of the sunken in living area and came back to her feet and ran trying to find the edge of the black. She exited back into the light after only a few steps only to be hit by three separate darts, one dart in her side and two in her left shoulder. She stopped and looked back towards the front doors. Advancing on her now was a drow clad in chainmail covered by thick black leather. Sword drawn, he advanced slowly or seemed to. A wave of dizziness hit her as she back stepped away from the enemy for the drow darts were dipped in a type of poison that put one to sleep.

Half-elf herself she sided with her elf cousins that drow were the most despicable of races. Anger rose and she wanted to kill this drow so badly. She tried to raise her bow arm but instead lost her grip on it and it fell to the ground. Her left arm was now numb and useless as her body succumbed to the poison. Now dizzier then before she saw what looked like two drow advancing on her though it was only one. Beyond him she saw other globes of darkness blink into existence around Gaebald and Eric. She tried to yell but instead sank into unconsciousness and slumped to the floor before any word left her mouth.

Eric had his hammer raised over his head and was about to drive home a killing blow on the skull of the downed orc in front of him when suddenly he couldn't see. Not knowing what was happening he finished the blow and heard the hammer hit home and the crushing noise it made on his enemy. He tried to look around to no avail. Two bolts entered his body, one in his lower back, the other in his left breast. He reached with his left hand feeling for the one in his chest. His hands wrapped around it and he yanked it free. He gave an enormous war cry and leaped forward bringing his warhammer sweeping across his body back and forth while advancing. He exited the globe of darkness and kneeling before him was a drow elf with scimitar in hand that had just ducked under one of his swings. Eric brought his warhammer up high thinking to smash this drow right through the floor.

The drow was the quicker opponent. He leaped up and towards Eric sending his scimitar into his gut. The hammer fell from Eric's grasp and hit the ground behind him with a resounding thud. Slowly his eyes went to the sword protruding from his stomach. Then he looked forward to the swords' wielder who stared back with an evil grin spread across his face. Eric smiled back revealing blood that was now flowing out of his mouth. Seconds ticked by then Eric, with both hands grabbed the drow by the wrist and pulled him closer sending the sword through his back. Quicker than the stunned drow could react Eric's hands went to the drow's face and with all the strength left in his legs pushed forward and down sending both combatants to the ground with him on top. Eric's thumbs found the eye sockets of the drow and pushed inwards. Screams erupted from the drow as his thumbs dug ever deeper into this one's skull. Another drow stepped in and kicked Eric in the head sending him off of his companion. This new drow stepped over his now dead companion and straddled his legs over Eric. Eric spit the blood from his mouth, looked up at the sword trained above him and its wielder, laughed and said, "Cowards." A second later this new drow thrust the sword into Eric's throat.

Freemund was engaged with an orc when the front doors burst open but was facing in that direction so he could see the new threat enter the room. He had never seen a drow before but knew of their description and having been around elves before he knew precisely what they were. He was fighting defensively trying to stave off his latest orc opponent and see the battle unfold. There was already one globe of darkness near the front door and as he looked to Gaebald, who was likewise engaged with an orc, two more appeared; one around Eric and the other around Gaebald and his orc combatant. He had to act quickly. He had to aid his friends. Another orc was approaching so two would soon press him. Before the second could engage he rushed the orc in front of him bashing his shield into his, then as the orc went high with his mace, Freemund dropped low and sliced at the kneecap of the orc. His strike was true and the orc's leg gave way to his weight and he toppled sidelong to the ground. Freemund was there in a flash reversing the grip on his sword and thrusting it down into the orc's chest. As he looked up expecting the other orc to be on top of him he saw a bright flash of orange erupt from a drow's hands near the back door. The ball of orange light and flame entered the globe of darkness that surrounded Gaebald. An explosion rocked the vicinity inside the globe and Gaebald and the orc were sent flying out of the darkness and across the room landing awkwardly against one another on the far wall; both quite dead.

"No!" Freemund screamed.

As the orc approaching Freemund neared its target another voice yelled out in a language that Freemund could not understand, "*Stop!*"

The orc approaching Freemund stopped and began backing from him with shield raised. The robed drow standing near the back entrance said something else he could not understand and the globes of darkness dissipated. Shield and sword still raised, Freemund quickly scanned the room. Gaebald lay dead against the wall to his right, Rowena across the other side of the room appeared dead and had several drow now standing around her, he could not see Eric though knew the area in which he was fighting beyond the central fireplace and was now only occupied by another drow with blood upon his sword and he recalled hearing earlier, just before the fireball had hit Gaebald, him yelling furiously.

R. A. HAYDEN

It hit him squarely; he stood alone against a room full of drow. At least one of which was a wizard. The robed drow turned to the one standing closest to him and began conversing in their strange language. This other drow was wounded on the right side of his face and his right hand was heavily bandaged. While they talked Freemund tried to think of something. He could dash into the kitchen behind him and try to defend through the doorway. At least then only one could come on at a time. That still wouldn't work considering the wizard and just then another robed figure entered through the front doors and stood among his companions who now all stood staring at him with swords in hand.

Just then Brosa of Drae addressed Freemund in the common tongue, "Greetings human."

Freemund did not respond as Brosa stepped closer while drawing his sword with his good hand. The other drow began sheathing their swords and the orc now back against the wall finally lowered his guard.

"I have a proposition for you." Brosa said drawing ever closer.

Bewildered by all of this Freemund finally answered, "What do you want?"

"Your head."

"Good luck."

"Ah, spirit. I like that. Especially from one so young."

Brosa stopped a few strides away. Freemund never lowering his guard looked on at his opponent sizing him up. Brosa took a second to look around at the many dead orcs on the ground then again began speaking to Freemund. "Surely you want to survive past this night?"

Freemund stern and resolute again didn't answer.

"Here is my offer. Defeat me and you live."

"What?"

"Take my life if you can and my partners behind me will simply walk away."

Jhaeros Drae shouted in drow, *"Quit playing and finish this."*

Without another word Brosa waded in. Seeing the advance, Freemund lashed out with his sword, which was easily blocked and countered. Freemund barely got his sword back in line to deflect the blow. Freemund acknowledged right away that this one was skilled despite the use of only one arm.

Brosa began circling to his right stepping over the dead orc at his feet then lunging forward with a quick jab that hit squarely on Freemund's raised shield. No novice to battle despite his young years, Freemund did not return the blow expecting that this drow wanted him to counter at that moment. His confidence rose while thinking that. He was trained after all by Oran Righe and Gaebald Hogg, two of the best and revered swordsmen in all of Casta. However, he had never faced an opponent such as this and three of his friends already lay dead in this very room.

Brosa jabbed at his shield again and this time Freemund answered with a quick riposte of his longsword followed by a lunge forward trying to bash Brosa with his shield. Brosa was quick to block the blow of the sword and stepped back too rapidly for Freemund to hit him with his shield then changed direction circling right and slicing down low forcing Freemund to drop his shield low to block then coming back with a high swing in at Freemund's head which was likewise blocked this time with his sword. Brosa stepped back disengaging from the duel.

"Impressive for a human. But not overly so."

Freemund came on then, swinging with great balance and keeping his shield in line to deflect any counters. Brosa expertly blocked every blow not bothering to reply with a counter. He kept backing and circling to his right. He took the steps up to the landing without so much as a glance down always keeping his guard and deflecting every blow coming his way. When he circled enough to be coming back down the steps that ran the width of the central room he reversed direction and jabbed out suddenly. Freemund blocked with his shield and answered with a sidelong swing of his sword that Brosa easily ducked under then stepped into Freemund while bringing his scimitar up in a stabbing motion right into the ribs and through, piercing his right lung, meanwhile placing his right leg behind and pushing him with his right arm sending Freemund right off the steps and landing heavily on his back.

Brosa looked on from the top of the steps. He watched as Freemund gasped for air that would not come with a punctured lung. He tilted his head as Freemund tried to look up at him, curious as to how long it would take for him to suffocate or bleed out. He could have ended it right there with another blow. He could have shown mercy to this youth. He could have been respectful to a fellow swordsman who proved more than a novice despite his age. He could have, but he didn't.

Jhaeros Drae surveyed the scene as his drow went about their business of hanging the humans from the exposed beams of this little Keep. He was quite pleased with himself despite his initial frustration and inability to blast through the heavily warded door. After his initial fireball spell, which should have splintered the door and sent half of he wall crumbling he was forced to cast a detection spell. The vision before him was like nothing he had ever seen before. Never had he seen so many magical wards placed on such a small structure. To not look the fool, especially in front of Brosa of Drae, he was forced to enact his most powerful spell in his repertoire. Despite the use of his disintegrate spell the door still held. After that there was nothing he could do but revert back to his weaker fireball spell and hope that the wards did not hold.

One of his soldiers addressed him from across the room, *"My Lord Drae. The elf bitch still lives. She is only unconscious and the big one's throat is cut too deep to support his weight if we hang him."*

Before Jhaeros Drae could answer a shout from another soldier standing vigil at the front door of the Keep interrupted, *"Lord Drae, torches are gathering outside of the town. The soldiers are gathering."*

"How many?" Jhaeros Drae asked.

"Too many to count from this distance my lord." He replied.

Brosa of Drae standing now next to Freemund after watching him breath his last after struggling for breath at the length of the noose now wrapped around his throat walked towards Jhaeros Drae and said, *"I warned you about their number. This should have been done quietly. This will not please Deathmar. He will need time to enact the portal to send us away."*

"Need I remind you of your lengthy duel with that child. Your games cost us entirely too much time."

"Not unlike your inability to gain entry. Not to mention the excessive noise."

"Enough!" Jhaeros pointed to the initial soldier who addressed him, *"Hang the elf in her sleep and the large one by his feet. Let his blood flow to the ground like an animal put to slaughter."*

Brosa realizing he might have overstepped his bounds but did not wish now to relent asked, *"What of our dead?"*

Jhaeros stepped closer to Brosa; an unusual move considering he was a wizard and not a fighter. If confrontation were to come he would want distance. Brosa could chop him in half before a spell could be uttered. Before Brosa could say anything else Jhaeros answered, *"We lost only one drow. Take him with us. Throw the rest on the fire. Let this place reek of burning hair and orc flesh."*

With that Jhaeros turned his back on Brosa and headed for the back door. Turning his back in such a manner was a grave insult. It showed those in attendance that he had no fear at all of Brosa of Drae. Brosa let it go. There time would come some other night and he knew that Jhaeros was about to take a verbal beating from his real master. Deathmar the Black would surely not be pleased with this lengthy and raucous attack. He watched as the soldiers finished hanging the last two and made sure to leave Deathmar's sigil written in blood on the wall opposite the front entry, in full view of all who would shortly enter and bear witness to the now fallen Silver Guard.

R. A. HAYDEN

CHAPTER THREE

Homecoming—Selmeril, 1014

HEADING WEST ALONG the road to Lanos, adjacent to and in sight of the Mehm River, Josef Righe hurried his team of two horses pulling his wagon as fast as they could possibly bear it. Near exhaustion the horses were going as fast as they were able and still Josef yelled and whipped the rains in his hands pushing them to their limit.

"Slow down father. You're gonna kill 'em." Oran Righe yelled from the back of the uncovered wagon where he was sitting to hold down their cargo, which had already threatened to slide completely out of the wagon. That would be unfortunate indeed considering they were hauling back two of their fallen comrades who served with them in The Silver Guard.

The two had fallen at the hands of some drow elf mercenaries they had come across in the Talt Mountains. The band of four had arrived in the Talt Mountains a week prior to investigate the disappearances of dwarves who had apparently gone missing from the hill dwarf clans who called those mountains their home. The truth of it was far worse than they could have imagined. Two entire hill dwarf clans had completely vanished without a trace. While moving through the mountains to warn and rally the other clans they came upon a sizeable force of drow and orcs. In the ensuing battle two of The Silver Guard lay slain.

Josef yelled back, "No time. We must get back."

Early that morning, well before sunrise, Josef had woken as if from a horrible nightmare. He immediately set to hitching the horses babbling it seemed to Oran that the Keep was under attack. He knew well that his father was not mad and knew of the wards set about their compound that would warn Josef if the Keep ever came under attack. Such was the design of specific wards he had cast upon their home but the urgency his father felt towards it had him more worried about him than anything else. Silver Guard Keep was well protected and their fellow members were there as well as near a hundred Castan soldiers in Lanos.

They had planned to be there that evening but here before the midday sun they were rounding the last bend in the road before Lanos would be in sight. Heading towards them was a squad of soldiers on horseback. As the group neared Josef finally pulled back the reins to slow his team. At the head of the dozen men was Sergeant Adley whom they knew well and had served at the Lanos Outpost for several years and fought alongside them multiple times.

Josef began before Adley could fully rein in his horse, "What is it Sergeant? What has happened?"

Sergeant Adley tried to reply, "We were just heading east to find you. Thank the gods you are here."

"Enough of that blather Sergeant. Tell me what has happened."

"I'm sorry sir. It's your house. Your men." The words were coming hard for Sergeant Adley to get out.

"Tell me straight you fool." Josef ordered coming out of his seat and onto his feet.

"Dead sir. Slaughtered in the night. I no not..."

Josef never let him finish his sentence. He sat back down and gave a great heave of the reins and forced his team of horses on. The Castan soldiers turned their horses around and followed in pursuit. Oran sat in the back of the wagon unsure of how to react. Here, lying at his feet were two of his best friends and now to hear that the rest of his companions were also slain had him beside himself.

Josef didn't bother slowing the wagon through town. The horses nearly clipped a passerby attempting to cross the mud soaked road. As they passed, the horses hooves and wheels of the wagon threw mud and water every which way, splashing all who were too close to avoid it. The whole town was out it seemed to Oran. No doubt congregating at the taverns to hear of the horrible news from the previous night.

As they neared the gates to Silver Guard Keep Josef could see Lieutenant Borin, the commander of the Lanos Outpost, step out onto the front deck through the double doors, which now barely hung onto their hinges. Before coming to a complete stop Oran hopped from the back and ran ahead of his father heading straight for Lieutenant Borin.

R. A. HAYDEN

At the top of the stairs Borin held out his hands attempting to block Oran from entry.

Borin, in as calm a voice as he could muster began, "Easy Oran. You don't want to go in there."

Hardly hearing, Oran pushed right past his upraised arms and entered the front door. He stopped on the stair leading down into the sunken hall. His eyes went to four bodies laying to the left of his vision. There in the far corner, each covered with a blanket, lay his fallen friends. Slowly he moved that direction circumventing the blood on the floor but not taking notice of the cut ropes still dangling from the ceiling beams. As he neared a voice took him from his thoughts.

"Oran. Is that you sir?" Harold asked after entering from the rear door of the Keep.

Oran looked his direction. Surely he thought that all had died. He walked to Harold and embraced his forearm with his outstretched hand just as Harold did the same to him. This was the usual greeting between Silver Guard members but Oran pulled him forward with his other arm embracing him in a hug as well. Then he pushed him back looking him in the face.

"Your wife. Georgette. Does she live as well?" Oran asked.

"She does sir. The others. They saved us." Harold explained as tears began to form in his eyes.

"What happened Harold? Who did this?"

Harold shrugged, "I know not sir. I know only of the beginning."

"Tell me."

"Well you see sir…" Harold began to explain but then both turned as Josef entered the hall followed close behind by Sergeant Adley and Lieutenant Borin. They stopped before the stairs, Josef staring hard at a distinct location on the wall while Adley and Borin took turns trying to explain the events of the previous night.

Oran released Harold and the two walked towards Josef. Josef didn't look their way in the slightest as he and Harold approached. He appeared oblivious to the words being said to him by Adley and Borin. Upon reaching the stair in front of his father he looked inquisitively at his father's face then turned to see what had his attention so fixed. There on the wall, so obvious now, Oran could not believe he had missed it. His attention had become transfixed on the bodies of his fallen comrades upon entering the Keep. On the wall opposite them, drawn in blood was a full circle about five feet or so in diameter and in its center was a solid circle with six triangles fixed at approximate locations around its perimeter to give the sigil the look of a sun. A black sun to be exact except this one was drawn in the blood of his fallen friends.

"We know this sigil," Oran proclaimed. "It is the personal sigil of Deathmar the Black."

"Yes." Josef answered as though Oran was asking a question.

"But why?" Oran asked.

Josef began walking closer to the image never taking his eyes off of it. "Isn't it obvious son?"

Oran pondered the question for only a second before coming to the conclusion. He turned his gaze on Borin. "Did you see any who did this?"

"Yes. Upon entering the Keep we discovered several orc bodies. Two of which had been thrown on the fire there." Borin pointed behind Oran to the fireplace, which wasn't currently lit. "We removed their filthy bodies and set them ablaze once more far removed from your house.

"No commander," Josef answered as he turned back, his attention now back on the quartet, "This is the work of drow."

"Drow? We saw no drow." Borin said as he looked to his side at Adley for support. "That's ridiculous. We are far too removed from their lands. A force of drow skulking about would not go unnoticed."

"I assure you commander," Josef continued, "Drow do not skulk about like some unruly orc or goblin band. They are the epitome of stealth and secrecy."

"You believe this is a retaliation for what happened in the hills?" Oran asked his father.

"It would certainly fit. Don't you agree?" Josef said as he turned once more to look upon the sigil.

Borin, not fully understanding all the implications of the conversation going on took a step forward, "There is more."

"What more?" Oran asked.

On the short ride from Silver Guard Keep to the home of Cecilia Alio, Lieutenant Borin and Harold filled in as many details as were known to Josef and Oran. Borin detailed the accounts of his men assembling and rushing to the Keep in force once alerted of the attack. He spared as many gruesome details as were possible of the condition in which they found the four Silver Guard who had been left to hang in the living area.

Harold added his details as to how it all began and the role in which he took as well as what he had seen when he and Georgette emerged from the safe room in the lower quarters once hearing the voices of the soldiers searching the compound. After that Borin described his men tracking through the fields as they searched for the perpetrators, which led them to the farm of Jon and Cecilia Alio. He explained Cecilia's recent loss of her husband and the role his men and The Silver Guard played in tracking down and killing the bulette who had taken his life. The state in which his men found poor Cecilia was not easy for him to describe.

The four arrived in front of the house after hearing the brief description and dismounted. Two soldiers were stationed on either side of the door leading into the farmhouse. They saluted as the lieutenant approached and meant to enter when Josef took his attention back the other direction.

"Lieutenant. What is that?" Josef asked as he walked the opposite direction of the house towards the barn.

Oran was on his heels likewise focusing his attention on a large burn mark on the ground. He kneeled down once beside it touching the mark with his fingertips then lifting them to his nose to sniff at the soot and mud. "Strange."

Borin and Harold met them next to the mark. Borin shaking his head and said, "I'm not sure. A burn of some kind."

"Strange don't you think," Josef began explaining as he too knelt down to inspect the mark more closely. "For there to be a burn here in the mud with no sign of tinder. Especially considering the amount of rain that fell in last nights storm."

"I hadn't given it that much thought." Borin explained, "Upon arriving here I did not notice it. It was still dark. The morning sun had not begun to crest the horizon. My focus was on searching the surrounding area for any sign of the attackers."

"This is your sign Lieutenant."

"I don't take your meaning."

"A portal." Josef stood and faced Borin.

Borin was shaking his head. "No. That cannot be. I've never heard of such a thing."

"There is much you don't know young man." Josef's tone was a bit harsh but before Borin could respond they were interrupted by Georgette who exited the front door of the house and sped her way towards them. Exiting the door behind her was Father Terrell, the local priest who lived in Lanos and held prayer seminars for the townspeople. He also served, as the town doctor for that was the duel purpose that most priests and clerics held.

"Thank the gods. Oh thank the gods. Josef, Oran you've returned to us." Georgette said as she neared the two men. She embraced Josef and then Oran with a hug.

"How does she fare?" Borin asked of her.

Before she could answer Father Terrell answered for her, "Not well I'm afraid. I gave something for the pain earlier though it doesn't keep her under for long. I've administered it multiple times since but she keeps waking up. Fortunately she is out now." He looked to Josef. "Now that you are here I'm hoping you might have something more potent."

"What are her wounds?"

"Well she is battered and bruised all over her body as well as cuts and some glass I had to remove. She has at least two broken ribs and three of her fingers I had to pop back into place." Father Terrell took a heavy sigh and shook his head before continuing. "She was raped quite brutally. Like nothing I've ever seen."

"Bastards." Oran interrupted while shaking his head and crossing his arms in front of him.

"Yes but strangest of all are the burn marks on her body." Father Terrell continued.

"What do you mean?" Josef asked.

"It's as though they were made with acid not heat or fire. She has one on her face and several spots on her body."

Josef patted Father Terrell on the shoulder as he began walking past towards the door. "I believe I can help with the pain and I have some healing salves to compliment yours. Unfortunately I'm out of healing potions presently."

Before he got to the door Father Terrell added, "She said she has a message for you from him."

"For me?"

"Yes. She said that he told her to tell you, your move." He said while shrugging his shoulders.

Josef's eyes went towards the ground. Lost in thought at the implications of the remark.

Borin addressed Josef, "Why would a drow elf tell you that?"

"He is not drow. They are merely his servants. He walks the world in drow from though he is not of their ilk. He is a dragon." Josef said as he reached for the latch to the door and pushed his way into the home.

CHAPTER FOUR

Funeral—Selmeril, 1014

THE DAY FOLLOWING the return of Josef and Oran Righe from the Talt Mountains the townspeople of Lanos and most of the soldiers garrisoned there gathered in the field in front of The Silver Guard private cemetery. It was well after the midday sun but still plenty of time before the sun slipped beyond the horizon. All of the storm clouds from the previous days had passed and the sun shined brilliantly on those in attendance. All in the town and most of the surrounding farmers had come out in show of support for those remaining in the Keep and respect for the fallen. The Silver Guard commanded the utmost respect from those living in Casta but especially to those in close proximity to them. Long have they served in defense of those who needed them the most and being that Lanos was the northernmost town in all of Casta and in close proximity to the Talt Mountains, where orcs, goblins, and a number of other creatures lived and liked to occasionally try to raid in the civilized lands of men, they were needed often.

The soldiers likewise had the utmost respect for The Silver Guard. More often than not The Silver Guard accompanied them or vise versa on some mission. Raiders from Cruz Kingdom directly north of them often crossed the Mehm River to pillage and burn. This was the main charge for those stationed in Lanos and they felt very fortunate to be stationed among such elite mercenaries. Many of The Silver Guard were former members of the Castan military and recruitment by Josef and Oran often came from those stationed in Lanos. Today the soldiers came out in full armor ready to bid farewell to those that many of them had fought beside.

The funeral procession started out of the front gates of The Silver Guard Keep with Josef and Lieutenant Borin leading the way down the small path that led to the cemetery. Behind them Oran, Harold and a host of soldiers carried coffins, six in total for the number of lost Silver Guard members, two fallen in the Talts and the remainder in their own home. Within twenty yards to the gate of the cemetery Sergeant Adley had his men set in lines on each side of the pathway with the remaining set in formation in front of the townspeople.

When the procession was in close proximity to his men Adley shouted the order, "Company! Order arms!"

All of the soldiers, dressed in their silver colored banded mail adorned with the symbol of Bahamut, one of the patron gods of Tomé and symbol for the infantry- men of the Castan forces, came to attention. They slammed their large shields to the ground and withdrew their short swords and raised them to the heavens in solute as the procession passed.

Inside the cemetery Father Terrell waited with Georgette while the coffins were placed next to their burial location. Once lowered the soldiers were ordered to lower their solutes so that Father Terrell could begin the funeral rites. Harold went to stand with his wife who had already begun to cry while Josef and Oran set themselves on either side of Father Terrell.

While standing there listening to Father Terrell, Josef lamented on how large the cemetery had become. As founder of The Silver Guard he had seen each one of those buried there put to rest. Fine men and women from a multitude of races who believed as he did that evil must be met with force whenever it is encountered. The sacrifice for such an endeavor was heavy indeed. Only a few of the over forty tombstones that made up the cemetery had ever seen old age. Most were taken in their prime, fighting the undead forces of the necromancers to the east of the Talt Mountains while others met their end fighting orc or goblin hordes, soldiers from Cruz Kingdom, werewolves, or vampires. Now six more would join their ranks. Slain by drow forces led by Deathmar the Black. As Josef thought about all of this he looked to his son. Oran stood stern and resolute among the tombstones. They were the only two Silver Guard remaining. Justice must be meted out he thought. Delivering on that justice was another matter entirely.

Oran sat at the table in one of the corner chairs as he looked to the small flames in the fireplace in Silver Guard Keep. Him and his father had recently finished a cheerless meal with Harold and Georgette following the funeral services for their friends. Plates and dishes were still on the table as no one saw a direct need to clean up and Georgette was tending to Cecilia, who they had moved to the Keep so that Georgette could play nurse to her. After the loss of her husband Cecilia had few else in town that would be willing to take on the duty. Oran was awaiting Josef's return from the kitchen where he had gone to grab another bottle of wine. They had already gone through two bottles reliving past glories and fond memories of their fallen friends. Harold was on his hands and knees working on trying to scrub out the bloodstains that stubbornly remained on the hard wood floor.

"Harold," Oran cocked his head in Harold's direction, "Put down the brush and join us. That incessant scrubbing sound is wearing on me."

Harold looked up and sighed. He had been trying for the better part of two days now to finish cleaning up the mess and supposed it couldn't hurt to rest. He placed the brush into the bucket and rose, drying his hands on the apron around his midsection and walked over to the large table. Josef returned from the kitchen at the same time carrying two bottles of wine.

Josef cracked the seal on one of the bottles and gestured toward Harold to hold out his glass. "Now this one is all the way from Feywood."

He filled Harold's glass and turned to Oran to do the same before taking his seat and filling his own. They raised their glasses in a silent cheer and took long pulls from their glasses.

"Mm, a fine vintage." Harold said while wiping his lip with his sleeve.

"Yes indeed," Josef explained, "Those Feywood elves do not barter easily. I'd have to say this was worth every bit of silver I paid."

Oran took another long pull and turned to Josef. "Shall we continue?"

"Yes of course. As I was saying, in the morning I will ride for Tomé." Josef reached for his pipe and began filling it. "I must speak with the heads of The Orders. Surely they will have some knowledge and then we can plan from there."

"You're forgetting something." Oran said as he moved to fill his glass again.

R. A. HAYDEN

"Yes, yes. I will ask for their assistance but I doubt they will provide much." Josef took a pull from his pipe and continued. "The Orders will not see this as a huge threat but a mere anomaly. We will likely have to recruit on our own."

"That's insane. No one is going to want to go after Deathmar the Black and you and I are getting far too old for this."

"You still seem very spry. You made short work of both drow and orc only a few days ago. Except for that one bastard who gave you a bit of a challenge."

Oran turned his stare towards Harold. "Harold, how old would you say I am."

"Well I'm not quite sure sir. Older than me." He pondered the question tilting his head side to side. "Forty perhaps."

Josef and Oran both chuckled at that remark.

"What is so funny?" Harold asked feeling embarrassed and taking another drink from his glass.

"I believe it is time you know more about us." Oran looked to Josef and cocked his head as if asking permission.

"Oh go right ahead. I'm not ashamed of my age." Josef said as he leaned back in his chair.

Oran began, "How long have we known you Harold? Six years is it?"

"About there sir. Me and Georgette had our shop in town for near five years before coming to work here."

"And in all that time you had never heard rumors spoken about us?"

"Well surely but they didn't seem plausible."

"And you never thought to ask any who lived here if they were true?"

"Not my business sir. I mind my own when I can."

Oran lifted his right hand and moved it closer to Harold. "You see this ring."

"Yes sir."

"This ring is very special." Oran began rubbing the ring on his index finger with his thumb. "It is magic. It's called a ring of regeneration."

"I'm not rightly sure what that means sir."

"Well similar rings you see, are worn to aid in healing. If you take an arrow to the chest for example." Oran lifted his shirt and pointed to a star shaped scar on his left breast. "You see there. I took that from a clever little goblin in the Talt Mountains. It healed in minutes after pulling the shaft out."

"Mind you Harold, he never should have taken that arrow in the first place. If he had been paying attention it never would have happened." Josef explained with a little laugh and shrug of his shoulders as he reached for his glass.

"Never mind him." Oran continued after taking another drink. "Where was I? Oh yes. This ring is extra special. It also slows the aging process."

"Slows sir?"

"Yes Harold. This year I will be celebrating my. What is it now? Two hundredth and twenty first birthday."

"Surely not."

"Oh yes my friend. It's starting not to work though you see. It has limits. I've begun aging normally again. Have been for years now." Oran took another drink while pointing his thumb at Josef. When he finished he said, "That's nothing compared to this old fart."

"I beg your pardon." Josef said while coming forward in his seat to join in a private laugh between father and son.

When they finished Harold asked, "How old would that make you sir?"

"Well let's see." Josef began counting on his fingers. "I had him when I was ninety so three hundred and ten or there abouts."

Harold began choking on the drink he had been taking. He couldn't believe what he had just heard. Josef looked to only be about sixty. Josef and Oran laughed at the spectacle. When Harold cleared his air pipe once again he asked, "So you had a child at the age of ninety."

"Well I did enjoy the ladies in my younger days quite a lot."

"So one of the rings you wear. Is one like Oran's?"

"No I'm afraid not. My situation is harder to explain." Josef began filling his cup from the final bottle of wine sitting on the table. He looked back to Harold and added. "Nothing nefarious, mind you. But that might be a longer conversation than this bottle can handle."

R. A. HAYDEN

CHAPTER FIVE

The Orders—Selmeril, 1014

EIGHT DAYS AFTER leaving Lanos, Josef Righe directed his horse through the front gates of Tomé, capital of the Castan Kingdom and home of some of the most influential factions on the continent of Drilain. Tomé has a population of over half a million. Mostly human but different races from all over Drilain can be found here as it boasts the largest center for trade of agriculture, livestock and metals as well as trading districts for magic both divine and arcane. Josef cared not for any such distractions on this trip to this most wondrous city, which he once called home. His purpose clear, he headed straight for the docks to catch the ferry to Creet Island, home of Hareth Academy of Wizards, named after its founder over fifteen centuries before, and the largest arcane academy on all of Drilain.

After a short ride from the docks after making the crossing to Creet Island, Josef dismounted, handed his horse over to one of the students so that he may be taken to the stables and entered the front doors to the castle. A couple of the older students recognizing him said hello as he passed. Josef often visited the academy and occasionally gave lectures in one discipline or the other for he was well versed in all and The Silver Guard were quite famous throughout Casta. Stories of some of their deeds throughout the last couple centuries were well documented and position as Josef Righe's apprentice had been filled several times by students from the academy.

Josef headed straight for the Headmaster's office. After rounding the corner that would take him there he could see Headmaster Usarus walking in his direction. He appeared ever the same wearing his flowing white and gray trimmed robes similar to the ones Josef wore though his were gray with white trim. He carried a white oaken staff though not for support as he had the gate of a much younger man, even more so than his long gray beard would suggest. In contrast Josef kept his facial hair trimmed and tidy and supported it in the fashion of a goatee and the staff he carried was of harden steel with two separate black leather hand holds so that the staff could be used like a staff or spear. One end formed a spike that was coated in silver while the other held a large uncut blue sapphire. Like the staff of the headmaster his staff was also quite famous and known to all at the academy as Etburn.

"Apologies my friend," Usarus began as they neared one another, "I had meant to meet you at the door but alas unruly students demanded my attention."

Josef was not surprised to learn that Usarus had known of his arrival. He had sent him a sending, a magical way of communication over great distances, the day after arriving back in Lanos to apprise him of the situation and little happened on Creet Island at any time that Usarus was not aware of.

Josef waved his hand in dismissal showing it was of no concern. As they stopped in front of one another Josef asked, "What of my request?"

"Straight to business as always."

"This is not business."

"Yes of course. I meant nothing. My deepest sympathies for your losses." "Thank you old friend. Now what can you tell me?"

Usarus stepped to the left of Josef and gestured down the hall with his staff bearing hand motioning him to walk with him and leave the vicinity of the prying ears of students passing in the hall. "Nothing as of yet I'm afraid."

The two continued walking down the hall and into the office of Headmaster Usarus as Josef digested what little information he was being told. Usarus had sent word out to all known contacts, of which he had many, regarding any knowledge of the movements or whereabouts of Deathmar the Black. So far he had learned nothing more than that which Josef already knew.

Deathmar was known to frequent Veszdor, the drow capital deep in the underdark below the Ashen Mountains. Deathmar was known to be aligned with House Drae, the third most powerful house in the city and was secretly the power behind the house if not ruling it from behind the scenes as Usarus suspected. Drow society is commonly ruled over by the females. Great priestesses in the service of Lloth, a most heinous and evil deity who has chosen drow as her champions in the material world and has gifted her females with extraordinary divine powers that they use to rule the underdark with the utmost cruelty. The fact that Deathmar the Black had been able to supplant the powers that be in one of the strongest houses in all of the underdark spoke volumes about his cunning and power.

"Yes Usarus I know all of this and it's very interesting but I need to go after him." Josef said as he paced back and forth in front of Usarus' desk. "This cannot stand."

"And what would you have us do?" Usarus said in calm and even tone. He understood very well the mood in which Josef was in. "Give you an army of mages to track him down and destroy him."

"Not all but a sizeable force so that we may strike back."

Usarus shook his head thinking of how to relay his thoughts without turning this into an argument. "Even if I could do that you know The Orders would never approve and you have no chance of succeeding. Attacking the drow in their lair is suicide."

"If the cause is just their sacrifice will be rewarded."

"What reward? They would have to win to be rewarded. In the underdark they would be slaughtered like so many sheep."

Josef stopped pacing looking Usarus directly in the eye. "You underestimate our wizards."

"No my friend. It is you who are blinded by recent losses. Such an attack could not be won. Our reach goes only so far."

"Usarus, if these were your friends, your family, you would feel as I do now and urge action." Josef said as a matter to end the debate.

"I have no doubt that you are right, however, I am not and must consider my responsibilities here." Usarus could tell that Josef was not happy with his response and knew what was to come next. Josef had on several occasions berated him for playing too much of a politicians role. Before Josef could give him a verbal lashing on politics he picked himself up from his chair and headed towards the door. "Come Josef. Let us seek further council. I will call The Orders to convene so that we may seek their wisdom on the matter."

Josef reluctantly headed towards the door as well. He knew he would have to talk to The Orders for that was protocol but he also knew that if Headmaster Usarus authorized a force of wizards to be under his command that The Orders could do little except complain.

An hour later Josef and Usarus entered the audience chamber where The Orders convened. It was a large room that started out in a rectangle with benches set in rows on both sides of the main aisle for audience members or witnesses to whatever business was to be discussed. The rows of benches sat empty on this occasion except for one scribe who was in attendance to detail the accounts of the meeting. The main aisle led to a table or bench, as it was refereed to, set in a half moon conforming to the contours of the wall behind it. Sitting behind this raised bench and sitting on chairs that raised their position far above the floor in the center were the members of The Orders.

Usarus moved around the right side of the bench and positioned himself in his chair set in the center. As headmaster it was part of his duty to oversee meetings of The Orders. His duties were to keep order as many a time great arguments had erupted in the audience chamber ending in challenges between one member and another. To either side of him sat four chairs, one for each discipline of magic, though the last chair to his left always sat empty for the chair was reserved for the necromancy discipline and the school had done away with that position at the beginning of The Hundred Year War over a thousand years ago. The other seven chairs consisted of five humans, a gnome from Feywood, and an elf from Kreewood.

Headmaster Usarus called the meeting to order then motioned to Josef standing in the middle of the room to begin. He began by scanning the room from left to right. Sitting above him were eight faces of those he knew well and respected for the wizardry skills and in his mind were deserving of the post of master for their respective school. However, he detested the politics that were involved whenever meeting with The Orders as a whole. Many times in the past he had come before The Orders seeking a call to action against one foe or another who was waging war or causing mischief for Casta. Many of those times he was refused at least in part to his preferred response to such threats. This was in part why Josef had formed The Silver Guard. Leading a group of mercenaries independent of the politics of the Castan Kingdom afforded him the chance to take action sooner rather than later. Without having to worry about whether their actions would be sanctioned by the academy, the churches or the King himself.

After scanning those in attendance Josef took a long sigh before beginning. He turned his gaze to Zachary Rischer, head of invocation and evocation magic and strong supporter and friend to The Silver Guard. He wanted to gain support as early as possible in the discussion hoping to sway the other members.

He began, "Friends and long time supporters for action against those that would cause harm to the Castan Kingdom. I come before you today to garner support for an expedition to the underdark in search of Deathmar the Black."

He let his request hang in the air a few seconds gaging the reactions of the members. He noted already a smirk on the face of Master Rischer and knew immediately that he could count on his support. Master Rischer was well known for being overly brash even foolhardy when it came to action. He had a knack for rushing into battle when he was younger, often putting allies in danger with his extensive knowledge and power over spells dealing with fire. Once he had joined Oran Righe and several other Silver Guard members in hunting down a trio of witches who were wreaking havoc on the border towns of Searcy and Casta. The battle was short lived for the witches but in the process of destroying them Master Rischer had burnt down two warehouses to their foundation. Over forty now, though still the youngest and newest member of The Orders, it seemed that none of that brashness had worn off. Josef turned to look at the four members opposite Master Rischer sitting to Headmaster Usarus' right.

Before Josef could begin again Mefeumon Strongtree, master of alteration magic for Hareth Academy and sole elf residing at the academy as a professor and voice for the Kreewood elves, interrupted him asking, "Forgive me Master Righe, I do not wish to seem rude but pertinent details as too how we know that this was Deathmar the Black would be helpful."

Josef, expecting this question but not exactly from this source and was surprised that Master Strongtree would be the one to question this fact. Next to Headmaster Usarus, Master Strongtree had been a member of The Orders the second longest. Close to the age of Josef for elves were a long-lived race naturally, he had known this elf since his time as a student in the academy. "Deathmar's sigil was written in blood on the wall in Silver Guard Keep."

"And what is this sigil?" Acton Denholm, master of the divination school asked.

Josef turned his attention and replied, "A black sun set in the center of a circle."

"And how do we know that this is the sigil of Deathmar? There are many sigils in the world. Perhaps this is simply something similar." Master Denholm said as he looked around the room for support.

Josef perturbed by the assumption and apparent lack of knowledge by Master Denholm in the subject concerning Deathmar the Black shot back, "His sigil is documented in the libraries of this very school." He took a step closer in his direction and added in a sarcastic tone, "Perhaps professor you need to brush up on your reading."

Master Denholm not wishing to sound the fool asked further, "If that is the case then why leave it? Why make oneself known?" He looked around hoping for support but the looks he received were not reassuring. Not wanting to concede his point he continued, "Wouldn't the real attackers want you to believe that it was someone else? Let us not forget that The Silver Guard has made many enemies over the centuries."

Josef was rethinking the amount of respect he had for all of the members of The Orders. Perhaps he should not have had so much for Master Denholm's skills in divination but instead concentrated on his apparent lack of common sense. Despite this he added, "There is also the matter that among the attackers were drow."

"I am terribly sorry Master Righe but if I may?" Master Bombrik Fastfuse, master of phantasm and the only other member of The Orders who was not human besides Mefeumon Strongtree, asked as he raised himself up in his chair and raised his hand trying to garner the attention of everyone in the room. Master Fastfuse was a gnome and with his diminutive stature and quiet voice he was often overlooked if a shouting match ensued.

"Please Master Fastfuse." Josef returned while motioning with his right arm towards Master Fastfuse urging him to continue.

"I do not wish to sound doubtful but it's my understanding that no drow were actually seen. The report from this Lieutenant Borin stationed in Lanos made mention that none of the attackers were seen except for the bodies of the orcs that your men dispatched."

Josef not realizing that Lieutenant Borin had made an official report to his superiors as of yet or that it had made it to Tomé had him on the defensive. He looked to Headmaster Usarus for answers but none were forthcoming. "I was not aware of this report but obviously Lieutenant Borin is mistaken." He would have to remember to have a little word with young Lieutenant Borin when he returned to Lanos.

"Well Master Righe as a matter of interest to us, how do you infer that drow were party to the attack?"

"Simple Master Fastfuse. There was one witness, a detail that apparently Lieutenant Borin left out."

"Apparently so. Please continue."

"Cecilia Alio lives on a small farm not too distant from my home. There she was attacked by Deathmar himself in the guise of a drow which as we know he is wont to do." Josef took a look over to Master Denholm expecting another question concerning this detail. When he could see that none were forthcoming he continued, "I would spare the worst of the details but she was beaten and tortured for information about Silver Guard Keep. After she was raped to add to her humiliation and purposefully left alive to deliver me a message."

"What was this message Master Righe?"

Josef not wanting to deliver the simple message actually left, lied, "To convey to me who was responsible by name."

"Why?" Yuliana Keats, master of abjuration and only female on The Orders asked. When Josef turned his attention towards her she continued, "I mean why let you know who is responsible? Deathmar the Black has not been known to frequent any lands this far south in over a century."

"Retaliation Madam Keats."

"For what?" Before Josef could elaborate she added, "I know well the stories concerning Deathmar the Black and know that most of the information we know about him comes from you and The Silver Guard when you encountered him a century ago but do you mean to tell us that this is a retaliation from all that time ago?" Master Keats finished having a look of suspicion.

Josef was waiting for this question. Now he could relay information that he knew Lieutenant Borin must have left out of his report as well. "Not at all Madam. Days prior to the attack in Lanos, my son and others of The Silver Guard had gone to investigate disappearances in the Talt Mountains."

Headmaster Usarus came forward in his seat. This was information that he had not heard of and it obviously peaked his interest. "Disappearances you say?"

"Yes Headmaster." Josef replied. "Rumors had reached Lanos of hill dwarf clan members that had gone missing. Thinking that these were the usual clashes between the dwarfs and orcs we set out to see if we could lend a hand. What we found was nothing of the sort. Instead we found that two entire hill clan tribes had disappeared without a trace."

"Without a trace you say?" Headmaster Usarus asked.

"Yes. No bodies, no burning, just empty villages. It was simple enough to deduce some of the tracks left behind were made by orcs but when have orcs ever just taken prisoners and without signs of any struggle from the dwarves. Truly confounded after the second village we hurried to a third we knew to be nearby. En route to that village we came across a force of drow and orc preparing to attack. I can spare the minor details here but we engaged this force. I lost two of my Silver Guard in the process but with the village informed the attackers were routed."

Yuliana Keats entered the conversation once more, "And you believe it is this same force that is tied to Deathmar."

"Yes indeed. Though routed not all were slain. Several drow escaped including one who had been badly injured by my son. It was this drow who Cecilia Alio identified by description of his injuries that was present when Deathmar defiled the poor girl."

Master Rischer stood up and said in a disgusted voice, "I've heard enough. Something must be done immediately."

"Calm yourself Master Rischer." Usarus said.

"No. This is ridiculous." Master Rischer put both hands on the bench in front of him and leaned forward looking directly at Headmaster Usarus. "Since when is the word of Master Righe not enough?"

Usarus shot back, "His word is not in question Master Rischer. From the second I heard this news I took it as fact." This elated Master Rischer to some extent and he sat back allowing Usarus to continue. "Attention however is in the details and the question is not who is responsible but what is to be done about it." Usarus turned his attention back to Josef and asked, "What would you have done Master Righe?"

The conversation that ensued went on for well over an hour. Josef asked for a sizeable force of wizards so that he may strike back at Deathmar in the underdark. The response and details of such an action could not be agreed upon. Though not wishing a frontal assault on the city of Veszdor it was his hope to draw Deathmar out and then destroy him. Most feared that this course of action was not plausible. Veszdor was too far removed and traversing the underdark, let alone attempting any kind of attack on a drow city by surface dwellers, was deemed not possible. In the end Josef received votes of support from Master Rischer and Madam Keats, the latter surprising him to some extent. He had hoped that Master Strongtree would cast a vote for him considering the long history between the Kreewood elves and the drow elves but that vote did not come. In the end it was decided that they must wait and see. Something Josef was not fond of doing. The Orders wished to draw him out from the underdark all together or find a way to track his movements should he come to the surface on his own. Something Josef believed was not plausible.

For one, Deathmar did not stay in his dragon form, an unusual thing for a creature that was so incredibly powerful and would leave himself vulnerable to attack in his smaller form. Though most would not think it possible for a dragon or any creature to make such a drastic change in appearance, dragons were among the most magically gifted creatures in the entire world and the strongest of them were capable of such magic. And two, Deathmar was one of the last remaining threats of dragon kind on all of Drilain, due in large part because he knew how to stay hidden. He spent centuries at a time without interfering in the lives of the kingdoms. Fortunately they did know that he favored drow and had a destination to bring the fight to him but alas it appeared that that option was off the table. At least as far as The Orders were concerned.

CHAPTER SIX

Considerations—Selmeril, 1014

ONCE AGAIN IN the office of Headmaster Usarus, Josef and he discussed the particulars of the meeting. Josef expected such a decision to be made by The Orders but that did nothing to hinder his anger.

"Patience Josef." Usarus counseled. "The events are so recent that they are clouding your judgment. You need to look to securing the safety of those remaining."

Josef insisted, "They will not attack again. He wants us to come after him."

"Precisely the point. You would be walking into a trap."

"No Usarus. It is he who underestimates me."

"I doubt that Deathmar underestimates much." Josef gave Usarus a quizzical look not fully understanding his meaning behind that statement. "Think about it Josef. Deathmar did not attack with you present. You and Oran defeated him once before. He wants the battle on his terms to ensure a positive outcome for him."

"Yes but I am not one to shy from confrontation. Especially not after recent events."

"Were The Silver Guard at its highest strength in its prime I have no doubt that you could find a way. But think about it. Only you and Oran remain."

Josef was beginning to think he was only getting these compliments in an attempt to subdue his attitude on the course of action he wanted to take.

Usarus continued, "Now let us take a minute to think about what else may be done in the meantime. Why don't you and Oran come and stay here?"

Josef dismissed the notion, "No I believe we are perfectly safe for the moment. They will not attack again as I have said. Besides a number of soldiers from Lanos Outpost are staying at the Keep and will remain at my insistence or Lieutenant Borin will truly earn my ire."

Usarus did not doubt that statement in the least. He already imagined the tongue lashing that this young lieutenant would be receiving upon Josef's return. He knew as well the attitude and relentless personality of his old friend. Never had Josef listened to the advice of The Orders. Much to the benefit of the Castan Kingdom he knew. Where he was in a position to play the political game to some extent Josef was free to act on his own. In times past Usarus had called upon his old friend in times when discretion was not to his liking. This was not one of those times for he feared for the wellbeing of Josef and Oran and did not want to see them dead at the hands of a despicable fiend like Deathmar the Black. He knew he had to urge patience.

Usarus stood from his chair and walked to a small cupboard behind his desk. There he pulled out a bottle of wine and two glasses, showing them to Josef. After the debate earlier Josef thought it was just the thing he needed to calm his nerves and motioned for Usarus to bring him the glass.

While filling the glass for Josef, Usarus said, "Consider this Josef. What harm is there in waiting?"

"You know well the answer to that. Six of mine lay dead and I will not let that stand."

"I do not mean indefinitely." After filling Josef's glass and then beginning to fill his own as he took a seat on the corner of his desk. Usarus continued, "Strategy and patience has long been your weakness." Josef looked as though he wanted to counter immediately but with an upraised hand to silence his rebuke Usarus elaborated, "Do not mistake me. Deathmar will pay for this. I do not care that he is one of our last known true threats from dragon kind but you are not considering him."

"In what way?"

"He is one of the last of his kind on Drilain and probably the oldest especially concerning black dragons. While their time has passed he has not maintained his position on being stupid." Usarus finished filling his glass and stood up again and moved around his desk and took his seat.

Josef pondered this while he took a couple drinks from his glass. Once finished he asked, "So your advice is to wait and watch?"

"If Deathmar has again come out into the world of men for whatever reason then perhaps we can find him and bring the fight to him on our terms."

"What of the meantime? Just wait for him to slaughter more innocents?"

"Not at all. Let us rely on the considerable resources we have and plan to take him away from where he is strongest. I will employ all the resources I have here in finding him and I expect you will do the same. In the meantime I also have a favor to ask of you."

"And what might that be?" Josef asked while expecting it to pertain to not going after Deathmar without the aid of Hareth Academy. He knew this was the likely measure he would have to take anyway. Though The Orders had denied him magical aid in the form of wizards and would no doubt advise the King of Casta to not lend him troops he had no doubt that the King would. They were on the best of terms just as he had been with every King that had served Casta over the past couple centuries. That combined with his fame and fortune he could have other mercenary bands and hirelings that serve Casta rally to his cause and thus force Hareth Academy's hand in lending aid after all. To not do so might cause too big of a rift between the academy and those they serve. Politics in the end would serve Josef's needs. While contemplating this he knew well that Usarus knew this to be the case as well and patiently awaited Usarus to make his pitch to not follow that course of action.

Usarus said, "I believe it is time for you to have a new apprentice."

"An apprentice?" Josef questioned not expecting that turn in conversation.

"Yes. I have found an excellent candidate for your next apprentice."

Josef brought his fine glass up to his lips slowly while trying to figure out this angle. He expected that Usarus wanted to put someone close to him so that he may have better eyes and ears on what he is up to. After taking a slow sip of his wine he asked, "And who is this candidate?"

"Oh you won't know him. Though you do know the family."

"What family is that?"

"The Shoone family."

Josef gave a little chuckle. "You jest."

"Not at all."

"Usarus, the Shoone family has never had a mage in their family." Josef moved forward in his seat and pointed a finger at Usarus as though he were to lecture him. "In fact they despise our kind. If it were up to the Shoone family Casta would go the way of Kodia."

Kodia is one of the kingdoms north of the Strymn Sea. Once Kodia had their own arcane academy in their former capital, Striphis City. Striphis City was once a melting pot of arcane and divine magic. Located in the Hodak Mountains next to Kreewood it also served as a crossroads for trade between the Kreewood elves and the human kingdoms to the south. Over two hundred years ago a great magical catastrophe occurred and all who lived in Striphis City were killed. Blame was pointed at arcane magic wielders and the Kingdom of Kodia banished arcane magic from its lands thus starting The Purge War. When the war was over the church claimed victory and arcane magic was outlawed and so Kodia became like it's western allies, the Kingdoms of Astoné and Aldar, who likewise distrusted wizards and their powers. In those three kingdoms the church rules over the lands more so than their respective kings.

"Nevertheless Josef, they have one now." Usarus looked to the corner of his office at a large crystal hourglass atop a shelf adjacent to his office window. Unlike other hourglasses this one did not mark the time of a mere hour but an entire day. Once the blue sand ran its course for the day the center of the glass containing the sand would magically flip itself over on a pendulum thus starting another day. Usarus had looked to it to figure out the time. "In fact the students are preparing for dinner as we speak. I imagine he is in the dining hall right now."

"He is a student here now?"

"Yes."

"What year?"

"This is his first year."

Josef gave a great belly laugh. "Ha. Now I know you jest."

"And why is that?"

Josef looked at Usarus and he did not seem to be joking in any way. "I have no time for a child. I thought you meant a recent graduate. One that may have excelled in one school or the other, which could be helpful to me as I would be to him. But a first year student. Not possible."

"I had hoped to persuade you to come stay here, with Oran of course, so that you may supervise his teaching first hand." Josef began shaking his head at that but Usarus would not be deterred. "But if that is not your wish than I have another option."

Josef interrupted Usarus before he could continue, "Forget it. First off I'm not a professor here. Second, you have the finest professors of any school. Why would I have to supervise the teaching of a child?"

"He is one of eight."

The smile on Josef's face wiped clean in an instant. After a few seconds thinking of what he had just been told a look of doubt crossed his face. "Wait, wait, wait. You are telling me that a child from the Shoone family line is one of eight at the age of what, ten or so?"

"Precisely." Just as Josef was about to blurt out something Usarus cut him off, "Let me fill you in. This is quite remarkable."

"Unbelievable you mean."

Usarus sighed and waited for Josef to stop. "May I?"

Josef recognizing the mounting frustration on Usarus' face picked the wine bottle up and filled his glass then relaxed deep into his chair. He thought this should be interesting indeed for this could not be possible. For a wizard to be named one of eight he would have to show some level of proficiency in all eight disciplines of arcane magic. To do so marked you as a sorcerer, a title that Josef did not like simply because he preferred to be called a wizard even though he long ago became very proficient in all disciplines. Most wizards, especially humans, due to their short life spans, never reach the rank of sorcerer. Actually most only ever become truly proficient in two or three disciplines. Usarus and he were sorcerers, which had everything to do with their long life spans. Usarus was well over five hundred years old and he was over three hundred. They have become so in tune with magic that it provides a measure of longevity. Essentially the magic keeps you alive as long as you do not abuse your powers. This too is a problem for most wizards. Magic is addictive and if you stretch your mind and body too far your own magic will kill you.

Usarus began, "I assure you this is no hoax. I was in utter disbelief just as you are now. We found him in one of our testing sessions in the regular schools in the city. As you know we test students there every year looking for hopefuls. After showing that he had a spark of magical energy within him he was brought here and put through the normal tests to see what disciplines he might be able to train for." Usarus paused a second for effect. "My friend, he passed all of them."

Josef now intrigued had to chime in, "But that young? That has never happened before. I know you were named one of eight while still in school but if I recall that did not happen until you entered your final year."

"Yes."

"How is that possible though? Someone in the Shoone family showing any magical talent at all would surprise me. They are huge supporters of the church and they don't even have divine magic running through their veins let alone arcane magic."

"Well this is were it gets interesting." Usarus came up out of his chair and reached for the wine bottle sitting on Josef's side of the desk. He had him now he knew. Josef would take an interest here and take this child as his apprentice. After filling his own glass he continued, "I did some digging here of course."

"Of course. And what did you find out?"

"He is not of Garrison Shoone's loins." Usarus took his own drink and let that set in. "Apparently Sydni Shoone, his mother, was unfaithful."

"Then who is his father?"

"That she would not divulge. You can well imagine the shock on that old Garrison Shoone's face when he found out that his son was able to cast magic. He knew then that the child was not of his line."

"I'll bet that went over well."

"That may be an understatement. He denounced the boy fully. Cast him out of his house."

"So the school stepped in as a surrogate I guess."

"Actually Sydni Shoone brought him to us. With payment in full for his entire education so that he might stay here."

"You took it?"

"Of course." Both Usarus and Josef shared a little laugh at that. "I know it is not needed. The intrigue around him alone secured a place for him here but it wasn't her money after all and Garrison Shoone is a right ass." Both shared a good laugh at that followed by a raise of their glasses.

"So what would you have of me then?" Josef asked.

"Well if you will not stay here then I wish for the boy to summer with you. I can watch over his training during the school year and he can get off of the island and see a bit of the world and be under your watch during the summer."

"With me. With everything I have going on. Surely not."

Usarus knowing that Josef was already intrigued and about to let go of his stubbornness made his final argument. "Look Josef. This matter with Deathmar is likely to take months if not longer. In the meantime I am asking this of you."

"With all this going on around me it will not be safe."

"You said yourself that Deathmar will not attack again. Not anytime soon anyway. He is waiting for you. If that day should come than I want you to contact me immediately and the entire force of Hareth Academy will descend on Silver Guard Keep. You know we can be there instantly using the portal at the school." Josef looked to argue more but Usarus cut him off again, "Just think about it. In the meantime I would like for you to meet him."

Josef sat with glass in hand and rubbed the beard on his chin contemplating what he should do for a long while. Finally he asked, "What is the boy's name?"

"Havander Shoone." Usarus replied knowing he had just sunk his hook.

Havander Shoone followed close behind an older student who had been dispatched by the Headmaster in order to bring him to his office. As they rounded the corner and entered the hallway that would lead them to his office Havander could not help but worry that something might be wrong with his mother. Perhaps word had come that his father had thrown her out as well or worse yet that his father had changed his mind about him. While he was worried for his mother he also did not want to leave school. He would much rather stay here than go and live with her if that were the case. The wondrous things he had seen since starting school in this castle and the lessons he received by his professors had him loving magic more and more with each passing day. He contemplated his options as they reached the door and the other student knocked. From behind the door he could hear the Headmaster bid them entry.

As the door swung open Usarus said, "Ah, at last. Do come in young Havander." Usarus turned his attention to the other student. "That will be all. Havander here will be a few minutes. You can go about your evening."

With a short bow to the Headmaster the other student exited while Havander eased his way past him, entering the room with his gaze locked on the floor. Once he fully entered the room he looked up to see another man standing next to the Headmaster. He was an older gentlemen dressed in robes of gray and trimmed in white. He was holding a most magnificent looking staff with a blue gem of some sort on its top the likes of which he had never seen before. With a wave of the Headmasters hand the door behind Havander closed shut. As it did he turned his head around to see that he was correct that with just a wave of his hand the Headmaster had closed the door from clear across the room. He turned back around with a smile on his face. Truly magic was a glorious thing to behold.

Moving around one side of his desk while Josef went the other way Usarus said, "Havander, I would like you to meet a good friend of mine." Once the two stood before Havander who had lowered his gaze once more Usarus continued, "Havander this is Master Josef Righe of The Silver Guard."

Havander's head snapped up in disbelief and locked eyes with Josef. He had heard of Master Righe and The Silver Guard in history class. Their adventures and deeds had been outlined in battles between Cruz Kingdom and Casta. He thought surely this could not be the same man. Those stories were over a hundred years old.

Josef stretched out his right hand. "Pleasure to meet you Havander."

Havander did the same taking a hold of Josef's hand and shaking. "The pleasure is mine Master Righe."

"Ah a firm shake and good manners. A good sign of character young mage." Josef took measure of Havander as they shook hands and noticed the blushing of cheeks at his referral of mage comment. The young boy seemed to be brimming with pride as his shoulders noticeably perked up. "Tell me Havander, how do you like it at Hareth Academy?"

"It is like nothing I could have ever hoped for Master Righe." They ended their handshake and believing now that this meeting had nothing to do with his family he removed those thoughts from his mind. "May I ask you something Master Righe?"

"Well of course. What can I answer for you?"

"Well sir, in history class we read about Master Righe and his Silver Guard and some of the battles they were in while fighting Cruz soldiers. He must have been your grandfather I imagine."

"Oh you don't say." Josef said while looking over to Usarus who had a large toothy grin clearly visible even under his enormous beard and mustache.

Havander not catching it went on, "Yes sir. They also said that The Silver Guard has been fighting monsters like vampires and werewolves for Casta since their founding. I'm sure you have got to have loads of details not in my books." Havander took a breath and continued, "Could you tell me more about The Silver Guard?"

"I would love to fill you in Havander but I'm afraid those stories will take some time and it is getting late for you. You have class in the morning after all."

Havander's shoulders slumped ever so slightly and he lowered his gaze for just a second before booming right back in and with his big blue eyes and locked stares with Josef once again. "Yes sir but you will tell me sometime?"

Josef almost startled by Havander's exuberance was on the defensive against this young child before him. How could he disappoint such enthusiasm? "Uh yes Havander. I will tell you sometime." Josef gave a little bow to Havander and stuck out his hand to shake once again. "Tonight though I just wanted to meet the young man whom I heard is exceptional in his classes."

If possible Havander was brimming with even more pride than before. He took Josef's hand in his once again and bid them both a good night. He exited the office and headed straight for his dormitory wanting to get in some studying before going to bed and perhaps brag to his classmates that he had just been personally introduced to a relative of the founder of The Silver Guard, Josef Righe, who bore the same name as what must have been his great grandfather.

CHAPTER SEVEN

The Fallen One—Selmeril, 1014

JOSEF RIGHE EASED his horse out of Clarcton Town along the Mehm Road, which continued on to Lanos. It was late and he could have decided to stay at the inn in Clarcton but instead decided that he would sleep outdoors tonight before making the final leg of his journey back home. He had been traveling for seven days after leaving Hareth Academy the morning following his meeting with The Orders. Although his meeting with The Orders had gone as he had expected he was still frustrated with their decision. Parts of what Usarus and he had discussed concerning the best route to strike back at Deathmar the Black made sense. The amount of lives that would be at risk on any kind of trek into the underdark was wearing on his resolve but still it was a risk he was willing to take. Ever the optimist when it concerned battle, Josef believed he could make it benefit his side. On the other hand he knew as well that if Deathmar was venturing into the affairs of humans in their lands and continued to do so then a fight on their terms would have a much better chance at succeeding. There were too many unknowns as of yet. Usarus assured him that every means he had in finding information out about his movements would be put to use. Josef did not believe that was enough though. While considerable resources were at play through Hareth Academy he believed he would have to rely on other means of information. One in which he had used on a couple of occasions despite the danger that it involved.

After leaving Clarcton well behind him he veered his horse off the road towards the Mehm River. He found a suitable spot to camp under a large sycamore tree close to the banks of the river. After seeing to his horse and gathering enough loose wood from the grounds nearby he settled in and lit a fire just as the last rays of sunlight disappeared. He took a quick meal of jerky and bread as he sat next to the fire with the sycamore and his horse tethered to it at his back. After, he gathered materials from his saddlebags he would need for the task he was going to perform.

He sat back in front of the fire cross legged and set before him two small cylinders with tiny elaborate designs engraved into their surface. Connected to the bottom of each and running from one to the other of the two cylinders was a copper strand connecting them together. Josef took a deep breath and visibly relaxed as he closed his eyes and began chanting in low murmured tones, too low for anyone to decipher had they been present. When he finished speaking he opened his eyes and saw the faintest of light emanating from within the cylinders. Then quick as can be the lights blinked out leaving Josef sitting in front of the fire knowing that his magical sending had been sent. With nothing more to do but see if he received a reply he packed up his tools, grabbed his pipe and tobacco and sat himself down in front of the sycamore with his back leaning against the tree. After lighting his pipe he reached up and grabbed Etburn, which was leaning against the sycamore, and laid it across his lap. There he sat quietly waiting and hoping this would not be a disaster.

Hours ticked by as Josef sat and waited. He had gathered more wood and stoked the fire a few more times in the passing time. The night was mostly clear with a few scattered clouds and the air was fairly warm for this early in the spring. On a couple of occasions he had heard rustling in bushes and some small creature making noise down at the banks of the river. Probably raccoons edging closer to investigate this human with his fire he figured. He was hopeful his wait was over when he had heard the noises but these were not the creatures of the night that he was waiting for.

Suddenly he felt it. He knew he was being watched. There was no answer to his sending. That would have come in the form of words echoing in his mind if he so allowed the sending in. He knew too that eyes were not directly upon him as though someone was watching him directly but rather someone was watching from afar. Always placed upon his person were wards of warning against scrying. These wards were not to block scrying, although he could have it so if he so wanted but rather they were designed to inform him when scrying was being attempted on his person. Very easily he could have dispelled the scrying attempt but that would defeat his purpose. He knew his audience was all too cautious to not take certain precautions so he let the scrying continue and tried to appear unaware that it was even happening. He reached for his pipe again and lit it with a conjured flame upon his fingertip and settled against the sycamore more deeply. He knew it would not be long now.

Josef's horse adjusted her stance and flattened her ears. She was aware that something was approaching even before Josef. The sign from the horse alerted him that he was no longer alone. The sounds of the surrounding forest quieted as well and the only sounds came from the crackling fire directly in front of him. He stared out over the flames into the woods along the Mehm River and waited. Seconds ticked by before Josef could hear very faintly the footfalls of the one who approached and then the firelight reflected back a glimmer of red off of a pair of eyes growing ever closer. Josef laid his pipe down and stood with Etburn firm in his grasp now and took a couple steps closer to the fire. His invited guest stopped within equal distance to the fire opposite him.

Standing not ten feet from Josef stood Braden Aranor. Commonly referred to as "The Fallen One." Josef examined him as Braden did the same to him. He looked the same as ever wearing similar attire to that which Josef had always seen him in. Clad mostly in black with gold trim on the parts of his clothing that could be seen under the long overcoat he wore that ran all the way to the ground. Over that and perhaps sewn in to the overcoat he wore a set of pauldrons also black and trimmed in gold that came up and formed a collar around the neck. Although black, the pauldrons shined brightly as the firelight glinted off their surface. An impressive sight he was as always but nothing stood out more than his red trimmed iris surrounding his large black pupils. The colors of the eyes were a trademark of all of his kind. While vampires could make their eyes appear as a normal humans would Josef had never seen Braden do so. In fact his eyes were more often almost completely red with only a small dot of black in their center. He expected that the lord and first of his kind of all vampires wore them proudly and without fear of anyone or anything knowing who or what he was.

Breaking the silence of the still night Braden said in his deep melodic voice, "Good evening young one."

Josef rolled his eyes and then said, "I could say the same." Josef disliked being called young one, which is something that Braden had always called him. In truth Josef looked to be in his early sixties though he was over three hundred years old. Braden on the other hand was well over one thousand years old and appeared to be in his early twenties. Shrugging off the thought Josef continued, "Took you long enough."

Braden's lips parted in a crooked smile on the right side of his mouth revealing one of his fangs. He was always amused at how Josef referred to him as though he would an old friend. He thoroughly enjoyed the banter between himself and his old enemy. "One never knows when you will be up to your old tricks. Perhaps you had set a trap and were trying to kill me once again."

Josef sighed and shook his head. "You know better than that. I made it clear and without reservation when I was coming for you."

"Yes I suppose you are right. Perhaps if you hadn't you would have had more success." Braden let that hang in the air for just a second before continuing, "Although I doubt it."

"As much as I love reliving old times I called upon you for a reason."

"Deathmar." Braden stated instead of asking.

In times past Josef would have been shocked and if it were someone else he was speaking with he still would have been. One thing he has learned when dealing with Braden is to never be surprised. "What can you tell me?"

"Very little I'm afraid. Still probably more than your little friends at Hareth."

Josef noticed that Braden's timbre in his voice changed menacingly when referring to Hareth Academy. Nothing ever seemed to unnerve Braden but he never disguised his contempt for the academy. Once a member of Hareth Academy and Master of Necromancy before his transformation to a vampire, something in which no one to this day knows how he did it, he now despised the academy for trying to take his life after learning of his transformation.

Josef asked, "But you do know something?"

"Of course. Information is power after all and I always follow the players of the game."

"Oh come Braden. You know I do not believe in your theories."

R. A. HAYDEN

"And why not young one? Is this attack not proof that Deathmar wishes to be a major player?" Braden was referring to what he liked to call "the game." He believed that there are powers on Drilain that thrive for nothing less than total domination of the continent if not the entire world itself.

Josef began trying to argue, "Because it does not make sense. Especially for Deathmar. No one had heard from him for about a hundred years or so."

Braden interrupted, "You mean not in the human lands."

Josef looked to him quizzically. "What do you mean?"

"Just because you and your Silver Guard defeated him once all that time ago does not mean he just slunk back to some swamp to lick his wounds forever." Braden let Josef think on that while moving to the side and grabbing a large fallen log and pulling it next to the fire effortlessly with one hand. Once there he sat and motioned for Josef to do the same. Reluctantly Josef edged around the fire and seated himself as far as possible on the other end of the log. Something that Braden noticed and smiled again. "Relax young one. It is not I who has ever come after you." Braden raised his hands out towards the flame and rubbed his palms together as though trying to warm his hands. Something that was of course not necessary for cold could never hinder him in any way. He merely liked to play the part and wanted Josef to relax a bit more.

"Please continue." Josef bade.

"Think about it young one." Braden started again without even looking in Josef's direction. He was content to look into the fire and explain as though having a conversation with an old friend instead of a once fierce enemy. "Deathmar is one of the last of his kind. Not only one of the last black dragons on Drilain but one of the last chromatic dragons as well. And let us not also forget that he is far older than even me. He has been a player of the game for a very long time but recently he has changed goals it seems."

"What does that mean?"

"Back when you encountered him before he was in the River Lands looking for information regarding the Ancient Dragon Kings."

Josef waved his hand dismissing the notion. "Bah. The ancient ones are long dead."

"Something I believe as well but something Deathmar has been obsessing over for centuries. He believes they went into hiding or at least one of them did at the end of The Dragon Wars and will someday return and when that happens dragons will once again rule over all."

"What does that have to do with now?"

"Well it seems he has finally given up on finding them and instead wishes to take on the role of conqueror himself."

"That still doesn't explain why he would assault my people."

"Doesn't it?" Braden asked and looked over to Josef. "What better way to announce you presence than to attack an old adversary, one in which defeated you in the past." Josef began to shake his head but Braden did not relent. "The infamous Silver Guard and their founder Josef Righe, hero of the Kingdom of Casta."

"No it was because we happened upon his forces in the Talt Mountains and stopped them from slaughtering dwarves is why he attacked us."

"He was not killing them. He was gathering slaves." Braden said in a matter of fact tone and then reached down to grab a large stick and began poking at the fire.

Josef watched and thought about the two dwarven villages that they had entered in the Talt Mountains. They were completely empty. No bodies and no signs of struggle or burning of the villages had been seen. After contemplating this he continued. "For what? Why take dwarves?"

"That I cannot answer yet. But it is not just dwarves. His little minions have been buying up slaves in Santon and The River Lands and raiding villages and towns of humans as well."

"How do you know all of this?"

Braden smiled. "I fancy myself the best player of the game and watch all pieces closely." He looked to Josef and saw a very unpleasant look on his face. "I ought not jest. I became aware when hill dwarf tribes in Sranihn Mountains also started going missing. This peaked my interest and I began investigating."

"So he is taking them back to Veszdor. Back to the underdark for some reason." Josef stated thinking that he could use this information to garner support for the mission he wanted in the first place. Surely the powers of not only Casta but also other allies would rally to the cause of so many being taken as slaves by drow.

"No actually. That is what I believed as well at first."

"Then where?"

"That I do not know. What I do know is that my sources in Veszdor where completely unaware of any influx of slaves in their city and hill dwarves from the surface and humans would not go unnoticed."

"But surely the powers in Veszdor would know something."

"I doubt they very much know what is going on. Deathmar is an unnamed power of House Drae for the matron mothers of the city would not allow him voice as a true power of the city. Whatever Deathmar and House Drae are up to they probably could not get it sanctioned by the powers above them."

"Well this tells me nothing."

"It tells us everything."

"How do you mean?" Josef leaned closer to the fire weighing heavily upon Etburn. What insight was he not seeing?

"It tells us that any conceived notion you had on striking back at Deathmar in Veszdor would not produce the desired result you had hoped."

Josef positioned Etburn to his forehead and leaned upon it thinking of the implications of going there and bearing no fruit.

Braden could feel the even heavier weight come crashing down on Josef. "While I have always admired your courage and devotion to those you care for as well as your straight forward thinking about an enemy, me included in the past, I believe you will have to wait this one out."

Josef sighed heavily and looked to Braden. He wondered if this was all a distraction. If indeed what Braden was telling him was true. "Why tell me all of this?"

Braden straightened and looked as though he wanted to laugh. "You called me lets not forget."

"Yes of course but why? With our history why help me?"

"Perhaps I am helping myself young one." Braden watched Josef closely as he thought about that.

"Always quizzical in the end eh?"

"No. Not this time." Braden paused as he pondered how to word this. He did not wish to insult his old enemy but he could tell that Josef was truly getting old. He knew his magic was beginning to fail and would not keep him alive forever. He knew that of Oran as well. The ring in which Oran wears was a gift of his to Oran unbeknownst to them. Through the many decades that their stories have been entwined with his he had truly taken a liking to them despite the fact they have tried to kill him on multiple occasions, one in which Oran almost did end his existence. "Like it or not young one, you and Oran are players of the game. Deathmar knows this and wishes to strike a decisive blow on any who could stand in his way once his end game is known to us. He wants you to come to the underdark."

"So do nothing?"

"We are doing something right now by not playing the game the way he wants. I suggest you take the advice of that old crab Usarus, which he no doubt gave you and wait this one out."

"Hah." Josef laughed. "That was one thing I didn't want to do."

"Yes I know but as much as I can't stand Usarus I'd have to agree with him on this. Deathmar will slip up it's just a matter of time." Braden stood up and threw his now half burnt stick into the fire and walked around the log to head back in the direction in which he came.

Josef let him go not bothering to turn and face him until he was almost out of the range of the firelight then called after him, "You never asked anything of me. What is in this for you?"

Braden turned his head around showing his eyes once again reflected in the firelight to Josef. "This is my game. I will not have some bloated old black worm decide the fate of the pieces."

After that last statement he turned and headed deeper into the darkness and was simply gone, leaving Josef to think about all that was said. Slowly the sounds of the forest crept back into earshot and Josef retrieved his pipe and lit it as he sat on the log. Puffs of smoke from his pipe mixed with the smoke from the fire for long hours through the night as Josef contemplated every scenario that was laid out before him now. In the end as the first rays of sunlight started to peak through the trees he rose up and started for his horse wanting to head back home to rest from this tiresome journey and perhaps begin refitting his laboratory to be more appropriate for an apprentice of a young age.

PART II

Rekindle

CHAPTER EIGHT

The News—Sadan, 1014

TWO WEEKS AFTER Josef's return from Tomé he sat in his laboratory searching through the many books he had and was coming up with a sort of lesson plan for his apprentice that would be arriving sometime in the first week of Silhad, the first month of summer. Earlier that day he had a conversation with Headmaster Usarus through a scrying crystal designed for two-way communication. Unlike their previous conversations over the past couple of weeks, which pertained to dealing with Deathmar and any intelligence on his whereabouts, Josef was relieved and even happy to let Usarus know that he would indeed take Havander Shoone as his apprentice for the summer. Although he had many apprentices under his belt and did guest lectures at Hareth Academy from time to time he had never had an apprentice that was this young. Neither had he ever had an apprentice who was one of eight. All of his prior apprentices were recent graduates of the academy who had excelled in multiple disciplines but never all eight. Now his youngest student ever would be here in just a couple months and Josef found himself slightly nervous and excited all at once. Research and teaching had always been a great love of his and he wanted to take the right approach with this young mind, who Usarus had relayed to him was excelling in classes beyond that of any first year student he had ever seen. Josef was taken out of his thoughts by a loud knock on the door.

"Do come in!" He shouted more than he meant to. Caught up in his process he did not want to be disturbed.

Harold opened the door to the lab and saw Josef set up on one of the long desks with papers, scrolls and books spread out before him. He had not looked up and continued scribbling on some piece of parchment while he simultaneously had his nose in a large book. "I am sorry to disturb you Master Righe but we may have a problem."

Still not looking up Josef asked, "And what's that Harold? I'm rather busy."

Harold crossed his hands before him at his belt line and walked into the room. As he approached Josef, he answered, "Well sir, it's Cecilia you see."

"What of her Harold? She's on the mend. She has had a good amount of color return to her complexion this last week."

"I'm afraid it's gone again sir."

"Gone." Josef finally stopped writing and looked up from his book. Harold looked to be in disbelief and in terrible discomfort. "Well what is it man? Explain yourself."

Harold swallowed hard. "She's pregnant sir."

Josef dropped his quill immediately thinking of the worst. He stood up and moved towards Harold. "Are you sure Harold?"

"She believes so sir and my wife agrees. They are upstairs talking to Oran now. He sent me to get you."

Josef moved right past Harold and out the door heading for upstairs. Surely this could not be. He reached the top of the stairs with Harold in tow. At the top of the stairs he could see Oran talking to Georgette next to Cecilia who was sitting in one of the lounge chairs with her elbows on her knees and her hands cupping her face. She was obviously crying. Josef couldn't help but think, hadn't this poor women been through enough. She was just up and moving about in the last week, aided considerably by the healing potions that Josef had recently procured on his trip to the capital. After finally feeling well enough to move about she was now facing the prospect of possibly being pregnant. He hoped dearly that it was of her husbands' doing.

Georgette moved to intercept Josef before he got to Cecilia when she saw him heading in their direction. Before he could even ask anything she immediately jumped to Cecilia's defense. "You keep your tone even sir or you'll find my ladle smacking you on the back of your head and you can cook your own dam meals."

Josef came to an abrupt halt taken fully by surprise by Georgette's tone. He looked over her shoulder to Oran who wore a small smile obviously amused by her authoritative way. Georgette was what they call a bit of a tyrant and motherly figure for all in the house when it came to the day-to-day living arrangements despite the fact that besides Cecilia she was presently the youngest one living there. That was part of her charm, Josef knew, but he also knew that he had been short with everyone the last couple of weeks and his attitude had been wrought with frustration over not being able to do much in the way of avenging his fallen brothers. Thinking back on it now he was surprised that Georgette had not smacked him with one of her ladles yet. He brought his hands up and placed them on either shoulder of Georgette who was standing right in front of him with a stern look on her face. In a calm and easy tone with a smile upon his face he said, "Now is no time for my silly rants but perhaps instead time for celebration."

Georgette raised her eyebrows in quiet surprise and let Josef move past her to Cecilia's side. He lowered himself to one knee and put a hand up to rest on her sobbing shoulder. "My dear lady. What is the meaning of all this crying?"

Cecilia removed her hands from her face as she looked up to see Josef staring intently and with great concern etched upon his face as though he was looking down on his own daughter. She was reminded of her husbands' father who was one of the kindest men she had ever met. Cecilia attempted to respond but instead fresh tears rolled down her cheeks and she covered her face again with her hands. Georgette moved to stand behind her and Josef could see he might have to get answers from her instead.

"Well Georgette, tell me what we know. Are you sure she is carrying?" Josef asked.

"As certain as I can be. I recognized the signs a few days ago but said nothing preferring to wait. Considering recent," she paused a second not wanting to upset Cecilia more, she wanted to use the right words, "Things I could not be sure at first."

"How do you mean?" Josef inquired further.

"Well she's been throwing up in the morn and late in the eve. Given all that's been happening with recovery from her injuries and all I'd hoped it was nothing until she came to me believing the same." Georgette looked down and stroked Cecilia's hair.

"Surely that's not enough to go on. This past month has been hard indeed." Josef interjected.

Georgette shook her head and added, "She's not bled in over two months. Since well before poor Jon passed."

"Well pleasant news then."

Cecilia looked up at that comment which threw her from her line of thinking. "What?"

"Perhaps Jon left you one last gift before leaving this world." Josef said hoping to raise her spirits.

"No. No. It belongs to that monster."

"Oh come dear we don't know that."

"Yes I do." Cecilia said in-between sobs.

Josef edged closer and around to her left side and put his arm around her and gently pulled her closer. She took to the support and leaned her head against his shoulder. "How could you know such a thing child?" He asked.

"Me and Jon had been trying for months and it had not happened for us."

"Well there you go. These things take time. Perhaps as his final act he was able to leave you with something of himself."

Cecilia shuddered a little less and her tears began to stem their flow. She began wiping her face first with her hand than using a handkerchief that Josef pulled as if from nowhere and handed her. "Do you truly believe that?"

"I believe it is a great possibility and a hopeful one as well. Don't you?"

Cecilia just looked into his eyes not sure how to respond. She turned and looked up to Georgette for further comfort.

Josef turned his attention back to Georgette as well. "Georgette."

"Yes."

"We will not mark this day with sadness but instead celebrate." He turned his attention to Harold. "Harold I want you to go into town and get anything Georgette requires for a fine meal and a large desert. After we will break open some wine and toast to Jon Alio."

Cecilia looked recovered and smiled just a bit. Josef motioned for Georgette to take his place beside her, which she did and embraced her in a hug.

"Now Georgette if you wouldn't mind taking Cecilia into the kitchen and take stock of whatever we need for tonight. Make whatever her favorite dishes are of course and let Harold know if there is anything we are short of."

The ladies moved off towards the kitchen with Georgette taking Cecilia's hand in hers and began talking about plans for what they might make. When they exited the room and out of earshot Josef turned to Oran. "Are we all that knows of this?"

Harold replied before Oran who didn't know the details and could only shrug. "No sir."

His soothing tone now gone Josef said, "Explain. Tell me who else may know."

Harold motioned towards the back door and began explaining, "The soldiers were here changing shifts when Cecilia first broke down. Two of them came through the back door to grab some belongings they had left on the table there."

"And they knew what she was on about?"

"I believe so sir. She was very upset and vocal."

Josef moved towards the front double doors which he had just finished warding the day prior after the replacements had finally been finished and hung properly. He opened the doors wide, Oran and Harold exited right behind him. Just as he had feared, Lieutenant Borin and Sergeant Adley were just exiting the town and approaching on the road with two other soldiers whom he assumed were the ones who overheard Cecilia.

Josef turned to Harold, "Go out back and round up the soldiers on guard there and tell them to walk around front. Tell them to grab all of their gear and that I need to speak with them."

Sensing the urgency in Josef's voice Harold moved quickly through the house and out the back door and gathered the four soldiers that were milling about. He hurried them around the house and motioned them to where Josef had directed the other four in front of the stairs. He moved past them and up the stairs and took his place again next to Oran and behind Josef.

Standing at the top of the stair Josef looked down upon the soldiers who had been standing vigil at Silver Guard Keep this past month and began speaking to them all, "Soldiers. I would like to thank you for your help in our time of need but I do believe we can take it from here. If you look behind you your commander is on his way this very moment to collect you. Do save him some time and please leave. Next time I'm in Willow Bark Tavern I'll buy you all multiple rounds of ale."

With that the soldiers raised a hearty little cheer and moved off and headed towards town. Josef could see the pace of Lieutenant Borin quicken when he saw his soldiers exiting the front gate. Oran closed the doors to the house and moved to stand beside his father. They could see and slightly hear the raised voice of the Lieutenant after his soldiers got done explaining why they were heading back to post and after he was done yelling all of the soldiers got in formation behind them as they headed back their way.

Josef turned to Harold and said, "Harold you might want to go back inside."

"Why sir? I don't understand what is going on."

Oran began to explain for his father, "Well you see Harold, the young and brash Lieutenant has just heard that Cecilia is pregnant."

"So. What is that to him?"

"They are going to automatically assume it is from her rape."

As if that should explain everything Harold still wasn't quite catching on. "I don't understand sir."

"Although the Lieutenant is in disbelief that what raped her was a dragon because he is ignorant and doesn't believe such a thing is possible he is going to want to take her."

"Why?"

"Well for one thing my father here chewed his ass up one side and down the other when he returned from Tomé for that impromptu and erroneous report he sent to his commanders in the capital." Oran gave a little chuckle at that.

"And the second sir?"

"The second Harold is that we do know that what they call dragonborn or half dragon half some other race is possible. In fact hundreds of years ago they were common in certain parts of Drilain but now as far as we know they are very few."

"So they want to take her for that?"

"They'll kill her for that Harold." Josef finished for Oran.

Harold looked back to the doors then forward again at the now close troops. Just as they neared the stairs and Sergeant Adley gave the order for his men behind himself and the Lieutenant to halt. Harold stepped forward to the left of Josef opposite Oran and rested his hand on the hilt of the small dagger he wore on his belt.

"What can I do for you Lieutenant?" Josef asked after giving Lieutenant Borin time to assess the situation before him.

Lieutenant Borin took a step closer putting one foot on the bottom stair and looked up directly into Josef's eyes, anger clearly etched upon his face. "My men here tell me that you have dismissed them from their post."

"Yes Lieutenant. There services are no longer required."

"And what makes you say that?"

"It's been a month since the attack and not a peep since. Perhaps your initial report was correct and it was just a raiding party of orcs from the mountains." Josef said putting emphasis on the end of that statement to sound sarcastic.

"Despite that you do not give my men orders." Lieutenant Borin insisted.

Behind him Josef could clearly see Sergeant Adley and a couple of the soldiers shift nervously in their stance. "Is that so Borin?"

Lieutenant Borin marked immediately the drop of his formal title and he narrowed his eyes. Quite intent on his actions he continued, "Yes that is so. Despite your reputation and that of The Silver Guard you are not of the Castan military and therefore have no authority over my men whatsoever."

"Yes, Borin but this is my property and I'll decide who is to be on it."

"Property that resides in the Kingdom of Casta in the town of Lanos of which I am the commander and will decide where my men are to be stationed." Lieutenant Borin took another step up and continued, "And now I hear Cecilia Alio may be carrying the child of her rapist."

"What of it?" Josef decided not to elaborate on any possibility that she may not even be carrying a child at all or that if so it could very well be from her husband. His patience was growing thin and he was not going to be questioned by this spoiled idiot who no doubt only got commissioned as an officer because of family ties and no real merit.

"I hereby order you to release her into my custody at once."

"Or else what?"

Lieutenant Borin took hold of the hilt of his sword and dared take another step forward. Oran had had enough of this and he likewise grabbed the hilt of the dagger he was wearing on his belt and advanced a step. Before the Lieutenant could utter anything he cut him off, "That's enough Borin. You and yours will leave now or I'll cut you in half."

"How dare you threaten an officer?" Not taking his eyes off of Oran who now only stood a few steps away up the long set of stairs yelled back, "Sergeant, arrest this man."

Oran looked to Sergeant Adley. A man he knew well who had served at Lanos for close to eight years now and had fought along side The Silver Guard on several occasions as had a couple of the men behind him. Adley considered his options and did not move.

Lieutenant Borin turned his head around. "Did you not hear me Sergeant? I said arrest this man."

Sergeant Adley puffed up his chest, looked Lieutenant Borin straight in the eye and said, "No."

"I beg your pardon."

"You can beg all you want but I'll not follow that order."

Lieutenant Borin drew his sword out of its scabbard while simultaneously Josef uttered a couple words into his palm and extended his arm in Borin's direction. A small amount of multicolored mist nearly invisible to the naked eye hit him in the face. He blinked instinctively and crunched up his nose at the peculiar smell. A second later his eyes rolled into the back of his head and he fell backwards onto the cobblestone walkway in front of the stairs. A couple of the soldiers drew their weapons but did nothing more as Sergeant Adley raised his hand up in a signal to halt. He stepped forward and leaned down over Borin. "Serves you right you little bastard." Then he looked up to Josef and asked, "How long is he going to be asleep?"

"Not long I'm afraid." Josef moved down to his position and uncorked a small brown flask that he pulled from one of his inner pockets of his robe. He crouched next to Borin and opened his mouth with one hand and poured a small amount of the liquid from the flask into his mouth. "There we go, all down. Now that should keep him under for a couple days I should think."

Sergeant Adley asked, "What was that?"

"Just something to help him rest. He seems of a mood and I haven't the time to argue with him." Josef stood and gave a slight nod to Sergeant

Adley. "Thank you Sergeant but you know when he wakes up he is likely to remember everything. He may put you under the lash for this."

"Bah. I've been lashed for less. I think it was time for him to be put into his place." Sergeant Adley then addressed his troops, "Men. It seems the Lieutenant is exhausted from his workload. Pick him up and go throw him in his bunk so he can sleep it off."

Four of the men moved to the Lieutenant and positioned themselves so that each could grab a limb. They hoisted him up while Sergeant Adley retrieved his sword and placed it back into its scabbard. "You men all go back to the barracks. I'll be by directly." When the men moved off he turned to Josef once more. "What now Master Righe? Is it true about the girl? Could she really be carrying a baby from Deathmar the Black?"

"Honestly we do not know as of yet but I'll not let anymore harm come to that girl on account of him. I thank you for your discretion Sergeant. I'll see to it that Borin is replaced here immediately."

"You can do that?"

Oran who had stepped down closer to them said, "Easily. That idiot really had no idea who he was talking to. I wouldn't be surprised if he is not busted back to third grade soldier after we talk to your guy's superiors."

Sergeant Adley thought about that and believed the assessment completely. These were after all The Silver Guard. Heroes of Casta whose friends in high places would no doubt see to it. "Let me know if you need anything in the meantime. I'll head back now and make sure the Lieutenant is comfortable."

"Not too comfortable I hope." Oran joked.

"Nah of course not."

Sergeant Adley headed back towards town leaving the trio standing on their stairs. When he departed Oran addressed his father, "What now you think?"

"Now we do as I said. We celebrate with the girls. I need the day to think this through. Harold."

"Yes sir."

"Do not let on to the women the gravity of the situation until I figure this out. Go inside and see that your wife has everything she needs for tonight's feast." He reached into his beltline and extracted a coin purse and tossed it to Harold. "Spare no expense and pickup a couple bundle of flowers for the women. We could use some more cheer around here."

Josef stood on the far side of The Silver Guard Cemetery waiting for the arrival of Headmaster Usarus. That morning he had contacted him and asked him to travel by portal to discuss the matter of Cecilia possibly being pregnant with a child by Deathmar the Black. Leaving Creet Island was not something that the Headmaster did often except to go to Tomé where he sat in as an advisor for the King when asked. The importance of this matter however would have had him demanding an audience with Josef had he not been invited. Josef waited at the appointed spot looking out over the fields behind Lanos. Before him a large circular area appeared looking very much like a vale of water standing vertically. Josef could see through it to the town beyond until Usarus stepped through and stood in front of it and then it winked out of existence as though it was never there leaving Usarus standing a few yards away from Josef.

"Well met Usarus. Thank you for coming so quickly." Josef said as he bowed to the Headmaster.

Usarus took some time to survey the scene around him. He looked to Josef standing in front of the cemetery and beyond to The Silver Guard Keep in the distance. "Yes well met but why did you have me travel here and not to the Keep itself?"

"You know you cannot use a portal to enter the grounds of the Keep. My wards prevent such intrusions."

"Of course but I could have shown up at the gate so that we may enter."

"I would prefer to keep this as quiet as possible for now. I do not wish those inside knowing of what we are to discuss. After we can walk up there and have a good midday meal. Oran has asked after you and would enjoy talking to you."

"Ah good but you are referring to the girl. You don't want her to know."

"Yes."

Usarus walked closer to Josef. "I see. This is unfortunate. I thank you for letting me know so quickly."

"I thought it best to have your support in this."

"And what support do you require Josef? This will not keep quiet."

"Surely not. The guards in town got wind of it already. Yesterday we had a little confrontation with them."

"Oh. And how did that go?"

"That fool commander of theirs demanded at sword point that we turn Cecilia over into his custody."

"I see. Where is he now? Hopefully not under of one of those tombstones behind you."

"No." Josef glanced back and looked over the tombstones of his fallen brothers then turned back to Usarus. "That fools' body would be an insult to my men if it had gone that way but no, he is merely sleeping in his quarters."

"I imagine you will have more problems when he awakens."

"Yes. He has become quite irrational in dealing with me since our dispute over the attack here but I wish for you to help me in that arena as well."

"More favors." Usarus reached up to stroke his long beard contemplating all the while the rare necessity of Josef asking him for favors. "What is it you need regarding the commander?"

"I want him replaced of course. The previous commander was well liked here and very competent. If he is available I would like to have him back. Talk to his superiors in Tomé. Tell them that I require this favor of them…"

Usarus interrupted, "Josef he is not necessarily wrong in wanting to take the woman if she is indeed pregnant with a child from Deathmar. His superiors will likely agree that he was right to try to take her."

"Possibly but not at the cost of a direct confrontation with me. You know this."

"Still when they hear of it fully they may demand that you give over the woman anyway."

"They can demand all they want. It won't happen."

"Meaning you will not give her over."

"Of course not. I hope you will convey that to them as diplomatically as possible when you speak to them."

Usarus again stroked his beard looking Josef over. Ever the stubborn one Josef was he knew. He was unsure on how this would play out.

"Alright Josef. The commander is the least of our problems. What of the child?"

"Cecilia will stay under my protection until she gives birth."

"You want her to carry it through to term then?"

"Of course." Now it was time for Josef to scrutinize Usarus. He thought the conversation would likely go this way but he would not be dissuaded from this. "What would you prefer to do Usarus?"

"If the child is indeed that of Deathmar the Black than most would not suffer it to live." Usarus was choosing his words carefully. He did not want a confrontation with Josef who was his oldest friend despite their obvious differences in important matters.

"I care little for what most would do. And besides we do not know that yet."

"What chance would you give it?"

Josef had thought long and hard about this the previous night. Trying to consider the timeline but he could not know for sure. "Dragonborn are rare but under the circumstances I would have to say fifty/fifty."

"Josef I do not advocate this personally but you know that all will say why take the chance. Why not simply end the pregnancy and spare this women the possibility?"

"Because Usarus, Cecilia Alio has been through enough. She has lost more than any due to recent events. First losing her husband than having to go through her brutal attack only to find out that she may be giving birth to a baby by the very bastard that raped her."

"Precisely the point. Spare her that outcome."

"Look Usarus. She has hope right now. Something hard to gain back after losing it. I'll not deny her that. Likely she will give birth to a child from her husband but even if we knew for sure that it wasn't I would not force the outcome if she did not wish it." Josef expected that last remark would surprise Usarus.

"I find that hard to believe. Deathmar has struck a devastating blow against your house and family. I do not believe you would suffer a child of his to live."

Josef stepped closer to Usarus and raised his tone slightly, "A child whose fault it wasn't."

"But Josef..."

Josef cut him off, "No Usarus do not mistake me. I am a killer of evil make no mistake. Head of a mercenary band who has for over two centuries assassinated any threat to rise up against Casta even when it was unseemly so that others would not have to get there hands dirty. I am not a murderer of children though."

"Alright my friend. Easy." Usarus could see he wouldn't get anywhere with this line of questioning. He raised his one hand not holding his signature staff and took a step back giving him more distance and indicating that he was backing down from this line. "We are only talking here. If the child is dragonborn what then?"

"Then Cecilia will likely raise it. She is of a kind heart and I can't imagine that she would kill it."

"But others will. That's the point. She will be endangering herself and you if you so decide to keep her under your protection."

"And why should that be? There are other dragonborn walking the lands of Casta even as we speak."

"Very few but yes. I concede that but all that we know of are of a dragon lineage that is not chromatic and even they keep their heads down and do not draw attention to themselves. Dragons are not well thought of from any line." Josef wanted to counter but Usarus did not let him. "Remember that town in The Broken Grasslands on the edge of The Dry Wastes that was completely destroyed by Bayorth the Copper?"

Josef nodded his head yes and knew where Usarus was going with this but Usarus continued anyway.

"Bayorth the Copper had long been an ally to Casta. The last true dragon to be considered such and so he walked freely without the guise of human form. That is until his son, his half dragon son got into a bar fight with Castan soldiers and was killed. Those idiots hung his body by the front gates and when Bayorth found out about it he destroyed the entire town and flew off with his son's body never to be seen again."

"Yes I know this but I still will not condemn this child. Especially not before he is even born."

"Fine Josef. I will concede this as well for now. So what else would you ask of me then?"

"Simple. I wish for the commander to be replaced and everything else to go on as they are now."

"The commander is easy but what else do you mean?"

"I will continue to inquire about Deathmar of course. I will kill him if found and opportunity presents itself therefore I will not be making any travel arrangements for the underdark. In the meantime I will be happy to take Havander Shoone as my apprentice as previously discussed." Josef motioned for Usarus to follow him to the Keep and they both began strolling along the path that would take them to the gate. Josef wanted to sate Usarus' curiosity he no doubt had about the Keep since he had not visited in a couple decades and introduce him to Cecilia so that he could gage her character and bare witness to the damage that Deathmar had left in the form of a large scar upon her right cheek. "Now we will make no declarations to Cecilia about anything. I wish to keep her hopeful and happy."

"Yes but as you said this news has already gotten out and will spread. You are sure to get inquiries from Tomé. The churches and others surrounding the King will not want to be left in the dark about a possible dragonborn from that of Deathmar."

"I will do my best to shield her from those and any word you might have in advance would be appreciated. She has strong support here in the form of my housekeeper, whom you've not met and fair warning she runs the house completely so be on your best behavior or she'll scold you as though you are a child."

CHAPTER NINE

Acquisitions—Sadan, 1014

A LOUD AND PERSISTENT knock pounded on the front doors of Silver Guard Keep the evening of the day following the departure of Headmaster Usarus taking Josef and Oran from their conversation after just finishing their dinner. Georgette and Cecilia were in the kitchen cleaning up and Harold had gone out to see to the animals out back. They could hear an unfamiliar voice asking for their help and to come quick. Oran went quickly to the door after grabbing his sword and scabbard from the weapon rack next to the door. Josef followed more slowly letting Oran get to the porthole before him. Oran threw the latch and opened it. There on the opposite side of the door Oran recognized the man pounding on the door as one of the soldiers who was present when Lieutenant Borin was taken away two days prior.

"What is it soldier?"

"It's Sergeant Adley sir. He needs your help." The soldier said in an excited tone.

Oran could well guess that the Lieutenant had at last woken from his slumber and they would soon have to be dealing with him. Fortunately they already had news from Usarus that their request for his replacement would be en route as soon as possible, which should deflate the little weasel. "Let me guess Sergeant Adley is getting the lash for his actions the other day."

"Yes sir. I mean no sir. It's far worse than that." The soldier said very animatedly.

"Calm down soldier. Tell me what's happened."

The soldier took a breath. "He is getting whipped sir but not with a lash. The Lieutenant ordered a bull whip to be used."

"What?" Oran grabbed for lock on the door and threw open the double doors. He grabbed the soldier by the top of his mail just under the chin and pulled him in close. "Explain!"

Stammering just a little the soldier went on, "The Lieutenant woke up not long ago and ordered the men into formation in the center of the outpost. Then he ordered men to apprehend the Sergeant and strap him to a wagon wheel. The Sergeant knew he was going to be punished and didn't bother putting up a fight at all. After he was strapped down the Lieutenant produced a bull whip and ordered one of the men to use that instead of the lash."

"Why didn't someone stop him?"

"All the other sergeants are out on patrol and no one else would dare go against the commander."

Oran released the soldier and took off in a run with Josef and the soldier following behind but Oran was quickly gaining distance on them. It was a few hundred yards to the gates of the outpost and Oran showed no sign of slowing. He couldn't believe that the Lieutenant could be this stupid. A lashing for disobedience was common punishment in the Castan military. Depending on the severity of the offense would determine how many lashes you got. It was a firm reminder to show who was in charge and stung like hell. While a lash would break skin the effects were short lived but to use a bullwhip was unheard of. In the proper hands a bullwhip could tear flesh down to the bone.

Oran continued running right through the gates of the large outpost. The guards were not at their posts in the towers adorning the walls and no sentries were there to stop him having all been ordered to the center square for assembly. He slowed as he rounded the corner of the barracks building and was in sight of the men all standing at attention with their backs to him listening to Lieutenant Borin lecturing them on obedience from the top of his stair leading to his private quarters. He moved to the left of formation of roughly fifty soldiers in attendance. This was a common number to be present at any one time for patrols were out constantly monitoring the borders of Casta, searching for bandits, and checking on the smaller farming communities to the south and east. As he reached the far side of the formation he could see the wagon next to the stables. As he got nearer the sight before him was horrendous. Tied to the back wagon wheel was Sergeant Adley hanging slack by his wrists

R. A. HAYDEN

and unconscious with blood flowing down his back and onto the ground. Multiple deep slashes ran across his backside. He ran over to his friend and lifted his chin looking for signs of life.

Sergeant Adley amazingly opened his eyes for just a second and smiled briefly after discerning who had a hold of him and then went back out. Oran turned his gaze to the Lieutenant who also took notice of his presence at that moment.

"Ah Oran Righe the subject of our conversation. You've saved me the trouble of coming to your home."

Oran stood and began advancing on the Lieutenant's position. He looked over to the soldiers all in line and pointed to the two nearest him. "You two cut him down immediately."

The two soldiers began to move in Sergeant Adley's direction but halted as the Lieutenant shouted, "Do not touch that man. I give the orders here."

Oran still walking steadily in his direction and slowly pulling his sword from its scabbard responded, "No longer Borin."

Lieutenant Borin not liking the approach of Oran Righe advancing on him with a weapon addressed his soldiers, "Men. This man means your commander harm. Take him now."

Oran stopped and turned, still twenty paces away from Borin and regarded the soldiers who still hadn't moved noticeably. Josef came into view on the right side of their formation along with the soldier who had informed them. "Soldiers!" He shouted loud so that all could hear. "Your commander has been relieved of his duty by order of The Silver Guard! Any man moves in my direction and you will share his fate!" Oran waited a few seconds and no man moved an inch. He turned back to Borin and continued walking. "Draw your sword you little whelp."

"Stay back old man." Lieutenant Borin shouted while drawing his weapon. "I don't want to hurt you."

Under different circumstances Oran may have laughed at that statement. Borin had no idea how right he was. While over two hundred years old he looked to be in his early forties but with the build and stamina of a much younger man. He had no more need for words and just advanced. Within a few paces Borin shouted again for his men but none came. As Oran neared, Borin came forward and attempted to slash right to left at Oran's midsection. Never slowing, Oran moved his right arm to his left with sword tip pointing down to block the assault and in the same fluid motion changed direction up over his head and brought his sword hilt smashing hard into the forehead of Borin, knocking him to the deck of the building, unconscious.

After kicking his sword away Oran again turned to the soldiers in attendance and walked back down the stairs towards them. He pointed in the direction of the two men he had ordered to cut down Sergeant Adley previously. "You two. I said cut him down."

Josef moved in front of the formation and began pulling forth bottles from the pockets of his robes as he went to help the Sergeant. Oran not quite finished stopped in front of the formation with sword still in hand and pointed to the man nearest him. "You!"

The soldier stepped forward. "Yes sir."

"Who held the whip?"

The soldier looked around nervously obviously not wanting to answer. When no word came Oran shouted even louder. "Who held the whip?"

In the front row two men over from the man standing out in front of Oran a soldier stepped forward and declared, "I did sir."

Oran walked over to stand in front of that soldier. "Good. I'm sure your Sergeant will want to speak with you when he is on his feet again. In the meantime," Oran pointed to one and then the other of the two men opposite him, "Escort him to a cell." When they hesitated Oran yelled, "Now!"

Those two men grabbed him up by his arms and began pulling him in the direction of their small jail all the while the soldier responsible for using the whip on Sergeant Adley was arguing, saying he was only following orders but Oran was hearing none of it. When he was out of sight Oran continued, "The rest of you. What I said is true. Your new commander is en route to Lanos as we speak. In the meantime you will strip former Lieutenant Borin of his armor and any further weapons he might have on him and throw him in the cell next to that idiot." Oran said while pointing in the direction the other soldier had just been led off to. "After that I suggest you find something constructive to do as your new commander will be getting a full report of todays actions upon his arrival."

Oran let that sink in while he looked over to Josef who was pouring liquid down the throat of Sergeant Adley. He knew it to be a healing potion and knowing his father it would be quite a powerful one. No doubt Adley would be on his feet in no time. Oran pointed to four more soldiers in the front line. "You four go get a litter so you can carry the Sergeant to Silver Guard Keep. The rest of you get out of my sight." When no one moved immediately Oran shouted again, "Now!"

The soldiers broke ranks. Most moving towards the barracks, those on duty headed towards their positions of responsibility and a few moved towards the Lieutenant to drag him to a cell. Most had heads bowed in shame and discomfort knowing they had just witnessed and done nothing for their beloved Sergeant who would have never allowed anything like that to happen to any one of them.

Oran retrieved his scabbard he had dropped on his approach to Borin and then went to his father who had Sergeant Adley on his side so that his back was not on the ground and his head in his lap. He took a knee beside them. "How is he?"

Josef grimaced slightly for an instant but replied, "I think he will be alright. That potion will kick in fast. Look you can see the wounds closing already." Josef pointed to the gashes, which were indeed slowly closing. "He will be out for a while though. Good idea to take him with us."

"I thought it best under these circumstances. Don't want to leave him here with these buffoons."

"That was a nice speech. Maybe you want to return to the ranks."

"Uh that would be a big no. Bunch of unthinking jackasses." Oran spit after the comment.

"I was surprised you didn't kill Borin."

"No I'll leave that for the Sarge here if he wants it."

The litter bearers showed up and as gentle as they could after applying some bandages laid Sergeant Adley onto it and hoisted him up for the trip back to Silver Guard Keep. They laid him down in a spare room and Georgette took to nursing him immediately. A couple hours passed and Oran had stayed by his bedside watching over him. Slowly Sergeant Adley opened his eyes and took in his surroundings. Finally focusing on Oran sitting at his bedside on a chair next to the bedside table with a single candle lit. He smiled a bit and asked, "You guys got a job opening?"

Oran smiled wide and laid his hand on Sergeant Adley's chest. "Just so happens we do."

Adley, Josef and Oran were sitting on the front deck of Silver Guard Keep waiting for Georgette to call them in for dinner while looking over the newly obtained gear that Adley had acquired from Armihrmond Firefist, the blacksmith and sole dwarf residing in Lanos. After healing fully from his wounds administered by his former commander Josef had sent him down to have new weapons and armor forged that were more befitting a member of The Silver Guard. Paid in full as part of his signing bonus Armihrmond had done an excellent job fitting Adley to an existing set of half-plate and matching helmet and forged a new longsword to replace Adley's short sword he previously carried. Josef had gone down to Armihrmond's forge when called at the appropriate time to add wards to the sword to increase strength and durability as he did for all weapons carried by members of The Silver Guard. Adley was still waiting for his shield, which he also preferred to use in battle but replaced his large tower shield, commonly used by Castan infantry, with a smaller design that would complement a more single combat style since The Silver Guard didn't really fight in a formation like the Castan infantry. Along with weapons and armor of his choosing he was provided a set of silver stakes, one of which was fitted with a handle and worn on the belt line like you would a dagger. Most Silver Guard members, including Oran, carried this signature weapon. Exceptions included but was not limited to members designing their own preferred semblance of the silver stake like Josef having Etburn's point dipped in silver or the spike on the back of the hammer carried by the recently fallen Eric Treby.

Adley held the stake out to Josef and asked, "What are these marks carved into this? I've always been curious."

Josef leaned up from his seated position so that he could grab the stake from Adley's hand. "Well you see here." Josef pointed to one of the markings on the side of the stake. "These are just smaller versions of the same runes or wards if you like that me and Armihrmond placed onto your sword. More necessary for this than your sword since silver is so soft. Essentially it makes it stronger and less likely to wear out."

Taking the stake back Adley asked further, "All magic than?"

"Yes indeed. I'll not have any of us go into a battle unprepared." Josef leaned back and out of the corner of his eye he noticed approaching

R. A. HAYDEN

horses coming down the road to Lanos. "Look there boys. I'd wager that is our new commander finally arriving."

Oran and Adley both turned their attention to the group of six riders closing in at a quick pace. They watched as they continued on towards Lanos. Once they reached the turn in the road that made its way up to The Silver Guard Keep they slowed and one rider broke free after giving some orders to the others and headed in their direction while the rest continued on into town. Even from this distance and with the light quickly fading to dusk they could recognize their old friend and former commander of the Lanos Outpost. All three stood up from their chairs and moved to the top of the stairs as he neared.

Smile wide and brimming with confidence he didn't even wait to fully dismount before starting in, "Well, well, well. What do we have here? A bunch of trouble makers from what I hear."

Oran moved first to meet him on the stairs and embraced him with the typical greeting of clasping each other's forearms. "Well met Lieutenant Payne."

"Oh watch yourself. It's Captain Payne now." Captain Payne proclaimed as he wagged a finger of his free hand in the face of Oran.

"Captain Payne you say. How did that happen?"

"Well you know these fools in Tomé can't get enough of me and my accomplishments after serving out here along side you boys hurried me along."

"You don't say. I see that some more gray hair came along with the promotion." Oran pointed to the hairline of Captain Payne.

Captain Payne grabbed at his short-cropped military haircut at the remark. "That's true enough." Though only thirty years of age, the same as Adley, Payne's dark hair had begun showing gray at a young age.

He moved up a couple stairs to embrace Adley who was next in line. "Seems you are out of uniform Sergeant."

Adley looked embarrassed to some extent. "Yeah about that. I placed a discharge request on the desk of the main office at the outpost. I've only a few months left on my current contract but I'd prefer to step down now."

"Seems to me Sergeant Adley that you finished your time in the infantry serving at my request as the personal guard to Silver Guard Keep." Captain Payne said with a wink.

"My gratitude Captain."

"Think nothing of it. I hate paperwork anyways. And besides I heard about what happened along the road. I figure you could use a few more months' pay along with whatever these jokers are paying ya. Make sure to stop by the quartermasters office for your pay as usual."

"You heard already?"

"Sure did. Heard it in Clarcton. News travels fast around here. Shame though. I was going to ask you to be my lieutenant."

Adley was honored by the proclamation. "I appreciate that sir."

"Guess we will have to stick to calling you Sarge." Captain Payne said as he finished the last few stairs and embraced Josef.

"Well met Captain." Josef greeted.

"Yes sir. My deepest sympathies for your recent losses." Captain Payne bowed his head in deep reverence before Josef. "I apologize for not sending word before now."

"Think nothing of it."

Captain Payne waved his hand dismissing the notion. "No it wasn't right. I'd like to pay my respects at a later time. Me and Gaebald had a couple good fights under our belts against that one werewolf causing problems south of here. We finally got the bastard though."

"Anytime you like of course."

"And to Jon Alio as well. He was a good man. Served under me here before he left the infantry to marry Cecilia."

"I'm sure she would appreciate that." Josef motioned towards the chairs set on the deck and all four moved to take a seat. Once seated Josef asked, "Can we get you anything? Sure you might like a drink after your long ride."

"No sir. Can't tonight. I should be at post already but I saw you guys sitting out here so wanted to give you word on what's happening."

"And what's that? Not sure how much you know."

Captain Payne leaned forward in his chair to see that the front doors of the Keep were shut. "I hear that Deathmar the Black, some dragon from your past has come calling you out. Can't say I know much about him. Hoping you can fill me in on that."

"Of course. What else?"

"I also hear that he may be father to what's growing in Cecilia's tummy and that you want to keep that as quiet as possible."

"I would appreciate that."

"Well I'll do my part in that but you should know something."

"Oh do tell." Josef's interest was peaked.

"The only reason they granted your request to have me sent out here instead of someone else is that I am a captain now. Normally a post like this isn't commanded by a lieutenant. They only let that slide because they know you boys are out here. In fact this close to Cruz and all the problems we've had with them we should probably have twice as many soldiers stationed out here as well."

Adley was shaking his head in agreement with that statement but that was not unknown to Josef or Oran either. Though The Silver Guard had always been few in number, those few were always more than capable of pulling more weight than the average soldier.

Captain Payne continued, "You're also the reason they don't assign mages and clerics out here. I mean why waste our own manpower when they know you guys will pick up the slack for free."

Josef nodded in agreement. "Yes this is not unknown to me. We don't mind."

"Well now that's changed. One of those riders with me was the newly assigned mage of Lanos Outpost."

Now Josef was even more interested. "And who might that be?"

"Escott Claridge. You know him?"

Josef pondered the name for a minute while stroking his beard. "I believe so. About your age, blonde hair. Good with battle spells and phantasm if I remember right."

"Yeah that's him. Seems like a good guy but I'd be willing to bet they sent him out here to keep an eye on ya."

"Did they ask the same of you?"

"Of course they did. That's why I'm willing to bet on him. They obviously don't know exactly how friendly we are."

"I can guess who they are but truly I'm not that surprised. So what are we to do about this?"

Captain Payne came up out of his seat and paced to the front of the deck and turned to face all three of them. "Nothing. You tell me what you want passed down and so be it."

Oran and Adley gave a good laugh at that and Captain Payne smiled and tilted his head to the side. Josef was a bit more serious looking though. Josef asked, "What of Escott?"

Captain Payne shrugged his shoulders. "It's my assessment that those stationed at this outpost have become fat and lazy. Present company excluded of course." Captain Payne nodded in Adley's direction. "Especially considering recent events I don't believe we have been doing enough patrols especially to the Talt Mountains where I hear dwarf allies of ours have come under siege by drow mercenaries under command of some fat lizard. You can be sure that I will not send my soldiers out there without aid from our newly assigned powerhouse of a wizard."

Now Josef did smile. "I'm truly glad we asked for you back."

"No sir it is my pleasure." Captain Payne looked around at the impending darkness that was fast approaching. "Now I'm off to my old post. It's getting late and I still have a former Lieutenant to scold." He gave another laugh as he moved towards the stairs.

All three stood and Adley asked after him, "What's to become of him?"

Not slowing Captain Payne continued down the stairs to retrieve his horse. "He'll be here a while yet. I've got to round up any of his other sergeants that I'm hoping are doing their job and are out in the field somewhere."

Adley responded, "They are actually. Sent them out myself."

"Good man Sarge." Captain Payne took to his saddle. "After that I'm sending them to escort him back to Tomé where he has more fun to look forward to. I brought my own sergeants with me so his will be reassigned as well."

Now Oran lay praise, "I'm impressed."

"Well didn't make Captain off of looks alone although they sure do help." The four shared another good laugh at that and Captain Payne finished with, "Let's have dinner tomorrow night. You're buyin."

Adley, Josef and Oran watched as Captain Payne departed giving his horse a good kick and sending him quickly out the gate. They knew that at the very least their short-term prospects just took a turn for the better.

R. A. HAYDEN

CHAPTER TEN

Orphans—Silhad, 1014

THE BUSTLING SOUNDS of the main trade district in Tomé had Oran in a splendid mood as he strolled down the street admiring the many carts and shops along its route. Earlier he and Josef had entered Tomé and Oran had seen Josef to the docks where he set off to Creet Island to retrieve his new apprentice who would be joining them for the summer months while his schooling at Hareth Academy ceased for the summer so that students could reunite with their families. As Havander Shoone was now technically an orphan after being denounced from his family by his father his only choice would be to stay at the school which was fine because the wizards there wouldn't let one of their own students make his own way on the streets but Oran thought it a good change that his father would take an apprentice so young. And if the talk he had heard about the boy was true about his talents then he could think of no better person than his father to help him reach his full potential.

Oran stopped at one cart and was admiring some expensive silks from Searcy. While not purchasing anything today, he was browsing in advance so that him and Josef could purchase early the next day and load up their wagon with exotic goods not found in Lanos and begin their trip back. Along with foodstuffs they also wanted to purchase some items for the women to lift the mood and give them, especially Cecilia, something to think about rather than the constant worry Cecilia had about her upcoming child birth. It had only been a couple months since they realized she was indeed pregnant and she was already showing the signs in the way of her stomach expanding and her morning sickness had been relentless. Georgette had explained to them that she had never seen any women go through so much vomiting and retching after only a couple months in. This had everyone in the house worried for her but they were all good at remaining positive around her and Georgette waited on her hand and foot.

While haggling with the merchant over the price of a bolt of red silk Oran felt the slightest little tug on his beltline under the light cloak he was wearing over his fine leather armor set. His cloak was draped over his right shoulder so he raised his right arm and where his coin purse should have been was nothing more than a knot of leather cord, which was securing it in place but the purse itself was gone. Quickly he turned around and saw a young boy slide under a rolling cart passing by on the thoroughfare.

"Hey you little thief!" Oran shouted as he took off in pursuit.

The boy, hearing Oran and now knowing he was being pursued dashed down a small alleyway in-between two of the merchant shops. He ran as quickly as his little legs would carry him. After passing the length of the building he was paralleling he turned right and then left as soon as he found another back alley path. As soon as he made that left he ran headlong into someone carrying a basket and bounced off of him into the adjacent wall and slid down to the ground unable to keep his feet while listening to the merchant telling him to watch where he was going. As fast as he went down he was back on his feet and running again. Crisscrossing this way and that. Whichever path seemed the easiest to gain distance hoping that his pursuer would give up the chase through the maze of buildings.

He glanced back every few seconds hoping to not see anyone coming after him. After one more turn he was exhausted and had to slow his pace. Believing he was in the clear after not seeing anyone or hearing any more shouting he began walking backwards down the alley just in case he had to sprint again he wanted to see if anyone was still following. Confident now after a few more seconds and hearing only the distant sounds of the hustle and bustle of the trade market he threw the coin purse in the air with one hand and caught it in the other while turning and walked right into the waist of Oran who was standing with hands on hips waiting for the boy to do so. The boy fell back onto his bottom into the muck. He looked up to see Oran's hand reaching down for him. He tried to turn over and regain his feet to dash away once more but Oran's reach was quicker and grabbed a handhold on the back of his filthy tunic.

"Let me go. Let me go. I didn't do anything." The boy yelled.

He tried turning and began hitting Oran's arm as best he could while shouting for help. Oran lifted the boy off the ground and with his free hand snatched his coin purse out of the flailing hand of the boy and released him sending him into the muck of the alley once more.

It was unsettling and embarrassing to be tossed around so easily but the boy figured that the beating he was about to receive would be worse. He raised his arms and hands to defend his face while scooting through the dirt and mud up against the wall of the nearest building.

"What's your name boy?" Oran asked while examining the little street thief who had amazingly been able to get his coin purse off of his belt with him hardly noticing. No easy feat considering his skill and knowledge in the art of thievery.

Oran kneeled down beside the boy when he didn't answer. "Look at me boy."

Slowly the boy uncovered his face and opened his eyes expecting that a punch or at least a slap across the face was coming next. When none came he looked past Oran and then left and right down the alley hoping that someone was visible and would stop this man from beating on a small child but none were in sight. With nothing else left to try he began pleading, "Ya got your sack back so no harm done. I'll be on my way never to be in sight of ya again."

"It's called a coin purse boy."

"What's the difference? No harm done mate." The boy inched his way down the wall trying to slide farther away in hopes of finding opportunity to run again.

"Mate? Where you from boy?" Oran probed.

"What do you care?" The boy asked defiantly. No time in his life had anyone cared so why would this man care.

"Look boy I'm not going to hurt you just answer my question."

"Yeah I know what that means. Means your worse than the others. Probably want to do worse than beat me." Not liking the prospect of that at all the boy reached into his tunic and produced a small blade hoping to fend off his attacker.

Quicker than the boy produced the blade, which was nothing more than a butter knife he had apparently sharpened on rocks or the like, Oran slapped it out of his hand and then grabbed him by the front of his tunic and pushed him against the wall and held him there.

"Lets try again. What's your name boy?" Oran asked very insistent this time.

"Willem alright. Now let me go." He said while trying futilely to pry at Oran's hand holding him against the wall.

"Where are your parents Willem?"

"Parents," Willem spit at the very mention of it, "Don't got none."

"Alright what's your last name Willem?"

"Don't got one of those either."

"You don't have a last name?"

"None I'd care to remember even if I could." Willem relaxed realizing the folly of even trying to wrestle away from this much bigger and stronger man. He knew he was stuck fast and would just have to take whatever comes.

"Okay Willem just be easy and I'll let you go. I just want to talk." As Oran finished his sentence he released the front of the tunic and stood back up expecting Willem to make another move but thankfully he did not. "How did you get all those cuts and bruises?" Oran asked while taking a good look at the boys many injuries including many scrapes and cuts on his legs and a large bruise on his left temple. He was also covered in dirt and filth from who knows where. His tunic he wore was full of holes and even more dirty than his skin. His sandals were barely holding together from some makeshift repairs with twine and string.

Willem watched Oran carefully as he stood up and took a step back from him. He needed to buy time he knew so he could make a run for it at the first opportunity. "What you care mister?"

"Well Willem a boy your size doesn't have any business being covered in bruises like that. Where'd you get 'em?"

"Some older boys a couple days ago gave me a right beaten for what coin I had."

"What are you about seven?"

"I'm nine."

"Nine huh." Oran repeated while contemplating on whether or not he was being told the truth. "Bit small for your age, aren't you?" Oran suspected he was younger for Willem was extremely small even if he was seven. He was obviously malnourished and looked on the verge of being sickly.

"Wouldn't know. Don't know any other nine year olds." He said showing a flare of attitude.

"Well listen son…"

"Don't call me that," Willem interrupted, "I ain't your son and don't figure I ever want a father again."

Oran could see that he had struck a nerve and didn't want to press the matter. He changed his line of questioning hoping to learn more without angering Willem. He held up his coin purse and examined the cut leather cord. "Almost got away with this Willem. What'd you need the money for? Food?"

"Food, no way. I don't buy food." Willem said very matter of fact.

"How do you eat then?"

"I steal food. I was savin up to buy me a proper dagger. Those are harder to steal."

"I see. And what was the dagger for?"

"Are you daft? Protection of course." Willem said while pointing to the large bruise on his temple. "You blind?"

Oran snickered a little at that. The boy had a confidence and way with his demeanor that had Oran a bit intrigued besides the fact that he felt sorry for the poor lad. No doubt he has had a harder run in life than most kids his age. "Let me ask you something Willem. Do you want to come with me somewhere and get out of this dirty alley?" Oran said while looking around at their surroundings.

"Oh I get it now. You're one of those church going types. Thinks he can save me." Willem finally took to his feat and leaned against the wall and crossed his arms across his chest. "Look mister I ain't ever going back to no orphanage. Ran away from the last one as fast as I could after my pa dropped me there."

"Your father gave you away to an orphanage?"

"That's what he called it but he took money from the man he gave me too."

"Why would he do that Willem?"

"He used to beat me a lot. My ma too. He beat her so bad one night that she never woke up. After that he took me there. Said it would be better for me. Those bastards beat me just as bad as he did. First chance I got I took off and jumped aboard a ship heading here."

"I'm sorry to hear that Willem. Where was that at?"

"Hovert."

"That's a long ways to travel. How did you survive on such a long sea voyage stowed away on a ship?"

"You kiddin. That trip was great. Best I ever ate. They was loaded with food."

"How long ago was that if you don't mind me asking?"

"I dun no. Couple years ago I guess."

Oran was contemplating a hasty move on his part. This was worse than he had thought. He couldn't in good conscious just leave this boy out here on the streets. Despite his obvious resourcefulness at such a young age he couldn't imagine that he would last that much longer. Too many bad people wandering the streets of Tomé that would take advantage of such a young boy in more horrible ways than he wanted to imagine. He was shocked that Willem had gone this long.

"Well Willem I have no intention of bringing you to an orphanage but I would like to bring you somewhere else."

"The law then? Figures. You know they'll just send me to an orphanage don't ya?"

"You've got a bit of wit about you don't you? I like that in my employees."

"What's that?"

"Employee. It means I'm offering you a job."

"A job." Willem said unsure of where this was going.

"It's what people do for a living. Like a shop keep or blacksmith."

"I know what a job is. I wasn't asking that. I mean why would you offer me a job and what kind?"

Oran believed playing to Willem's ego would get him much farther than any other tactic. "I'm in the market for a good thief." Willem's facial expression looked perplexing to Oran but he knew he had his attention. "That was quite the grab you made from me. Anyone else and I dare say you would have gotten away with it."

"Yeah but I didn't."

"With a little training I'd bet you'd be much better at your trade. What do you say Willem?"

"Training? You mean you actually want me to steal?"

"One never knows when they need to acquire something in an unconventional way."

R. A. HAYDEN

"Un what?" Willem asked truly unaware of what that meant.

"To steal something is my point Willem. Is there anyone else you steal for or anyone who looks after you or are you all on your own?" Oran inquired because sometimes disreputable characters liked to employ the young for purposes such as thievery in order to keep themselves out of the lime light. Thieves' guilds and gangs liked to recruit young as well.

"Just me. Don't care much for people. They are always looking to cheat ya or beat ya down."

Oran enjoyed the irony of that statement considering cheating is paramount to stealing. He thought better of bringing it up though. "You see Willem I work for an organization who specializes in acquiring things from time to time and someone with your skill would be an asset."

"Special something or other, acquiring. Look mister you want me to steal somethin for ya or not?"

Oran appreciated his straight forwardness and indeed wanted to move this along. "Eventually. First as I said you will have to be trained up a bit so that you don't get caught like you did today."

Willem unfolded his arms and brought his left hand up to his chin and rubbed it as though he was in deep thought. The spectacle of this little red haired, freckled child covered in filth thinking so hard as though he had so many other options almost made Oran laugh but he remained stern faced as to not belittle Willem.

"Let me get this straight. You actually want me to be a better thief and take from people?"

"Yes." Oran lied.

"Well I got other stuff to do ya know. What's to say this is better?"

Oran just found the heart of the matter. He untied what was left of the leather strap securing his coin purse and pulled forth a single gold coin. The look on Willem's face as his eyes went wide told him he had just hit the mark. "I pay my people in advance." He tossed the coin to Willem who snatched it out of the air and held it close to his face to examine it thoroughly. Oran imagined how wide his eyes might of went if he had gotten away with his coin purse because the looks of it were deceiving. Although it appeared full and to the naked eye probably held a large handful of coins the truth was that it was enchanted. It was actually an extension bag that Josef had made for him. The extradimensional space inside the leather pouch actually held more than ten times what it appeared to be containing and all of the coins inside were gold.

Willem said excitedly, "I've never held one of these before. The best I get is silver and even those are rare." He continued examining a few seconds more and then looked to Oran. "This is a trick. No one just gives away gold."

"No trick Willem. I'm not giving it away. I expect you to be a good worker and follow my lead. If you can't than you won't work for me for long and you can return to where I found you."

Willem was still very wary but what options he had were lousy. At the very least he thought he should see where this leads. If nothing else maybe he would get another chance at that bag holding even more gold than the one coin he now had. "Alright. What do I do first?"

Satisfied with coercing the boy to come along made Oran feel good. Now he knew he'd have to string him along until the next day to start their trip back to Lanos. At the very least he thought that Josef's apprentice would have someone to talk to on the trip. "First I don't do work on an empty stomach. You hungry Willem? I know a good place not far from here."

"Sure I guess." Not wanting to sound overeager although he was starving. He hadn't eaten more than a crust of molded bread in the last day.

"Good. We'll talk business over a good meal and then see to getting you a bath and some good clothes."

"A bath. Are you serious?" Willem said in disgust.

Oran thought that funny and didn't try to hide his laugh. "Yes Willem. I'll not have someone who works for me looking shabby." Oran stepped closer and reached to the shoulder of Willem's tunic and pulled a piece of drying mud from it and threw it to the ground.

Willem felt embarrassed and crossed one leg in front of the other while dropping his head and examining his clothing.

Oran recognizing this and not meaning to shame the boy reached under his chin and lightly lifted his hand to raise Willem's head so he could look him in the eye. "No shame boy. We'll get you dressed in proper clothing and cleaned up so no one would think to see coming for their stuff. You see, training already."

Willem's face brightened at the prospect of that statement. He moved along Oran's side and kept pace as they began walking down the alley. When he reached where his knife was lying on the ground he stopped and bent down to pick it up.

Oran stopped as well and reached his hand out to Willem. "Let me see that."

Tentatively Willem stretched his hand out and let Oran take it.

Oran examined the blade and then threw it into a pile of garbage next to a building and then turned to Willem. "My people don't use garbage. We'll get you a proper dagger soon enough."

Now Willem was truly excited. He couldn't wait to have his own proper blade. He stood there thinking while Oran began walking again. When he got a few strides ahead of him he shouted after him. "Wait. What do I call you? Boss?"

Oran turned to Willem. "My name is Oran Righe. Pleasure to meet you Willem."

Willem skipped to catch up and then moved past Oran and continued down the alley. As he passed he said, "Na. I like Boss."

The Hareth Academy ferry was closing on the docks of Tomé after making the trip across the bay from Creet Island. Josef and Havander leaned against the rail waiting for the ship to finish the short journey and throw lines to tie up so that they could gather Havander's belongings and make their way to where Oran was suppose to meet them. Havander was excited to meet another member of The Silver Guard and upon hearing that it would be the legendary Oran Righe had him even more excited. Upon meeting Josef for the first time he believed that he must have been a descendent of the founder of The Silver Guard. Upon hearing the news that he was indeed the original Josef Righe from some older students who had overheard him having a conversation with one of his classmates about meeting him had him searching for answers for months on to how that was possible. In the library of Hareth Academy he came across many possible ways as to how someone could extend their life span and last night he had questioned Josef thoroughly on how he did it but got only vague answers as his new Master skirted the question.

"Master Righe can I ask you another question?" Havander asked as a crewman aboard the ferry threw the first line to the dockworkers waiting to tie them up.

"Of course Havander. As I've said you need not ask for permission. That is what I'm here for." Josef replied and was not surprised in the least that Havander had yet another question. Since their reunion last night at dinner he had asked him an endless list of questions it seemed. There seemed no end to the information that Havander wanted to know and Josef took that as a great sign for his thirst in knowledge. Josef was also impressed as to how courteous and respectful Havander was when inquiring. At least the Shoone family had taught him manners before disregarding their child.

"We learned in history class that Oran Righe is your son. Does that mean he is as old as you?" Havander asked hoping that it was not getting tiresome or rude that he was asking again about his Master's age.

Josef laughed and reached an arm out putting it around Havander's shoulders and began guiding him towards the ship to shore bridge that was being lowered so that they could make their exit from the main deck. "No Havander. Oran is not quite as old as I am."

"But I don't understand that Master. I know from our readings that Oran Righe is your son and that he took part in battles that were over a hundred years ago." Havander looked up to Josef looking for conformation.

Josef shook his head yes.

"Well he is known to be a great warrior and not a wizard so how is that possible for him?"

As they put feet onto the dock Josef tossed a coin to the baggage men who were to grab Havander's chest and bring it ashore and then turned his attention back to Havander. "That's a good question Havander. You are right that Oran is not a wizard but there are ways for those not of our ilk to extend their life. You will have to ask him sometime but I'd prefer you wait until you get to know him better if you don't mind. He's a bit more touchy about his age than I."

"Yes Master." Havander said still not sure he'd get a straight answer on the subject.

Josef recognized the frustrated posture of Havander after his reply and continued, "All will be revealed in time Havander don't you doubt. Your questions now should be more focused on your tasks to be had over the next couple of months and I believe you will be pleased about what I have in store for you."

The two of them kept stride to the end of the dock and stepped onto solid ground once more. Josef scanned the area of the road looking for Oran and at last spotted him pulling up the wagon fully stocked it seemed and with a horse tied to the rear of the wagon with full saddle and harness. Josef thought that strange since there should be no need for them to acquire a horse and they had planned to shop for what they planned to bring back home together. Josef lead Havander in the direction of Oran with the large chest of Havander's being toted close behind by two dockworkers. As they neared, Oran jumped down from the seat upon seeing their approach.

"Sorry I'm late." Oran said.

"Not at all. We just arrived ourselves." Josef replied while scanning past Oran to the wagon even more stocked than what he had planned.

"This must be Havander Shoone." Oran said while putting his hand out to Havander.

Havander took Oran's hand and shook vigorously. "I am sir. It is a pleasure to meet you. I've heard so much about The Silver Guard. It's hard to believe that I have this opportunity."

"Oh very polite isn't he?" Oran said while looking to his father.

"Indeed." Josef pointed Etburn in the direction of the wagon drawing Oran's attention in that direction. "What is all this? I thought I told you I wanted to browse the trade district with you."

"Yeah about that. I got up extra early and figured I'd get most of the work done." Oran explained while scratching the back of his head.

Josef could tell he was leaving something out. He was so obvious. "I see. I figured you'd have a good tear through a couple of the taverns last night." Josef wanted to say brothels but younger ears so near by curbed his language. "Didn't think you'd be up early enough for all this." Josef pointed to the wagon indicating the large amount of supplies, which was more than they had discussed.

"Yeah I went a little overboard on some things but we'll use it all the same. Don't forget we have extra mouths to feed now."

Josef did not miss the reference to mouths but asked instead, "What about the horse? Why are we in need of another horse? There is still enough room in the wagon for us three after all."

Oran scratched the back of his head again but just as he was about to begin speaking he was interrupted. "Here ya go Boss. Thought you might want one." Willem said as he suddenly appeared next to Oran. He thrust a crab apple into the palm of Oran and took a bite of his own." He looked up to Josef and over to Havander and continued, "Who they?" He said spitting a few bits of apple out of his mouth while trying to speak.

Oran looked at his own little apple than back to Willem. "Where did you get this?"

Willem pointed back in the direction he had come from. "Man with a cart full of them back there."

"Uh huh. Did you pay for it?" Oran bent down and stared hard into the eyes of Willem.

"Uh, sure Boss. Why not?"

"What did I tell you? We don't just steal whenever we want."

"I just said I paid for 'em."

"Yeah I don't think so. We are going to have to work on your lying as well it seems." Oran stood up straight shaking his head only to catch the bewildered look on his father's face.

"Who is this?" Josef inquired pointing down at Willem.

"Oh apologies. This is Willem." Oran then addressed Willem. "Willem this is my father, Josef Righe and Havander Shoone."

Without exchanging pleasantries Josef persisted, "That's not what I meant Oran. Why is he here?" Josef looked down at Willem who took another bite of his crab apple then threw the rest away while giving Josef a scrutinizing look as though measuring him up for a fight.

Oran began explaining, "Willem here is now in our employ."

"Since when?" Josef chastised sounding flabbergasted at the notion.

"Since last night."

Josef shook his head and grabbed Oran by his arm and pulled him away from the boys. "We need to talk."

Oran let his father pull him away and turned back to Willem. "You two get acquainted. We'll just be a minute."

Once out of earshot at least enough for Josef anyway he pulled up from their hasty retreat away from the boys and began again, "Explain yourself."

Oran was suppressing his nervous laughter at the sight of his old man so flustered. "What? What's the big deal?"

R. A. HAYDEN

"The big deal. Are you serious? We are not running an orphanage."

"Hey don't say that around Willem. He's rather touchy about those."

"You've got to be kidding me. Where did you find him?" Josef turned around looking at the two boys now shaking hands and introducing themselves.

Oran had turned around as well and saw Willem reach very cleverly into the beltline of Havander as he turned to motion to his chest and extract something. Knowing his father undoubtedly saw it as well he winced knowing that would not be good for his argument. "He found me last night."

"So."

"So he needs our help."

"Help with what? Take him to his family or caretaker."

"He has neither."

Josef lowered the tone in his voice hoping to sound rational about the situation. "Oran we cannot take on every hard case we come across. What are we supposed to do with him?"

"Train him of course."

"Train him to do what? He's a little thief."

"Precisely. So was I for quite a time if you remember."

Josef rolled his eyes. "That was over two hundred years ago and your were just rebelling against my teachings."

"Not quite that long ago. I continued for quite some time after I started as well. And besides my skill in thievery has gotten us out of some pretty hairy situations if you remember. Besides he's quite good."

"Yeah I noticed." Josef pointed back to where the two boys were standing. "But how good could he really be he's only five?"

"I guessed seven but he says he's nine."

"That's not the point." Josef proclaimed then stopped his line of thinking confused by the apparent age that Oran had just declared. He scanned Willem looking for any signs that he might have halfling or gnome blood coursing through him.

Before Josef could berate him more Oran began explaining, "Look father. You see that bruise on his temple?"

"How could I miss it? Looks like he got beat with a club."

"Very likely. That's only one of many. You should see the rest of his body. He's been living on the street since he escaped slavery that his father sold him into in Hovert. He escaped and travelled all the way here and has barely been surviving for over two years now or so he claims."

Josef shook his head not willing to give in just yet. "He doesn't look that bad off. How could he afford such nice clothing if that were the case?"

"I bought those for him last night." Oran now began to raise his tone expressing his seriousness in the matter. "I fed him, took him to a bathhouse, and bought him everything he is now wearing. He's going with us."

Josef recognized the finality in his son's tone but still shook his head in disbelief. "I don't like this. I don't want a little thief running around the Keep."

"He's more than that I can tell. He's ambidextrous as far as I can tell and he's got a wit about him far above his years."

"Can he read?"

"No he's had no schooling." Oran waited for the inevitable eye roll he knew his father was going to make. "He can count though and says that's all he needs to count all the gold he's going to get."

Josef threw his free hand up into the air. "That's just perfect."

"Think of it this way. You have your apprentice and now I have mine. While the two boys are not in school or training they can play and keep each other company."

"Yeah but I know you. The schooling will come down to me and I need to be paying attention to Havander."

"Not so. He can go to the little schoolhouse in Lanos after we catch him up a little and Georgette will undoubtedly help out with that. She loves kids and the gods know Willem could use some of her strict discipline and love."

"You've thought this all through then 'eh?"

"Yep." Oran replied with a wide smile and moved back towards the children leaving his father behind. Oran shouted back, "Now come on we still have to stop in the mage trading district. I didn't acquire anything you said you needed from there and we've a long road ahead of us."

Oran stopped in front of the boys and held his hand out to Willem. "Give it."

"Give what?"

Oran just cocked his head and narrowed his gaze waiting for Willem to comply. After a few seconds Willem sheepishly reached into a pocket and produced a small linen pouch of some sort and handed it to Oran. Oran snatched it out of his hand and threw it to Havander. "I believe you dropped that Havander."

"Oh thanks Master Righe." Havander replied.

Oran turned his attention back to Willem. "You hear that. A little respect goes a long way. Don't forget that because that will be part of your lessons to come."

Willem thought about that for just a second and then turned an eerie gaze towards Havander. "Nope I still prefer Boss."

CHAPTER ELEVEN

School In Session—Silhad, 1014

HAVANDER LOOKED UP from the large tome of dwarvish language that he was studying, to Josef who was carousing Havander's first spellbook and nodding along in silent satisfaction with what he was finding on the pages. "Master."

"Yes Havander." Josef replied while not looking up from the pages.

"I know this is my first day and I don't want to sound ungrateful but I can't help but wonder what the purpose is for me to learn dwarvish?"

Josef looked up from his reading. "Why are you finding it difficult? I told you not to go any further than what we had discussed earlier. Repetition is key to learning a new language."

"No sir. I mean yes, it is difficult. Their use of symbols is so different from what I know but that's not what I mean."

"Oh. Please go on." Josef closed Havander's spellbook and moved from his desk that he was sitting at to the large table that Havander was sitting at in the laboratory turned classroom of Silver Guard Keep.

"I'm a bit lost to the purpose. After all there are spells that will allow me to read this quite easily."

"Yes I know." Josef held up Havander's spellbook to draw his attention to it as he seated himself opposite him. "And I see in here that you have already begun learning that spell."

"Yes sir."

"I take it from the notations in here that you have already been able to cast four spells with relative ease."

"That's correct as well sir." Havander was surprised that Master Righe had been able to deduct that from his scribblings in the margins that weren't meant to be understood by anyone other than him.

That is remarkable Havander. I believe I was only able to cast a couple spells to satisfaction after my first year at Hareth. I see as well that you can cast the spell required to read that entire book if you so wanted, which is precisely the point of the lesson."

"The point sir?"

"Yes Havander. It is not enough to rely on your magic for everything. Remember me saying that along the road to Lanos?"

"I do sir."

"That unfortunately is one area that I fear is often neglected at Hareth Academy. While their intentions are good they are sometimes remiss about teaching restraint in the overuse of magic."

Havander thought about that for a second and wanted to defend his professors at the academy who had treated him so well. "Perhaps but everything we learn at Hareth Academy is not magic. We have history and language classes there as well."

"Yes indeed and in your third year I believe you can take a language of your choosing but think how much better off you'll be if you already know one by then but that is besides the point. My point is that magic like many other things takes a certain amount of energy. Energy that is precious to you. Overuse of magic will leave you exhausted."

"How do you mean sir?"

"Well you may have not noticed it due to your age and only casting spells of minor difficulty albeit impressively but casting spells or attempting to do so beyond your own experience and power can have disastrous results. It may even lead to your death if not careful."

"That's horrible sir. They never told us that."

"Well no I expect not." Josef noticed the discomfort in Havander's face and certainly didn't want to discourage him. "Not to worry young apprentice. You have no fear of that outcome this early on in the game."

"But why wouldn't they tell us that?"

"Let me explain. Magic is like anything else. Too much of anything can be bad for you. It can leave you exhausted or worse. The mage who uses his magic to the extent far beyond his ability will quickly find his powers diminishing because their body cannot keep up with the demand and toll that magic can take on a person. It is for this reason that I wish for you to learn dwarvish. Knowing it without having to use magic will save you in the long run."

"I think I see sir."

"Not only that but we have many dwarf allies here in Casta. Before long you'll see many dwarves who travel to Lanos for trade from the Talt Mountains. They know common of course but being able to speak their tongue will show to them that you have respect for their culture and respect to a dwarf is very important as you'll come to find."

"I see now sir. I'll continue with this vocabulary."

"Good. Good. You continue with that until lunch and than after we'll practice with what you do know and see exactly how proficient you are."

Havander put his face back into the pages as Josef moved again back to his desk. Once Josef got there it was his turn to interrupt Havander. "One more thing Havander."

"Yes sir."

"After you've more or less learned dwarvish we'll switch to learning goblin."

"Goblin sir?"

"Yes. It's also just as advantageous to know the language of your enemies as it is your allies."

Sweat rolled down the forehead and into the eyes of Willem, stinging them as he finished depositing another scoop of straw and horse manure into the wheelbarrow. He silently cursed his seemingly bad luck, as this was the third day in a row since arriving at Silver Guard Keep that he was forced to clean up the horse stalls. He wiped the sweat from his brow and blinked his eyes repeatedly trying to lessen the sting of the sweat in his eyes. When he could see clearly again he looked out the stall door to the back deck of the Keep where Oran, Sarge, and Cecilia sat in the shade enjoying some kind of cool drink that Georgette had prepared. There, perched under the roof of the deck in the shade and out of the blistering summer heat they sat and joked and laughed while here he was ankle deep in horse manure slaving away.

Willem yelled out across the yard, "You know Boss this isn't what I had in mind when I agreed to come out here to the sticks!"

Oran shouted back, "Hey less talking more shoveling!"

"But it's hot."

Adley replied for Oran, "Well it wouldn't be so bad if you had done it this morning instead of lying about it." Oran and Adley shared a little laugh at that obvious statement.

"I wasn't talking to you Sarge!" Willem hollered back.

Cecilia was laid back with cold drink in hand and her feet propped up on a bench that Adley had slid over to her so that she could put her feet up while listening to the back and forth between the boys. She was thoroughly enjoying the heat of the day despite the discomfort from being pregnant that all women went through especially on really hot days but she found that she preferred the heat at least for today and was laughing along with the boys who were talking behind Willem's back as he worked in the stalls. "I like how he calls you Sarge like Captain Payne does when he comes to visit."

"Yeah seems that one is going to stick with me. At least with Willem. He likes nicknames for people for some reason." Adley took another drink. "At least it is better than Boss."

"Hey there are a lot worse things he could be calling me so Boss is alright." Oran proclaimed.

Cecilia looked back out across the yard and listened to the muffled cursing coming from the stalls as Willem went back to work. "Do you think you are being to hard on him Oran?"

"Not at all my dear. What that boy needs is some responsibility along with proper discipline."

"I'm sure but after going through so much at such a young age do you think it likely that you'll push him away. Besides he's so small to be doing all that work by himself."

Oran shook his head. "He's only doing two stalls and they aren't that dirty. Harold took care of all the rest this morning like always. Willem is exaggerating on how bad it is. With this heat maybe he'll learn that he should do them at the proper time."

The three of them sat and watched as Willem closed the door to the stall and began awkwardly moving the large wheelbarrow full of manure and soiled straw towards the dumping site. He was having a hard time of it being too short to properly lift the back legs of wheelbarrow so that they wouldn't scrape on the ground. As he tried to make the turn around the stalls the wheelbarrow overbalanced and tipped, spilling its contents onto the ground. Willem let out a tirade of curses and kicked the wheelbarrow.

With a little nervous sounding laugh Cecilia said, "Oh the poor dear. Maybe I should help him."

"No don't you dare." Adley said while putting his arm out to block Cecilia from getting up.

"Oh but look at him. He's going to throw a fit." She said while frowning trying to hide the laughter inside from watching the show that Willem was putting on in the yard.

Adley looked back to Willem who retrieved his shovel and was now beating the wheelbarrow with it. "Perhaps I should give him a hand."

"Yeah we don't want to lose him completely before tomorrow." Oran said while snickering.

Cecilia watched as Adley jogged from the deck to Willem and snatched the shovel out of his hand before he broke the handle and then asked, "What's tomorrow Oran?"

"Well can't keep him doing chores forever. Havander's turn tomorrow anyway. Willem and I will be having a bit of fun learning about weapons. Something he'll be more interested in than his chores and alphabet lessons with Georgette."

Later and after the long summer day had finally quieted its relentless heat and the cool of the evening set in Georgette and Cecilia were finishing their usual walk around the perimeter of the Keep when they came across Willem sitting alone in the dark on the back deck. They exchanged knowing glances and approached him.

Georgette kneeled in front of him and the chair he was sitting in and put her hand on his knee. "Willem is something wrong?"

"What do you care?"

Georgette not surprised by his tone or choice of words did not shy away or raise her voice in this instance. Willem had been very standoffish since his arrival and the walls he had set up around himself were strong indeed. "Well Willem I care a great deal."

"Whatever Mom." Willem said in a sarcastic tone while turning his head away.

Georgette had heard him use that name for her once before during their school lessons and she did not dissuade him from calling her that despite his sarcastic tone that time either. Not being able to have kids of her own after going through a failed childbirth some ten years earlier was something she often grieved. Despite his obvious try to get a rise out of her she found she liked being called Mom even if he was trying to be spiteful. Nevertheless she used her hand to move his face forward so that she could look him in the eye. "You know Willem if you keep trying to push people away that are trying to care for you eventually you'll find that it will work."

Willem crossed his arms across his chest. "You don't care for me. All I do is get yelled at and made to do chores."

"Well perhaps if you weren't taking things that didn't belong to you or making a mess we wouldn't."

"That's what Boss hired me for."

"Boss, oh Oran." Georgette looked back to Cecilia standing behind her after figuring out the reference and shrugged her shoulders then turned back to Willem. "That may be Willem but not from us and I doubt very much that that's all that Boss wants from you."

"Well what else could he possibly want?"

Georgette thought about the best way to approach this, as obviously Oran had not done enough explaining to Willem about exactly where he was. She raised both arms out wide as though trying to encompass the entire building. "Do you know what this place is Willem?"

"It's a Keep or so I'm told."

"Not just any Keep. This is Silver Guard Keep."

"Never heard of it before I came here."

"Well Willem this is home to some of the best warriors and wizards who have ever walked Drilain."

Willem pointed with his thumb back behind him, "These guys?"

"Yes Willem, these guys. Josef Righe is the founder of The Silver Guard."

"The old guy?" Willem knew very well the name of Josef but didn't want to refer to him by name. He liked him least of all for the comments he had made about him when he thought he was out of hearing.

"Yes Willem the old guy. Only the very best are asked to train here."

"That's the point. I'm not training."

"You don't think so?"

"No."

"Well when you got here you were even skinnier than you are now. Working on chores is a fine way to build muscle and get stronger. Then there is your schooling with me and Oran, I mean Boss."

"Yeah which I'm no good at."

"Actually Willem you are doing quite well for someone who has never had any form of education before." Georgette stood up hopeful that maybe he would latch onto something she had said. "You need to look past the obvious Willem. I'm sure," she paused for a second thinking about the right name, "Boss is hoping you will figure this out on your own." With that Georgette leaned down and kissed him on the forehead and moved away towards the back door of the Keep.

Cecilia followed suit and likewise moved over to William and kissed him on the forehead then whispered, "Boss said you start weapons training tomorrow." She gave Willem a little wink and was happy to see a smile appear on Willem's face and then she followed Georgette in doors.

Havander slammed his hand down hard on the desk next to the four wands that were causing him so much frustration just as Josef entered the door to the laboratory. Josef stopped and blew across the top of his teacup to cool the hot liquid and then proceeded towards his desk in a very nonchalant way. "Something wrong Havander?"

Havander was standing with hands on hips now looking back and forth from his opened spellbook to the four wands. "I still don't get it Master Righe."

"What don't you get exactly?"

Havander was frustrated as this was not the first time or even the second time that Josef had asked him the same thing over the last week concerning this particular problem. "You say that I'm doing my new spell correctly but I still can't figure out what all four of these wands do."

"Yes you are doing it correctly."

"Then why do you say that I'm wrong in my answers?"

Josef placed his tea on his desk and then walked over to the desk to join Havander. "You are not completely wrong. Two of them you have identified correctly."

Havander pointed to the two on the left. "The wand of light and the wand of magic missile."

"Yes."

"But I'm not doing anything different so why am I wrong about the other two?"

"Well perhaps you should be doing something different."

"But that doesn't make sense either. That would alter the spell."

"Don't think of it as altering the spell. Think of it as being so familiar with it that you can look past an illusion meant for you to believe that they are something else." Josef patted Havander on the shoulder when he noticed the spark of clarity appear on his face. He moved back to his desk to sit and watch the young mind figure it out.

Three hours later Havander declared very excitedly, "I got it. Finally I got it."

Josef put down his third cup of tea he had just finished since giving him the hint he needed to solve the identification of the wands and started Havander's way. He was about to end the session since they were already well past Havander's bedtime but thankfully he did not. Josef believed it was important enough to Havander that he would have been angered so he let him continue. "Well don't keep me in suspense what do you know?"

Very excited Havander began explaining, "Okay. Well we know that these two are light and magic missile." He pointed to them and then picked up the third in line. "I believed this to be a wand of mending but it's actually nothing. Just an unfinished wand made of some wood I can't identify but it is indeed not spelled with anything. It is only made to look so."

"Very good. How about the fourth?" Josef knew this was the hardest to identify and hoped that Havander had gotten it right as well.

Havander put down the third wand and picked up the fourth. "This one, which I thought to be spelled with shocking grasp is actually the wand of mending."

"Impressive Havander. Now how did you figure it out?"

Havander let go of his tension and misgivings and visibly relaxed. "Finally. Okay." He picked up the third wand again. "This one I compared to the other two which I already knew to be correct and the slightest of differences in it's aura eventually led me to believe that it was a false aura as my research into phantasm aura spells indicated." He pointed to the phantasm tome on the desk."

"Very good as well but what of the fourth?"

"That one was the hardest. It's aura shone as true as the first two wands telling me that it was indeed spelled with something but it was slightly off."

"How do you mean?"

"Well it's hard to explain but it felt like it was stronger than the others. Like there was more than one thing going on. Twice as strong I guess."

"Yes exactly Havander. So what did you have to do?"

"It had a similar feeling to that of the third but also under that I could feel something else. I figured it had a false aura placed on it as well but had a true aura of it's own underneath. I simply had to look past the false one."

"Bravo young man." Josef was pleased beyond belief. For Havander to be able to discern a false magical aura over a real one having only learned to identify magical objects a couple weeks prior was beyond impressive. "Now we will discuss tomorrow the importance of phantasm spells and why wizards use them so often to hide their secrets but for now it's off to bed with you."

Lanos was bustling with dwarf traders on the last week of Selilimar as it often was on the last week of summer. Oran and Willem were walking back from the far end of town, where the dwarves had put up their tents and carts for trade, and Willem was busting with excitement over the dagger that Oran had purchased for him. While they walked he was examining every detail of the ornately carved handle and running his hand across the overly thick backside of the curved blade. The blade curved forward like a kukri, though certainly not as large, while the handle curved the opposite direction. It was sharp only on the one side with the blade set into the hilt that extended on the backside of the blade giving it extra thickness for strength as well as giving it an unusual look. Though Oran believed that Willem should have picked a more traditional dagger, Willem was fixed on the dwarven craftsmanship that went into the making of this one and Oran would not deny him his first choice of weapon.

As they reached the general store and took the stairs to the landing running along its front Oran stopped and addressed Willem, "Alright quit fawning over that blade for a second and give it to me."

"What? Why? I just got it."

"You're not going to need it for what you are doing next and besides it's not a toy."

"I know it's not a toy but I like the way it feels in my hand."

"I'll give it back after. Now hand it over."

Reluctantly Willem placed it back into its equally ornate metal sheath and handed it over.

"You know when Josef gets back from delivering Havander back to school I'll have him spell this so that its even better."

Willem's eyes went wide and he jumped up a little in excitement. "Really? Spell it with what?" Since living at the Keep Willem had begun to understand a lot more about magic and felt privileged, though he didn't often show it, to be among those who could count themselves among students of The Silver Guard.

"Well for now he'll just make it stronger than it already is." Oran took the blade out of it's sheath and examined it again himself. "With your fascination with daggers and the ridiculous cost of this thing I'll not have you break it."

"Can he spell it with other stuff too?"

"Someday maybe. For now you are to keep it put away. It is not for practicing."

"But why not?"

"Because first we are going to continue your training with the practice swords. After you get better at that we are going to move onto the other practice weapons."

"I want to learn how to fight with daggers."

Oran shook his head. "You know fighting with daggers alone is a hard thing to master. You'll always have a disadvantage of reach over your opponents."

"Yeah but I'll be faster. Those wooden sticks we practice with are heavy enough as it is. Using real swords are going to be even heavier."

"Fine, fine. We'll talk about this more later. For now I have something for you to do." Oran waited while two townspeople passed and then drew

Willem closer to him with his arm. "I want you to go into the store and steal something."

Willem shouted with joy, "What? Really?"

Oran pressed his finger to his lips, "Shh. Keep your voice down."

Willem leaned in close. "Okay but really? I finally get to steal something."

"What do you mean finally? You've been stealing from Havander all summer."

"I have not."

"Okay, okay we'll talk about that later too. Right now I want you to go into the store and steal something."

"What?"

"Whatever you want. Whatever catches your eye and you can get away with. I'll wait out here."

"Okay I'll be right back."

Willem walked quickly to the door of the store then straightened his tunic and entered the front door all proud and distinguished like. Oran shook his head watching the spectacle of the little thief and then took a seat on the bench next to the wall of the store and waited.

Only a couple minutes passed and Willem exited the store in the same manner and then rushed over to Oran. "Okay now what?"

"Well show me what you got."

Willem put his hand into his beltline and produced a set of thimbles in a small linen pouch, then reached into his sleeve and took out two knitting needles and a set of sewing needles and handed them to Oran.

Oran looked in disbelief. "Is that all?"

"Nope." Willem handed the items to Oran and then took out a handful of rock candy from his pocket. "Got these on my way out."

Oran couldn't believe he did all that so fast. "How did you manage that and why all the sewing stuff?"

"Well I figured Mom could use the sewing stuff. She likes that sort of thing and Mr. Barrie's candy is the best so I got that for us."

Oran shook his head again for two reasons. One at how Willem had slowly over the summer started referring to Georgette as Mom and two at how happy Willem was for doing such a despicable thing. "Alright Willem now I want you to take these back in the store and give them back to Mr. Barrie."

R. A. HAYDEN

"Yeah right."

Oran stood up and held out the items to Willem. "I'm very serious Willem."

"But why? He didn't see anything. He was helping another customer and Mrs. Barrie was nowhere to be seen."

"That's not the point Willem." Oran grabbed Willem's little hand and thrust the items into it.

"Boss. I don't get it. You told me too."

"Yes and if you say that to Mr. Barrie I'll deny it and he wouldn't believe you anyway. Now I want you to go back in there and give this stuff back and apologize."

Willem looked from the stuff in his hands to the door and then back to Oran who looked positively angrier than he had ever seen him. Angrier looking than when he took his stuff in Tomé. "Are you coming with me?"

"Yes. To make sure you do it. Now turn around right now and walk in there. I'll tell you the point of all this after."

Willem hung his head in shame and kicked at the ground once then moved towards the door with Oran right behind him. Mr. Barrie was just finishing up with his customer and upon noticing the two approaching gave a cheerful welcome. "Ah Oran and young Willem good evening to you."

"Good evening to you sir." Oran said and then took Mr. Barrie's hand over the counter and gave it a good shake.

"What can I do for you two fine gentleman today?"

"Well actually we are here to return something to you."

"Oh. Something wrong with one of your purchases?"

"Not exactly." Oran looked down to Willem who couldn't see over the counter even if he wasn't hanging his head in embarrassment. "Willem do you have something for Mr. Barrie?" When Willem said nothing Oran changed his tone considerably and even startled Mr. Barrie a little. "Now Willem!"

Willem placed the items in his hand on top of the counter without looking up and mumbled something indecipherable

"Look up Willem and use your words." Oran demanded.

Willem looked up and could see a confused look on Mr. Barrie's face. "I took these without paying sir. It was wrong and I want to give them back."

Mr. Barrie looked to Oran who gave him a wink and pointed to the ruler sitting next to Mr. Barrie's hand. "I see Willem. Well I thank you for your honesty but I'm very disappointed in you for taking them in the first place."

"The candy too Willem." Oran said.

"Oh yeah." Willem reached into his pocket and produced the rock candy and placed it on the counter as well.

Mr. Barrie was shaking his head now in disbelief that he had taken all that in the short time he was in here before without him noticing. "Well young man this cannot be tolerated. Do you know that?"

In a meek and defeated voice Willem replied, "Yes sir. It won't happen again."

"Well I should hope not. Hold your hand out." Barrie pointed to the top of the counter.

"My hand sir?"

"Yes Willem put your hand right here."

Willem placed his hand on the counter and Mr. Barrie picked up the ruler. He would have been happy with just the apology but he knew Oran wanted him to give him a good smack so he grabbed Willem's tiny wrist and gave him a good smack across the knuckles. "Now let that be a lesson to you."

Willem recoiled his hand and grabbed at his knuckles. He couldn't believe such a small whack could hurt so badly. After shaking his hand out a bit he looked up to Mr. Barrie again. "It won't happen again I swear."

"Well good enough." Mr. Barrie said and then turned to Oran.

"Thanks Mr. Barrie." Oran said and he scooped up the rock candy and handed Mr. Barrie a few coins easily paying twice the amount they were worth. "I'll just take these. His grubby little hands were all over them. I'll have him come by later if you want and help you sweep up the store."

"Oh that would be great. How about just after sundown."

Back outside Willem was still rubbing his sore knuckles and was angry as well. "You said you'd tell me the point Boss."

"Yes Willem." Oran motioned for Willem to keep pace as they began their walk back to the Keep. "Let me tell you something about the Barries. Before they opened up that store quite a few years ago they lost nearly everything they had in their other business. If fact they struggled for quite a long time. They put all their hopes into starting new out here in Lanos and thankfully it worked out for them."

"I don't get it."

"Well you see Willem, just because they are well off now doesn't mean that they deserve to be stolen from." Oran explained.

"But you told me too."

"Yes Willem I did. But if I told you to do something that you thought was wrong would you do it?"

"I dun no."

"That's the point Willem. There will be a time when you may have to steal but you need to be able to recognize when that is. Like back in Tomé when you were stealing for you own survival. I would not harshly judge you then and I did not if you recall. I only asked you to steal here cause I knew it was safe but think about when it is not safe and I'm not around to bail you out. Your actions are your own. You cannot blindly follow what others tell you. Not even me. Do you understand?"

"I think so. But that's confusing."

"In time you'll be able to judge when such actions are appropriate and when they are not. I don't expect you to follow through immediately but you know as well as I do that the Barries are good people and don't deserve to be taken advantage of."

Oran tossed a piece of the candy in the air in front of Willem who easily caught it. Oran smiled and tossed a piece into his mouth as well. "Mm. Good stuff."

"I told you Mr. Barrie's candy was the best."

CHAPTER TWELVE

Ahead of Schedule—Fhurin, 1014

I T WAS A beautiful fall morning in the hills around Lanos. The first rays of light were just starting to creep through the branches and soon they would begin their work of relieving the grasses and leaves of the morning dew clinging to them in the early morning mist. Hidden behind a small copse of trees and brush overlooking a shallow valley with the smallest of little brooks running north towards the Mehm River was Willem and Oran readying to strike their prey down.

Oran leaned in close to Willem's ear and whispered, "Just like we've talked about. Aim for the body. It's a much bigger target. Take in a good breath and squeeze the trigger as you slowly exhale. Don't pull it or your aim will not be true."

Willem was in a stance with one knee touching the wet ground aiming a medium crossbow out into the valley. Tucked in tight to his shoulder with his right cheek resting on the stock. Steadying himself proved difficult for although it was not a large crossbow it was still very big for him and he did not want to miss so he took some extra time waiting for his prey to inch ever closer. He had his prey in sight and just when the opportunity seemed to be at its best he took his breath and released it slowly while squeezing the trigger. The twang of the crossbow string sounded loud in the ears of Willem in the still morning silence but it was too late to alert his intended target.

Oran stood after the shot and examined the results. "Well done Willem. First shot. Come quickly." Oran moved out of the brush and rushed to the turkey still thrashing and trying to run away. Without hesitation he lunged onto the turkey, grabbed its neck and quickly snapped it, releasing the animal from any unnecessary suffering.

Willem caught up to Oran just as he made the twist of the turkey's neck, which was quick but loud. The snapping sound had him wince in the slightest moment of disgust but upon seeing the joy in Oran's face as he looked up cleared any doubt of wrong doing, which Oran was constantly testing him on.

"Look here Willem." Oran positioned the turkey so that they could examine the shaft of the bolt protruding from its right side. "Excellent shot this. You pinned his wing to his body so he had no chance of escape. That's why he thrashed around briefly in a circle trying to take flight with only the one wing."

Willem leaned down and stroked the feathers of the turkey. They felt very soft and warm. He ran his hand up to the shaft of the bolt and then asked, "Now what do we do with him?"

Oran looked around the valley and noted the position of the rays of sunlight coming through the trees. "Well it's still early yet. I thought we'd be out all day looking for some birds. What do you say we get this big guy back to Georgette and have a delicious turkey dinner tonight?"

"Really? That sounds great."

"Well you'll have to help out of course. Your kill you know."

"So what does that mean?"

"It means that now I have to teach you how to clean it and you'll also have to pluck all it's feathers out."

"Ew gross."

"That was a wonderful meal Willem." Harold said as he pushed his empty plate away from him and leaned back in his chair.

"Thank you Harold." Willem replied while holding his extended gut. He couldn't remember ever eating as much and felt as though he couldn't keep it down but was happy for the compliment.

Georgette got up from her chair next to Harold while gathering up his plate. She walked past Harold and Oran and then grabbed the plate in front of Willem as well. "Yes indeed Willem and thanks for all the help in the kitchen today."

"Yeah that was fun cooking everything except for the plucking. Why do birds have so many feathers anyway?" Willem asked aloud to everyone.

In reply he got mottled laughs, as everyone was so full that laughter hurt the belly. Even Cecilia gave out a little laugh, which was something that she hadn't done much these past few weeks. Cecilia watched as Georgette continued to grab other plates so she pushed herself away from the table and began to rise, thinking to help Georgette.

Georgette noticed her and waved for her to sit back down. "You sit down and rest dear. I can handle all of this. Willem here will help me."

"I will?" Willem protested.

Georgette placed her free hand on her hip and looked down on Willem giving him a stern look. "Yes you will."

"Oh it's no bother. I can at least get my own dishes to the kitchen. I feel I need to stretch a little." Cecilia declared while pushing her chair back even farther to make room for her enormous belly.

Just as Cecilia was moving past Josef, who was sitting to her left, he began to protest and reached for her arm as a resounding splash hit the floor. Silence followed for the briefest of moments as everyone tried to register what had just happened. Cecilia grabbed for her stomach and let out a horrific scream as a pain unlike any she had ever felt erupted from deep within her. Josef was by her side instantly holding her up and waving for Georgette. Georgette dropped the plates in her hand and rushed to the other side of Cecilia.

"Uh, what just happened?" Willem asked aloud.

Georgette took charge of the situation. "Silence Willem." She turned to Harold. "Quickly Harold I need hot water immediately. Heat some up in the kitchen." Then to Oran, "Oran hurry, open the door to her room."

Oran ran quickly to Cecilia's room and Adley was in pursuit of Georgette and Josef hoping to help as they escorted her towards her bedroom. Cecilia was clutching her stomach and screaming in-between breaths of air. They hustled through the door and laid her down.

"Oran get me some more blankets from the chest at the end of the bed." Georgette stepped back a second assessing the situation. "Alright Josef and Oran you stay. Adley go help Harold at once."

Back out in the main hall Willem stood over the area in which Cecilia was standing. As Adley came running back across the floor towards the kitchen Willem stepped in front of him. "What's going on Sarge?"

"Cecilia's water broke. Her baby is on the way."

"Water. That don't look like water Sarge." Willem pointed to the large pool on the floor. "That looks like blood."

Adley stopped in his tracks just as he reached Willem wanting to reassure him that it wasn't. "It's okay Willem I believe a little blood comes out as well."

"Un no Sarge that's almost all blood."

Adley moved over to the pool. Shadowed from the light by the table and chairs it was hard to tell at first but upon closer examination Adley could see that it was indeed almost all blood. He scanned the path back to Cecilia's room and sure enough there were drops of blood leading all the way to the now closed door of her room.

Harold and Adley waited patiently for hours around the hearth of the main hall. In hushed tones they talked about the relentless screaming emanating from within Cecilia's room. Thankfully Willem had finally given up his watch and slipped into sleep though not willfully. Adley had carried him downstairs a couple hours previous to lay him in his own bed. Even from downstairs, the shrill cries of Cecilia could be heard by Adley's ears while he was briefly down there.

"You know dawn will be approaching soon. Surely this cannot go on for much longer." Adley declared much later.

Harold shook his head indicating he did not agree. "When Georgette tried to have our first baby she was in labor for near two days."

"I did not know that. I thought Georgette could not have kids."

"After that she could not have anymore. It was too much on her body." Harold explained while trying to not reveal the sadness he felt within himself though it had been many years since that fateful night.

"I'm sorry to hear that my friend. What of the child?"

"A boy." Harold smiled at the memory. "Born too early though I'm afraid. I was a father for only a couple days before he passed."

"My apologies Harold. I did not mean to pry."

Harold stoically waved off the notion. "It was years ago. We have found since then that family runs deeper than just blood." Harold leaned over and patted Adley on the shoulder. "I worry about Cecilia though. She has not been pregnant for near as long as my wife was even though the size of her belly would argue otherwise."

The sound of a baby's first cries interrupted their conversation. Both Harold and Adley stood and walked towards the door of Cecilia Alio's room. They waited patiently outside the door, for Georgette had scolded both of them earlier for entering even though they only wanted to help. Adley was surprised at the time of the rebuke of Harold but Harold was not. Georgette had played midwife to a few of their friends from times past. After the loss of their own child she always kept Harold out of the room perhaps to shield him from seeing another child born before it's time.

The door swung open and Oran exited wiping his bloody hands with a towel and shaking his head at the sight of Adley and Harold. "She didn't make it."

All three hung their heads low but lifted again as Georgette came behind Oran with a baby swaddled in a blanket that Cecilia and her had made for the arrival of the child. Georgette was smiling wide looking down at the face of what appeared to be a very large bundle, considering the child was just born, but also crying over the loss of her friend. Georgette stifled back her tears and came closer to Adley and Harold. She positioned the crying bundle so that they could see his face. "Gentlemen I'd like you to meet Marcus Alio."

Adley and Harold both sighed with relief at the sight of the baby's face. They had discussed earlier that if the child was indeed dragonborn as they had feared then he would likely take on many of the traits of a dragon such as scaled skin. Harold moved closer and with his finger tickled the under side of Marcus' chin. For a brief second Marcus opened his squinted crying eyes revealing the darkest black orbs that Harold had ever seen.

"So what do we do now?" Adley inquired of Josef after the realization that Marcus was indeed the son of Deathmar the Black and Josef was able to converse after seeing to Cecilia.

"Shh. Keep your voice down." Josef answered while looking to the door to Georgette and Harold's room.

Georgette had retired to her room with their newest arrival after preparing him some formula that she hoped he would accept. Thus far it didn't seem to be working as his crying could be heard beyond the door, clear as day.

R. A. HAYDEN

"Apologies." Adley looked around from Josef to Oran and finally Harold standing next to him. "Surely we cannot let anyone else know of this."

Oran crossed one arm under the other using it as a platform to rest his other arm on so that he could rest his chin on his upraised hand. "We cannot hide a dragonborn child forever. What he is will be known soon enough."

Fearing the worst Harold flew to the defense of Marcus. "It's only his eyes. Surely we can explain that away some other way."

"No Harold it is not just his eyes." Josef relayed to Harold and Adley. "His nails on his hands and feet are as black as his eyes and the skin running up his spine is dark in color."

"Well what does that mean?" Adley asked.

"It means that likely his nails will be more claw like as he matures and he will do so rapidly if Cecilia's fast pregnancy is any indication. His spine will likely end up protruding or at the very least be covered in scales as well." Josef replied.

"How can you know this?" Adley persisted.

"I have met a few dragonborn in my time. All very different from one another but most exhibit traits of the dragon parent far exceeding what we have seen from Marcus."

"Well perhaps that is a good thing. He need not walk around shirtless." Adley suggested.

"That's all well and good but he will still show his other signs." Josef could tell that Adley wanted to continue arguing his point so Josef continued. "He may as well, start showing other signs as he grows. Dragons mature extremely quickly in comparison to their long lifespans. They must do so to survive. Like a dragon I guess that Marcus will do the same. We simply don't know what else may come about in terms of his physical form."

Harold stepped forward. "Me and Georgette will take him. We will hide if need be."

Josef never surprised of the bravery of Harold anymore stood from the table he was leaning against and placed his hands on his shoulders. "That was not my meaning. I would never ask such a thing of you."

"You know you need not ask." Harold interrupted.

"Let me finish." Josef released Harold and leaned again against the table. "We are all of like mind here. We will not forsake the child despite his origins. That is not who we are and I for one will be damned before I let someone, anyone, come into our house and demand terms of us."

"That's all well and good father but we need to prepare for the inevitable." Oran said.

"Yes Oran. This will get out and sooner than we like I'm sure." Josef stood up again and began pacing back and forth along the length of one end of the center tables. "We need at the very least for it to be on our terms."

"What do you mean?" Oran asked.

"No one knows yet. Cecilia could still be pregnant for all anyone knows. She still had at least two months before she was due to give birth."

Adley was shaking his head now. "Her screams were loud and for hours on end. Likely someone heard."

"I don't believe so or the guards would have shown up. It was late and we are a far peace from the edge of town." Josef reasoned. "If that is the case than we will deal with it sooner rather than later but for now we plan on this."

"Okay what then?" Oran began asking just as the crying ceased from the bedroom.

"She did it." Josef looked to Harold who wore a proud expression on his face. "Okay no one knows of Cecilia. She has not been in town for well over a month to my knowledge so she will not be missed. That will give us time to plan our next move."

"What of Cecilia though? She must be laid to rest." Oran said.

"Yes of course. Tonight we will send her on her way. We will bury her next to her husbands plot on the outskirts of their property. I believe that is what she would have wished."

Oran, Harold and Adley shook their heads in agreement then Adley asked, "What of today?"

"We need rest for one. Adley I hate to ask but could you stand staying awake a bit longer and taking watch out front so we are not caught unaware to anyone approaching?"

"Of course."

"Watch for Willem. He will be awake soon no doubt. Make him stand watch with you. I'm sure that will keep you awake." Josef actually

R. A. HAYDEN

smiled at that. Something he rarely did if ever when concerned about Willem. He then turned to Harold. "You will have to help your wife. I'm sure she is exhausted as well. Me and Oran will try to rest for a couple hours and relieve the both of you."

Harold nodded his agreement and moved towards his bedroom door while the others went on about their assignment. Before he got there Josef stopped him once more. "Harold."

"Yes sir."

"Congratulations Harold."

"For what sir?"

"Well it seems you are a father now."

Harold smiled at that but then shook the notion away. "No sir. It seems we all are."

CHAPTER THIRTEEN

The Lie—Fandril, 1014

"YOU KNOW FATHER, Usarus may not go for this." Oran said while looking across the open field outside of The Silver Guard Cemetery. "This is likely to get ugly fast."

"We have prepared for this as much as we can. Delaying any longer with the inquiries we have had from the capital and Hareth can no longer be ignored." Josef explained.

Josef and Oran were waiting at the intended meeting spot where Usarus would once again enact the portal of Hareth Academy and meet with them to discuss the topic of Marcus Alio. They were able to delay the telling of his birth for near a month but with so many having seen Cecilia and how large she had become it was reasonable that many knew she would give birth early.

"Look there father." Oran pointed to Lanos. Emerging from in-between two of the buildings was Captain Payne followed closely by Escott Claridge. "Seems Usarus has made this meeting known to his little spy in Lanos."

"Yes indeed. I'm not surprised. I doubt Usarus will show up alone from Hareth either." Josef proclaimed.

Oran just shook his head. It was hard to fathom how so many interested parties were seemingly scared over the birth of a single child. He contemplated what they were about to try to accomplish as Captain Payne and Escott neared. When they were close Oran moved to embrace his friend. "Greetings Captain."

In typical fashion Captain Payne greeted Oran with a forearm shake. "And to you." He hesitated a moment before continuing. "It seems I've been summoned to be representative of the Castan military in this meeting."

Josef shook his head in agreement of Casta's choice. "That was inevitable Captain. I do apologize for not informing you myself but best to get this over with all at once."

"Yes. But still I don't appreciate taking orders from Hareth." Captain Payne turned to regard Escott who had informed him of his role in this.

Escott began, "You…"

Captain Payne interrupted Escott, "No Escott you will keep your mouth shut throughout this meeting!"

Josef and Oran were both surprised at the verbal beating it seemed that Captain Payne had just administered in just one sentence. Escott put his hands into his robes and stood silent while exchanging a threatening stare down with his Captain. No doubt Captain Payne had already had a disagreeable conversation with him about this. They both wondered if there was a struggle for power going on in the Lanos Outpost between the two. While Captain Payne was in charge and Escott was merely an advisor sent by Hareth Academy there was always the debate on who really held the true power behind Casta. Whether it was their formidable army or the wizards who ran everything from behind the scenes. In any case it seemed that Captain Payne believed it was the former.

The water like image marking the opening of the Hareth portal appeared before the quartet of onlookers and as Josef suspected not only did Usarus step through the portal but two others appeared as well.

Hallam Leighton, head of the Order of Bahamut, stood to the left of Usarus. He was wearing the traditional priest robes of Bahamut. They were dark gray in color underneath, with a lighter gray top that overlapped the under robe. Every seam on the robe had ornate designs hemmed into the stitching and he wore a large silver pendant of Bahamut displayed proudly on his chest. He also carried a large warhammer; a typical weapon of clerics serving Bahamut although this one was likely more than it appeared considering he was head of the order.

To the right of Usarus was Patience Thorp, head of the Order of Pelor. Oran could not help but let his stare linger on Patience for longer than was appropriate, something that did not go unmissed by Patience. Her attire was scantily clad next to the priest of Bahamut and Oran wondered if this was becoming typical of a priestess of Pelor. Her outfit consisted of a low cut top connected to a corset that went only down to the hips and then connected to a loincloth that went down below the knees leaving her long and shapely caramel tinted legs bare until they met up with her high boots of matching color and design. The only part of the outfit that was not revealing were the arms that were part of the top leaving both of her arms covered except for her hands. To top it all off she wore pauldrons and matching crown both gold in color matching her entire outfit, which was all trimmed in red.

Usarus took in his surroundings and noted the distance set between Captain Payne and Escott Claridge. He noted as well that Captain Payne had taken up a position standing next to Oran who was clad in full armor with his magnificent longsword strapped to his belt, a sword unmatched in power in all of Casta for it was heavily enchanted. A gift that Josef had given his son early on.

Rainclouds gathered behind his hosts moving in their direction and he hoped that unlike the fast approaching weather that this meeting would not turn dour. He approached Josef and bowed slightly to his old friend. "Well met Josef. Shall we begin?"

"Yes indeed. Welcome all." Josef said while returning the bow. "As you all well know by now the child born of Cecilia Alio is unfortunately not of her husband. This has been a matter of concern for us most of all especially considering the affront made against us by Deathmar the Black and his minions. Unfortunate as well because Cecilia Alio has been a dear friend to us and she has passed beyond this world."

"She did not survive the birthing then?" Usarus asked Josef.

"No I'm afraid she has not."

"What of the child? Is there no doubt?"

"There is no doubt. He is dragonborn." Josef replied while looking as sour in his expression as he could.

Patience Thorp asked, "How will the child survive?"

Surprised by the concern in her voice, both Usarus and Hallam Leighton turned to regard her. She was the representative for Pelor, god of the sun, and Deathmar the Black had chosen his sigil as a black sun, mocking and indicating a direct challenge to those serving under Pelor. Without a word they turned back to Josef but the looks she received from the two were not unnoticed by the always-perceptive Patience Thorp.

"The child is under the care of my servants for now." Josef explained.

R. A. HAYDEN

Hallam Leighton weighed in, "Perhaps that is unwise."

"How do you mean?" Josef asked.

"Perhaps the child did not survive the birth as well. Perhaps he should just expire. It may be better for all concerned."

"That is tantamount to murder." Josef said.

"Better that he grow to the monster he will become?" Hallam retorted.

"That is a good point Father Leighton." Josef felt as though poison were spewing from his lips. He knew well that he would have to play this one close to the vest though if Marcus were to have any chance of proving himself as anything other than a son of Deathmar and the vile evil nature that accompanied that fact. "I would have you think on something else though."

Usarus' interest was peaked. He firmly believed that Josef would not give up the child as indicated by previous discussions they had on the subject. "Tell me Josef. What would you recommend?"

"Bait of course."

"Bait?" Usarus did not expect this in the slightest. He feared direct conflict. Perhaps there was hope that him and his old friend would not have to be at odds.

"Yes bait. We have been searching for over half a year now for any sign of Deathmar the Black with absolutely no sign of him or his followers. Word of a son by his loins will spread far and wide." Josef could tell by the quizzical expressions of Patience, Hallam, and Usarus that they had not thought of that option but Usarus also looked skeptical. "Even if he believes it is only a bad rumor perhaps it will lure him out so that we may all take in the glory of ending the only known threat by black dragons."

Usarus surely did not expect this. He believed it was a stall tactic on the part of Josef but at the same time even if Josef's words were false in conviction, the truth of the matter might still prove valuable. "What of his care in the meantime? I suggest holding him at Hareth Academy."

"Who do you suggest would take care of him?"

"We would hire a midwife of course. There is no shortage of women we could hire in the capital. Even those willing to take care of a doomed child for a healthy price."

Josef shook his head at the notion. "I thank you for the thought but as it has been our burden to see him into this world so too should it be to see him raised."

Hallam Leighton weighed in again, "This is false then. Why care for the child of your most hated enemy? Why not release yourself from the burden?"

"Because Father Leighton I said so." Josef did not wish to further explain his reasoning especially to one who has already proven to him that he would have killed Marcus already.

Taken back slightly Hallam was astounded by the straightforwardness of Josef. "Need I remind you that you do not dictate policy in Casta? If we decree that the child will come with us then it will be so."

"I believe if you look back in the records of Casta than you will find that I have dictated policy in a fair amount over the past couple centuries. Defying me on this would not be to your interest." Josef finished with placing Etburn further in front of him.

Catching the subtle implications of Josef's words and movements, Hallam picked up his hammer, which was hanging by his side and placed it onto his shoulder. As he did he noticed Oran and Captain Payne rest their hands on the top of their respective sword hilts.

Surprisingly to Josef, Usarus deflated the debate and the mounting tension out of the hands of all. "Very well Josef. Your plan has merit. I would add only one thing."

"What would that be Headmaster?"

"As you say we have looked for Deathmar for a long time now. The previous time you encountered him was a hundred years ago and no word from him in our lands until this past year had happened. It is likely that this will not work or that Deathmar would even care is up in the air. If it turns out that it does work you will take aid in destroying him from us." Usarus pointed back to his travelling companions.

"And if it doesn't work?" Josef knew there would be a caveat to this. He imagined well what it would be.

"If the child turns out to take to his father's nature than you will destroy him." Usarus let that sink in. "You understand what I mean? You are putting all in your home in great danger taking this on. We cannot know how inherent the evil is within the child. It is a great risk."

"I understand fully Headmaster."

R. A. HAYDEN

"I must protest." Hallam insisted. "You Usarus also do not dictate policy in Casta. The decision is not yours alone. The church will not stand for this. At the very least the child should be brought back to Tomé."

"Enough Father Leighton." Usarus responded in an even tone. Usarus walked in-between Patience and Hallam and recalled the portal back to Hareth Academy then turned to Hallam. "You can debate further back in Tomé now or I'll see you when you arrive on foot if you like." Usarus gave a nod to Josef and stepped through the portal.

Hallam was fuming now and seemed on the verge of striking but thought better of it looking at the formidable trio standing before him. At last he turned around and walked through the portal. Patience wore a little grin thinking the show quite amusing. She in turn bowed to Josef and gave a wink and a smile to Oran before departing as well.

Hallam Leighton entered the office of Headmaster Usarus, leaned his warhammer against the desk and then took a seat not bothering to wait for Usarus to close the door behind them or waiting for him to be seated either. "This is an outrage Usarus. Once word of this spreads there is nothing that either of us can do to stop anyone else for trying for the child."

"Calm yourself Hallam. I have insights I wish to share that you have apparently not thought about." Usarus grabbed a decanter of brandy and two glasses on his way to his desk and placed one in front of Hallam then filled it with the potent alcohol. His hope was to calm Hallam's nerves and wine didn't seem strong enough at the moment.

"Well go ahead then. Tell me."

Usarus took his time and finished pouring his own glass as well before elaborating. "This works to our advantage if you would clear your head and think this through."

Hallam took in a deep breath and then picked up his brandy and took a healthy drink. The sting of the alcohol on his throat was actually soothing to his now sore throat after arguing in the corridor with Patience Thorp about her complicity with Josef Righe's plan. "Alright. Continue please."

"Direct conflict with Josef Righe at this time is not advantageous to us in the slightest. He is far too powerful." Usarus raised his glass in a motion of silence as Hallam did the same and seemed to want to argue the point. "Let me finish. You have only been the head of the Order of Bahamut for a couple years now correct?"

"Yes, but that is hardly the point."

"I'm getting there. Patience Thorp is in a similar situation correct?"

"Yes."

"I have been head of Hareth Academy for over three hundred years and I tell you now that Josef Righe taking care of a dragonborn, even one sired by Deathmar the Black is not our greatest concern. You know well of what I speak."

"That is besides the point."

"It is exactly the point. War is coming. It has been far too long since a full out war between Casta and the necromancers and witches of the east. The wall being erected by the Iron Hall Dwarves is near completion. Something our enemies do not wish to see completed."

Hallam took another drink. He was still unsure of what Usarus was getting at. "The wall is still years away from completion and one has nothing to do with the other."

"What do you think would happen if we demanded the child from Josef?"

"Well after today I imagine he would refuse."

"Exactly. This ruse of his to use the child as bait is exactly that. A ruse. He would not turn over a child of any race knowing full well that it's life would end at our hands."

"For the greater good."

"Josef does not think that way. While the child is innocent we know well what he will become. Dragonborn of metallic decent are barely tolerated let alone one of chromatic descent."

"Then why the stall? Why not simply take it?"

"Josef Righe is the second oldest human wizard in all of Drilain to my knowledge. Only I am older. We did not get this way by mere happenstance. Only a powerful wizard or many could take him on directly and that would benefit him. Besides, he is my friend."

"Others will try."

"I doubt it. Josef and Oran Righe are living legends known not only in Casta but all of Drilain. Going against them now directly could spark a sizeable conflict. One in which our true enemies of the east will take advantage of."

"Surely not. They are but a handful in a Keep that barely begs that title."

Usarus shook his head and took a good swallow of his drink. Apparently he would have to hold the hand of Hallam through this. "Did you not see how that Captain took to their side immediately when tensions rose?"

"I did."

"And Patience Thorp would not even speak against them."

"What of it?"

"Such is their legend. They have fought and many of The Silver Guard have died over the centuries in defense of Casta. Now if Casta were to declare them criminals for not following the orders of Casta they could spring up support that you could not even imagine."

Hallam smiled catching on to Usarus' way of thinking. "You mean to let time dwindle their reputation. No one will follow someone who takes the side of an evil dragonborn."

"Precisely. Though I do not think it will come to that. The child's nature will come forth eventually. When that happens my old friend will not fail in his duty. He is merely blinded by the innocence of a baby. In the meantime let us look to the east. This child is of no concern to the safety of Casta presently."

Josef's thoughts were interrupted by Oran who had sidled next to him on the back deck of the Keep. His thoughts were far away and he hadn't even noticed Oran exit the back door of the Keep and move to join him under the cover of the porch. Perhaps it was the sound of the drizzling rain and distant thoughts that had kept him unaware of his approach or perhaps he was just getting old. A thought for another time he reasoned.

"It is late father. Adley and I will keep watch tonight. Perhaps you should get some rest." Oran said.

Josef smiled. He was thankful for the concern of his son. "A watch is likely not necessary my son."

"Oh? I thought after today you would be wary about unwanted visitors." Oran referred to the meeting with Usarus, Hallam Leighton and Patience Thorp. "Have you come to some realization about our present situation?"

"Perhaps. Is Adley up then?"

"Yes. Everyone else has turned in. He is sitting inside."

Josef stamped out the remaining tobacco in his pipe on the railing then asked, "Go get a bottle of wine from the cellar will you? I'll join you in a second."

Oran nodded and headed in. Josef took a few more seconds listening to the calming sound of the small raindrops dripping off of the roof in front of him and finalizing his reasoning for the conversation to be had with his fellow Silver Guard members. Then he headed in and bolted the heavily fortified door and with a minor spell lifted the locking bar and put it in place without physically touching it. Satisfied he joined Adley sitting in front of the fire just as Oran showed up with the bottle of wine and three glasses.

Oran filled the three glasses and then took a seat as well placing his feet up on the table, which Georgette would have been furious about were she awake. "Well let's have it then. What do you know?" He asked of his father.

Josef looked to Oran and then to Adley and felt a great sense of pride. While they were the only three Silver Guard remaining they were formidable. Even Adley who had only joined recently had fought alongside them for years while stationed at Lanos. While not as finely tuned in the sword as his son he was a ferocious fighter and would take two hits to his one if he knew it would win him the fight.

Oran he knew was still the best swordsman in all of Casta and perhaps much farther but though his son would never admit it he was beginning to slow. The ring that had kept him so young and vibrant for so long was slowly fading and would soon be no aid to him at all. Josef knew not how to replenish it's magic for it was unlike any other ring of regeneration he had ever seen and it's maker was unknown to them or at least they would not speak their guess out loud. Other rings of regeneration or rings of healing, as they were more commonly known, only healed wounds inflicted on the body but did nothing to stop the aging process. Time it seemed was beginning to catch up to them. While he would still probably live for another century or perhaps even longer while his magic still ran true he would be without his son in only a few short decades.

Josef began, "Well I do not believe that Usarus believed us about hoping to use Marcus for bait."

"If that were the case wouldn't he have had a lot more fight in him today?" Adley asked.

"No Adley I don't believe so. In fact I believe he saw right through it. Remember now he has known me for over three hundred years. He was my Headmaster when I was but a first year student at Hareth."

"I didn't know that."

"Few do. Oran and myself might be the only two who do know that except for Usarus himself of course and anyone curious enough to look back in the Hareth Academy history."

"Then why let us keep Marcus without further debate?"

"Usarus is always looking far into the future unlike myself. He no doubt knows something I do not," Josef thought on that for a second, "Or it could be that after our many debates he has finally come to the realization that I wouldn't bend on this and truly fears a conflict between the two of us. Regardless of his reasons I am thankful. I do not wish conflict were I think there should be none so I will not search further for his reasoning."

"But what if this is to just draw you into this false hope?"

"It doesn't matter. Locked away in here there is little any can do without giving us ample warning. If that day comes we will deal with it."

"Then what would you have us do father?" Oran asked.

Josef took a deep sigh. "I believe it is time I take a verse from Usarus and look further into the future." Oran and Adley looked to each other not sure of Josef's meaning but he continued, "We must secure the future of The Silver Guard."

"You wish for me to begin recruiting then?" Oran rationalized.

"No Oran I believe we have the recruits that we need already." Josef lifted his glass pointing at the door of Harold and Georgette's room.

"What? No?" Oran's voice was harsh and loud. Realizing it he lowered so as not to wake Harold or Georgette. "You can't mean to train Marcus in anything."

"And why not?"

"For a multitude of reasons. How about that he really is the son of Deathmar?"

"That is not the child's fault."

"Nothing is his fault but what if he does turn to evil? We will have to put him down. That will be all the harder if we are the ones to train him."

"I don't only mean him. You have Willem and I have Havander as well."

Oran threw his arms in the air in protest. "Even at their age it will take years and that's fine but what do we do in the meantime?"

"We do as we have always done. We aid Lanos in time of need and our other neighbors. We will keep out feelers for any word of Deathmar. While here we train our apprentices."

"We would do that anyway. What of Marcus? Do you really intend to train him as a wizard? That might very well be the straw that brings not only Hareth but the churches and the King down on us as well."

Josef was a bit surprised at how concerned Oran was but he would not relent. "Yes I will if he has the aptitude for it. If not than you and Adley will teach him the way of the sword."

Oran rolled his eyes and Adley actually smiled being happy that he was brought into the debate at all. Josef watched and waited and gave a slight chuckle before taking a drink of his wine.

"What is so funny?" Oran asked.

"I said it was time I look to the future a bit more. I never said it was going to be boring."

CHAPTER FOURTEEN

Sarge—Sadan, 1015

"WHAT DO YOU think Sarge?" Captain Payne asked atop his mount while looking down at Adley who was examining some tracks.

Without looking up from the one clear track in the mud Adley responded, "I'd say we are lucky that the spring rains have let up for a couple days or these tracks would have washed away completely. They are extremely light. As though they barely touched the ground."

"What do you make of that?"

"I believe it confirms my suspicions of the bodies we have found in the two farm houses." Adley stood and looked up to Captain Payne. He was hoping to not confirm his suspicions, as he was sure Captain Payne hoped as well.

"You believe it is a vampire then?"

"Only thing I know of that can travel that fast on foot and wears boots. I believe that the slaughtered families of those two farms were butchered in the way they were to hide the true identity of the attacker. Sloppy work really. Can't think of anything else that would have drained them of blood before ripping the bodies apart." Adley took his reins of his horse and mounted alongside Captain Payne and the other four Lanos soldiers accompanying them.

Captain Payne looked in the direction that the tracks were leading. "No other farms or villages southeast of here. If it keeps running that direction there won't be anything else for it to feed on." Captain Payne focused his direction directly south and pointed. "There is a small village about a days ride from here. That's gonna be the only opportunity to feed unless it wants to run straight onto Iron Hall and try it's luck there."

"I believe it is a she. Tracks are too small for the boot print of a man and there is a distinctive high heel in the back indicating a woman's boot. Likely turned not long ago. Vampires are not this sloppy and don't kill this regularly out of sheer hunger. This one has not learned to control itself yet."

Captain Payne nodded his agreement. He looked behind him to his four soldiers and beyond to the direction they had come from. They were three days southeast of Lanos. He hadn't expected that they would be hunting down a vampire when they had first heard the news five days ago that a farm in the vicinity of Lanos has been attacked and all residents were killed or he would have brought more men. Although him and Adley had been on hunts for vampires with other Silver Guard members in the past neither him nor Adley had ever killed one themselves. He looked over to Adley and admired his newly crafted and untested shield strapped to the right flank of his horse. It was an astonishing piece of work that Armihrmond Firefist, the dwarven blacksmith in Lanos, had created for him. It was of teardrop design with small silver spikes protruding from its gleaming surface. In the center was a larger spike also made of silver. He thought to himself that it was good that at least one of them was prepared for such an enemy. "What do you think Sarge? This is more your area of expertise now."

Adley appreciated the praise but knew the challenge set before him would be difficult without the aid of more seasoned vampire hunters like Oran and Josef. Nevertheless he was Silver Guard now and would not shrink before it. "It's early now. We will never find where the vampire has gone to ground in time. Once night hits we will be at its mercy in the wilderness." Adley thought about the erratic behavior of the one they tracked and reasoned a sensible option. "If this vampire is indeed new I believe it won't be able to control its hunger. The village is its closest option to sate its appetite. I say we push on and set up an ambush."

Captain Payne nodded his approval. "Like old times." He gave his horse a good kick and headed out with all speed. Adley and the troops followed close behind. They would have to hurry if they were to reach the village before nightfall.

Hours later the six riders entered the village of Ecrin. It was a small farming village nowhere near the size of Lanos thus depicting it as a village and not a town. It had one tavern surrounded by the personal homes of the village inhabitants running down the small main street with a sizeable barn on one end that acted as the business place for the town blacksmith and stable man. The sun had already gone past the horizon so they hurried their horses into the barn. There was no one present to greet them so they took to securing their horses in the barn themselves. Likely the blacksmith was already at the tavern and from the sounds of it as they passed so was most of the village as that was the usual custom of most villages.

Once the horses were secure Captain Payne looked to Adley to confirm their game plan. "What do you think? As we discussed on the road."

"Yes. The village opens up nicely to the east. If she comes in at all she will likely come from that direction." Adley unstrapped his crossbow and quiver and then went into his saddlebags and took out a large leather toolkit. He kneeled on the ground and spread the kit out in front of him. Inside were flasks, ointments, vials of potions, two silver stakes, and three throwing knives. It was a customary toolkit that Josef provided for all Silver Guard members. Of interest to him now were the silver stakes and the three throwing knives that were also made entirely of silver. He handed one out to each other member of his party and then grabbed the bolts out of his quiver. "Now these bolt tips are also silver. I'll take only one and once spotted I'll take the first shot." He handed three each to the other three men who would be using their crossbows. "Remember silver is the only thing that hurts these bastards and it won't do so for long unless you can get them straight in the heart."

One of the soldiers asked, "That'll kill 'em right?"

"No but a shot directly to the heart will paralyze them. The silver just slows their healing process and burns them. Your normal weapons will only inflict damage for a brief period. You have to cut off their heads or let them slowly burn in the sunlight to truly kill them." Adley looked to each man hoping to see that his words were hitting home as to how dangerous an opponent they were facing. "Remember they are faster than you can imagine and if one gets a hold of you they can rip you apart with their bare hands."

"Remember as well that their senses are powerful. They can see in the dark and hear us way before we could hear them. I want no talking and no noise. Wait for Adley to make his move and we back up from there." Captain Payne added.

Adley stood up and nodded his approval of Captain Payne's words. Then set into motion the plan they had discussed having a clearer picture in mind now that he was in the village.

Captain Payne took one soldier with him into the tavern to ensure that their quarry wasn't already inside, which they doubted but also to try to keep the villagers from action or alarming their prey as to their presence. Two men with crossbows went to the other end of town and managed to climb onto the roofs of the two buildings at the end of the main street. Thankfully the roofs were made in such a way that they could not be seen if entering the town from the east. Adley ordered the last man to the second story of the barn to be his eyes and cover him from up high with his crossbow. With everything set up as well as could be, Adley took a seat inside the barn making sure he had a clear view of the village street laid out before him so that he could see anything coming into the village.

Tense minutes ticked by at first for Adley as well as the soldiers. Adley found himself shushing the man in the hayloft above him a few times for moving and causing the boards to creak in response. Minutes turned into an hour and then two though it felt much longer. Not surprising to Adley only one pair of people had exited the tavern in that time and crossed the small dirt street to their home directly opposite the tavern. It was normal for villagers to spend many hours drinking after a long days work out in the fields and it was a beautifully clear night to do so. From his distance of approximately thirty yards Adley could hear the muffled laughter and goings on inside the walls of the tavern. He imagined Captain Payne was having a much easier time waiting this out. He hoped as well that the two inside weren't just getting drunk after a hard days ride.

Just as Adley pulled both of his arms back to stretch his shoulders he saw distant movement in the darkness beyond the lightly colored dirt street. Unsure at first for it could be anything he waited for a clearer sign of what was moving in the darkness beyond his sight. Coming into view slowly was the outline of a figure strolling towards the street that ran down the middle of the village. Adley picked up his crossbow and fit his bolt tipped with silver into the flight groove while never taking his eyes off the approaching figure. When the figure came near to the end of the darkness and the beginning of the light that shone from the torches set about the town, like lanterns would hang in more prosperous towns and cities, it stopped. Adley crept closer to the double doors opened in the barn making sure to stay in shadow. In one arm he had his shield, which he leaned against the wall of the barn then took up his crossbow with both hands. Just out of the light he could not be sure what he was looking at. Only that it had the size and shape of a person. Adley listened to the sounds coming from the village tavern just as whatever it was he was looking at must be doing. Patiently he waited while hoping that his men would not give away the game by making a raucous or nervous movement of any kind.

Into the light stepped a woman clad in high boots, tightly fitted trousers with a large belt and buckle now shining in the torchlight, and a ruffled collared blouse which used to be white but was caked in dirt and who knows what else. Even from this distance Adley could see that her skin was pale white. Her face was framed with long brown curly locks dangling down to her shoulders. Her chin was dark in appearance as though covered in something that her cheeks were not. Adley watched as the women lifted her chin into the air and sniffed at the night air then tilted her head from one side of the village to the other taking in the sounds coming from the tavern or at least that is what Adley hoped for he could not hear anything else from his vantage point.

With an alluring like stroll the women moved to Adley's left towards the walkway running down that side of the street. She stepped onto the boards that acted like a sidewalk running along the entire length of houses. At each house she stopped and peered into the unlit windows. Apparently not satisfied with what she sensed from within she crept ever closer towards the tavern. As she neared, it appeared to Adley that she was fidgety in her head movements and was licking her lips. Even more clearly to Adley now was that she was indeed covered in dirt. Even her curly hair had remnants of dirt clinging stubbornly to it. Were it not for her shabby appearance Adley surmised that she would be quite beautiful given her lithe form and confident stroll.

Out of the corner of his eye Adley noticed the soldier set onto the roof on the right side of town leveling his crossbow in her direction. He could not see the other but since she was on his side of the street he had probably not noticed her.

Adley silently worded to himself, "Wait, wait. Let her get closer to me."

Still apparently unaware of him and the soldier aiming a crossbow at her the woman came within arms reach of the tavern. She crept closer to the building staying in shadow so as not to be seen through the windows. A step more and she would come into view being lit up by the torch lit outside the tavern. She took the step as Adley placed his finger on the trigger of his crossbow. She did so to get a view inside the clouded window of the tavern. Adley waited and watched. Strangely the woman leaned against the wall with her face hugging the wood sniffing like an animal sniffs out prey hidden from its view. When she finished she stepped back a step from the wall coming into full view of the torchlight and smiled revealing to Adley a pair of pearly white fangs glistening in the moonlight.

Without a second thought Adley pulled his trigger releasing his bolt and then dropped the crossbow immediately. At this distance it was a remarkable shot that took her in the shoulder spinning her to face Adley's direction fully. She let out a horrible scream and tore the bolt from her arm. Smoke rose up and out of the wound as well as off of the bolt's tip made of silver, which had reacted with the vampire's blood.

Adley with shield in hand now stepped out of the double doors of the barn into the light of the moon and torchlight and advanced slowly. Seeing her attacker the vampire threw the bolt from her hand just as another bolt flew over her right shoulder and stuck into the wood of the walkway. The soldier behind her had fired his shot but she didn't even register it. She focused clearly on Adley and started to run in his direction. Adley did the same while unsheathing his sword.

The soldier in the barn fired a shot at the vampire now racing at Adley. The bolt hit her in the left shoulder but she seemed to not notice at all. The two combatants didn't slow. In the middle of the street they collided. Adley knew better than to test his strength against a vampire. Even a smaller woman who was unarmed would seem to any that Adley would just bawl her over but this was a vampire not any mere woman. Her hands and teeth were her weapons and with the added strength that comes from vampirism it was her that could have easily bawled over Adley. Adley was the wiser combatant though. Just before they collided he brought his shield into line and let her crash into it. Adley accepted the blow, which sent him shooting backwards. He used the momentum from the collision to go to his back and roll coming up to his feet in a perfect defensive stance with shield in line again and sword raised to strike.

The woman vampire was not so fortunate in the collision. She ran headlong into the shield not knowing the danger that it posed to her. The largest of the spikes on the shield hit her squarely in the right breast impaling her and a couple of the smaller spikes tore into her flesh as well. One even hit her in the face as she ducked to land the blow to Adley. She recoiled in pain looking to the smoking wounds now coming from her body. It took many seconds for the pain to subside and for her to regain her wits.

"You'll pay for what you have done witch." Adley said as he advanced.

The vampire focused again on Adley. She bared her fangs and went into a crouch, extending her hands out like weapons. The commotion behind her of people exiting the tavern alerted her to danger from behind. She glanced back just as a another bolt entered the back of her right thigh. It stung like the others and she ripped it from her body and then did similarly with the one still protruding from her shoulder. She surveyed what was behind her. There were two men standing on the rooftops with crossbows trained her way and two soldiers ahead of the crowd exiting the tavern with swords in hand and advancing in her direction.

She turned back to Adley and thought of her options. She looked left and right to the buildings but the houses were built so close together there were no alleys to escape into. She lunged instead at Adley who lowered his shield once again accepting the blow and sliding backwards in the dirt after the impact. The vampire recoiled her hand in agony from punching directly into one of the smaller silver spikes. Adley advanced and took a swipe with his longsword, which she deftly ducked under and then grabbed at the edges of his shield. Even through the pain of holding onto the silver trim of the shield she hung on and ripped it from Adley's arm sending him tumbling towards the double doors of the barn. More crossbow bolts came at her and missed their target as she threw the shield and advanced on Adley who was once again rising.

Just before Captain Payne reached her position she took off in a sprint faster than any human could ever manage right at Adley leaving Captain Payne's swipe with his sword hitting nothing but air. She hoped to crush his skull with her bare hands before he could bring his sword to bear. Instead Adley rose while reaching to his belt and pulled forth his silver stake. Just as the vampire reached with her hands and grabbed him by his helmet he thrust upwards with the weapon digging it deep into her chest cavity and straight into her heart.

She released Adley involuntarily as her body began to spasm. Adley pulled her in close and refused to let her hands get to the hilt of the stake. Her screams became gargled as she stopped moving. Adley held her up waiting for her to go completely limp in his arms. He knew he had hit the mark. The fight was over.

Unsure of what they had just witnessed the townspeople gasped in horror. For all they knew these soldiers had just murdered a woman. Slowly they crept closer as Adley brought her body down to the ground keeping his hand on the stake the whole time. As Captain Payne and his fellow soldiers came closer with the townspeople right behind them the smoke rising from the vampires wounds and the stake still in her chest could be seen clearly but they had never seen a vampire before and they began murmuring amongst themselves of murder.

Captain Payne hearing this turned around to silence the crowd. "Silence." He yelled gaining the attention of the townspeople. "What you just witnessed was an act of heroism by none other than a Silver Guard member who just saved you all from a vampire we have been tracking for days."

Still unsure of how to react the townspeople whispered loudly between one another while trying to fathom the meaning behind it while Adley ran his finger along the left cheek of the vampire uncovering her face from her brown locks. He couldn't help but think to himself that he was correct in that she was beautiful. He thought to himself how unsettling it is that something so beautiful could be so evil. He shook the notion away and retrieved his sword. He walked back to her body and thought of the families in those farms that were horribly massacred as he brought his sword down across her neck severing it cleanly, garnering another gasp from the crowd. Only then did he retrieve his stake from her chest.

Captain Payne and the other soldiers who were now all in attendance raised their swords in salute and gave out a cheer. Adley merely examined

R. A. HAYDEN

his stake, which was still smoking from the vampire blood that was coating its surface. The crowd began to cheer along with the soldiers.

Captain Payne started issuing orders to his men. The body would need to be burned as was custom when killing a vampire and they would see to it. He wrapped his arm around Adley and ushered him towards the tavern. "You need a drink my friend. They have the most wonderful ale made with honey. You have to try it."

"So you have been drinking?" Adley asked.

"Of course. It would have looked suspicious if we hadn't had at least one."

Adley smiled at that as he bent down to retrieve his shield while walking towards the door to the tavern. "Just one huh?"

"Well maybe two." Captain Payne laughed and smacked Adley on the back. "You'll have to catch up Sarge."

When they reached the door Adley turned around and raised his shield to the crowd who now cheered in celebration. Beyond those nearest him he could see the soldiers and a few townspeople gathering the body and the head of the vampire. Beyond them standing next to the side of the barn he thought he saw two glints of red shining off of the light from the towns torches. He tried to focus more on that spot and as he did a man clad in a long black overcoat trimmed in gold with matching pauldrons stepped out into the light. With no more than a crooked smile and a nod the man returned to the shadows. Adley knew not what to make of him and entered the tavern on the insistence of the villagers all-clamoring to buy him a drink.

CHAPTER FIFTEEN

Details—Sadan, 1015

ORAN AND WILLEM were on the front deck of Silver Guard Keep watching through the dreary rain as Adley and Captain Payne approached on horseback. Oran ordered Willem, "Go get the gate for them."

"But it's raining."

Oran gave Willem a look indicating it was not up for debate and with a little huff Willem ran down the steps towards the gate. Oran watched as Willem opened the gate for the two who had been out hunting down some kind of murderer who had butchered a family not far from Lanos. The two passed Willem with thanks and praises for getting the gate and kept right on moving letting Willem close it behind them. Willem ducked and dodged the mud kicked up by the horses as they spurred them past him. Oran could tell he was cussing and he thought it quite amusing.

"Well met Oran." Captain Payne said as they neared the cobblestone walkway leading up to the steps.

"Yes indeed. Successful hunt I gather."

Adley answered, "Yes but not at all what we had expected."

"It rarely is." Oran replied. "Well put your horses up and meet me inside. Dinner will be ready in a while. We can discuss the details over some wine so you boys can warm up."

Adley and Captain Payne walked in through the back door a few minutes later and waiting for them by the warm fire was Oran with full glasses. They dropped their gear and unclasped their rain soaked cloaks and hung them by the back door then took to their seats with their fine drinks waiting.

"Ah good man. That hits the spot." Captain Payne proclaimed.

"I'm glad you two are back. We are a little short handed here right now." Oran said.

"Oh how so? Where is everybody?" Adley asked.

"Well Harold is in the kitchen helping Georgette with Marcus as she finishes dinner but my father had to go to Tomé. Personal invitation from the King."

That had Adley and Captain Payne stop in mid drink. Ever since they had their meeting with Usarus and the representatives from Bahamut and Pelor churches there had apparently been debates in the capital over whether or not to order The Silver Guard to hand over Marcus. Apparently not from the three they met with, according to Usarus but from many other members of the academy and churches. They figured it was just a matter of time before the King stepped in.

"Not to worry." Oran continued, "Usarus assured my father that it is more of a formality than anything. The King cannot be seen as never having had personal assurances from us that all is well. My father and the King go back a long ways."

"So when will he be back?" Captain Payne asked.

"He plans on staying until it is time for Havander to join us for the summer. That way he can deal with all the inquiries and reassure all the naysayers that all is well. He also plans to look into finding any information he can on the whereabouts of Deathmar the Black. In the meantime we are without his company for a couple months and I feel better having you two around with him absent."

"That's not that reassuring. What if he gets into trouble with none of us there to back him up?" Adley said.

"No one would dare challenge him I assure you. He has spells that can transport him far enough away if anything does happen. More likely that someone would cause trouble for us here with him absent."

Adley mulled that over but thought it more likely that Josef would not hold his tongue if anyone made any threat towards him or them. "Well anything else we missed?"

"No. Just glad to have you back. Now tell me. What was all the trouble about that had you gone for so long?"

"Terrible business. Two families slaughtered." Captain Payne answered before Adley could respond.

"Oh. I assume you caught up to who did it?"

"Not a who. It was a vampire."

"A vampire. Wow!" Willem was overcome with excitement and interrupted the conversation. "Did you catch it?"

"We did young Willem though it's nothing to get excited about. Vampires are horrible creatures and very hard to kill." Adley explained.

"You killed it too. I heard vampires are next to impossible to kill."

"What do you know of vampires Willem?"

"I know they are undead that fly around drinking the blood of men. They live forever and only sunlight can kill them."

"Oh you don't say." Oran said. "What else do you think you know?" He finished sarcastically.

Willem catching the sarcasm responded, "What? Am I missing something?"

Oran looked to Adley and Captain Payne who wore curious smiles thoroughly enjoying Willem's confusion. "Well I suppose this is a good time for a lesson. Let me tell you about vampires Willem. First of all they don't fly, unless they know magic maybe, but they can move with blinding speed. They are incredibly strong and yes they do live on blood but they can live off of any type of blood though they prefer human."

"Why is that?" Willem asked.

"Well they were all human once so it is believed that that is why human blood nourishes them the best."

"So other races can't become vampires if they are bitten?"

"That's not how one becomes a vampire but no other races cannot become vampires."

"That's not what I've heard. I heard if they bite anything and they live than they can become a vampire." Willem said very matter of fact.

"Not at all Willem. You see the first vampire was a human. He is known as The Fallen One. He was once a member of Hareth Academy in charge of necromancy. The last person to be assigned to that post as it were. After he turned vampire the academy deemed that necromancy would no longer hold a seat on the council of The Orders."

"So if he was the first then how did he become a vampire?" Willem said while posting both his elbows on the table. Fully entranced by the story.

"No one knows Willem. We only know that he was the first. No one has ever been able to figure out how he did it. Other vampires were turned by drinking a lot of another vampire's blood. As we understand it one must be drained of most of their blood to the point of death and then drink the blood of a vampire. You see their blood is magical and yearns for a host body to thrive in but it cannot do so if all of your blood is present. Their bodies are essentially dead which is why they are considered undead. That and they have a natural ability to control other undead things."

"So if only The Fallen One can create vampires then there must not be a lot of them right?"

"No that's not what I meant. Once you are a vampire you can turn others but The Fallen One was the first. And it is never a guarantee that it will work. Sometimes the blood fails to take over in time and one dies. But it is believed that since he was human when he became a vampire that that is why only humans can be turned."

"Okay. But if they are so powerful then why don't they rule the world?"

"They have weaknesses. Like you said sunlight can kill them, which limits them to only being active at night or out of direct sunlight at least. Silver hurts them which is why we all carry silver weapons."

"So that is why we are called The Silver Guard?"

Oran tilted his head back and forth thinking of an answer that would suffice. "Well yes and no. The Silver Guard was founded by my father to aid Casta in hunting down and fighting against the undead. Silver is a tribute to the god Bahamut who opposes the undead which is why we believe it hurts some undead creatures. Sunlight is the symbol of Pelor who also opposes the undead which is why some undead cannot stand sunlight."

"So we only fight against the undead?"

"Well no. I'm just giving you some highlights. There is a lot more to it. Basically we stand in opposition to all evil or try to. Whatever we can do to help the good folks of Casta."

Willem turned his attention back to Adley. "So what about your vampire? How did you guys manage to kill it?"

Captain Payne again answered for Adley. "Actually Willem, Sarge here killed her all by himself. Mostly anyways."

Oran was impressed. "Do tell Sarge."

Not one to boast Adley shrugged and downplayed the story. "I believe she was newly turned. That is why she was on a tear. A practiced vampire would never have made the mistakes this one made. We set a trap in Ecrin and managed to take her down."

"He's just being modest. Me and my men barely did anything. Sarge here did all the hard lifting. It was quite impressive." Captain Payne slapped Adley on the back of the shoulder spilling some of Adley's wine in the process.

Oran was even more impressed now. They had done well in accepting Adley into the fold. He would have to get all the minor details later for Harold exited the kitchen with serving dishes in both arms and Georgette followed with Marcus in her arms. Best not to sully dinner with talk of death.

Josef waited near one of the doors inside the palace that lead out to one of the gardens for the King to join him. Two guards had escorted him to this spot and indicated that that is where the King wished to meet him. The King, followed by Headmaster Usarus, Father Leighton and a quartet of guards, rounded the corner leading down the marble hallway that lead to where Josef waited. The King was much as he remembered. He had not met with him in over ten years but he looked much the same. He wore modest clothing and no armor or weapons save for a dagger strapped to his beltline. He had always admired the King for remaining so humble even though he was perhaps the richest man in all of Drilain, living in the biggest palace surrounded by every luxury one could imagine. In his heart he was a soldier first and had often lamented on not being able to be in the field more with his adored soldiers. After his father passed some twenty years ago he had to give all that up and take on the duties of King. Before that he was most often in Iron Hall with the dwarves or the Casta outposts now lined up behind the wall being constructed between the southern tip of the Talt Mountains running all the way south to Prurst Peaks in order to bar the powers from the east from ever invading Casta.

"Well met Master Righe." The King said as he embraced Josef in a hug.

Josef felt awkward about the greeting and found it hard to hug back holding Etburn and being unaware that it was coming. They had always been friendly but he was not expecting a hug. "Your majesty." Josef finished with a bow after being released from the embrace.

The King turned to his entourage and stated, "That will be all."

"Your majesty…" Hallam Leighton started but was interrupted by the King.

"I said that will be all."

Josef watched as Usarus and Leighton slowly turned to head back from where they had come. The King also pointed to his guards including the two who had escorted Josef to depart with them.

Once alone the King addressed Josef while pushing open the double doors leading to the garden. "Shall we walk in the garden? I know it is raining but I have a lovely gazebo that will shelter us and I need some air after that appalling meeting. I would also like to stay away from prying ears."

"As you wish your majesty." Josef bowed again.

"Oh stop with that nonsense. It's only the two of us here. Norwin or Abram if you please."

Surprised once again by the courtesy of the King he followed Abram into the garden. The rain was barely drizzling and the gazebo was within sight of the doors so they needn't be drenched in any case. He walked alongside the King down the stone walkway through the wonderful garden, which was in full bloom. They walked in silence admiring the flowers and hedges and the King looked up to the sky more than once drinking in the fresh air. As they neared the gazebo Josef decided he would not drop the formal title of King despite the wishes of King Abram.

Once inside the gazebo the King took a seat and indicated for Josef to do the same in the seat opposite him. "Much better out here. I tire of meetings with men in positions of so called power. Lords and priests all squabbling over the stupidest of things."

Josef smiled at the King's candor and said, "I apologize if any of that is to do with me and The Silver Guard your majesty."

"I'll not bandy words with you Josef. There has been many complaints coming my way about this child of your keeping."

"I see your majesty. What am I to make of that?"

"I care little of what you make of it." Direct and to the point the King laid it out flat. "You can tell them all to go jump in a lake for all I care but you should know that your reputation is being slandered."

That did not surprise Josef but he was surprised at the King's attitude towards his advisors. At the very least he expected to be scolded for not coming to him for advice on the present situation. "What of your feelings King Abram?"

"I believe this could have been handled better but I'll not second guess your actions. The Silver Guard has long been one of the spear tips against those that threaten the way of life in my kingdom. I remember my father's father telling me about stories of you and Oran and I've seen your men in action years ago as you know, in the east. You have also been there to advise me in matters I deem important when asked."

"I appreciate that but what of the child?"

"That is exactly my meaning. There is no honor is putting a child to the knife no matter his origins. Had you done so I would have judged you harshly despite what advice I would have gotten against that course."

"I appreciate that as well."

"Well now let me finish. If what these fools advise me on is correct than the child will grow to some horrible monster and if they are correct than it falls to you to correct your actions. I don't believe that is the case though. Nevertheless controversy will always follow that child. Any slip up by him when he is older will be detrimental to his well being."

"You mean to let him grow up then?"

King Abram gave Josef a scrutinizing look. "I fear not for the safety of my kingdom from the likes of a child of any origin." King Abram let that hang in the air hoping to let his attitude be fully known. "Besides he is in your care and I've never known you to take any action that did not merit praise."

"I thank you for your words. It is of great relief."

"They are not mine alone. Usarus and Leighton have weighed in and are on your side though I suspect the other opposition to this came from their big mouths letting it be known to their underlings. Now everyone knows about it. All the guilds and many lords are in opposition to me standing idly by."

Josef was surprised that Leighton would speak up for him but not that Leighton let it slip to others so that they could voice his true opinion

R. A. HAYDEN

through proxy. "Your trust will not go unnoticed. You may call on The Silver Guard whenever we are needed."

"That may be sooner than you know if Usarus and Leighton are correct." King Abram declared.

Unsure of the meaning behind that statement Josef inquired, "How so?"

"Well they believe, as well as many others that a war is coming. A true war not the typical squabbling between us and Cruz or orc raiders from the Talt Mountains."

"It has been many years since an all out war between kingdoms has broken out. What are the details your majesty?"

"I do not believe it is an imminent as they would have me believe. They, and I mean Usarus of course, is looking at recent actions as being more than just posturing."

"Posturing in what way?"

"Well there is a lot of posturing going on. Coming from the necromancers of the east of course. There has been an increase in the number of undead marching against the wall. I do not believe it is a prelude to all out war yet but merely a way for the Lich Mayre to slow our progress."

Josef knew well of the Lich Mayre. He was the self-proclaimed King of the lands east of Casta. He controlled the human necromancers and their tower located east of the wall and the foremost enemies of Hareth Academy. For centuries he has wanted the lands of Casta as his own and has been trying relentlessly to take control of it. Casta has repelled every chance he has taken against the kingdom aided considerably by Hareth Academy, the churches, and the Iron Hill dwarves. His armies consisted of men, necromancers and even witches, which were not numerous anywhere else in Drilain except for within his lands. His greatest army is headed by a death knight general who commands a legion of undead soldiers and almost every other mentionable kind of undead except for vampires. Unknown to many was that The Fallen One and the Vampire Nation loathed Lich Mayre and from behind the scenes corrupted many of his attempts to expand his lands.

"What do you make of the posturing King Abram?" Josef asked

"I believe that war with the necromancers is inevitable of course but there is a lot going on elsewhere as well. As we speak the kingdoms of

Searcy and Feywood are under assault by the sea devils from the ocean, Kodia and The River Lands have several lords fighting battles between themselves, and Deathmar the Black has taken it upon himself to show that dragons are not out of the equation. All of these are not related of course but opportunity is knocking for our enemies to get into the game."

"My world is far less hectic it seems."

"I envy that of course. But I wish for you to take away that you may be needed but for now look to yours and should the time come that we do find Deathmar I insist that you come to me before acting out alone. I'll not let you shoulder this without considerable aid."

After finishing their discussion in the garden, Josef stayed in the palace for many hours that evening shadowing the King and hearing about everything of the goings on in the world. He even had dinner with the King and his family. Long has the line of Abram defended Casta and it seemed to Josef that it would for much longer, as long as King Abram's line continued.

R. A. HAYDEN

CHAPTER SIXTEEN

Third Year—Fhurin, 1015

HAVANDER SAT IN the history classroom with his fellow classmates waiting for their professor. There were twenty students in all, though last year they had twenty-two. Apparently two of their classmates after their second year were evaluated for their magical talent and were deemed unworthy of continuing their education at Hareth Academy. Havander knew this was common after the second year but the two who had not made it on to the third year were friends of his and he would miss them in class. Of those remaining he had but one true friend. Aelehli Ambervale sat next to him now. She is half-elven and is fifteen years old which is older than any other third year student in their class. This is not completely uncommon especially for those that are not human though all of the other students in the class were the same age as Havander. Aelehli's magical talent was not noticed as early as others partially because of where she grew up. She lived on the border between Searcy and Casta. If she lived near Tomé her talents would have been noted earlier due to the fact that the professors there scoured the nearby cities and towns for any with magical talent every summer. Her father was an elf from Feywood and her mother was human. They were well off and after discovering her talent her father insisted on relocating to Tomé so that their daughter could get the very best education for magic wielders.

"Good afternoon class." Professor Dukes stated as he entered the classroom. "Sorry for my tardiness but first day and all has many demands."

Havander liked Professor Paton Dukes very much and his lessons over the past two years had been very informative. He watched as

Professor Dukes walked past him and Aelehli sitting in the last row of desks and made his way to the front. Along with being the largest classroom in Hareth Academy as it had desks for as many as thirty students and could accommodate many more if necessary, it also held the largest collection of books in the castle other than the Hareth library.

"Welcome to third year history." Professor Dukes began after he laid his parchments he was carrying onto his desk. "Now as you undoubtedly already know this is your last required history class. There is a fourth history class that you can elect to take later but my advice to you is to take it your final year as most students do. The reason for this is that the fourth term history class is extremely easy with no tests to speak of and is more a less a rehash of your first three years."

Professor Dukes waited until the class got done with its oohs and ahhs before continuing. "Yes, yes I know it sounds very appealing. That is why I recommend students wait until their final year to take that class. It allows more time for you to prepare for your final test to become a full member of Hareth and earn your title of wizard or wizardess. My advice is to take advantage of that because no matter what year you have to be enrolled in a minimum of four classes no matter what. In the meantime in this class there will of course be tests and the content we will cover is numerous to say the least." Professor Dukes pointed over to his fine collection of history books and others on the left side of the classroom.

After pointing out the large collection of research available Professor Dukes continued, "Now in your first year we covered the history of Casta and the second we covered the history of other kingdoms in Drilain but in this class, since you are all now really coming to terms with your individual talents in magic, we will be covering the history of magic and it's three primary origins. Can anyone tell me what they are?"

Many hands shot into the air including Havander's and Aelehi's but Professor Dukes called upon a student in the front row.

"Go ahead my dear." Professor Dukes said.

"There is arcane, divine, and witchcraft." She replied.

"Yes very good. For the first part of the term we will be discussing arcane since that is what you are here for and then we will follow with divine magic followed for a short amount of time on witchcraft. Today we will cover just a short overview of each before we delve into specifics. So can anyone tell me as to why we would be spending more time on arcane and divine magic over that of witchcraft?" The classroom was silent and no one raised a hand except for Havander. "Okay Havander go ahead."

"Well Professor, Master Righe informed me that witchcraft is not well thought of and most arcane and divine magic users consider the practice evil." Havander answered.

Havander hadn't noticed as Professor Dukes did, the amount of eye rolls and slight head shakes that the rest of the students did when he had answered. Professor Dukes thought it slightly amusing but resigned to talk to Havander after class about it along with something else he wanted to address to him.

"That is partially correct Havander but not fully." Professor Dukes began his pacing down the center aisle separating the two sides of the classroom as he often did while lecturing. "You see students witchcraft draws a perplexing issue with arcane spellcasters and divine spellcasters but that is not the only reason we spend such a short amount of time on it. One very good reason is that we know so little about it. Witches are not very numerous. They have no great schools such as this one or libraries revealing their secrets. Partially because of differences between witches and other magic users there has always been great conflict and to be honest witches have lost all of those big confrontations. They have literally been hunted down and killed."

"That's horrible." One of the students replied out loud.

"Yes it is." Professor Dukes replied. "But like my other classes I will not hold back on telling you the truth or my version of it anyway. I do not believe in sugar coating things as others might. To do so is a discredit to your education. In this class you will find a very bloody history between all three magical disciplines and theories behind the reasoning for those histories. The Purge War is a prime example as discussed last year."

Aelehli raised her hand and asked, "Professor you said there is a difference between the three. What did you mean?"

"I'm glad you asked. Being arcane magic users yourself you know or at least you should by now, that our magic is believed to be derived mostly from the god Corellon. It is our belief that he cast magic into the world, along with some other gods, so that we may use it as we see fit. Divine magic wielders on the other hand believe that their magic is derived directly from their chosen god and that they are but a conduit for their gods will. Given that, can anyone tell me where witches derive their power from?"

The class sat silent and no one could provide an answer or think of the reasoning behind the question.

"It is both." Professor Dukes answered for the class. "It is a common belief that witches do both. They are capable of wielding their own magic as well as gaining aid from higher powers and not just gods but also demons, devils, and a few others. This also adds to the reasoning why most consider the practice evil."

"Professor wouldn't that make them twice as powerful?" A student asked.

"No. Good reasoning but no. You see there are many different ways to do the same spell in some cases. I dare say that there are actually differences in ways of doing the same spell between what arcane school you go to and new ways of doing spells are being discovered even as we speak. How proficient you are in one practice or another might also determine how you cast a spell. In the beginning for instance there are many material components that go into spell casting. As you progress in your own magical talents and become in tune with whatever spell you are trying you will likely find that you can do away with the material component all together.

The class looked a bit confused and Professor Dukes realized he was going off on a little tangent. "Let me be a little more specific. Everyone here has classes in divination since that is the one universal arcane discipline and thus you have mandatory classes in divination. You have all practiced being able to detect if some object actually contains magic within it. Clerics can do the exact same thing though they go about it differently. Now does that mean one is more powerful than the other? I tend to believe that it doesn't."

Havander asked, "But how would a witch go about doing that same spell?"

"Another good question and what I'm not one hundred percent on for that particular spell but I will tell you that I was witness to a witch casting a spell of read languages once." Professor Dukes could tell that the class was intrigued by that so he continued, "I witnessed a witch attempting to help me and some other associates of mine at the time to decipher a coded message for us in a language that she did not know. Now imagine this. She lit up some strange looking piece of rope infused with something and breathed in the heavy fumes, then wafted the smoke all over the pages of writing while chanting something I didn't understand. Not only could she read it but also all of us present who breathed in the smoke, even non-magic users, could read the text. Now which would you say is more powerful?"

A few of the Havander's classmates answered at once, "The witch."

Professor Dukes gave a doubtful expression as he continued pacing and answered, "That would be up for debate and I doubt there is one true answer." The class was confused again as far as he could tell. "Let me elaborate. I am good with alteration magic, which of course where the read language spell comes from for arcane wielders. I can cast read languages quite easily on myself or another person if I want but I have to do so separately between individuals. Now what the witch did made it so we could all read at once but her method took far longer so which would you say is more powerful?"

That sparked a bit of a debate and the entire class got involved though in the end there was no one answer which Professor Dukes explained that that was the case in most instances when trying to decide which way of doing magic was more powerful and he sited more references between divine and arcane magic.

At the end of the class session Professor Dukes asked Havander to remain behind. Once everyone left Professor Dukes walked to the desk in front of Havander and pushed the seat aside and leaned against the desk. "So Havander how was your summer?"

"It was good sir. I continued my lessons with Master Righe and even started being able to decipher dwarf writings way better which is helping me a lot since I took dwarven language this year. I believe I'm further along than anyone else in class. Even the older students." Havander answered and sat up more straight in his chair being very proud of himself.

"Yes that's partially what I wanted to talk to you about Havander."

"What's that sir?"

"It's hard to say this without sounding like an ass but I believe it is better you hear it from me rather than your fellow students." Professor Dukes raised his eyebrows and looked down upon Havander hoping to get his attention fully. "You need to quit bringing up Master Righe when you give answers to questions."

Havander was confused and didn't understand. "Why is that sir?"

"Please don't misunderstand Havander. What you have going with Master Righe is incredible. Believe me I wish I could take some lessons from him. But no other student here has a master yet. A master and apprentice relationship is generally not forged until after you graduate Hareth and become a full member." Professor Dukes waved his right arm around the classroom indicating the entirety of it. "None of your fellow students here have a master and the benefits that the relationship provides."

"But many of the students here have their parents which are magic users." Havander replied.

"Yes but not all and I shouldn't be telling you this but given your maturity for your age I believe I can tell you that most of them are novices at best and a true master and apprentice relationship cannot be had between parent and sibling in most cases. I believe I can also tell that you know that you are more capable than most and adding that to the benefit of having someone like Master Righe teaching you puts you well above the rest of your class."

"Why are you telling me this professor?"

"Because Havander you and your classmates are getting to the age when rivalries start to form and lines are drawn. I can tell you now that other students don't like being outdone so often."

"But I'm not trying to do that."

"Oh I know son. And believe me you are doing great but young students tend to disregard that and begin bullying the better student to make themselves feel better."

Havander recollected some instances where he believed other students were short with him for no apparent reason and it suddenly became clear to him that the professor might be correct. "What should I do sir?"

"Well some of what you will experience with other students is inevitable as far as them being jealous or envious of your skills but one thing you can do is stop using Master Righe's name when you give answers. On the other hand I don't want you to be discouraged when you do have a confrontation with another student or students for that matter. I am not saying this to be harsh I only want you to realize the situation so that you can continue on your path."

Havander felt deflated and encouraged all at once. On one hand he was being praised and the other being told it was to his detriment. "Any advice beyond that professor?"

"Yes actually. Were I you I would keep taking evocation classes with Aelehli. That is truly her calling and she is better than you so maybe it will keep you grounded." Professor Dukes moved towards Havander and gave him a laugh and a small push on the shoulder with his fist trying to bring some levity to the conversation then returned to his leaning position on the desk.

Havander felt somewhat agitated by the realization that other students would look down on him for his successes and not at all comforted by the advice he was receiving. If anything he wanted to excel even more. He raised himself from his seat and said, "Well if there is nothing else I should be leaving."

"Actually no. That was just a side note. I have something of greater concern I wish to speak to you about." Professor Dukes indicated.

Seeing the now serious look in his professor eyes Havander took to his seat again. "What is that professor?"

"How many classes are you taking this year Havander?"

"Six."

"I see. Why so many?"

Havander thought the question odd. There was more than enough time in the day. Each class period was less than a couple hours most of the time and there was plenty of time between classes to reach the considerable distance between where some classes were held throughout the expansive castle and the buildings not connected to the main structure. Even on days when some classes were held somewhere else on the island other classes allotted time for those situations. "I have time. Why not six professor?"

"I was afraid you might ask that Havander." Professor Dukes shook his head and his facial expression expressed a bit of outrage. "Look Havander it's not a huge deal now but you need to think of limiting your classes."

"Why is that sir?"

Professor Dukes held up his hands in a defensive posture. "Again I am telling you this because of your maturity level," he paused for a second, "but there is such a thing as doing too much when it concerns magic. Frankly I'm angry that another professor has not told you as much. I'm only the history teacher and we practice no magic in here otherwise I may have thought about it sooner."

"Well Master Righe has discussed it with me."

"Good, good." Professor Dukes felt some relief that at least his master has shown some semblance in honesty with Havander. "He is not wrong Havander. As you know it is required at Hareth that every student take four classes every year and half of those aren't magical in nature like this class, yes?"

"Yes sir." Havander answered.

"Well that's usually all any student takes. Some elect to take five and sometimes six is allotted but usually to students older than your. Do you know why?"

"Master Righe told me that magic has limits and it is hard on the body."

"Exactly Havander. Exactly. Take heed of what he has taught you. Doing too much magic or magic beyond your control can be bad for you."

"But I feel fine."

"Oh I imagine so. You are still young and learning skills that don't require that much magic. You are still getting tuned into your abilities but the lesson is sound and I believe it is never too early to learn this despite what others may say."

"What might others say?"

"Well some would say that you should always push your limits. That pushing the limits of magic is necessary to achieve your highest potential. And while that is not always wrong, what is the hurry? You are a third year student and only go to school another five years after that before you go out on your own with a master or continue your own education here at Hareth with so many others learning from one another or your own studies."

Havander contemplated that reasoning and had always imagined he would remain the apprentice of Master Righe beyond Hareth Academy. Although Hareth Academy was amazing and many recent graduates and even older members of Hareth stayed at the school or revisited the section of the castle for those that were no longer students, he imagined a place for himself at Silver Guard Keep. To be a member of The Silver Guard had now been a dream of his ever since he learned that Master Righe was to be his master. "What is it you suggest professor?"

Professor Dukes took in a good breath and said, "I want you to drop one of those classes. Take five, which is more than enough to keep you busy. In fact it gives you more time to concentrate on the ones you have rather than spreading yourself thin on multiple disciplines."

The concern in the expression of Professor Dukes and the reminder of the same lesson that Master Righe had told him his first summer with him was more than enough to take heed to the precaution. "I appreciate the concern professor and it makes sense. It may take me a couple days to decide what class to drop."

"Thank you Havander. Remember you have five years after this so string classes together as you can and it will help you excel in those disciplines."

As Havander exited the classroom and saw Aelehli waiting for him, he decided right there that evocation would not be the one class in which he would drop. If the other students were indeed having so much trouble with him excelling, he'd at least like to have one friend who didn't mind.

CHAPTER SEVENTEEN

Teenage Boldness—
Shalladrin, 1019

IN TYPICAL FASHION of a glorious midday during summer, Willem strolled towards the general store in Lanos to deliver to Mr. and Mrs. Barrie a basket of vegetables from Georgette's garden. Always having more than they could consume at the Keep she often sent extra to the Barries to sell or keep for their own, as they like. As with most days in the month of Shalladrin the sun was shining and Willem was in a great mood having finished his early day weapons training lessons with great success. He had now been training with Oran, Adley, and occasionally Captain Payne for six years now. Most of his training came from Oran of course but depending on what was going on in the vicinity, like today, Oran was absent having to give way to the demands of The Silver Guard and their expertise in matters concerning enemies of Casta. Willem felt especially proud of himself today for having bested Adley twice during their training session. He knew of course that they weren't dealing with real weapons and Adley was absent of using a shield but his confidence had never been higher. He was daydreaming while he stepped onto the deck of the general store that served as part of the sidewalk through Lanos, about being able to best Oran one day when he overheard two Lanos soldiers sitting on the bench outside the store's front door talking about Marcus.

"You know they say that dragon child has fangs on his upper and lower jaw now." One soldier claimed.

Hearing dragon child mentioned, Willem slowed his pace to a slow walk and listened further.

The other soldier shook his head in disgust. "They should've killed that thing as soon as they knew what he was."

"No doubt. Why would any sensible person let something like that live? You know if they let it get any bigger it's likely to sprout scales all over its body. Maybe even wings and then fly about killing everyone who lives there." The other soldier responded. "Dam fools all of them."

"Excuse me." Willem said while stopping right in front of the two soldiers. Once they turned their attention to him he continued, "You know I've heard it's always better to mind your own when you don't know what you're talking about."

The two soldiers looked Willem up and down and one responded quite rudely, "Mind your business runt."

Willem smiled at the comment. He was ridiculed so much for his height that now he welcomed it. Among the many lessons Oran taught him, sizing up your opponent was key to victory in any fight and apparently these two had no idea who he was and they looked at his small stature and young age as something to be completely dismissed. In a stuttering and mocking tone Willem persisted, "I do apologize soldier sirs, but I heard that Casta is getting desperate for soldiers and took to hiring orc scum like yourselves."

Completely shocked by this young teenagers attitude they both turned to regard him and one began to stand up. After he left his seat and before he was fully standing, Willem dropped the basket in his left hand and before it hit the deck he caught the soldier with a blinding right cross, hitting him in his left temple and sending him careening into the wall of the general store. Shocked, the other soldier only stood and took a couple paces backing away from Willem in the process while watching his companion regain his composure.

"You little bastard." The soldier he had struck said as he shook away his apparent dizziness and lunged forward with both arms outstretched.

Willem jabbed with his right fist catching him squarely in the nose, watering his eyes and then following through with an overhand left catching him in the opposite temple he had hit previously and sending him back into the wall once again. Before he could react further he followed with a vicious uppercut with his right hand under the chin and sent the soldier tumbling down to the seat he was previously occupying with no apparent control over his legs. After sliding down the wall and more or less bouncing off the bench he fell to the deck unconscious.

The other soldier stood shocked for a few moments while looking down at his companion. He looked up to Willem who with both hands at his waist motioned him forward with his fingers while smiling ear to ear. With a furious growl he waded in with a jab of his own followed immediately with another and then a left cross. All of which hit nothing but air as Willem dodged every one without so much as a step backwards then caught his new opponent with a right uppercut sending him backwards.

Willem smiled all the wider if that was possible as the soldier regained his composure. The soldier put his hand to his mouth and wiped blood away from his lips coming from his tongue, which he had bitten down on. He spit blood out of his mouth and onto the ground next to the deck and pulled his shortsword from its scabbard.

"That's a bad idea friend." Willem replied while reaching to his back and pulling forth his curved dagger that he had only recently been told he was allowed to carry on his person as was seen fit from Oran.

Just before the soldier came forward with a lunge of his sword they were interrupted. "Halt!" Captain Payne yelled while hurrying to the side of the deck.

The soldier immediately halted his movements and stood at attention. Willem did no such thing and kept his defensive stance and watched Captain Payne advance out of the corner of his eye while keeping most of his attention on his opponent in front of him.

Captain Payne took to the deck with one long stride from the street. One of his sergeants was right behind him and did likewise and now the two stood in-between Willem and the soldier standing at attention. Captain Payne grabbed his soldier by his breastplate and pushed him against the wall. "What in the nine hells is this about?" He looked down to the unconscious soldier and then back to the one still standing. The soldier was unable to find his words so Captain Payne yelled out to Willem, "Willem what is going on here?"

Willem could feel that many eyes were watching him. Behind him Mr. and Mrs. Barrie had exited the front door of their store and looked on with concerned expressions. Likewise across the street a couple other townspeople looked on and Armihrmond Firefist stepped out of his blacksmith shop with hammer in hand. With the tension eased Willem slid his blade back into its sheath strapped across his lower back then finally answered, "These two believed it was funny to joke about killing Marcus."

Captain Payne raised his brows in response to the answer and then narrowed his gaze, effectively staring down his soldier. "Is that so?"

"Not exactly sir." The soldier embarrassingly replied.

"Not exactly but something along those lines 'eh?" Captain Payne shouted into his face. He released the soldier and took a step back. Then turned to Willem. "You would do better young man to report such senseless remarks to me or one of my sergeants is that understood Willem?"

Not waiting for a reply Captain Payne went back at his soldier. "As for you and your friend." Captain Payne stepped over to him and gave him a nudge with his foot. "Five lashes each. Maybe that will be enough of a reminder that we do not talk about killing children and certainly don't engage in brawls with teenagers. Sergeant take these two back to the barracks and see it done."

Willem picked up the basket of vegetables and handed them to Mrs. Barrie. "Sorry about that. Couldn't let that one stand."

Overhearing that remark Captain Payne advanced on Willem and grabbed him up by his earlobe. "I'm not done with you either." He started dragging Willem by the ear across the deck and heading back towards Silver Guard Keep. When they reached the ground he released his ear and pushed him a little forward of himself and pointed towards home. "Keep moving."

Willem didn't protest and it certainly wasn't the first time that Captain Payne had grabbed him up by his ear. The two of them walked with a quick pace through the front gate of the Keep and headed straight for the doors. At the top of the stairs Havander was sitting and reading a book in the shade. He didn't even register that they were near him although he knew they were there.

As they reached the top stair Havander asked, "What'd you do this time?"

"None of your business." Willem stopped and looked over to Havander. "That books a little small for you ain't it? Usually see you reading huge tomes of nonsense."

"Well it's about halflings that's why it is so small. I'm surprised you didn't recognize it. Isn't your family all halflings?" Havander replied without missing a beat.

Willem only smiled at the remark and then kept moving. He was in enough trouble and didn't need to get into another verbal sparring match with Havander at the moment. Plenty of time for that and he knew he would have the last word at some later time. Willem walked right through the front doors and continued on through the back door with Captain Payne right behind him. Everyone else was out back he knew. As they came onto the back deck Adley noticed immediately the guilty look on Willem's face and the stern look on Captain Payne's face.

Adley set down his glass of water and asked, "What happened?"

Captain Payne saw Georgette, Harold and Marcus out in the garden and he pointed in their direction. "Go help them while me and Adley decide your punishment Willem. We don't need your play by play."

Willem shook his head and headed back out to the garden without a word. When he was out of hearing distance Captain Payne turned to Adley and in a low voice said, "That was incredible. You should have seen him."

"Wait I thought he was in trouble."

"He is and you should find some way to punish him but what he did was amazing to behold."

Confused Adley asked, "Okay what happened?"

Two of my soldiers who just joined us on rotation made some off handed remarks about Marcus. Willem heard it and decided to confront them."

"And how did that go?"

Captain Payne excitedly answered, "He was incredible. They didn't even touch him. He laid one out unconscious and was giving a beating to the other when I decided to intervene before it got ugly."

"He did this with you present?"

"No he didn't know I was coming. I was walking into town from post and watched at a distance. Once blades were drawn I stopped it from going any further."

That had Adley angry immediately. "One of your men drew down on Willem. Who?"

"Oh don't worry. He's getting the lash along with his friend. Probably even as we speak but I'm telling you I've never seen a child beat the crap out of two trained soldiers before."

"Well he's hardly a child anymore. Just looks it."

"I know. I'm not sure I want to spar with him anymore." Captain Payne laughed at the remark.

"I know how you feel. He got the better of me earlier today. He's so fast I can't keep up anymore. Only way I can best him is if I rush him and overbear him with my size. If he were wielding real blades I'd be in a ton of trouble."

"Why the hell hasn't Oran ever taught us to fight like that?"

"He has. We simply don't have his speed and reflexes. He sees everything coming at him. And it doesn't matter what weapon he's using. He's equally good with staff, sword, axe. You name it. You should see him shoot a bow now or throw his daggers. I swear he never misses."

"Well I'm done. Let me have the illusion that I can still best him."

"He still can't get Oran but I've noticed Oran having a difficult time with him as well. Especially of late. Oran's left knee has been bothering him something awful."

Captain Payne hadn't heard that news about Oran. Oran had always been in the best of shape. Never complained ever about any kind of injury and was never feeling under the weather.

Adley asked, "What should we do about this situation?"

"I don't know. That's up to you to figure out. He is still young so we can't very well let it be. Don't be harsh though. I'd of done the same thing had I heard it. I can't have him waylaying my soldiers whenever he wants though. Makes us look bad if a teenager can beat us down. Do me a favor though."

"What's that?"

"Let him know I'd of done the same thing on the sly. I've got to head back and make sure those two boys got their lashing."

Captain Payne turned to leave but Adley called him back before he got to the back door. He pointed out towards Willem and Georgette was in his face with a finger right under his nose obviously lecturing him. The muffled sound of her raised voice could be heard and it sounded as though he was getting a good earful.

"Huh. Perhaps you won't have to punish him after all. Looks like he might be getting enough of that." Captain Payne said then turned again and left while laughing.

CHAPTER EIGHTEEN

First Hunt—Shalladrin, 1019

"QUIT BICKERING." ADLEY yelled at Havander and Willem. "You two have been at it all day and I feel like my head is going to explode."

Riding behind Adley throughout the entire day, Havander and Willem were constantly arguing about one thing or another. Apparently not being able to play practical jokes on one another, which was their usual way of getting at each other when at the Keep, since they were moving on horseback led them to have a verbal sparring match that had been going on for hours.

Adley stopped his horse upon reaching the top of a small hillside. Below his vantage point was a large depression in the landscape. Four farms could be seen in the distance, more or less equally separated from one another and there was a small stream running from east to west, which separated the two northernmost farms from the two in the south. Along that stream, thick vegetation grew and a mixture of deciduous trees including maple and birch. Havander and Willem positioned their mounts next to his and took in the scenery.

"Beautiful area isn't it boys?" Adley asked

"Uh yeah but what are we doing here? This is a long way to travel for training." Willem replied.

Adley turned in his saddle towards the two of them. "Who said anything about training?"

Confused, especially since Adley had told the two of them to take everything with them that they would need for training early this morning before they left home, Willem said, "If we aren't training then why did you make me carry this spear all the way here? I don't even like using spears." Willem held up the spear he had been carrying that had been cut down to size to better accommodate his stature.

"This isn't training Willem. We are here on a mission."

Overcome with excitement now Willem started, "What? About time. What are we after? Bandits? Murderers? No, please tell me its vampires."

"Kobolds actually. And no of course not vampires. You wouldn't stand a chance."

"Kobolds?" Willem said. "You mean those little walking lizard things?"

"Yes."

"But that's no fun. I want a real challenge."

Havander weighed in, "Actually kobolds are devilishly tricky and are more than a mere nuisance. In large numbers they've even been known to attack small villages in the night."

Willem made a face at Havander as he was explaining when he was looking in Adley's direction. "Okay know it all. Don't ya at least want to face something bigger?"

"That's enough Willem." Adley insisted. "This isn't a joke. Like Havander said kobolds can be quite deadly and you should take this seriously. Reports of kobolds killing and taking livestock in this area has reached Lanos and I told Captain Payne that we would handle it."

"Does Master Righe know about this?" Havander asked.

"Actually he heard about it first and thought it would be good for you two. He's busy with some other business and could use the time away from your classes. Besides learning in the field in my opinion is more effective than sitting in a classroom thinking about theory."

"But I haven't prepared any spells for this." Havander responded.

"Ha." Willem laughed.

"Shut up imp." Havander countered.

"Knock it off." Adley bellowed. "Plenty of time for preparing. We've a few hours until dark and we won't be hunting them at night. They can see far better in the dark than we can and you two have no idea what you're doing anyway. Now start getting serious. We have to talk to the local people first to find information out. Try to pay attention."

With that Adley gave his horse a good kick and started down the hillside towards the nearest farm. Havander and Willem quickly followed suit. Willem was excited and longed for confrontation. Havander was obviously more cautious and was thinking about the wisdom of this move to be searching for fights when him and Willem were so young and inexperienced.

Adley, Willem, and Havander spent a couple hours going from farm to farm questioning the people who lived there and indeed all four of the farms had indicated having problems with what they believed to be kobolds. The farm farthest away from their previous vantage point, on top of the hillside, had the most issues. They had reported seeing kobolds on a couple of occasions and over the past couple weeks many of their chickens, eggs, and even the family dog had gone missing.

The family living at that particular farm was beyond grateful that one of The Silver Guard had come to help them with this trouble and offered them a place to stay and all the hospitality they could handle. Adley refused to the dismay of his travelling companions and insisted they stay outside to better see if they could find any trace of their quarry. It wasn't only that but from inside the house they most likely wouldn't be able to see or hear anything and he didn't want Havander and Willem to be so accustomed to people opening up their doors to them. Although he didn't figure that this trip would be arduous in any way, he believed the two could use some time away from their comfortable living arrangements at the Keep and despite the fact that this was an actual mission it was also good training.

Adley took a look around the farm and the surrounding area, as far as he could see anyway, with the father of the household while Havander and Willem took care of settling their horses in the barn. A couple hundred yards removed from the farm stood a good size cluster of trees, mostly oak, with lots of cover and removed very little from the trees that ran along the banks of the stream to his north. He imagined that was a good spot for a small band of sneaky kobolds to set up a living area. Easy access to the stream and they could hide along the stream and travel to all four farms in the area unseen. Without so much as a single track to go on he figured it was the best spot to search in the morning.

Later that evening after they had enjoyed a good meal provided by their hosts that the family insisted upon, the three of them sat around a small fire, each leaning against their perspective saddle that the boys drug from the barn to use for something to lean against if not an all out seat. Adley had explained to them that it was a good idea for a more comfortable position and with kobolds lurking about they didn't want any of their gear in their saddlebags going missing. They had taken up position about twenty yards removed from one corner of the barn at the edge of one of the farmer's fields. They had no cover but could see relatively well in the moonlight: the house, the barn, and the other pens where pigs, chickens, and goats resided.

Havander sat reading his spellbook by the firelight and a candle lantern while Willem and Adley spent the first couple hours of the night talking about campaigns and enemies that Adley had faced, including his hunt where he faced a vampire single handedly and more recently a vampire that Oran an him had chased around the city of Palo. Willem was always intrigued by such stories and sat at the edge of his seat not wanting to miss a single detail.

"Sarge, who is Deathmar?" Willem asked after Adley finished giving the story of the vampire in Palo that Oran dispatched after they cornered it in a warehouse.

Havander's ears picked up hearing the name and he too looked to Adley who looked a bit surprised from the question. Havander had asked Master Righe about Deathmar after hearing it used by Josef and Oran but he never got an answer from his Master so he took it upon himself to look up what he could find himself at the library in Hareth Academy. He was surprised to find that Deathmar was a dragon and one that liked to insert himself into the affairs of men often over the centuries. He knew too that Marcus was half black dragon and later had heard the rumors that Deathmar was his father.

"Why do you ask Willem?" Adley responded.

"I've heard the soldiers talk of course. That's why there's so much worry about Marcus and why I had to fight two of them last week." Willem could tell he hit the mark from Adley's expression and uncomfortable posture as he repositioned himself to get more comfortable. "I'm right ain't I? That's Marcus' father."

Adley looked across the flames and saw even Havander put down his spellbook and lean in closer. "That's not for you two to worry about."

Havander asked, "That's why Master Righe is busy of late and why Oran is gone from the Keep too isn't it?"

Adley could tell he wasn't going to be able to hide much from these perceptive teenagers. Perhaps it was time they had heard that story but he couldn't believe it was going to come from him alone. "Look you two know that Marcus is dragonborn, yes?" Both Willem and Havander shook their heads in response. "Well the rumors you've heard are true. Deathmar the Black, as he is known, is his father."

"But how did Cecilia ever meet him?" Willem questioned.

"Believe me Willem, Cecilia never met Deathmar on purpose if that's how you want to put it." Adley took another long sigh and continued, "Deathmar the Black attacked Silver Guard Keep just before the two of you came into our lives. During that attack four Silver Guard members and my friends were killed at the hands of Deathmar and his allies. During that time Cecilia was also impregnated." Adley waited hoping he wouldn't have to elaborate on that last point.

"Against her will?" Willem asked.

"Of course it was against her will you idiot." Havander said.

Ignoring Havander, Willem continued, "But how is that possible? Dragons are huge."

"Don't you ever read anything you are suppose to? You should know all about dragons by now. And kobolds too for that matter." Havander said in disgust.

"Enough Havander." Adley intervened before Willem could retort. "You see Willem, dragons are beyond magical. The so-called intelligent dragons that practice magic like other races can change shape to that of a man or the like. They do so to hide their true form especially since most dragons were hunted down centuries ago. Deathmar as it happens walks the world in the form of a drow."

"Why a drow?" Havander asked.

"Well that's who he has aligned himself with. They took part in the attack against Silver Guard Keep all those years ago."

"That's why Oran left. I heard him mention drow." Willem pointed out.

"Oran is just following up on a lead. Apparently some drow were sighted in The River Lands. He went with some wizards from Hareth to check it out." Willem and Havander looked concerned to Adley. "Not to worry. Oran isn't going to face Deathmar alone. He's just looking for information. Besides, Josef is tracking him with one of his crystal balls or something like that. Havander you probably know about that kind of stuff more than I do."

"So hold on. What's that mean for Marcus? Is he going to turn into a dragon someday?" Willem asked.

Havander just shook his head but Adley answered, "No of course not. That's not how it works. That is however why his eyes are the way they are. It's also why he is so big for a mere four year old and why some of his teeth now look like fangs."

"Is that why he can growl the way he does when he's mad and his fingernails always have to be trimmed so they don't look like claws?"

Adley went on to explain in detail how some dragonborn look more like that of the dragon parent while others take on more of an appearance from their other parent. He gave more insights into why Deathmar would be fighting with The Silver Guard and outlined some of the other enemies that The Silver Guard has. In the end Willem seemed all the more excited to become a member while Havander was more concerned with the details surrounding Marcus and their need to take care of him as he grew. In the end Adley had to cut the conversation short for these two could have apparently talked about it all night and they had work to do in the morning.

"You have first watch Willem. Wake me in three hours." Adley said.

"Three hours. What am I suppose to do in the meantime?"

"Keep watch like I said. Stay quiet and look out for kobolds trying to sneak up on you in the night. After three hours wake me up and I'll take over. Havander can take the last shift after me. If you see anything wake me straight away. No heroics."

"That's not funny."

Adley lay down onto his bedroll and took out his cloak from his saddlebags to use as a blanket. He laid his head against his saddle using it like a pillow and closed his eyes. "It's not a joke Willem. Given half a chance kobolds are capable of killing so stay alert."

"But..."

"Shh. I'm sleeping."

Havander thought it funny but knew too that Adley was not joking but he followed suit and lay down onto his bedroll. He fell asleep musing over Willem worrying over kobolds catching him unaware.

Havander woke Adley and Willem as directed before the first rays of sun peeked through the tress. He spent his watch preparing the spells he thought would be most beneficial in fighting kobolds. Although he was schooled in all forms of magical discipline except necromancy, he was not overly proficient in any one area since he tended to jump from discipline to discipline between years at school because unlike other students he was able to cast in any sphere of influence. As beneficial as that may be it left him lagging in the number of spells he can cast in any particular area. Nevertheless he believed he chose well and had a wand of magic missiles to offset his lack of attack spells.

Adley had informed Havander that Willem had awoken him during his shift to look into the animals being overly noisy. Sure enough the two had investigated and as far as they could tell scared away whatever it was that had spooked the animals in their pens. It was behind the pens that they were to begin their work of hunting down the kobolds.

Adley led the way with crossbow in hand, leaving his shield behind, preferring to be armed with something he could use at a distance. Willem followed close behind with spear in hand and Havander followed armed with his wand and dagger he carried, which wasn't good for much other than ceremonial purposes or preparing items for spells and potions.

It was still extremely early. They had woken and not taken breakfast or even bothered stowing their gear. Adley wanted to be out hunting before the family was up and about and didn't fear for their gear in the hands of the seemingly noble family.

Behind the pens for the animals Adley quickly found little tracks belonging to kobolds. It appeared to him that there were three of them. Even in the lowlight of the morning it was easy to discern that they had came from the stream and headed back that way once interrupted. They followed the tracks to the tree line. Under the cover of the trees the tracks led to a small game trail that the kobolds were using to move back and forth between farms. Tracks could be seen going either direction along the southern edge of the stream.

Adley was kneeling down looking at the tracks and Willem was doing the same. Havander stood behind the pair looking into the dense underbrush for any sign of movement but could see nothing and hear only the sound of birds awakening from their slumber and beginning their daily rituals.

"Look here boys." Adley said in a hushed tone. "As I suspected they are using the cover here to move back and forth between farms." Adley pointed to his right. "That way leads to the other farms."

"So we follow the trail that way?" Havander reasoned.

"No I don't think so. If they were held up somewhere in that direction they may not have need to travel further in the other direction. There are no farms in that direction and yesterday I noted a spot that looked ideal for the little rats. It had excellent cover and from that vantage point they could look out over this farms open fields and see any danger coming there way for great distances."

Havander and Willem shook their heads in agreement.

Adley continued, "Now I know we went over this yesterday but I want you two to understand. This isn't a game. These things will kill you given a chance. Do you understand?"

Both Havander and Willem said in unison, "Yes."

"Take my meaning. We are not here to capture or question. If you see one you kill it. I know you are both young but Josef believes it is your time and I agree. Time to start leaving childish things behind. It is a dangerous world we live in and The Silver Guard is on the forefront of keeping it safe for the common folk." Adley looked from one to the other and was not surprised to see Willem slightly smirking and appeared anxious in anticipation of a fight. Havander was much more reserved but he too shook his head yes.

"Okay look, kobolds are notorious for setting traps and ambushes so be mindful of where you step. I'll lead but keep your eyes peeled and watch where I step. Be as quiet as possible but if you see danger don't wait for me. Havander I mean you most of all. You have that wand so don't be afraid to use it."

"Wait I need to do something." Havander said then tucked his wand away and began casting.

Once finished and seeing no notable changes in anything Adley asked, "What was that?"

"Just a minor shield spell. Mostly for protection from magic but it also helps in deflecting any type of missiles thrown or shot at me."

Adley smiled and nodded in appreciation for Havander's skill but Willem shook his head. He looked Havander over and standing in front of them, with Adley wearing his usual armor except for his helmet and shield and himself wearing mostly traveling clothes but over that he wore a leather cuirass, bracers and greaves, he thought Havander was out of place wearing his traveling robes.

Adley gave the order to move once Havander finished and he continued down the game trail. He was mindful of where he stepped and took his time. The light was fast approaching which made things easier to spot and Adley believed the timing of the early morning was the best time to catch the kobolds off guard. Doing most of their hunting and scavenging at night would hopefully leave them tired and settling down to rest making them unaware of their pending doom.

The trio travelled for quite some distance. Adley believed they were probably about halfway to the copse of trees where he believed them most likely to be hiding out when he stopped the boys behind him suddenly with an upraised hand. He believed Havander and Willem were doing well although Havander was having trouble navigating some of the thick brush and sticker bushes, which continually snagged on his robes. Nonetheless he extricated himself from them each time and with minimal noise. Adley waved the boys up to his location and pointed out a snare about waist high for him.

"You see here. We are getting close." Adley said while pointing out the snare.

"What is it?" Havander questioned.

"It's a snare. Cleverly hid too."

"Meant for us?"

"No. We could just slip it right off unless you were sprinting down the trail. It's meant for deer or possibly a coyote if any are about. You see the animal slips it's head through this opening and the line is pulled tight around their neck." Adley grabbed the snare and untangled it from the bushes that were concealing it and then gave it a tug. At the other end it was secured to a small birch tree. "The animals are too stupid to pull it off and will strangle themselves trying to pull away or just be stuck here until the kobolds come to finish it off."

Adley pulled his sword and cut the thick line then tossed it to the side. After, he continued along the trail and after another hundred yards or so stopped the boys again. He pulled his sword again and pushed it through what appeared to be a solid patch of grass. He leaned down to it and pulled the piece of turf away revealing a foot hole just large enough for him to step into with sharpened spikes made of wood pointing upwards to impale whoever was unfortunate enough to step into the hole. Willem had advanced on his position and after seeing what was revealed pointed his spear in two other locations ahead of them on the trail that looked similar.

"Very good Willem." Adley whispered. "How did you spot them?"

In an equally hushed tone Willem explained, "No other grass around. Look where we are. Not enough light for grass to grow. The brush and trees block it all out."

Adley put one of his gloves on just in case the spikes had any poison on them and pulled them from the ground. He did the same with the two traps farther along the trail and disposed of the spikes by throwing them in the nearby stream.

They kept following the trail until once again Adley stopped. The tracks stopped in the direction they were heading and veered left onto a much less used trail heading away from the stream. Through the brush and trees Adley could see the trees he had noticed the previous day which confirmed his theory of where the kobolds might be hiding. He advanced more slowly taking care not to make any noise. Havander and Willem followed until Adley stopped shy of coming out into the open. Before them was approximately twenty yards of open ground between where they now stood and a set of trees thick with brush around its perimeter.

"You see that stand of trees." Adley pointed out. "All of that cover around it is not natural. Look you can see excess foliage that has been added to the existing plants. Cut down from somewhere behind us to add cover and shield any from seeing into their lair."

"So what do we do? They will see us coming if we just rush across the field." Willem said.

"Unavoidable. Can't see any from here but don't doubt that they'll have at least one lookout. Probably high in the branches so watch out for incoming missiles." Adley explained. "I'll go first of course. Follow close behind. I'll push right through the brush and hope there is more clearing behind the first layer. Then it's all out from there. With any luck they will be resting and we will catch them by surprise. Don't wait for them. Attack as soon as you can."

"Wait." Havander said. "I think I can help. What if I can provide cover in the way of fog?"

"Fog?" Adley asked.

"Yes. I can cast a spell that will bring up a veil of fog between us and there. They won't see us coming."

"We won't be able to see either. Plus it's going to be a nice day. No reason for fog." Willem complained.

"Well if it's like we hope there won't be many up right now and look the morning mist is still rising from the grass. Perhaps the lookout will not think too much on it. They're not that smart and it might just be more confusing than seeing us three sprint the distance there. At least they won't see us until we've reached the trees."

"Very good Havander. Get your bearings. It's a straight shot there. Follow me closely and hopefully there won't be anymore of those foot traps in the grass. With a little luck we will get the first shots off." Adley said.

Havander stood ignoring the smart aleck look from Willem and began casting. About halfway through his words he threw a pinch of some dried material out into the field that Willem and Adley found peculiar with its obvious green coloring but they didn't know what it was. When Havander's words finished the mist still hovering in the field just above the grass grew thicker in appearance and then rose up into the air slowly. It grew in thickness and it looked as though the grass beneath it was spewing out clouds of vapor. The fog engulfed the area between them and the stand of trees and when it reached well above Adley's height Havander said, "Go."

Adley took off out of the brush at a jog with crossbow leveled out before him. Though he couldn't see more than a couple feet in front of him he knew he wouldn't need to until he cleared the other side. Willem followed a couple paces removed to his right and Havander followed directly behind with wand leveled right at his back.

With their sight dulled all of their hearing seemed more in tune. They could still hear the morning songs of the birds among the branches and the rustling of their feet through the dewy grass as their feet sped through it. When they neared the edge of the trees they were surprised to not hear an alarm sound. Adley did not wait and pushed through the brush with the fog now filtering through. As if on queue of the first couple branches breaking under the weight of Adley's feet a shrill shout of some apparent language unknown to them sounded from high in the branches above them.

Havander stopped in his tracks and pointed his wand up into the branches of the large oak in front of him. Without ever seeing his target he spoke the command word igniting the power in his wand three times in succession just hoping he was aiming in the area close to something. Having never aimed a spell at any living creature hoping to do harm and it had him exhilarated and shocked at the same time.

Adley heard Havander's words behind him and the noise of his spells hitting the branches above him but he did not slow. A rock, no doubt thrown at him from a sling bounced harmlessly off of his armor. He ignored it completely and exited the brush and just as he had hoped, the area under the long branches under the oak was a dry patch of dirt surrounding the enormous trunk of the main tree. Directly in front of him from a whole dug into the ground, kobolds began springing out in multiple directions. Unsure of what was happening they looked in all directions. The first one to spot Adley leveled its spear and sprang in his direction only to be blasted away by a crossbow bolt that hit it directly in the chest. Adley dropped his crossbow without slowing and slashed with his longsword at the next kobold in line who had advanced only a couple steps before meeting the fine edge of Adley's sword. Faced with a ferocious enemy apparently appearing from nowhere within the boundaries of their home the kobolds scattered trying to gain some ground and assess the situation.

Willem saw as Adley dispatched two kobolds with the quickness and efficiency of a veteran warrior. It was like no other sight he had ever seen and it spurred him into action as one kobold darted away from Adley right in line with him. At the last second it noticed Willem and raised it's spear but it was too late. Willem's spear entered its midsection and it was pushed backwards onto the ground under the weight of Willem's forceful thrust.

Seeing one of their fellow kobolds dying on the ground with a spear sticking into it the next two kobolds that were darting out in a similar direction came at Willem. One held a spear like the previous kobold and the other pulled forth a form of a blade, which wasn't much more than a sharpened piece of scrap metal in the semblance of a primitive blade.

Willem tried pulling his spear out of the body of his first kill but it was stuck and when he pulled on it he lifted the small kobold off of the ground. Small himself for a human, it was still no challenge to lift the three foot tall creature off of the ground but he could not wield it that way and so Willem let loose of the shaft as the two newcomers came on. The next kobold in line lunged with his spear in an upward direction towards Willem's face. Willem, with his fast reflexes saw the attack for exactly what it was and lifted his left forearm up at the precise moment to hit the shaft of the spear just aft of the blade and lift it harmlessly above his head while grabbing at his curved dagger behind his back with his right hand. Now with his preferred weapon in hand he slashed the dangerous looking weapon right across the face of kobold. The slash cut deep, Willem knew, and after the slash he rotated with the weight of the swing leaving the kobold to clutch at its face while Willem got in line for his next opponent. The kobold with the crude dagger came on jabbing his blade forward.

Willem could see Adley out of the corner of his eye engaging another kobold that was trying to exit the whole in the ground while backing away from his attacker. Always just out of reach of the clumsy jabs, Willem felt cocky as he continuously backed and then began to circle as he neared the edge of the dirt under the oak and before he entered the tangled mesh of brush at it's perimeter. Just as he was about to counter the kobold standing in front of him trying futilely to catch him, the kobold was blasted away by a missile fired from Havander's wand.

"Hey that one was mine." Willem complained as he looked to Havander standing just a few feet away from him.

"He's not dead. That'll just stun him." Havander shouted.

Willem turned back to the kobold blasted away and landed incidentally next to the kobold he had slashed across the face and was still clutching at its wound. Before it could fully regain its feet Willem was on it pushing it back down to the ground with his knee and slashing it across the throat. In what seemed a continuous motion Willem then reversed the motion of his blade and caught the other kobold clutching its face right in its earhole. The tip of his blade entered deep into its head piercing through skull and entered its brain.

After witnessing the efficiency and brutality of Willem ending the two kobolds he was engaging, a rock skipped right off of his magical shield not an inch from Havander's face. Had he not enacted that shield spell earlier he knew he would have at the very least been knocked unconscious. He looked up to the branches and at last caught sight of the rock thrower. Just as he set another rock into his sling Havander pointed his wand and enacted his wand's power once more. Finally catching the kobold in the hip as it tried to dart off of the branch he was on, to avoid the magic missile racing up at him. The kobold fell to the dirt face first. Quickly it rolled over onto its back and began scurrying away from Havander who was closing fast with wand in hand. Just a couple of feet away now, Havander blasted the kobold right in the face with the magic of his wand. Normally a magic missile spell is not deadly but in such close proximity to such a small creature and being shot right in the head it was like being hit with a punch delivered from a ogre. Blood spurted from it's eyes, nose, and ears as its head bounced off of the solidly packed ground.

Caught up in the moment Havander was pleased from his quick decision-making but as he looked around to see Adley slay the last of the kobolds he couldn't help but feel sorry for the diminutive creatures. Nine lay dead under the eaves of the branches of the large oak. Looking back down to his one kill made him shudder for a second but he quickly regained his composure as Adley waved him and Willem over to the hole that the kobolds had dug under the oak tree.

Back at the farmhouse, the family met Adley, Havander and Willem with cheers and congratulations. Adley explained to them the reasoning for the smoke in the distance. After ensuring that there were no other kobolds hiding in their underground lair the three of them had drug the bodies of the kobolds out from under the trees and set fire to the corpses for easier disposal. The father of the family ensured them that it was quite all right and that he would follow through with disposing of any leftover remains into the hole they had dug under the oak and have it filled in after.

Not long after the three were back on the road to home. "You know you two just earned your first bounty." Adley proclaimed to his two young friends.

"How's that?" Willem asked

"Well it's a standing order in Casta as well as other kingdoms that the killing of creatures like kobolds, goblins, orcs and many others earns you a reward for each creature killed. Normally you have to provide proof but I'm sure Captain Payne will take my word for it."

"Proof in what form?" Havander inquired.

"Well if it's a bounty on a known criminal you have to bring back the body of course but for other creatures you have to cut off their ears for an actual account of how many bodies there were."

"That's gross." Havander said in revulsion.

"It's not that bad. You just put them in a sac. Ears are mostly cartilage and don't bleed much anyway."

"It's still gross." Havander repeated.

"Split three ways?" Willem asked.

"Ha." Adley laughed. "No I guess you two can split it though I killed the majority. I get paid regularly by Josef and Oran anyway."

"When do we start getting paid regularly?" Willem asked hopeful of a desirable answer from Adley.

"When you become full members of The Silver Guard of course."

"Didn't we just do that?"

"No. This was merely another step in that direction." Adley looked to Willem riding alongside him and noted his usual sour expression when not getting his way. "Not to worry young man. It shouldn't be long now."

CHAPTER NINETEEN

Expectations—Sraes, 1021

JOSEF WATCHED AS Marcus held the wand of divination before his eyes, examining its smooth surface and delicate design. When he was finished inspecting it he thrust his right arm out and spoke the command word that should have activated the magic held within the wand. Seconds ticked by as Josef and Marcus awaited any kind of response from the wand. When nothing happened Marcus again spoke the command word and still nothing happened. He elicited a little growl and bared his fangs in frustration. He tried three more times in succession. With each try his voice grew louder and raspier and still nothing happened.

"Enough Marcus." Josef instructed. "It does not appear that it is going to work at this time."

"I don't understand Master Righe. You said I have magic within me but still the wand will not work. Am I saying it wrong?"

"No you are not saying it wrong and you do indeed have magical properties flowing through you though apparently not the kind needed to elicit a response from the wand." When Josef finished he snatched the wand from Marcus' hand and walked towards his desk in the classroom of Silver Guard Keep.

Seeing and hearing the obvious disappointment in Master Righe's expression and voice gave Marcus a feeling of deep disappointment within himself. Master Righe had explained to him that the wand he was attempting to use was the same that students at Hareth Academy practiced with to find out if they had the skills required to become mages. Apparently divination magic was the most commonly used magic among wizards and was more or less universal in its usage to any type of mage. If that were the case and if he did indeed have some form of magical properties within himself, as Master Righe had often said, than he couldn't understand why the divination wand did not work in his hands. Without waiting for Master Righe to turn back around Marcus exited the classroom, slamming the door behind him as he exited.

Josef heard a knock on the door of the classroom. Deep within his thoughts it took him several seconds to respond but finally he uttered, "Enter."

Harold walked in and came up to his desk. Laid out in front of Josef were maps of various kingdoms in Drilain and check marks were etched on numerous locations on the maps. Recognizing the frustration on Josef's face he asked, "Is everything alright Master Righe? You've missed the midday meal again."

Josef took himself from his thoughts and finally looked up to Harold standing before his desk. "I do apologize Harold. I hope Georgette didn't go through any trouble on my account."

"Not at all. Just cold meat sandwiches but delicious none the less as all of my wife's food is." Harold responded as he inadvertently looked over his shoulder to ensure Georgette had not entered behind him and hear him utter the word "just".

Josef recognized the response to his words and gave a little laugh. Something he sorely needed in his time of frustration. "I'm sure they were. Was that all?"

"Actually no sir. I'm a bit worried about Marcus and was hoping to find out what you may have said to him this morning."

"Why? What has he done?"

"Oh nothing sir but he won't talk to anyone. Me and Georgette have both tried but he is visibly upset about something."

"Is he crying?" Josef asked thinking that an absurd possibility.

"Of course not. As you know he hasn't cried since he was a babe but he is on about something."

Josef thought back to his meeting with Marcus this morning and he shook his head at his own rudeness and lack of consideration considering young Marcus. "I'm afraid I may be the cause Harold. Where is Marcus now?" Josef asked as he stood from his chair.

Marcus was sitting on the back deck of the Keep. Keeping to the shade and searching through a large tome sitting on his lap and sometimes focusing on Willem and Oran who were sparring in the training yard. It was remarkable to him how the two could go at each other so furiously without hurting one another. Both wielding two short practice swords so as to not hurt one another but neither giving ground other than to maneuver to try to outdo the other. Even at his young age Marcus knew he was watching something spectacular and without comparison to others he had seen wield swords.

"May I join you?" Josef asked as he sat next to Marcus.

Marcus shrugged his shoulders and turned the page.

Once fully seated Josef pointed to the book in Marcus' lap. "What have you got there?"

Marcus wanted to ignore Josef but instead thought it better to at least acknowledge the Master of the house. "A book Willem leant me so that I may learn about the races of Drilain."

Trying to keep the conversation light Josef waded in. "Oh yes. You know, me and Oran wrote most of that book together. I do apologize for the drawings. I drew most of them and I'm sure you can tell I'm not much of an artist." Marcus did not give any indication that he had even heard him so Josef continued, "Anything in particular you are looking for?"

"Dragons." Marcus responded.

Taken back Josef asked, "Why would you want to do that Marcus?"

"You know why."

"Indeed." Josef whispered more to himself than Marcus.

Thinking about it now he should not have been surprised that Marcus would wish to learn more about dragons. Though only six years of age Marcus was smarter than any other child he had met his age and more mature than many children older than him. Far more mature than Willem was when he first moved into the Keep and larger as well. His dragon heritage had him maturing faster than that of a human child. Though they had never lied to Marcus they had never fully told him the details of his origins. He knew of course that Georgette and Harold were not his parents and after hearing the news more than a year earlier he had stopped referring to them as mother and father. For a long time after he was curious about his real parents and they had told him every detail about Cecilia Alio of course but only that his father was some dragon who did not know of his conception.

"Well you'll not find any information in that book about dragons I'm afraid." Josef said and then took in a deep breath while thinking about letting Marcus in on more of his story. "If you wish I have other books that can tell you what you wish to know but first I must apologize for my actions with you this morning. It was not my intent to upset you."

"It's not your fault I have no magic." Marcus said while still not looking in Josef's direction.

Josef used his finger to direct Marcus' face towards his by pushing his chin in his direction. "Is that what you think I'm frustrated about?"

Marcus looked down not wanting to lock eyes with Josef and merely shrugged his shoulders again.

"Oh dear boy. That is not the problem nor would it be your fault or anyone's fault for that matter. Besides you are only six. That stupid wand I had you using isn't even used on children as young as you."

Confused but hopeful Marcus finally looked into Josef's eyes. "Really?"

"Yes really. I only hoped because of your heritage and maturity that it might show in you sooner rather than later." Josef explained although he was truly frustrated that Marcus could not make the wand work but more of his frustration came from Marcus as a constant reminder that Deathmar the Black was still out in the world somewhere and after more than seven years of searching for him they were no where closer to finding him.

"So I may still have magic in me then?"

"Marcus as I've said you already do." Josef had a good idea and a way to stall some of the conversation as to who his father truly is. "Come with me Marcus. I want to show you something." Josef stood and headed back towards the classroom.

Once inside the classroom Josef went to the bookshelf and pulled forth a tome detailing many of the known dragon species in general but not the histories of known individuals. He laid the large leather bound book, with a depiction of a golden dragon etched into it's covering with gold leaf used to give it the desired color, in front of Marcus on the table.

While moving over to the other side of the classroom to gather more things Josef began explaining. "That book there is the one you are looking for. I must be completely honest with you though Marcus. You may not like what you find."

Marcus ran his hands over the dragon on the front cover. He marveled at the artistry that went into making it. "What do you mean Master Righe?"

Josef returned to the table with a clear jar containing some liquid, a glass of water and a piece of some strange looking leather he had recovered from under his potion lab setup. "Because Marcus, after I show you what I'm about to and after you read that book you will have more questions about who your father is. More specifically what kind of dragon he is." Josef arranged the items on the table and pushed the two books towards the opposite side of the table then turned back to Marcus. "What I'm about to tell you might go against what Georgette and Harold would want me to. Do you understand?"

"Yes."

"Now I'm leaving it up to you whether or not you want to tell them and you can decide that after. Either way it is your decision. I ask only that you keep in mind that none of us told you about your specific dragon heritage because we did not want to worry or scare you. Do you understand that?"

"Not really Master Righe."

"Well first off, not all dragons are good."

"I kind of assumed all dragons were bad. That's why no one wants to talk about my father."

Josef was surprised by the response. "Oh not at all Marcus. Many dragons are good. They range in a multitude of colors and different kinds of dragons have different magical abilities. We call the good dragons metallic dragons. They are gold like the one on the front of the book, silver, copper and a couple others. Each one is different in size, shape and a variety of other things. You'll find their specific details in that book."

"What about the bad dragons?"

"Well that's where the conversation gets uncomfortable I'm afraid. The evil or chromatic dragons are red, white, green, blue and black." Josef put greater emphasis on "black" hoping that Marcus would catch on and he didn't disappoint.

"Black like my scales in the middle of my back and my finger and toenails." Marcus reasoned.

"Yes Marcus. Well actually the claws of dragons are probably all black but the scales beginning to grow down your spine are an indication of what kind of dragon you came from."

"Does that make me evil than Master Righe?"

Josef kneeled down in front of Marcus and grabbed him by his shoulders. "No dear boy. Not at all."

"But…"

Josef interrupted, "You listen now. The things I've told you and when most people talk about different races they are talking in general. What makes a person or a dragonborn in your case what you are, is the decisions you make in life. For example goblins are evil correct?"

"So that book says." Marcus pointed to the book he was reading earlier. "The lessons I've had with you and Master Oran have always been that way as well."

"Yes I'm sure we have said that and most of the time we would be right but not always. That's what I mean when we say in general. But I'll tell you something. I once saw a goblin shaman pull an arrow from a wounded Castan soldier on a battlefield. I was too far away to do anything and thought the man doomed for sure. What he did next surprised me beyond belief. Though the soldier had undoubtedly killed many of the goblins and orcs around him, the shaman cast a healing spell on the soldier. When he was finished he nodded in reverence to his enemy and walked away." Josef finished with releasing Marcus and standing back up.

"So that goblin was good."

"Maybe not entirely. He did fight against us in the battle but when the fighting was over he saw no further need of killing or even hurting that wounded soldier. Instead he showed honor towards the man and understanding for the soldier's suffering. That is an act of kindness. An act of good you see."

"That's confusing Master Righe."

"Of course it is. The world is not black and white, right or wrong, even good or evil. It's a combination of them all. I do believe however that there are races that are inherently good or evil. Demons and devils for example live only to cause suffering of others but take humans for another example. Everyone else who lives in this house is human and we would consider them good, yes?"

R. A. HAYDEN

"Yes of course."

"As well as everyone who lives in town except for Armihrmond Firefist of course, yet most of who The Silver Guard fight against are human or were human before they turned into the undead by mostly human necromancers, which we consider evil. Humans are perhaps the most confusing of all. I've seen humans do both the most honorable and horrific things to others."

"So how does one know?"

"In time you will understand better. In any case I want to get back to your frustration over thinking you do not have any magic within you."

"Yes please."

Josef smiled at the confused look on Marcus' face. He had to remind himself that he was only talking to a child, albeit a large child. Josef pulled over two chairs from the table behind him. He faced them towards each other and sat in one and indicated for Marcus to take the other.

"Now lets start here." Josef reached out and grabbed a hand of Marcus' and pulled it closer to him. "You see your nails are black and thicker than humans yes?"

"Yes of course."

"They seem to want to grow into claws. Something you have obtained from your dragon heritage. If you want when you get older you can grow them out and they will probably be formidable weapons."

"But that's not magic."

"Now hold on I'm getting there. You know of course that you are larger than a human child of your age. Not only in height but you have a very wide frame as well. You are already much larger than Willem was when he came to live here and he was older than you are now."

"Yeah but Willem is short anyways."

"Ha." Josef laughed and leaned back in his chair and covered his mouth trying not to laugh further. "Yes he is. You will probably be taller than him very soon." Josef laughed some more thinking of how Willem would have been surprised to get jokes thrown at him from Marcus just like everyone else. "Now where was I? Oh yes. You are growing extremely fast. That is why you are in so much pain some nights. Your joints and bones hurt from the rapid expansion. I believe you will have a bone structure far superior in strength to that of a human when you are fully grown."

"The scales sprouting from my back hurt somethin awful."

"I imagine so. It won't last forever Marcus. All children go through it. You are just going through it younger and faster than other children. That is why it hurts so much."

"Georgette worries somethin awful."

"I know but still that is not the good stuff even though only with that I imagine you would be a tremendously good warrior when you are older if you want."

"But what else is there?"

"Well you know you can see better in the dark than any human can right?"

"Yes but is that magic?"

"Why not?" Josef uttered a couple words and all the faerie fire torches in the classroom went out leaving them in almost complete darkness. The only light emanated from the cracks above and below the exit door. "What do you see Marcus?"

"Everything mostly." Marcus answered after he scanned the room. "It looks mostly gray and white though."

"You see, I can't see anything. Only your outline from the light behind you." Josef finished with uttering the words of a spell again and all the torches lit back up.

"I'm still not convinced that that is magic. Many creatures come out at night that can see in the dark or so Oran and Harold have told me."

"Ah but I'm not done." Josef grabbed the piece of leather still sitting on the table and slid it closer to Marcus. "This is a piece of wing from a giant bat. It's very durable and strong." Josef then grabbed the clear jar. "Cup your hand so none spills onto anything."

Marcus did so and Josef poured a small amount of the liquid from the jar into his hand. Marcus just looked at it. He didn't understand what he was supposed to be seeing. "Do you feel anything Marcus?" Josef asked.

"No."

"Now pour that liquid from your hand onto the piece of leather there."

Marcus did just that and was immediately shocked by the reaction. The leather began to shrivel and smoke. The liquid seemed to burn right through the leather and even began scorching the table underneath it.

Josef grabbed the glass of water and first poured it over the leather to dilute the powerful acid and then into Marcus' hand.

"What was that?" Marcus asked in a surprised tone.

"That was acid Marcus. Strong acid at that, yet look at your hand."

Marcus examined his hand and other than a slight redness to his skin he couldn't see anything and certainly didn't feel anything. The leather next to him on the table on the other hand was burned and shriveled into almost nothing. "How did you know that wouldn't burn me?"

Josef lied in part, "Because you are part black dragon Marcus." Although black dragons do have those abilities he wanted to make sure that Marcus did as well so not long ago he had collected trimmings from his nails, hair, blood, and a skin sample while he slept heavily under the influence of a sleeping potion that he had given him when he could not find sleep due to the horrible pain he was suffering from his rapidly growing bone structure. Josef had used those samples to run experiments on the extent of Marcus' abilities. "Black dragons are essentially immune to all forms of acid. You are also very tolerant to many types of poison. All black dragons are Marcus."

"That was incredible. Is that all?"

"Well black dragons can spew acid from their mouths but it doesn't seem you gained that ability. Fortunately I would say. It doesn't mean that that is all there is of course. Your abilities will grow, as you get older. I imagine that you will be larger than most any human and stronger. If you wanted you could be a formidable warrior as I have said and probably use magical items that others wouldn't be able to use due to your natural dragon magic."

"You mean I can start training with Willem?" Marcus said excitedly.

Josef did not miss how quickly Marcus became excited over warrior training compared to magic training. "I had hoped to start you in training with magic next month. You know Havander graduates Hareth Academy next month and will be staying with us permanently afterwards. That was one reason for my disappointment this morning to be honest. I had hoped to have two students under my roof but if you so wish than you can start training with Willem if you like."

"I would Master Righe."

"We'll have to convince Georgette of course."

That took some bluster out of Marcus' spirits. Georgette was very protective of him. He was still excited to be able to swing a sword as well as Willem and Oran do one day. "I'll go talk to her at once." Marcus started for the door.

"Wait Marcus." Josef called after him. "What about your books here?"

Marcus ran back to the table and picked up both books then looked up to Josef who was standing once again. "Thank you Master Righe. And don't worry. I'll keep this conversation between us."

Josef watched as he exited and considered the possibilities. He really did want to train Marcus in the ways of magic and hoped that his skills would blossom when he got older. On the other hand he could imagine him being a very effective warrior, as most dragonborn are that don't acquire the skills necessary to perform magic from their parents. Either way he has the potential to be one of the most formidable Silver Guard members ever and a most devastating weapon against the likes of Marcus' father if they ever find him.

CHAPTER TWENTY

Graduation—Silhad, 1021

OUTSIDE OF THE Test Maze, as the students at Hareth Academy often called it, Havander waited with Professor Dukes at his side for his final test at the school he had called home for the past eight years. It was late in the day and Havander was one of the last three in his class to take his final test. The other two were at different locations on the island testing at those sites set aside for such occasions. Tests were not all the same. In fact they were designed specifically for the skillsets that each student was most accustomed to. Though the school only used three locations for testing, what was inside each area could drastically change from student to student. Havander knew that the Test Maze was generally thought of as the hardest of the three locations to test in, though the professors denied it. Havander knew as well that the Test Maze was used primarily for students who excelled in evocation and alteration magic.

As time grew closer for him to begin, Havander grew more anxious. The tests were designed to be hard. Hard enough to even kill in some situations. Last year one of the students had perished during his final test, the first time it had happened in twenty years but having a death occur so recently had Havander worried.

The instructions were simple. There was one entrance, which Havander and Professor Dukes were standing in front of at the moment, and one exit. You merely had to make it out the other side to pass and be honored as a member of Hareth Academy. What wasn't simple was not knowing what you would face. It could be anything from traps, to illusions, to all out confrontation with something that was sent there to kill you for its freedom. Creatures such as kobolds, goblins, orcs, stirges, and a host of others were possible encounters that a student might face and one didn't know which, if any, they would have to encounter.

Each student had to decide which spells they believed they would require in order to pass the test. As most students didn't know that many spells at this juncture in their arcane studies it wasn't that difficult to decide. Most students had their entire repertoire at their disposal but not so for Havander. Over his eight years at Hareth and the summers in-between with Master Righe he had more spells to choose from than any other student. What he did not know was that he actually had more spells at his disposal for the final test than any other student in the history of Hareth Academy.

You had the option to bring your spellbook with you of course but memorizing new spells took time and most students opted out of taking it. They relied on what spells they did have memorized so that they wouldn't be encumbered by carrying more than they needed. Unfortunately, besides a dagger or a staff, that had to be non-magical, that was all you were allowed to take with you. No other magical items such as wands, rods, scrolls or potions. You had to rely on your own personal magic to pass.

"It is time Havander." Professor Dukes announced taking Havander from his thoughts. "I'll see you on the other side young wizard." Professor Dukes said though Havander would not be considered a wizard until the test was concluded. In his mind though Havander was more than capable and he had no doubt that he would succeed.

Havander watched as Professor Dukes turned to the double doors and spoke the command word that allowed entry. The doors squeaked open and Havander entered.

Headmaster Usarus, Master Rischer, and Master Righe watched through a scrying pool large enough for the three to comfortably stand around as Havander entered the front doors of the Test Maze. Behind them other professors and heads of The Orders did similarly to the two other students whose tests had just started. The tests had been going on throughout the entire day and as this class of twenty was larger than a class size in a generation, the tests were taking longer than usual. That was to the enjoyments of those watching. They all thoroughly enjoyed watching the students, which they had cared for over the past eight years; take their final steps into earning the rank of wizard.

Not only could they see the students but they could also hear them. Hear them at least as much as someone listening to a low conversation from the other side of a room. Headmaster Usarus looked up to Josef in admiration for Havander as he cast his first spell before ever taking a step in either direction afforded to him at the beginning of the maze. All three could hear well enough to know that he had cast detect magic. Although from his present position it would not afford him any insights to what lie within, it was however an excellent idea.

After casting and seeing no effect whatsoever from his first spell attempt, Havander took in his surroundings once more. He was standing in a hallway of what looked like an ancient castle. The inside walls matched those outside on the perimeter of the circular structure. The large gray brickwork appeared to be old. Parts of it were crumbling away and their litter was scattered about the matching floor. Moss and green looking slime edged its way into the mortar between the large gray stones. Even though there were no torches in sight the hall was somehow lit with an eerie low light that appeared to come from the ceiling down even though Havander could not really see the ceiling as it was cast in shadow far above him.

All of the students knew that the professors and masters of the school watched as they progressed through their test through scrying pools. It was actually the only hint that the students had as to what spell not to prepare. There was no need to ward oneself from scrying or cast a spell in order to detect it. Knowing that Master Righe and no doubt the Headmaster as well were watching him he quickly decided to go right. It was early in the game and at this juncture he figured it a coin toss so it didn't matter either way.

Havander noted that the sides of the hallway were not similar in shape. The inner wall ran straight and if the remainder of the Test Maze was the same than everything would be squared off. The perimeter was circular though and as he walked, the wall to his right inched ever closer to the inner wall, forcing a choke point. He could see ahead that the wall on his left ended leaving more than ten feet between it and the circular wall to his right that continued on past the finish of the inner wall. He decided to be as cautious as possible and followed closely the curve of the outer wall so he could see further around the corner when he reached it.

Havander moved slowly, wary of traps that might be non-magical in nature. He actually wished at that moment that he had Willem's skill of noticing such things. As he ended the length of the first wall he could see another wall after that protruding towards the outermost wall just as the first one did. He had another choice to make. Continue following the perimeter or take this first left. He decided to continue following the perimeter. Since he had not gone far it would be easy enough to backtrack as long as the walls didn't start shifting or some such nonsense.

As his vision cleared the next wall in line he could see the length of this hallway and guessed it was about the length of the one he had first entered. At the far end of it he could see what appeared to be a human skeleton sitting against the wall. He thought that odd indeed that it would be sitting and not crumpled on the floor in a heap of bones. He decided to cast a detect undead spell.

Headmaster Usarus couldn't believe what he had just heard as Havander finished casting his next spell. He recognized the spell as detect undead and was a wise choice on the part of Havander but he was pretty sure he heard him cast it with a necromancer's incantation rather than with divination. Many spells had multiple ways in which to cast them but necromancy was not taught at Hareth Academy. He thought to question Josef on it but held his tongue as the skeleton rose up after hearing Havander at the other end of the hall. On the opposite side of where Havander could see, the skeleton had a sword, which it picked up as it rose and began walking in Havander's direction.

All three watched tensely as Havander began casting again. At the end of his short incantation a magic missile shot forth from his right hand and blasted the skeleton in the chest sending its bones scattering about the floor before it got anywhere near Havander.

Havander was surprised at how easily the skeleton went down. He thought perhaps it wasn't constructed well considering this was a test for

R. A. HAYDEN

students. Nevertheless he moved towards it cautiously while pulling forth his dagger. Upon closer examination he could tell that the skeleton was actually not human but probably that of an orc considering it's large lower jawbone and canines much larger than that of a human. He kicked the skull aside and bent down to pick up the sword that was left on the ground. Though not well versed in the use of a sword he did have some weapons training with Oran and Adley at Silver Guard Keep. He mostly trained with a staff but he imagined he had more weapons training with a sword than his fellow classmates and it never hurt to have a weapon in hand.

After rounding the next corner he was faced with a couple different dead ends. With no other option he reversed direction and decided to try the first hallway that he could have made a left onto after rounding the first corner of the hallway entrance. He assumed that he had made almost half of a circle following the perimeter so the complex was perhaps not as large as it appeared from outside. He knew it couldn't possibly be as easy as just keeping to the edge though and was not surprised that he had to turn around.

Once he reached the hallway back near where he had started he had second thoughts about trying the perimeter around the other side but in the end decided against it. Somewhere he imagined he would have to work his way towards the middle and this hall was his only option other than trying the other side. He decided to once again cast detect magic. Skeletons after all couldn't be the only things lurking in here. He was pleased with himself for his decision as he noticed a glimmer of magic on the right side of the wall approximately halfway down the length of this hallway. Slowly he crept towards it not knowing if it was a trap or something more nefarious. Once he was within a couple arms reach of the glimmer still visible in his eyesight he picked up a stone from the floor and tossed it in front of the wall. Nothing happened. The stone just skipped off of the ground before settling so he picked up another and tossed it directly at the wall with a little more force. What he heard brought a smile to his face as this stone hit the ground as well but it did so on the opposite side of seemingly solid wall.

"He is doing well." Master Rischer stated. "If he takes a right after passing through the illusionary wall he'll have circumvented the entire left side of the maze."

"Yes although it isn't much of a maze. It only takes a few turns to reach the center." Headmaster Usarus said in an irritated tone. He was not happy with the non-answer that Josef had given him earlier when he inquired as to how Havander knew a necromancy incantation for detecting undead.

Havander prodded his newly acquired sword through the illusionary wall before him. He did not know how to make the illusion dissipate and he did not want to walk into anything so he took his time. He even picked up a couple more stones and tossed them through the wall. When there was no obvious response he gathered his courage and stepped through. On the other side he was faced again with a choice of left or right at the end of the short hallway he was now in. He crept closer to the end of the hallway and peered both ways. There appeared to be nothing as far as he could tell. He decided to go right once again. Better to map out in his mind what he knew from one side of the complex rather than possibly start all over by looking where he had not been.

This new hallway continued for some ways. He did not wish to exhaust his spell casting capacity by continually casting detect magic so he kept one hand on the wall to his left as he continued slowly. After three left turns and before he took his first right, an awful smell came drifting down the hall. It was unlike anything he had ever smelled. The only thing he could compare it to was rotting meat. He continued even slower trying to cover his nose with the sleeve of his robes. Although probably not as pungent to other people, Havander could not stand the smell of things rotting or feces which he could tell was certainly mixed in as well as he neared. Even cleaning out the horses' stalls at Silver Guard Keep had him lose his breakfast more than once and this was far worse.

The end of the hall ended with only one option of turning right. Still covering his nose he peeked around the corner. What he saw in the opposite corner of his position in the large room defied explanation. He was unsure as to what manner of creature it was or why it would be rutting around in what could only be described of as the rotten remains and waste of numerous kinds of creatures. There were body parts of numerous creatures strewn about in close proximity to the creature. From his vantage point Havander could see a leg of some hooved animal, intestines, feathers, and blood spattering the wall and ground next to it. The creature itself was disgusting to view as well. It was as large as three men with two front legs helping two other long appendages, extending from its back, which ended in barbs or spikes of some sort that pulled the rotten flesh and guts into its massive maw. Its body was fat and rotund and its mouth seemed an extension of its body. The only real distinguishing characteristic of it was a strange tentacle protruding from its apparent backside that had three large eyeballs near the end of it. Thankfully for Havander it was looking to the other side of the room and not the entry point he was staring at it from.

After looking at what he thought must be an animal he leaned back against the wall still covering his nose and trying to figure out what he should do next when he heard a familiar language coming from elsewhere in the room. He dared another peak around the corner and standing in the far right hand corner of the room were three goblins. Behind them was a hallway and above them, written in dwarvish was the symbol for exit. He looked back to the other creature and he noticed as well a sign above it written in dwarvish indicating an exit. He hadn't even noticed the hallway behind the creature when first he looked upon it. So grotesque was the sight and smell emanating from it that he hadn't looked past it.

Leaning once again against the wall and trying not to wretch he considered his options. Two exits. One exit had three enemies before it and the other with only one, although it seemed far more formidable. He thought about trying to become invisible and simply walk past all of them but he didn't know if the strange creature in the corner could see right past that illusion and he wasn't proficient in that spell so he hadn't bothered studying it before his test. He knew of a sleeping spell he could cast at the goblins but figured that it couldn't be that easy. This was his final test after all. He didn't believe he could just put them to sleep and walk right out. The fat creature in the corner didn't look to be nimble and wasn't moving at all even with the goblins standing in the same room as it. Then it came to him. He had an idea.

"What is he doing?" Master Rischer asked of Josef.

Josef said nothing and just watched as Havander's form changed from that of a human in full robes to that of a hobgoblin wearing dirty leather armor. It was a risky spell to try to alter oneself in appearance especially as young as Havander was. The spellwork could generally be seen through especially by anyone with a strong will of their own such as the three masters looking on through the scrying pool. They could tell what he was trying to appear as but could also see glints of him. Nonetheless Havander strolled across the room with confidence shouting and pointing his sword in the direction of the otyugh in goblin, *"What are you three doing? Kill that thing."*

The goblins looked to one another unsure of what was happening. One of them addressed Havander who for all they knew was a hobgoblin and far superior to them due to his size, *"We told to wait and kill anyone try to pass."*

Havander addressed them more seriously and louder, *"Fools that is your true mission,"* He said while pointing at the other creature, *"Once it's done eating it will come for you."*

The largest of the three goblins walked towards Havander with sword in hand. *"Who you? We told by human that we wait for human."*

Just before reaching the goblin Havander enacted another spell quietly so that the goblin would not hear, even though he doubted that the goblin would understand the language of casting anyway. Even before Havander and the goblin were within sword reach of one another the goblin visibly changed his facial expression to what Havander noted as a smile. His charm spell had apparently took effect rendering the goblin under his influence.

"Did you not hear me fool? I said attack that disgusting thing." Havander ordered.

Not needing anymore prodding the goblin turned to its friends and issued the same order. The three of them advanced slowly on the otyugh with their short swords raised.

"Well this is certainly an interesting turn of events. Everyone else just bypasses the otyugh all together." Master Rischer said in an excited tone.

"Exactly the point Master Rischer. Havander is well out of his league trying to deal with that otyugh." Headmaster Usarus said in a scolding tone.

Josef said nothing and just watched as the three goblins advanced. More or less nestled in a corner the otyugh just watched and waited for the goblins to get within striking distance of its tentacles.

R. A. HAYDEN

Havander walked closer as well but much farther back than his new allies. The otyugh appeared not to notice and kept shoveling the gore in front of him into its mouth. What Havander did not know was that the otyugh could not advance much anyway. Underneath its massive body and behind its other two limbs was a third that was chained to the ground. The length of the chain allowed movement but even at its full reach the otyugh could not reach the other side of the room. All Havander had to do was turn around and walk out of the exit with the goblins distracted.

Two of the goblins moved to as much of the sides of the otyugh as possible while the third that was under the influence of Havander's spell advanced towards its center. Goblins are not normally brave creatures but when numbers favor them they will attack. Even though the otyugh outweighed each of them by ten fold, it didn't look like much more than a big garbage disposal.

The three masters watched tensely awaiting for the chaos to unfold.

"*Kill!*" Havander shouted.

The goblin directly in line with the creature's mouth pressed forward. Once it was well within range of the otyugh's tentacles, both shot out faster than the goblins knew possible from this fat disgusting pile of filth. The tentacles latched onto either side of the goblin. With his arms pinned and unable to fight back the goblin could do nothing but cry out in pain from the long spikes attached at the end of the tentacles, which now dug into its flesh. The otyugh pulled the goblin towards its mouth, which it now opened wider, revealing long rows of rotting but nevertheless sharp teeth.

Seeing its friend in trouble and about to be placed into the mouth of the otyugh the goblin on the left surged in and stabbed downward into the flesh of the creature. The tentacle on top of its body containing its eyes swept in the goblins direction hitting him across his midsection and sent him into the wall. Meanwhile it pulled its intended victim into its mouth and crunched down ending the screaming of the goblin with two massive bites.

Havander was amazed at how easily the creature took down one goblin. Not waiting for the other to react or the one now against the wall to regain its senses he began casting. He extended his right arm sending a magic missile directly into the body of the creature. If it could feel any pain it certainly didn't show it.

The otyugh turned in the direction of the third goblin sending one of its spiked tentacles in his direction. Thankfully for the goblin it swiped with its sword at the same time the tentacle reached out for him. The blade cut into the flesh of the beast and it recoiled but instead of retreating began moving in the goblins direction.

Havander was no longer under the guise of a hobgoblin after enacting his last spell but thankfully the goblins didn't recognize the shift back to his natural form. They were too engaged with their enemy. Havander took advantage of the turn that the creature had made toward the goblin and launched a more powerful spell. After using the spell components in the appropriate manner he cast the final word of the spell and this time a green glob of acid shot from his outstretched hand. Thankfully for the goblin now cornered by the otyugh the acid struck right into the body of the otyugh and had an immediate effect. The sound emanating from its mouth must have been what it was like for it to scream although it was gargled as it still had the first goblin it had dispatched in its mouth. It turned in Havander's direction while the acid continued to burn into its skin.

Hearing the awful sound coming from the otyugh took both goblins by surprise. The second goblin had regained his senses and seeing his other friend taking advantage of the distracted monster had him doing the same. They both jumped in at the otyugh now trying to pull itself towards Havander. Their swords both stabbed deep in the creatures flesh. The otyugh began thrashing around, slamming its own body into the solid stone and gore beneath it while lashing out wildly with its two spiked tentacles. The goblins amazingly ducked each time and continued slashing with their swords taking hunks of flesh out of the otyugh.

Inspired by the courage of the goblins Havander kept firing magic missiles into the pained creature hoping to keep its attention on him. It didn't seem to work but anything he could do to help was the only thing on his mind. The goblin's luck on the left of the otyugh ran out finally as the tentacle on that side wrapped around its body. The spikes dug in deep though it didn't matter much. The otyugh lifted it to the max reach of its tentacle above the ground and slammed the goblin head first into the ground ending his life.

"This goes too far. He has advanced too close to the otyugh. It can reach him now if it so wishes. Havander needs to give up and run." Usarus declared.

"It is not for us to decide. Besides the otyugh will never break his bindings. As long as Havander stays out of reach a while longer he will exhaust his spell uses and be forced to try the exit available to him." Master Rischer expounded.

Josef said nothing but his eyes went wide as Havander finished casting another spell. Out before him a spectral hand appeared. Josef immediately noted the stares of both Rischer and Usarus on him. Once again Havander had enacted a spell of necromancy. One that should probably be out of the reach of Havander's power, not to mention the only way he could have learned it was from Josef.

Havander thrust his sword into the spectral hand's grasp that he had just enacted and sent it with a thought above the creature. The otyugh was distracted from him once again as it corned the last goblin against the wall. It had one tentacle extended towards the wall to act like a barrier while the other swept in landing a blow with its spiked end into the face of the goblin. Half of the goblin's face was torn away including his eye. As it screamed in horror the otyugh grabbed him up with both tentacles and pulled it into its mouth.

Now alone Havander played out what he hoped would be his final move. The sword he was carrying was a longsword, which had considerably more length than the short swords carried by goblins. It was now in his spectral hand above the creature, poised to strike. On Havander's silent command the sword was thrust downwards impaling the monster right in the middle of its back all the way to the hilt.

Havander lost control of his spectral hand just as the otyugh began thrashing about wildly once more. He felt dizzy but elated that his plan had worked. He watched as the thrashing continued. He hoped it was enough to kill the stubborn creature. Finally the thrashing stopped as the tentacles with the eyes locked onto Havander. The otyugh let out another horrible scream in his direction and began pulling itself towards him.

While advancing the otyugh used one tentacle to grab at the sword in its back and pulled it out and then launched it in Havander's direction. It skipped off of the wall behind Havander; badly missing but a second later it was followed by the body of its last victim. The torn carcass of the goblin hit Havander in his legs as he tried to jump over the flying goblin missile. He landed hard on his face.

Another wave of dizziness came over Havander. This one derived from the impact of his head hitting the ground. He shook it away and reached up wiping the blood from his nose. He looked at the blood on his hand and a feeling of ferocity came over him. The otyugh was just about within striking distance of him when he jumped up and cast a continual light spell right into the eyes of the monster that had so earned his rage. As the creature recoiled from the light, losing sight of its prey, Havander ran around its left flank in close proximity to it while enacting yet another spell.

He touched his thumbs together and spread his hands out like a fan. When he reached the final syllable of the spell a searing hot wave of flames erupted from his hands engulfing the otyugh entirely. Havander kept moving to its backside all the while shouting in defiance of the creature that still continuously thrashed around. After what seemed like forever to Havander, the otyugh finally crashed to the ground unmoving. Only then did Havander relent. When he was finished he fell to one knee and clutched at his chest while gasping for breath. When he felt mostly recovered he looked behind him to the exit sign and forced himself to his feet and walked staggeringly towards it.

"I want an explanation Josef!" Headmaster Usarus shouted at Master Righe in his office.

Immediately following the test that Havander had just passed in a most extraordinary way Headmaster Usarus insisted on having a private conversation with Josef in his office.

"I'll not be spoken to in that tone old friend." Josef countered.

Usarus seemed about to explode. His face was flush and he slammed both fists down onto his desk. Josef waited as Usarus played out his anger. Finally Usarus looked back up to Josef and raised his hands in submission and took his seat while taking steadying breaths.

R. A. HAYDEN

"Okay old friend." Usarus said somewhat sarcastically. "Explain what we just witnessed. Havander did not learn necromancy spells on his own nor did he learn any while here at Hareth."

"You know the answer to that. I taught him of course." Josef said while finding his seat opposite of Usarus.

"Why would you do such a thing? You know we do not condone the teaching of necromancy to students."

"Oh come now Usarus. Was it not you who personally animated the skeletons used in every test today? Sounds like hypocrisy to me."

Once again Usarus raised his voice though not to the full extent as before. "It is not hypocrisy. Students are forbidden from learning such skills. I'll not have another Braden Aranor happen under my watch."

"One has nothing to do with the other. Braden Aranor was not a student when he discovered vampirism. He was the last master of necromancy at this school."

"Yes and he was the most proficient necromancer student this school had ever seen thus earning him the rank of Head of Necromancy in The Orders at a far younger age than any prior or after his time." Usarus argued.

Josef shrugged his shoulders. He had no real argument other than to trust in the heart of his apprentice. "What do you want me to say Usarus? It is done. And I might add it was you who tested him for every known discipline of arcane magic when he first arrived at the school. You want that I should deny him the practice. Both you and I, as well as others in this school are capable of casting necromancy spells."

"Not a good point Josef. Necromancy is far too influential on a young person's mind. It corrupts and deceives one into thinking they are the master of death itself."

"He has not learned skills that would allow him to raise the dead or create undead monstrosities. He has merely dabbled in the art."

"That didn't look like dabbling to me. He's too young to even be able to cast a couple of those spells he used and he cast from seven of the eight different disciplines in the timeframe of a short test."

Josef actually gave a little laugh at that. "You know as well as I that he could have cast from all eight."

"This isn't funny Josef."

"Oh come off it. It was you who knew he was unique well before you ever introduced him to me. Hareth Academy taught him far more than

I did in the last eight school years than I did in the last seven summers. You should be proud. We have another human sorcerer in our midst."

"Hmph sorcerer. He's far too young to gain the title."

"If memory serves you were a sorcerer at his age as well Usarus."

"Yes but not with that much proficiency. I merely knew I had the capability to do so. I did not truly begin to dabble in necromancy until I was far older and wiser."

"What of it then? Would you deny him a place here as a member of Hareth. It is Hareth's rules that grant him the title. If you so worry about him being corrupted by his own power than he will need our guidance more than ever."

Usarus leaned back in his chair rubbing his temples with his fingers. He knew very well he could not deny Havander anything. He was much beloved among the staff of Hareth Academy. Even if he could he knew Havander planned to stay as the apprentice of Josef anyway. He would become a member of The Silver Guard just as he had always suspected those years ago when he first introduced Josef and Havander. He did not foresee Havander becoming this powerful at such a young age though. Neither did he foresee Josef raising a black dragonborn in the midst of everything else going on. Usarus felt overwhelmed at the moment. "Fine my friend. This is out of my hands as it were. Yet I wish you to stress the importance on him of limiting his use of power. As you well know it can destroy him just as easily as it could give him great power."

CHAPTER TWENTY-ONE

Birthdays—Fhurin, 1021

"THEY ARE WALKING up the road. Hurry everyone come inside." Georgette hollered out the back door of Silver Guard Keep to Josef, Oran, and Adley.

The Keep was more full of people than usual. Georgette had collaborated with Josef on a surprise for Willem, Havander and Marcus. Being that Havander and Marcus both had their birthdays in Fhurin, the first month of autumn, and Willem never truly knew when his was when they first took him in, they had decided to celebrate all of theirs together. Earlier that day Harold had talked the boys into going fishing so that Georgette and Mrs. Barrie could prepare everything for the party in secret.

Havander was the only one who truly needed convincing since he hardly pulled himself away from his studies all summer, determined to learn as much as possible in the least amount of time it seemed. At last Josef stepped in and ordered him to go.

Now the time was upon them as the boys reached the bottom steps. Along with celebrating their birthdays, Havander and Willem were to be inducted as full members of The Silver Guard. Among other things their gifts consisted of a brand new set of custom leather armor for Willem along with twin blades designed specifically for him, while Havander was to receive a makeshift cloak more to his liking than the traditional robes worn by wizards. Beneath that he would also be getting a set of leather armor for his chest piece anyway, though it wasn't as intricate or designed for much more than appearance unlike Willem's whose armor was designed for stealth and quickness besides the protections it offered. Along with that they would receive full sets of clothes that matched their new outfits provided by Georgette who had a considerable hand in their design from Mrs. Barrie. Not to leave out Marcus he would also be getting new clothes and his first set of practice armor. Georgette had argued against it but Harold won out in his choice to give Marcus his first blade as well.

Havander was the first to push through the doors of the Keep with Willem and Marcus right behind aided considerably by Harold who rushed them through trying not to drop the considerable catch of fish he was toting. All of the torches and lanterns were out. Even the braziers set about the corners of the fireplace in the center of the main hall were out. Unsure of what was happening both Havander and Willem grabbed for their blades. All at once the lanterns and torches lit up from a command word from Josef and a great cheer of congratulations met them at the top of the stairs, by more people than any of them had seen at the Keep at one time.

Georgette was first to meet them as she ran to the stairs embracing Marcus with a hug while Havander and Willem replaced their blades in their respective sheaths. Havander and Willem looked to one another in disbelief. Along with the usual inhabitants of the Keep, Captain Payne and choice members of his soldiers, the Barries, Escott Claridge, and Armihrmond Firefist alongside an unknown dwarf to the two of them, were all in attendance.

Georgette grabbed them both by their hands and pulled them down the stairs towards the crowd. As they neared the central fireplace Adley came forth providing each with a full mug of ale and then gave Marcus a glass of cider. Set on the tables surrounding the fireplace was the largest feast the three had ever seen set out in the Keep and on the table to the left was three sets of clothes, armor and various other packages lined up.

"What is going on?" Willem asked.

Oran stood on top of a chair in the center of the back of the room and shouted for everyone's attention. Once everyone quieted Oran began, "Friends and neighbors we have met here today for a few reasons. First everyone here would like to wish the three of you a happy birthday."

Everyone in the crowd raised a mug and cheered for the three then took a drink. Willem not wanting to miss out tipped his mug up as well.

"Second we want to congratulate young Marcus for being the youngest person to ever start training to become a member of The Silver Guard."

Another cheer and hug from Georgette had Marcus blushing.

"And finally I need to hurry this up because Harold looks as though he is going to drop all of those fish."

The crowd laughed and Harold shook his head in agreement while urging someone to give him a mug as well.

"No, finally we are here on a serious note to welcome Havander and Willem as honorary members of The Silver Guard." Oran finished with a sincere bow to his young students.

The crowd cheered even louder aided considerably by Captain Payne who likewise stood on top of a chair yelling and then chugged the rest of his ale.

Shouts from Armihrmond and the soldiers urging the boys to do the same erupted. Willem turned to Havander and they clashed their mugs together and followed suit.

After the initial shock and personal greetings and congratulations from everyone in attendance they were treated to their new clothes and armor and Georgette insisted that the three try them on immediately. Marcus was the hardest to pull away from his other gifts and continuously stuffed candy and other sweets into his mouth provided by the Barries as Harold and Adley pushed him towards his room. He was also the first to emerge in his new outfit, having only to go to his room upstairs and aided by Harold and Adley in securing the armor on properly. He strolled out in his padded leather armor set puffing his chest out. The armor was far too large for him and was made so on purpose by Armihrmond since everyone knew he had a lot of growing to do and was doing so rapidly. Nonetheless he looked quite the little soldier in his armor.

Josef whispered to Armihrmond, "Hopefully he doesn't outgrow that too fast."

Armihrmond responded, "No matter its only for practice. Wait till you see what I've got in store for him once he's grown."

"We've not asked for that. What if he turns to magic later?"

"Ha. Look there old friend. That's a warrior if ever I've been seein one. And I make all your boys' armor. You contract out with someone else and I'll be takin it all back."

Josef looked back to Marcus just as Harold kneeled in front of him and waved Captain Payne over who was holding Harold's gift for Marcus in his hands. He had to agree with Armihrmond's assessment. Marcus did fit in well as a warrior.

As Captain Payne handed the short sword over to Harold, Marcus' eyes seemed to light up even with his dark orbs. Harold started, "Now Marcus I want you to listen carefully. This is no toy. You are not to swing it about anywhere unless on the training grounds with Oran, Willem, or Adley. Do you understand?"

Marcus couldn't wait to get the sword in his hands and his fists clenched and unclenched in anticipation. "Yes sir."

"If you do so I'll have to take it away and Georgette is going to give both of us a royal ass whippin." Harold alleged and behind Marcus he could see Adley nodding in agreement. "Careful now." Harold added as he held the scabbard out so that Marcus could pull the sword from it.

Marcus was giddy with delight. The sword in his hands was relative in size to a longsword might be in a fully-grown person's hands. Harold knew he would outgrow the sword eventually but he had Josef go through the process of enchanting the weapon as he did with all of the weapons for Silver Guard members. Marcus held it up before his dark eyes and examined the work. The duel edged blade was of typical design, not flashy or overly ornate. The cross-guard was fairly straight forward as well, not overly large but not as short as the crosspieces of a Castan infantry sword either. The grip was black and fed into the silver pommel, which was rounded on the end and sported the only design on the sword in the form of grooves etched into the metal running lengthwise until it reached the ball on the end.

"Can I go practice?" Marcus asked.

"I don't see why not." Harold replied.

Marcus took off like a bolt towards the back door, not bothering to sheath his new weapon. Harold and Adley were in hurried pursuit and as they passed Georgette who stood with hands on hips giving each of them a stern look. They hung their heads averting her gaze and then picked up their pace.

R. A. HAYDEN

Willem and Havander both reached the top of the stair at the same time coming back up to show off their new attire. Josef and Oran shared a glance of appreciation for each other's insights into designing the outfits between one another.

Willem and Havander walked over to Josef and Oran who were standing with Armihrmond and his guest. Upon reaching them Oran held out a leather toolkit to Willem, and Josef did the same for Havander. Both knew what was inside having seen the same kind of toolkit among Adley's things.

"Alright more daggers. I know just where to put them." Willem announced having already strapped his curved blade to its accustomed place across his back beltline and as his new armor sported a strap across his chest from his left shoulder down to his right hip, over the four gold buckles running down the middle of his chest that locked the four tiered plackart across his chest and abdomen, he thought he could secure the throwing daggers there.

Willem's matching armor was all dark brown leather with gold colored buckles and metal work to bind it all together. It comprised of matching pauldrons over each shoulder that snug tightly to the rerebrace over the upper arm. Each arm supported a matching vambrace and the legs matching greaves. Attached to the plackart were faulds that hung down to his mid thighs.

"Looks like it's missing something." Oran said while examining the fit, especially the plackarts, which stood out having no weapons strapped across them.

"Right my new silver stake. I'm not sure where I'll put that." Willem said while examining the three pockets that were attached to the strap that ran across his chest.

"No not what I was thinking. Though I don't know where you will put that either." Oran grabbed a belt from Armihrmond and handed it to Willem. Attached to the belt were two short swords with extra long hilts and a loop connected to one side of the single edged blades so that one may twirl the blades in their hands if they so wished.

As Willem excitedly strapped the blades around his waist Armihrmond said, "Now I don't know why you wanted blades that thin. Look more like toothpicks if you ask me but don't ya be doubtin they are as strong as any other blade that met my forge. Made the grips extra long so you can use two hands on one if you have to defend from a heavy blow."

Willem finished strapping the belt to his waist and then pulled forth both blades. His fingers went automatically to the loops that acted as the crosspieces and began spinning them. He spun twice and admired the balance that each blade had.

"Fine blades Armihrmond. Better than any I've ever wielded." Willem placed his blades back in their sheaths and then moved to Armihrmond to give him a forearm shake.

"Oh Willem. This is my nephew by the way. Denstrom Firefist. His father is chief to the Firefist clan in the Talts."

Willem extended another shake to Denstrom. "Pleasure."

"You weren't kiddin Armihrmond. This boys no taller than us and half the weight easy." Denstrom joked though Willem wasn't exactly that short.

All in attendance shared in the laugh except Havander who was searching through his toolkit.

"Aye but wait until you see him use those blades. That'll give your head something to think about." Armihrmond declared.

"Good idea. Where is Sarge?" Willem asked.

"Out back practicing with Marcus." Oran answered.

"Why didn't you say so? Let's go Denstrom." Willem said as he began moving past his audience.

"Hold on Willem." Josef called after him and everyone else following except for Oran. He picked up a coat from the nearby lounge chair and threw it at Willem. "That there is from Adley."

Willem examined the coat quickly and then threw it on. It was of matching color to his fine suit of leather armor except it was trimmed in a dark forest green. It had a high collar and hidden inside pockets, perfect for a little thief like Willem who liked to conceal everything. "This is perfect." Willem said.

"Good. Now go tell him that." Josef said as he turned back towards Havander who was still searching through the items in his toolkit. "Here Havander. This is from Adley as well." He handed over a dagger with an ivory handle. "It's not spelled yet like Willem's blades but I thought you might want to have a hand in that."

"This is most gracious Master. I would have never imagined." Havander thanked as he took the long double-edged blade out of its sheath and examined the thin blade and then the ivory handle with silver pommel. The dagger was exceptional and he would have to remember to keep it clear of Willem and his love for unique blades.

"Well tell me what you think of your new attire. More fitting than the robes you have grown to dislike?"

Havander looked down to his new set of pants and leather tunic. His pants and knee-high boots were of matching dark gray in color. The tunic was dark blue and had a matching cloak with hood. The cloak was trimmed in the same dark gray as the tunic and had a circle design stitched into the shoulder and a matching design stitched into each forearm of the tunic.

"I like it very much Master." Havander said though not very convincingly.

"What's wrong Havander?" Josef asked.

"It's nothing Master."

"Come on. Out with it."

"I was looking through my new toolkit and I believe I'm missing something."

Josef knew already that that was what Havander was looking for previously. "I know Havander. You're not getting one of those unless you absolutely insist."

Havander was shocked to some degree. All members of The Silver Guard carried the same silver stake. "I don't understand master."

"It's quite simple Havander. You are not that great with melee combat with a sword or dagger so I found something more befitting to your fighting style. It also matches the new look." Josef finished with reaching out his left arm and presenting Etburn before Havander.

Now Havander was truly in shock. He looked over Josef and Oran's shoulders to those who were not presently outside watching Willem spar with Adley. Georgette was finishing preparations so that the meal could begin and everyone else was in their own conversation and not paying attention to the three of them. He looked back to Josef. "You can't mean it sir. I cannot."

Oran cleared his throat and stepped closer to Havander. "Listen son. If you are to take our name as the three of us have discussed then it is only befitting that you carry a weapon befitting of the name."

"But Etburn was a founding member of The Silver Guard. He forged the staff himself. I'm not worthy to carry such a famed weapon." Havander argued.

"Actually Markus Etburn could not forge this weapon on his own. He wasn't much of a mage. To be honest he was more warrior than mage." Josef declared.

"Marcus? Like our Marcus? Is he named after Markus Etburn?" Havander inquired, having never heard of his first name before. In history he was always referred to as Etburn alone.

"No they spelled it different and our Marcus is named after Cecilia's father."

"But still that can't be. He is famed for his magical abilities and the forging of this staff." Havander looked from Josef to Oran.

"Don't look at me." Oran said. "I never knew the man. He passed before I was born."

Josef stepped in, "Havander, Markus Etburn was not a mage of any kind. He was an elemental. The only lightning elemental I've ever seen or heard about. He didn't cast spells. His one power was total dominance over lightning. He could use it at will with little cost to his strength. It was as easy for him to cast lightning as it is for Oran here to swing a sword."

Havander was in disbelief. He knew of elementals of course. Elementals were not of this plane and consisted primarily in the form of air, earth, fire or water. Wizards who could summon an elemental quickly found themselves with a powerful ally or a disastrous event if they could not control it. He knew too that certain individuals could be considered elementals. Individuals with a talent towards a particular element and can only cast spells pertaining to that element. Master Rischer of Hareth Academy was often talked about behind his back for being a fire elemental although he was not. He was however more in tune with spells dealing with fire than most wizards. Etburn, according to the history books concerning The Silver Guard had always been referred to as though he was a wizard. "Than how did he create the staff?"

"I created it for him. His dying wish was that his power could be harnessed and used by other generations of Silver Guard members."

"But how? That's impossible."

"It's a transfer of magical energy spell. Few in this world are capable of such a spell. To take the power of something or someone as strong as

Etburn and transfer it into something else without losing it or killing yourself in the process is beyond exceptional."

"So the weapon is sentient with the soul of Markus Etburn?"

"No that's different. The staff is not living and has no will of its own. I merely transferred his elemental energy into the staff."

"So it only casts lightning?"

"Well yes and no."

"What do you mean?"

"It didn't work fully. The staff's power can diminish but it takes a very long time to do so."

"How do you get it back to full strength."

"That's easy. Simply walk out into a lightning storm."

"And let myself get hit? I don't think so." Havander protested not liking the sound of that outcome in the least.

"It doesn't hurt you. That was really what I mean by yes and no. It is an additional bonus behind this staff. It allows more than being able to cast lightning at will. As long as you have it in your grasp no lightning based spell can harm you. It's absorbed into the staff."

"That's incredible." Havander said in awe.

"Yes and it's a great advantage in a spell duel. Not only that but other energy based spells will hurt you less."

"Less?"

"Yes. The staff or your body, as long as you are holding onto it, will absorb some of the power of a spell. Minor spells like magic missile will seem like virtually nothing to you. More powerful spells however are beyond its ability to absorb all of their power."

"But Master Righe what about you?"

"Oh my spell abilities are far beyond yours Havander. I have much less need than you for a staff such as this. It is time it had a new owner. One I know will protect it with his very life."

Oran weighed in again still sensing a reluctance to take Etburn from Havander, "It's not like this is negotiable. You'll take it as a condition of your acceptance in The Silver Guard."

Josef was surprised by the ultimatum but it seemed a good tactic to end the debate.

Havander could see no lie in Oran's eyes as he made his declaration. He searched for the confidence within himself to be worthy of such a prize possession. Finally he reached out his right arm. Josef placed the staff in his grip. Immediately Havander could feel its power as though it was coursing through his veins. His hair stood on end and his teeth locked together. He could feel them grinding together as he tried to separate them. What felt like minutes passed in just seconds. When it was finished he felt rejuvenated as though he had just woken from a full nights rest.

Oran extended his left arm. "Welcome to the family Havander Righe."

Havander embraced Oran and instantly Oran shot away from him and landed next to the table ten feet away.

"Oh yes. I guess I'll have to show you how not to do that." Josef said while trying not to laugh.

Havander ran to Oran to see if he was all right but Oran protested, "Don't touch me. I'm fine. Just a little shock is all."

Willem and Oran were outback sparring as the party continued not long after Oran shook all the cobwebs from his head after receiving a waking shock from Havander. They had a crowd urging them on as steel clashed against steel. Willem was feeling overly cocky with his new blades in hand and Oran could tell he was overstepping just a bit too much. Oran was using two normal short swords from their personal armory, which was not his favored weapons but he could use them as effective if not more than Willem. Oran however could feel the years catching up to him finally and it took most of what he had to keep Willem at bay anymore. He still had a couple tricks up his sleeve though and on one encounter he feigned an opening for Willem to strike, which he tried to take advantage of and instead ended up the with pommel of Oran's right hand weapon hitting him in the temple and laying him flat.

Breathing hard to little degree Oran stood over Willem and said, "Not bad but you have one enormous problem still."

"What's that?" Willem asked even though he already knew the answer.

"Your ego of course." Oran said while extending his hand to assist Willem to his feet.

The crowd cheered and the ale was flowing quickly at the climax of the sparring match. Georgette appeared out of the back door and announced that dinner was ready. The crowd started filing in but Oran halted Willem so that they may have a chat together.

When everyone was inside Oran lay down his swords on the deck and took a ring from his pocket. "Here I want you to take this."

Willem took the ring and looked to Oran. "Jewelry is not really my style Boss."

"It's not just jewelry. It is spelled or enchanted. However you want to say it."

"Truly. Why give it to me?" Willem said as he examined the ring.

"Because you've earned it. And because you are going to find that now that you are a full member you are going to be facing enemies that have advantages over someone such as us."

"Yeah but our swordsmanship is enough. Besides I'm not a huge fan of magic."

"Oh really. Is that why you begged me to have Josef spell that ridiculous curved blade of yours with a defiance spell so that you are immune to fear and compulsion spells?"

"Hey Havander used that stupid charm spell on me once and had me running errands for him and cleaning his room. I don't want that to ever happen again."

"Good point but if you weren't so susceptible to your own whims or distractions those spells wouldn't work on you effectively. But that will be the least of your problems when facing those that wield magic. Besides, I believe you will like this." Oran finished indicating the ring that Willem was holding.

"Why? What does it do?"

Oran took the ring back from Willem. The band on the ring was black leather with small silver colored studs placed evenly around its perimeter on both edges. Wrapped around the center of the leather, in an embrace, was a silver spider whose legs wrapped completely around it. "Now you'll probably have to wear this on your thumb like I do. I took it off of the pinky of a drow. I don't know how he wore it there. It feels too awkward on my fingers given its unusual width. But don't worry, the spider will magically resize its legs to fit whatever digit you put it on."

"That's creepy."

Oran placed the ring on his thumb and moved over to the outside wall of the Keep. Like a spider climbing up a wall, Oran crawled up the sheer surface. At about twenty feet high he flipped over so that his boots were flush to the wall along with his backside and he waved with one hand showing that you could indeed let go to some extent. After, he slid down the wall like a spider sliding down a piece of its webbing.

"I don't know what to say. I can't believe that's even possible." Willem said in absolute awe as Oran placed the ring back in his hand.

"Say nothing to no one." Oran suggested.

"What do you mean?"

"Well you don't want everyone knowing your secrets. Josef doesn't even know I have that spider ring."

"Really?"

"Oh yeah. I've gotten into places that were supposedly impregnable with that little thing. Josef still doesn't know how I did it. I merely shrug and say trade secret. It also allows you to jump a bit higher or further depending on the situation as well. Something to do with what kind of spider it was modeled after."

Oran discovered after having its properties identified by a wizard in the trade district of Tomé, that the ring was modeled after a so-called jumping spider that dwells in the underdark.

"So all that time we spent using grappling hooks to get over walls and climbing in high windows was useless."

"Not at all. Those are good skills to have. I keep those sorts of things with me when I go out on a mission though I rarely use them. It helps keep the illusion alive for others."

"So you are just a big liar." Willem accused sarcastically.

"I like to refer to it as a clever assassin. Or thief if you like. Depends on what you are doing."

"Can I try it?"

"Uh, not now. Georgette is gonna come yelling for us anytime I can feel it. Tomorrow I'll teach you how to use it. In the meantime tuck it away. Like I said you don't want everyone knowing what you can do."

At dinner Havander called everyone to attention. "I have an announcement to make if you please." Everyone quieted down and

R. A. HAYDEN

looked Havander's way. "First I would like to thank everyone for this wondrous day. Thanks to Georgette and Mrs. Barrie for a fine meal. Thanks to everyone for such wonderful gifts. Most of all I would like to thank Josef and Oran Righe for my induction as a member of The Silver Guard."

"Here, here." Adley yelled and then took a big drink from his mug.

Everyone else did the same and when finished Havander had to quiet the room back down once more. "Hold on I'm not done. Now as many of you know I was orphaned before I met Master Righe and by his acceptance I was welcomed into this family. In honor of that, after discussing it with Josef and Oran, we have decided that I shall take on the name of Righe from this day forth." Havander finished with raising his mug in a toast but the reaction he got was not as forthcoming as he had hoped. Everyone was filled with the same question that did not already know of the announcement. Adley, Harold, and Georgette knew but everyone else was dumbfounded and those who knew had apparently not thought about it.

Willem broke the awkward silence with the obvious question, "So wait. Does that make Josef or Oran your father? Or is it both?"

Josef spit out some of the wine he had just taken a sip of waiting for the awkward silence to break, which brought a great cheer and laughter throughout the hall.

"And how does that work anyway? Can anyone do that?" Willem asked further through the laughter.

"Why do you ask Willem?" Havander questioned expecting another punch line coming.

"Well I don't remember the last name of my parents. Could I take another last name?" Willem continued.

Josef stood while still wiping the wine from his goatee. "First off lets say I'm the step father and Oran can be the much older brother. Sound fair. Now Willem would you like to do the same?"

"Are you kiddin. I'll take Lindsey after Mom and Harold over here. I don't want any of that mess you three got goin on." Willem finished with reaching over and grabbing Georgette sitting next to him and kissing her on the cheek to the roar of laughter and cheers from their guests.

Josef slumped his head in mock embarrassment. "Well said young man."

When it quieted to a dull roar once more and Georgette was finished hugging Willem he couldn't help but try one more jab. "Hey Sarge what's your last name? You want to get in on this?"

Oran spoke up before Adley could answer, "Uh, he doesn't like to tell people his last name. Sounds too much like a girl's name."

Without missing a beat Adley responded, "You mean like Lindsey."

In-between the raucous laughter Willem could hear Havander. "Ah short little Lindsey girl."

Marcus exited the front gate of the Keep with his new armor and sword strapped to his side. It was after midnight and all who did not follow the party down to the tavern were asleep at the Keep giving Marcus the first opportunity he had all day to practice with his newly acquired weapon without being told to be careful. He often slipped out at night over the past year since he had so much trouble sleeping. He enjoyed walking the perimeter of the Keep and looking for the creatures of the night. With his keen night vision the dark didn't bother him at all and he actually preferred it to the daytime.

On this night Marcus went to the far side of The Silver Guard Cemetery so that he could do battle with imaginary zombies and ghouls. After dispatching one particularly troublesome creature he stopped his make believe battle upon seeing a man approaching him from town. Drunks often spilled out of the back of the taverns in Lanos as Marcus had learned during his expeditions through town when he was feeling extra adventurous but this man was walking in a straight line directly at him as though he was taking a midnight stroll of his own to a predetermined destination.

When the man got close enough to be heard without shouting he addressed Marcus. "Pleasant evening isn't it young Marcus?"

Marcus raised his sword in front of him with both hands. He didn't recognize the stranger in the least. "Do I know you?"

"Oh please forgive me. Of course you wouldn't remember. I haven't seen you since you were a babe."

"Who are you?" Marcus asked not lowering his blade.

"You are right to be wary but not to worry I'm and old friend of the Righe's. In fact I just came from the Willow Bark Tavern where Oran is still celebrating with Willem and Havander. I thought I would stop by the Keep to visit Josef if he was up and about."

"He's gone to bed I think."

"Oh best not to wake him then. It's fortunate that you are up and about tonight though."

"It is?"

"Yes indeed. It's my understanding that it's your birthday."

"Not quite but we celebrated it today along with Willem and Havander's."

"Lets see that would make you seven I believe."

Marcus lowered his sword. This man's words had disarmed him to some extent since he was so familiar with everyone.

"I see too that you were presented with a wonderful new weapon."

"Yes sir. My father gave it to me as a gift."

"So that you can begin your training no doubt."

"Yes sir. I'm supposed to start tomorrow if everyone is not too hung over."

"Ah a very perceptive and knowledgeable young man you are becoming. Well I'd best not keep you up all night chattering then. It's fortunate I caught you out then so not to wake everyone at the Keep. I've brought you a gift as well though I'm not sure that Georgette and Harold would approve of it."

"What is it?" Marcus said with renewed interest after hearing it might not be approved by his mother and father.

The man kneeled down and produced a small dagger, sheathed. "It's not as large as your weapon you hold there but alas Harold did not tell me that he was getting you a weapon."

Marcus took a step closer to better examine the hilt of the dagger sticking out towards him. There was enough light from the moon and stars that Marcus could see color this close up and the red gem that made up the pommel of the dagger shined brightly even in the lowlight. Marcus looked up to the man's face and could see the red trim around his dark pupils, which matched nicely to the gem in the dagger.

"This is really for me?" Marcus asked incredulously, knowing that the red gem in the pommel was indeed a ruby and a sizeable one at that. It was obviously very expensive.

"Why yes of course but I would ask one favor."

Marcus found that comment a bit dubious and he backed up a step. "What's that?"

"Well your family in the Keep doesn't see me often. Not nearly as often as I see them but I would not like to spoil my invitation back so I would just have you keep it a secret so that I don't earn the ill will of Georgette or anyone else. Could you do that?"

"I guess so." Marcus replied, confused a bit by the stranger's last statement.

He tossed the dagger to Marcus and revealed a grin showing his fangs that went unnoticed by Marcus, as he was too busy catching the dagger. "A bargain well struck then."

Marcus unsheathed the dagger. It was a small dagger, which would make it easier to conceal. He liked the feel of it in his hand and the design was unlike any he had ever seen. There was no crosspiece and the design on the grip was made of solid steel with various designs running down the handle.

"I'll return back to the tavern now to check in on our friends. I'd hurry off to bed if I were you so that you are rested for tomorrow. Please remember to not leave that lying about so that anyone can see it."

"I will sir. And thank you."

"One more thing Marcus. And this is of the utmost importance. If you are ever in serious danger, you need only speak my name into the jewel pommel and I'll be able to be at your side very soon."

"What is your name sir?"

"You may call me Braden." The Fallen One said as he turned and walked back towards town, leaving Marcus alone once again.

PART III

Battle

CHAPTER TWENTY-TWO

Firefist Troubles—Fhurin, 1021

D ENSTROM FIREFIST WAS anxious to get back to his village and his pace quickened, spurred by the onset of the road leading to where his clan's village was nestled in-between two peaks in the Talt Mountains. Travel had been slow the week prior as not far east of Lanos the roads ceased to exist and the trees thickened with the onset of the low hills set before the mountains. The Firefist Clan had built a road traveling most of the width of the valley, running west to east, which their large village lay within and it was this road, which Denstrom and his companions had just come upon. The legs of the horses bearing his newest allies were thankful for the quickened pace due to the need to stretch their legs after riding alongside the ponies that Denstrom and three of his clan members were riding and didn't offer many chances for their longer stride.

Willem spurred his horse along and caught up to Denstrom leading the company of dwarves as well as himself, Oran and Havander. "How much further my friend?"

"Couple a hours now. Oran knows. He has been inside my village many times." Denstrom replied as he looked back in his saddle to those trailing close behind him.

"Beautiful valley this is." Willem said as he admired a glimpse through a break in the tress at the tall peak to his right. "You know this is my first trip into the Talts?"

"Aye, so you've mentioned. Unfortunate it is that you are here for battle and not to take in the sights." Denstrom lamented.

Denstrom's purpose in visiting Lanos the week prior was not just a friendly visit to his uncle, Armihrmond, but rather the need to ask The

Silver Guard for assistance. The Firefist Clan had been under siege for the past month by an enemy unfamiliar to them. They had been battling orcs, who often attempted to pass their valley so that they may raid in the human lands to the west. All hill dwarf clans battled with orcs on a regular basis, but this particular orc raiding party had allied itself with something as yet unseen and their purpose seemed not at all to pass through the valley but to eliminate the dwarves all together.

"I do not mind Denstrom. As I am officially a member of The Silver Guard it is an honor that my first real mission is in service to the Firefist Clan." Willem asserted.

Denstrom turned around in his saddle once more looking to Havander who was riding farthest back alongside Oran then turned to Willem, "Not sure your mage shares the sentiment. Pity Josef could not make the trip. My father had hoped to see him once again."

Willem smiled at the remark. "Ah, he's just not used to the road is all. And I'm sure he figured he'd have more time with his books before starting out a mission."

"What of you?"

"Trial by fire as Sarge would put it. I long to test my newly acquired equipment forged by your most generous uncle."

"Hah. Generous you say." Denstrom shook his head. "Do you have any idea how much he charges you boys when making armor and weapons for ya?"

Willem's facial expression changed to one of a questioning frown. "Hadn't really thought about it. I didn't pay. Mine were a gift."

"I do. He told me as much." Denstrom finished with a hardy laugh as if in some private joke that Willem didn't understand.

"I don't get it Denstrom."

"Oh it's nothing lad. You know my uncle could once of been chief if he so desired."

"No I did not know that."

"He is the eldest between my father and he."

"Why isn't he then?"

"Long story but lets just say he caught a traveling bug in his youth. Found it was easier to take gems, gold, and metal from enemies rather than mine them. Preferred it so much he never returned to take his place as chief when his father passed on leaving it to my father instead."

"Why not return now? He's past age of adventuring it would seem."

"Because lad. He's got you boys paying his outrageous prices. Always a good metal worker that one, but he's got his own gold supply coming from The Silver Guard. Has for years." Denstrom finished again with a good laugh and spurred his pony on even faster to hasten the trip through the winding road.

Oran, Willem and Havander followed Denstrom as they entered the hall of his father, Dalin. Outside, the village was bustling with activity as the dwarves, both Firefist Clan members and dwarves from close by clans who had come at the call of Dalin Firefist to join in the fight against the orcs now pressing from the east. All were preparing for battle and adding fortifications to the perimeter of the large village.

Firefist Village, as it was called, was the largest hill dwarf village in the Talt Mountains. There fighting strength boasted over a hundred fighting dwarves whereas most other clan villages were small in comparison having usually around twenty fighters. Other villages were often higher up in elevation as well for easier access to the ore and gems they loved to mine. Unlike mountain dwarves, who built huge underground homes and tunnels and whose numbers could be in the thousands, hill dwarf communities preferred to have a lifestyle consisting of the open air alongside their much smaller mines. They also enjoyed mining from streams and the ability to take advantage of the bounty that the forest can provide such as game and in a small measure farming opportunities.

When Denstrom entered the main hall, which was the largest building in Firefist Village, consisting of a mead hall, which served as a central meeting place and was large enough for most of the village to linger so that all the dwarves had a place to share drink and mull over the days activities, he found his father and other clan chiefs surrounding a table with a map laid out.

When the four neared they caught Dalin Firefist's attention. "Ahh my son." Dalin left the table and embraced Denstrom. "Good that you have returned." He looked over to the familiar Oran and his two companions. "And not empty handed as I knew you wouldn't. He moved to Oran and welcomed him as well. "It has been long since my eyes have been upon you boy. Welcome."

Oran smirked at the term boy. It had been many years since he had laid eyes on Dalin Firefist and he knew he had aged considerably in appearance since last he saw him, although Dalin was probably not aware that Oran was probably older than he was but the sentiment was welcomed. "Well met Chief Firefist."

Dalin pushed Oran back from his embrace. "What have you brought with you?" Dalin then moved to stand in front of Willem and Havander. "And who be these youngsters?"

Oran introduced, "Dalin this is Willem and Havander."

Dalin shook hands with Havander and then Willem but before releasing Willem's hand he turned to Oran. "Bit young wouldn't you say?"

Oran and Havander shared a smile as Willem shook his head at the comment.

"I assure you Dalin, he is of fighting age." Oran said.

"Well I mean both." He said releasing Willem's hand and stepping in front of Havander once more and inspecting him further. His eyes went to Etburn. "Is that eh...?"

"It is." Oran confirmed.

Dalin stroked his long gray beard. "Well I had hoped Josef would show but seeing this has lifted spirits. We are going to need its power I assure you." Dalin finished with going back to the map and waving them near as he waved the clan chiefs back a step.

"What are we dealing with?" Oran asked as he looked down upon the map clearly showing their position and what appeared to be a large force shown on the map to the east with twice as many markers indicating apparent size of force.

Dalin turned to his son. "Did you not tell them?"

Denstrom replied, "As much as I could unless something else has come to light."

Oran looked to the concerned look on Dalin's face. "What is it?"

Dalin stroked his long beard again. "We don't know exactly."

"How do you mean?" Oran asked skeptically.

"I mean we truly don't know. The orcs send out small bands taking to the higher ground. Once we engage them they run like cowards and so we pursue. Then something as yet unseen assaults my men. Whatever lends strength to this orc hoard will not show itself."

"But you know there are orcs here." Oran said while pointing to the orc position on the map.

"Yes. And their numbers have swelled since I sent Denstrom for you. They stand over three hundred now. They have rallied more orcs and goblins to their ranks since we first encountered them."

"How do you know this?" Oran asked.

"Scouts or scout I should say." Dalin hung his head at having to remember the passing of more of his men. "We sent out six a week ago. Two pairs of three to better fight should they meet resistance. Only one returned and not unscathed. He returned heavily wounded but with the information about the enemy numbers. He passed shortly after his report from his wounds."

"What took your men if not orcs?"

"As I've said we have no idea. My scout reported not seeing what it was."

"Then how do we know it isn't just orcs?"

"Bah, orcs aren't that clever. They've made attacks as well but not in a pressing fashion. They are luring us out instead of their usual manner of fighting outright. Then whatever it is that is helping them attacks from the shadows. Never giving sight as to what it is. If it were just orcs my men would have routed them." Dalin declared with a firm nod.

"At night then?"

"No. During the day as well."

Oran looked to Willem and Havander to gage their reaction but none was forthcoming on their inexperienced faces, then back to Dalin. "I see your men preparing outside. What is your plan?"

"Well, we attack in force. Whatever it is can't kill us all."

"And what of the orcs beyond the pass?"

"We head straight for 'em."

Oran was shaking his head before he even finished. "I would ask a brief interval so that we may ascertain what it is we are up against." He said while pointing to Havander and Willem to indicate them all.

"If you are to do that you'd better see this." Dalin stated.

Oran, Havander, Willem and Denstrom followed Dalin to an adjacent room. Inside was the body of the scout who had passed the previous day. They were preparing him for funeral and thought to proceed with it that evening before heading out the next day. Dalin hoped the act would help enrage his fellow dwarves at seeing the passing of one of their own.

"Look here." Dalin said as he rolled the body over to its side revealing huge gashes running down his back. "He said it struck from behind as he attempted to run. He slid down an embankment after receiving the blow and ended up in a stream far below."

Oran leaned close to examine the wounds. The large wounds looked to be made by natural weapons and not that of a sharpened blade although individually they could have been inflicted by a sword but that was unlikely. Four similar marks ran the length of his back, two on either side of his spine.

Dalin said as Oran looked to the wounds, "He didn't last long once he got here. He could tell us nothing of what did this to him. He confirmed only that the orcs were gathering for an assault.

"What do you think Boss?" Willem asked as he too leaned in for a closer look before Dalin let the body lie flat once more.

Standing straight once more Oran said, "I'm not sure. My first thoughts were of a vampire even though attacking during the day is not typical of them. They can stand the daylight for only brief amounts of time and why one would ally with orcs is beyond me, so it must not be the case. That and they wouldn't typically bother with dwarves. They prefer to hunt humans. The wounds would indicate some form of large animal with huge claws to be able to inflict such large wounds. It would have to be intelligent though for it to form a bond with orcs otherwise their numbers would be in jeopardy as well." Oran then asked Dalin, "Have there been any orc bodies found?"

"None other than the few my men have dropped in the passing days." Dalin answered.

Cagorn Rockripper walked through his encampment admiring his swelling numbers around their fires. Many orcs have arrived along with goblin slaves to bolster his numbers for the upcoming battle with the dwarves of the Talts. Long has he waged skirmishes against the hill dwarf clans and long have those efforts not warranted any true benefits other than the occasional win in a skirmish. How he hated the stubborn dwarves and wished to supplant them as the ruler of the mountains.

With the Firefist Clan wiped out he could look to securing his position as chief among all of the orcs in the mountains. He brimmed with pride from recent advances but also impatience as he entered a large tent at the far end of his encampment.

Upon entering the large tent his eyes went immediately to the two occupants within. Both in a trance and unaware of his presence it seemed to him as they both looked into the flames of the fire in the center of the circular shaped structure and chanted words unknown to him while their eyes penetrated unseen events to his eyes, in the flame. He began pacing back and forth in the area afforded to him not wanting to disturb for he had seen and heard this before. One witch sitting before the fire was an orc and one he had taken to bed previously. She whispered in moments after their passionate embraces that if Cagorn Rockripper were ever to climb higher in standing than he must withdraw from the shamans advice who had so instructed and advised him on the ways of war in the past and embrace a new power. One of power within himself aided by witchcraft.

Thinking on this now and the fruit it had just begun to bear, Cagorn Rockripper's gaze went to the other female in the room. A human witch, who he had reluctantly met at the insistence of his lover, Katlika Saurtaker. Katlika had claimed that an acquaintance of hers could spur his intent on victories in the Talts. So far the human had been right but Cagorn's bloodlust urged him to press on the dwarves now before more clans could rally to their cause.

Finally finished with her chanting, Merill Siske finally acknowledged Cagorn Rockripper's presence. "Good evening my Lord." She said while bowing her head in reverence to the impressively sized orc pacing before her and her student.

Cagorn disregarded his witch's demeanor and began asserting, "It's time for assault. My numbers swell."

Already recognizing the tone of Cagorn's statement and growing tired of having to quell his moods and need for action, Merill decided it was time to let this impudent orc know who was truly in charge. "I've heard your arguments on the matter and my answer is still no."

"No?" Cagorn questioned.

"That is correct my Lord. You must heed my decision." Merill confirmed.

Cagorn felt like exploding. Never had a female, let alone a frigid old woman like the one sitting cross-legged in front of him ever tell him how things were to be. He looked over to Katlika for answers and when she stood resolute in her teacher's words he turned his attention back to Merill. "You forget me. I make decision not you."

Merill stood as if from a chair and not the hindering position in which she was sitting, cross-legged. When she stood fully she raised her tone considerably. "No my Lord it is you who are mistaken. You serve a higher purpose and one I don't need to disclose to the likes of you."

Enraged, Cagorn's hand went to the battleaxe strapped to his waist. Before he could pull it from his beltline though, his throat became restricted and he was lifted into the air by seemingly unimaginable strength. Materializing before him was the creature beholden to his human witch. Black of skin, like the darkest charcoal and standing a foot taller than he, the creature held him aloft without any real effort; his claws clutching at his throat and threatening to tear flesh. The astral walker's face was clear of any emotion and his white orbs showed not the slightest sign of life.

Merill watched as her servant took charge of the orc commander. Her assassin, conjured from the lower planes was at her command alone and through his efforts the dwarves were in disarray. It would not be long now until they tried a full assault on the orc encampment and because of her efforts their numbers swelled giving them considerable advantage in the open field. Attacking the dwarf homes where they were well defended and held advantage was not to her liking and an outcome she would not let this fool, Cagorn establish.

After considerable time of hanging in the air fighting for breath, Merill finally ordered her assassin to release Cagorn. He fell to this knees gasping for breath. Without waiting for him to recover she started, "As I've said these pitiful mountains can be yours. You have only to heed my council. Question me again or make move against me and my friend here will end your miserable existence and we will appoint a new chief." Merill moved to the side of her astral walker caressing his strong arm down to his enormous claws, which made up the entirety of the digits on his hand.

R. A. HAYDEN

CHAPTER TWENTY-THREE

Silver Versus Silver—Fhurin, 1021

RAMSAY PINKERTON WATCHED at the rails of the ship as the lines were cast from crewmen to dock workers as the ship his men were using as transport docked in Palo. Him and his men were en route from the Kingdom of Kodia to the wall built by the Iron Hall dwarves to aid Casta in repelling the undead forces of the east. Well known throughout the kingdoms was that the Lich Mayre and his necromancers were increasing their affront to the eastern border of Casta. As leader of The Order of Silver, and sworn enemy of the undead and arcane magic, especially necromancy, it was their charge to meet the assault despite the fact that Kodia was no friend to Casta or the wizards who claimed it as home.

Ellen Nubula, a silver dragonborn, approached her commander at the rail while the rest of their charges began readying for departure. "At last we will see if the rumors of this black dragonborn are true."

Ramsay, while never taking his eyes off of the docks or looking to his most devoted cleric responded, "It is but a side note to the glory that awaits us."

Ellen could not agree with her human commander in this assessment, although she would not argue his point outright. As her and her brother were from a silver dragon lineage and in her eyes the chosen of their god, Bahamut, they sought to destroy dragons and the kin of chromatic origin above even that of the undead. "It is no small thing my lord. My gratitude for agreeing on the northernmost route to the wall instead of docking in Tomé."

Ramsay turned his attention to his men gathering on the deck. Their number, including him, measured twenty strong. Among the mercenary band were two clerics, including Ellen who added to her divine magic with traits from her silver dragon lineage, and their eldest member Riston Browning who held considerable power aided by their chosen god, Bahamut. Perhaps the most impressive and Ramsay's biggest asset among his troupe of humans was his second dragonborn, Jorah Nubula. Ramsay watched as Jorah picked up a crate of supplies, which should have easily taken two men to lift. He hefted it onto his shoulder and headed towards the docking bridge, which had just been lowered. Ramsay knew that if they were to confront The Silver Guard then Jorah would perhaps prove the most effective weapon against their famed swordsman, Oran Righe.

Ramsay hoped it would not come to full out confrontation due to The Silver Guard's reputation and devotion to fighting the undead but he could not ignore their apparent lack of morals concerning the taking in of a black dragonborn. Such a sin was unforgiveable and it supported their claim that arcane magic was corrupt and perhaps Josef Righe had finally succumb to its influence. In a few short days they would certainly find out where The Silver Guard's hearts truly lay.

Adley and Marcus exited the front door of the Keep on their way into town to procure some more arrows from Armihrmond. They had been working on Marcus' archery skills the past few days and in the process had broken many of the tips from the shafts. As they neared the bottom of the large staircase Adley halted Marcus by grabbing him by the shoulder. In the distance, coming up the road Adley could see a large force upon horseback heading into Lanos. Two of the riders were bearing standards, which even at distance Adley could tell was the symbol for Bahamut but not the same symbol used by the Castan military. It had far more detail and instead of the silver dragon's head posted in the middle of a shield, these standards were of nothing but a full image of the god himself set against a blue background.

"What is it Sarge?" Marcus asked looking to what Adley was obviously criticizing in the distance.

"I'm not sure Marcus. Wait a second."

The pair stood by the stairs while Adley's gaze never left the approaching riders. As they drew nearer Adley could distinguish two of the riders from the others. Silver in color matching the armor sets worn by most of the procession. One in particular stood out. Even at this distance Adley could tell he was far larger than the other riders. That and he was riding a clydesdale, obviously to support his large frame. They were generally used as draft horses and in some cases heavy war- horses by kingdoms in the north. Clydesdale horses were rare in the south and Adley had not seen one for years. Even more rare was his rider of course. With his massive frame and silver coloring, which Adley first thought might be part of his armor, there could be no mistaking him now as riders veered from the main road and headed straight for the Keep. Two silver dragonborn approached with a host of humans at their sides.

Adley grabbed Marcus by both shoulders facing him in his direction. "Marcus hurry, get Josef."

"Why Sarge? What's going on?" Marcus asked with a confused look.

"No questions Marcus. Just go and tell him its urgent. Now!" Adley shouted while pushing Marcus back up the stairs. When Marcus began moving on his own Adley added, "Do not come back outside. Wait for us to enter."

Adley turned to the approaching riders and straightened his sword on his beltline then left his hand resting easily on top of the pommel. Unfortunately the gates were open, as they often were throughout the day, which Adley now wished was not the case. Riding in formation of two side by side with a depth of nine except one strangler in the rear pulling along a pair of pack horses he numbered them at nineteen. Adley did not like the odds. All of the riders were human, save two, who rode directly behind the lead riders.

As they hardly slowed to enter the gates Adley could see more clearly that these dragonborn were quite different from Marcus. Their dragon heritage showed distinctively, giving them a look of humanoid dragons. Adley believed one was female but the massive one to her left was obviously male. He patiently waited for them to get within distance of speaking range rather than to start shouting or try to halt them in any way. As they neared they slowed to trot and the two dragonborn fanned out to position themselves at the sides of the two human riders in front, making their ranks four abreast.

Within fifteen feet of Adley the apparent leader of the group held up his hand indicating a halting motion. Silence followed as the four in front were sizing up Adley. The only sounds were that of the horses' heavy breathing.

Finally breaking the tension Adley spoke first. "Good evening gentleman. Something I can help you with?"

The large silver dragonborn spit in response off to his left and then smiled, obviously pleased with the sight of only one human standing in front of him to oppose them.

Adley saw the apparent insult from the corner of his eye but never took his eyes of the human in front of him whose horse was slightly ahead of the rest.

Ramsay broke his silence after examining the small Keep and the guard standing out front, a couple steps up from the ground. He noted before speaking, three flags displayed out front of the Keep to his right. One was the symbol of Bahamut, one for Pelor, and the other for Corellon the god of arcane magic. "Do I speak to a member of The Silver Guard?"

"You do sir. Adley by name. May I ask your name and on what occasion you seek out The Silver Guard?" Adley responded politely even though he didn't figure this to be a pleasant visit. Now looking at these men close up he could tell more clearly that they wore armor more typical of the north and he recognized their standards more clearly as ones used in the Kingdom of Kodia.

"I am Ramsay Pinkerton. Commander of The Order of Silver." Ramsay replied.

"And what can I do for you commander?" Adley asked again while taking note of the coincidental similarities in their house names.

"We have heard rumors en route to the wall that a black dragonborn is in the area." Ramsay lied. Word had spread beyond Casta and reached his ears in Kodia months before. "Can you shed light on these disturbing rumors?"

"Of what importance would that be to you?"

"Is that not obvious?" Ramsay remarked looking to his right at Ellen Nubula.

Adley inspected Ellen Nebula. He had never before seen a female dragonborn of any lineage. Now in close proximity he could see her eyes glaring down at him intently. More reptilian than human, unlike Marcus whose eyes were nearly all black and did not take on the appearance of a reptiles eyes. She was larger and stouter than a human woman. Adley imagined that scales must run throughout the entirety of her body if her hands, arms, and head were any indication as to what lie beneath her clothing and armor. After his inspection Adley turned his attention back to Ramsay. "There is no threat from a black dragonborn here. I assure you if there were we could aptly handle the situation."

"You did not fully answer my question." Ramsay declared.

"I gave the only warranted answer." Adley said pointedly.

"You dare raise tone at my commander." Jorah Nubula spoke up while edging his large horse forward.

Adley turned his attention to the large silver dragonborn to his right. "I wasn't speaking to you. Mind the manners the rest of your companions share."

Jorah dismounted immediately, not bothering to grab the large morningstar strapped to the side of his saddle. He stepped in front of his mount with hand on hilt of his longsword strapped to his waist. "You spin words fool. Speak true words or ready for eternal silence."

Adley squared to Jorah fully. The dragonborn was almost a full foot taller than Adley and twice as wide. Unlike the female dragonborn his hands ended in four digits instead of the usual five of a human. At the end of each were vicious looking claws, which were weapons in it of themselves. Like the female, his head was more dragon like. He had a short snout, a mouth lined with sharp fangs, and two spiked ridges running up his forehead, which gave way to scales that appeared softer and resembled long hair falling behind his enormous head and running back behind his shoulders.

Even if it were just Jorah and not the eighteen behind him, Adley would not have acted any different. This was his house. "I am ready for such an end. Are you, worm?"

Adley pulled his sword as Jorah did the same. As the two took a step closer they halted suddenly as a voice louder than humanly possible pierced the air. "Enough!"

Josef exited the front doors of the Keep. The doors slammed shut behind him without him ever touching them and the locking bolt could be heard slamming into place. All eyes went to him except Adley and Jorah who did not break stance and longed for embrace of battle.

"To whom do I speak?" Josef shouted once again in his normal voice while coming to the top of the stairs.

"Ramsay Pinkerton. Commander of The Order of Silver." Ramsay shot back.

"And what reasoning would you give, Ramsay Pinkerton, for descending on my Keep in force and letting one of yours attack one of my men?"

"This man offers insult to reasonable question." Ramsay said while pointing to Adley.

"What question?"

"We inquire about a black dragonborn."

"What of him?"

Ramsay was reluctant to continue for a moment. He did not think Josef's answer would be so forthcoming. "You do not deny that one is here?"

"I'll not deny that fact." Josef announced.

"That is sacrilege. If…"

Josef interrupted Ramsay. "Shut your mouth commander."

Ramsay was completely taken back now, as were his men. No one spoke to him in such a way. In the lands of Kodia, The Order of Silver was treated with the utmost respect like The Silver Guard of Casta. The Order of Silver was renown for their dealings with anyone who defied the church especially those of arcane nature, which earned them an auspicious reputation throughout Kodia.

Before Ramsay could clear thought as to the insult inflicted upon him, Josef continued quite loudly, "I see you fly a banner for Bahamut. Is it his will that you would harm a child for?"

"If ever a viper is encountered, even one recently hatched, it must be stamped out." Ramsay replied.

Josef shook his head at the reply. "Then it is you who would commit sacrilege. Your dogmatic view, of the tenets of Bahamut, is beyond approach. Now leave my gates and do not return."

Ramsay actually gave out a laugh in reply before speaking once again. "I see but two standing in our way."

Josef raised his brows at the reply and shook his head in response. He pointed over the heads of The Order of Silver. Ramsay looked back and in-between his men he caught view of approximately an equal number of men to his own exiting Lanos on horseback bearing the standard of the Castan calvary.

When Ramsay turned his attention back, Josef added, "If you believe that unfair I will gladly halt their approach. You and yours can see how you fair against the likes of just us two. I doubt very much that your two clerics there," Josef pointed to Riston Browning and then to Ellen Nubula, "Will be of much help to you."

Tense moments passed while the riders approached quickly from the rear of Ramsay's men. He did not believe in the boast by Josef in the slightest that they would only face the pair of them. Deciding better of it and finding the answers he wanted anyway he turned his horse about ordering Jorah to mount up in the process.

Finally Adley lowered his guard as Jorah did the same taking to his horse once more after. Before he departed though Adley stepped closer. "I'm sure we'll meet again."

"You'd best hope not human." Jorah responded.

"Oh no, we will. Be sure of it." Adley finished with a smile.

Ramsay Pinkerton paced as well as he could in his tent with Ellen, Jorah, and Riston standing before him. Him and his men were forced to travel south after their encounter in Lanos. Ordered by the Captain of the Lanos Outpost that they were not welcome in his town. Had the numbers of soldiers at the outpost been less Ramsay's temper may have gotten the better of him and combat would have indeed ensued. An outcome that Ramsay surely did not want before this trip began. Their plan was to take up arms against the undead assaulting Casta but Ramsay's temper towards his perceived lack of respect had surely drifted his intentions. Not only the disrespect from The Silver Guard but also the Captain from Lanos when they verbally sparred.

"Commander." Riston Browning started as his commander quit pacing and contemplated their next move. "I would advise course against fighting the Castan military forces."

Before Ramsay could say anything Ellen spoke up, "You would advise retreat from those dogs?"

"Our intentions here were to aid Casta in fighting the undead. Not to turn course and join them in their assault." Riston argued back.

"We would be doing no such thing. We are far removed from the wall." Ellen countered.

"If we engage now we will be forced into a hasty retreat. We could not stay within Casta and we cannot fight their entire military. We would be unable to help at the wall."

"Coward." Jorah insulted.

"Enough!" Ramsay interjected. "I am of a mind that the Casta military can do their own fighting on the wall. If they would stand idly by and let an arcane magic user issue them orders from no position of authority than they are not worthy of our aid."

"Commander. Josef Righe is not just some mere arcane magic user. You know this. He commands great respect in these lands." Riston tried to reason with his commander's intentions.

Ramsay turned an evil looking glare on Riston. "You fear this man?"

Being no novice caster of divine magic, Riston was well known for being brutal in battle against enemies deserving of his wrath and that of his god. One thing he was not though was a fool; given to letting his emotions rule his actions.

"No commander I do not. But neither am I certain that victory could be obtained while so many soldiers stand at his side." Riston said while standing stern and resolute before his commander's gaze.

Before Ramsay could continue further a soldier from outside of the tent asked for entry and after permission from Ramsay, Davion Braxton entered the tent.

As Davion, Ramsay's most trusted scout entered, Ramsay questioned him for his report immediately. "What news Davion?"

"It was as you suspected commander. Entering the day prior to your arrival garnered much information."

The Order of Silver landed in the city of Palo with twenty men but wishing to have a good outlook on what they were walking into beforehand, Ramsay had sent Davion into town alone to gather information.

"Well let's have it than." Ramsay ordered.

"News to lift troubled mind apparently."

Davion was often forward in his dealings with others. A trait that had earned him rebuke from Jorah on a couple of occasions. Despite this they often found common ground as their lust for bloodletting matched one another.

Davion continued, "Only two Silver Guard are actually at their Keep. The rest, numbering only three, have gone to the Talts to help some dwarves with orcs."

"Josef and this Adley?"

"Yes. The only others at the Keep are the boy and two servants."

"News to lift the heart indeed." Ramsay nodded his approval garnering smiles from Jorah and Ellen. "And what of our pursuit? Are The Silver Guard present?"

"The soldier is but not the wizard."

After their departure from town Captain Payne had taken a number of men alongside Escott Claridge and Adley to pursue The Order of Silver to ensure they passed long out of reach of Lanos.

"What else?" Ramsay inquired further.

"That Captain and his wizard ride along as well. Their number stands at thirty-three. They stay at distance of course, not wanting to invoke a fight but to ensure our departure."

"Clever. What of the Keep now?"

"Guards will post from Lanos. We will not be dealing with the wizard alone."

Ramsay turned his attention back to Riston. "What of the wizard? Is he still tracking and attempting to scry like a coward?"

"I have felt no intrusions since we set camp. However he could not see or hear what goes on here. I have blocked such intrusions which is probably why hc has halted." Riston looked to Ellen for confirmation which she gave nodding her acceptance as to his reasoning.

Ramsay began pacing once again while searching his thoughts for the proper path. He did not want to engage the soldiers following. He believed his men could take the soldiers but open battle would lead to discovery and then they would be forced to flee Casta before more from Lanos arrived in greater number.

Ramsay stopped pacing once more and issued orders to Davion. "Slip back to Lanos. Watch from afar. We will continue southeast in the morning giving illusion we go towards the wall."

"Just watching then?"

"If opportunity presents itself than do what you do best Davion."

CHAPTER TWENTY-FOUR

Bait—Fandril, 1021

WILLEM WATCHED AHEAD of him on the road heading east of Firefist Village as he, Oran and Havander rode along the road. Oran was riding in the lead position with Havander behind him, leaving him in the rear. They had traveled out on horseback after three days of scouting the woods on foot in the hills surrounding Firefist Village for any sign of the mysterious attacker who had been plaguing the dwarves with no success. They had run across plenty of sign from orcs who had previously passed on both sides of the steep valley but always no more than that. Dalin Firefist was growing impatient and urged for a frontal assault on the orc encampment before their numbers could grow beyond chance of victory. This was perhaps going to be their final effort at drawing out whatever it was that had already claimed numerous dwarf lives.

The hope was that they would be attacked. Something Willem did not favor even though Denstrom and a good number of his boys followed off of the road and far enough removed as to not be detected. If he was to battle he would assume do it outright and favored the plan for a frontal attack on the orc encampment. Oran insisted on one last attempt as they were unsure as to what they would be facing out in the dense forest and since no one had seen it and lived they assumed it was a spellcaster of some sort. Able to make itself invisible or making the orc attackers invisible at the very least. Either way Havander was continually casting a detect invisibility spell so that their attacker would not get the first shot in before they were aware.

Suddenly Oran halted his horse from the front of the line and looked intently to his right, up the steep slope. Before Willem even turned his head in that direction his horse was struck with not one, but three arrows on his right side. One arrow narrowly missed Willem's leg and the other two pierced his horse in the neck. Willem's horse reared up and toppled to its left. With the quickness and agility far removed from most mortals Willem dislodged himself from his saddle before the horse hit the ground. He landed with a roll taking himself far enough away from his horse as to not be trampled or trapped underneath it. As he regained his feet his matching set of blades came into his hands as though they had always been there.

Willem surveyed the scene quickly. Oran and Havander were dismounting and dodging more incoming arrows from the bank now in front of Willem. He looked to his horse still thrashing to some extent but obviously wounded beyond help.

"Bastards." Willem breathed out quietly before sprinting headlong into the brush and taking to the hill just beyond the underbrush surrounding the road. He could hear Oran and Havander shouting from behind him to wait but he did not heed their calls. He was intent on blood.

The ascent was not easy, especially with orc arrows coming at him now but Willem dodged left and right, from tree to tree, never slowing. After rounding one particularly large cedar he caught sight of his enemy. Two began descending towards his position followed quickly by a third. At last his blades would be tested.

The first orc in line took a swing with his heavy sword as Willem neared. Believing it had advantage of the high ground and seeing such a small human coming at him he was confident of the impending kill. Willem dodged left letting the sword pass narrowly by his face then extended his right arm up into the lower jaw of the orc. He did not linger or try to finish. He extracted the blade still on the run leaving the orc in his wake as the second neared.

Seeing his orc companion fall enraged the second orc in line. He gave out an undecipherable curse, as Willem did not know the orc tongue nor would it have mattered. The orc's blade went up high and came down just as the two neared. Willem went to one knee and brought up his left blade to deflect the blow as his right arm swung in at the knee, cutting deep and toppling the orc to his back. With swiftness he brought his right arm back up and reversed grip on the hilt of his sword and drove the blade home in the orc's chest.

Willem registered Oran shouting behind him and saw streaks of lightning flash up the hill past his position hitting the trees. He didn't linger or look back but continued on to the third orc in line who now had two more orcs starting the descent behind it. He was halfway up the hill and wouldn't give advantage up of his quickness at dispatching the foolish orcs rushing at him.

The third orc took a heavy sidelong swing at him overbalancing itself on the steep decent. Willem simply ducked and brought his right blade up following the clumsy swing and pierced the orc all the way through the neck with his thin blade. He held the orc up and took cover behind him as an arrow came in striking the orc in the back. Willem then freed his left hand by sheathing his sword and pulling forth a throwing dagger from the strap across his chest. He let the orc he was holding up topple as he released the dagger, hitting the next orc in line directly in the face ending the fight for him as well. In quick succession he lobbed two more into the next orc as they advanced on one another. Both struck home dazing the orc as it looked down to his chest to examine the blades now protruding from him. Willem never slowed as the orc fell to his knees and sliced with his sword taking the head from the orc as he passed.

More of Havander's lightning flashed by Willem as he neared the top of the hill, giving him much needed cover. Finally he reached the top and found himself on the defensive as five more orcs rushed at him as he crested the top. The two nearest his position came at him at once swinging wildly with their weapons. Willem rolled backwards nearly taking him back down the hill but the blades swung harmlessly by. Once on his feet again he reversed momentum, jumping straight back into the pair of orcs from his crouched position and thrust both blades out in front of him striking true, one on each orc, ending their fight at the same time.

Willem sidestepped to his right while extricating his blades from the chests of his two most recent opponents. He quickstepped around the trunk of a tree letting it take the barrage of the next orc's swing. Believing Willem continued on that path the orc thought to cut him off by going the other way. Willem however stepped back from the tree while sheathing both swords this time and taking out two more throwing daggers from the lining of his jacket. Two orcs instead of the one came around that side of the large tree but no matter. Willem let fly one dagger after the other catching one in the eye and the other in the shoulder. He followed directly behind his throws, not wanting his targets to be able to recover. Within striking distance Willem unsheathed his swords once again while taking swipes at both orcs in the process. Blood spurt from the necks as both orc heads toppled from their perches. Willem casually walked around the tree after, with both blades in hands finding one lone orc left staring at him from ten feet away.

The orc could not believe what it had just witnessed. They thought their prey would be easy targets and yet this one human alone took out the rest of his band. He knew then that they should have followed orders and retreated after taking their first shots. Nevertheless he gave out a war cry and waded into battle with the little human hoping to avenge his friends.

Willem let the orc play out his rage. He didn't bother blocking the blows but stepped clear of each one while sidestepping back to his left. He deftly avoided the bodies of two of the orcs he had fell earlier as the orc kept swinging, always a split second behind him. When Willem was done playing he finally stepped in and blocked one blow with his left sword and drove his right blade directly into the orc's heart and extended his reach back away from the orc and kicked him off of his blade.

Willem looked around the hilltop at the blood pouring from the orcs onto the dark earth and pine needles littering the forest floor. He then looked up to the trees as a calming breeze wafted through the trunks of trees. It was strangely silent it seemed to him considering the noise that had just taken place. Willem took in a calming breath of air and released slowly.

A small branch on the ground broke right in front of Willem unexpectedly. Oddly enough it looked as though something had stepped on it but there was nothing there. Reacting as quick as he could Willem brought both of his blades up in front of him defensively just as a massive blow, which would have struck him in the chest but was instead absorbed to some extent by his blades. The weight of the blow however knocked the blades back into Willem, as did the fist of his attacker. Willem could barely register the large black humanoid looking creature materializing before his eyes as he was vaulted backwards from the blow taking him right over the crest of the hillside.

Just before Oran reached the top of the hill, taking the same route that Willem had ascended with Havander following close behind, he saw Willem fly backwards from the top of the rise to his left, and land heavily on his back before starting to roll backwards down the hill. After hitting one tree with a glancing blow Willem continued downward another ten feet where his momentum was finally stopped by another tree. He rolled onto its base of roots groaning and spitting dirt from his mouth. Assured that he was at least alive Oran continued on.

Oran took the last few strides that took him to the top of the hill and saw before him three orc bodies directly in front of him and among the bodies a large humanoid of unknown origin stood looking directly at him. The creature was much larger than Oran. It was perhaps twice his weight and easily a foot and a half taller. Its skin was black as night, which did nothing to obscure the corded muscles that rippled through its entire frame and mostly unclothed body. Most impressive and worrisome were its claws. At the end of each of its two arms its hands looked more like weapons as each finger looked to be more claw than finger. Oran briefly recalled hearing of a creature similar to this. One from the lower planes he believed. Astral walkers they were called.

A blast of lightning sent forth from Etburn by Havander, arced past Oran's left shoulder, hitting the astral walker as it took its first step in Oran's direction. The astral walker barely recoiled from its power as the blue-white streaks of lightning danced over its dark skin. After quickly shaking off the effects the astral walker reached down and grabbed a hold of the nearest orc body lying at its feet. He hefted the orc like a missile at his prey.

Oran shoulder rolled to his right clearing the orc body with ease but the orc body slammed into Havander's shield spell that he had enacted. Although the body of the orc did not come into contact with Havander himself, the force from the weighted body against the shield was enough to send Havander reeling backwards down the hill behind him, leaving Oran alone with the astral walker on the top of the hill.

The astral walker came forward towards Oran. Oran, hoping to get a better measure of the creature sidestepped to his right taking the path around the same large tree that Willem had taken earlier. Oran hoped his pursuer would follow leaving his backside to Havander or Willem, if they recovered, but the astral walker, like the orcs previously, stopped and then sidestepped itself around and away from the tree and waited for Oran to come around. Oran stepped passed the decapitated bodies of the fallen orcs by Willem's blades and stood once more before the astral walker that waited patiently.

Oran waded into melee. Hoping to counter and see the battle capability of the astral walker he stepped ever closer. He was not disappointed as the astral walker lunged forward raking the air with its claws at the end of its right arm. Oran jumped back out of reach and hoped it would continue with another strike but his attacker did not. No fool to battle apparently and recognizing that it was against a seasoned warrior the astral walker stepped back as well after it's initial miss.

The two combatants sidestepped more, mirroring each other's movements away from the where the orc bodies lie. Suddenly the astral walker lurched forward again with a massive downward strike with its right arm followed quickly with a sidelong swing of his left. Oran dodged both and swung a backhand swipe with his sword after the second strike, which was easily blocked by the claws of the astral walker's right hand.

After blocking the astral walker jumped backwards disengaging himself from the melee. He looked to his claws and where Oran's sword had sliced into them. His claws were harder than any natural creatures. Any normal blade would bounce right off leaving barely a mark. The astral walker was surprised to see deep cut marks in three of his claws. This was no ordinary swordsman he faced, nor was his weapon. He looked back up to Oran stepping in slowly and measured with his magnificent looking longsword. The astral walker thought it was time to stop playing and came forward as well or tried to as suddenly his body was racked with another blow of lightning energy.

Seeing his opponent stunned instantly from Havander, who had now crested the hill once more Oran engaged, stabbing his blade out in front of him. The astral walker was not as hindered as he had hoped and it jumped further back out of range and looked to Havander's position.

Like a dart shot from a blowgun, a needle shot forth from the mouth of the abomination straight at Havander. Havander could not even see the fast flying and thin missile. Havander stopped suddenly as two feet before his eyes a needle, as if from nowhere appeared before his eyes, stuck in his invisible magic barrier. If it were not for his magic that dart would have struck him right in-between his eyes inflicting who knows what kind of damage on his person from the strange weapon. Relieved and furious all at once Havander enacted the power in Etburn sending shot after shot of lighting at the astral walker. The astral walker however changed tactics. Now on the defensive it dodged every blast of lightning coming at him while simultaneously staying out of reach of Oran and the swings from his blade, which were barely missing him.

After narrowly dodging another of the lightning blasts the abomination took a chance of a swing of its own at Oran disregarding the effect it knew the blade could have on its claws. Oran was perhaps a little anxious having his enemy on the defensive but his own defensive posture was not gone. He took the weight of the heavy blow, catching the claws with his blade, but the force behind it knocked him backwards sending him to his back. Oran used the momentum to roll back to his feet expecting the astral walker to be quick on his heels however the astral walker had took off in a sprint after Havander.

Havander shot more balls of lightning as the astral walker approached him with all speed, which it narrowly ducked or dodged the balls of lightning energy coming at him. Havander began backing up, even starting back down the hill. As the astral walker got close to striking distance Havander reached into Etburn exuding his influence on the staff calling forth an extended stream of lightning instead of a small ball of its energy. Several streaks of lightning reached out grabbing hold of the astral walker and stopped it in its tracks.

Havander let a war cry as the astral walker screamed out in pain, revealing finally some form of communication, from the relentless streaks of power arcing across his black skin. The abomination fell to one knee but held itself upright with and extended arm balancing itself on the ground. With a feral growl the astral walker reached down into itself and lunged forward from his kneeling position and backhanded with all of its strength at the wizard now inflicting pain upon it.

The astral walker's blow and determination would have surprised Havander if he had time to better recognize the quick movement. As it was, the blow struck Havander's shield with such force that it broke the spell and he took some measure of the blow sending him backwards once more. Thankfully for Havander the blow was a backhand otherwise the sharp edge of the inner claws would have been tested against his magical protections set upon his cloak and clothing.

Oran took a swing of his sword at the back of the abomination just after Havander was sent flying once more. The blade struck flesh making the astral walker arch his back in pain. It recovered quickly though and turned once more on Oran. The astral walker came forward with a series of strikes. Oran dodged all with his agile footwork, not wanting to force another block with his sword, perhaps sending him careening backwards once more or worse forcing his blade from his hands. He waited for the ferocity of the astral walker to play out so they could reset their match.

Oran's opening came before he would have thought possible. While the astral walker took swipe after swipe with his claws, inching ever forward, it screamed out in pain once more. Willem's blades now dug deep into each shoulder blade. Willem had taken the hillside once more and was hanging on with all of his strength to his blades while hanging a couple feet off of the ground after jumping onto it's back. The astral walker thrashed and spun while trying to reach to his back to extricate his newest attacker and pull out his blades.

Oran took advantage once more swiping low with his blade slashing the astral walker across the belly. Blood as black as the astral walker's skin oozed out of the wide opening. The astral walker stopped and looked down to its intestines now threatening to follow suit. It clasped at its belly with its claws.

Willem let go of his blades and pulled forth his curved blade as quickly as his feet once again touched the ground. He slashed down and across, cutting deep into the back of the kneecaps of the astral walker forcing it to its knees.

Oran lunged forward with his superb blade covered in black blood right after it fell to its knees and his blade went into the chest of the astral walker. It must have a heart in the same place as him, Oran thought, as finally the astral walker quit fighting and fell over sideways before it could reach for the blade sticking from its chest.

Willem returned to the body of the astral walker after yelling down to the road at Denstrom and his men upon hearing their shouts from below. Oran and Havander were kneeling down examining the body.

"Well what is it?" Willem asked as he leaned down and began pulling his second blade back out of the left shoulder blade of the astral walker.

Oran reached to his chin, rubbing his short stubble as he thought about the answer. "I believe it is an astral walker though I've never seen one before."

"Astral walker?" Willem asked further. "Demon, devil or what?"

"Neither actually." Oran confirmed after looking to Havander who confirmed his suspicions with a nod. "Legend says they are assassins created by the gods in a war they had against the primordials."

"What would gods care about battles between orcs and dwarves?" Willem questioned after finally getting his stuck blade to release from the body.

"They wouldn't." Havander stated as he pulled forth his ivory handled dagger and cut from the neck of the astral walker an odd looking medallion. "Strange."

Oran leaned closer to look at the medallion that Havander was inspecting. He grimaced and shook his head unsure of the meaning of what Havander held. "What do you think?"

"This is witchcraft."

"Witchcraft?" Willem asked.

"I believe so. Its markings are unclear to me but it doesn't look arcane."

"So how do you know?" Oran questioned.

Havander stood and took a good look over the entire body of the astral walker from his standing position. "If this thing is from a different plane it should have dematerialized when it died."

"D what?" Willem said with a confused look.

Oran was shaking his head yes in regards to Havander's logic.

"Things from the other planes don't belong here you see Willem. They cannot access our plane without assistance from here. Demons, devils, elementals and apparently this thing should return to their plane once they die here." Havander explained.

"So why didn't this thing?"

"I believe because of this." Havander held up the strange medallion with words and markings etched onto its hard ceramic surface. "It would take a witch of considerable power to summon a creature as powerful as this. Then they bind it to this world with something like this."

"Alright. Let's assume you are right. Why would a witch do that?" Willem asked.

"Well my unschooled friend," Havander started sarcastically, "Witches are known for having servants or slaves to their will, who will carry out deeds for them and to act as protectors or bodyguards."

"Or assassins." Oran added.

"Exactly." Havander replied. "Many witches who are in league with the necromancers to the south use undead creatures. Summoning this thing however and bending it to your will would require a witch of considerable power."

"Any importance in all of that?" Willem asked.

"Perhaps." Oran replied as he moved to Havander and took the medallion from his hands. "The necromancers have been increasing their harassments to the building of the wall to the south. Perhaps this is another of their ploys towards a war against Casta, which many believe is coming."

"Why not just go around the wall and use the passes themselves?" Willem inquired.

"Because orcs and goblins rule the lands east of the mountain passes. They aren't fond of the undead either. However if they can be infiltrated and their forces used to battle the dwarves who have long acted as a defense to Casta's eastern borders, those who rule in Casta wouldn't bat an eye. Orcs and dwarves have been fighting each other forever." Oran finished just as Denstrom reached the top of the hill and examined the dead bodies that lay out before his friends.

"So what's next?" Willem asked as he finished cleaning the black blood from his second blade and placed it back in its sheath.

"Simple." Oran stated as he placed the ceramic medallion on top of an exposed root from a nearby tree. He then took out his signature silver stake and brought it down hard, using the pommel to smash the medallion to pieces. "We tell Chief Dalin it's time for war." Oran finished as he looked up to Denstrom who nodded in anticipation.

All on top of the hill turned their attention to the body of the astral walker after the smashing of the medallion as its body began to smoke at first then it seemed to filter itself through the ground like water running, fighting to get through a small drain. When at last it stopped there was nothing left except for the blood that had drained out onto the ground away from the body.

Katlika Saurtaker watched from the corner of her hut as Merill Siske paced frantically back and forth before the fire set in the middle of the hut while stroking and examining a ceramic medallion hung across her neck. She had been pacing for many minutes uttering words that were undecipherable to Katlika. Katlika had switched from common to orc and back again trying to calm her mentor and once tried to grab a hold of her, which earned her a smack across the face.

Suddenly Merill stopped and fell to her knees screaming while looking into the palms of her hands that now held the medallion still hanging from the chain around her neck. Before Merill's eyes the ceramic disk cracked apart. First splitting in two and then crumbling further away until it was nothing more than dust sifting through Merill's wrinkled old fingers.

CHAPTER TWENTY-FIVE

Protector—Fandril, 1021

MARCUS WAS RELIEVED to finally be out once more among the forest creatures of the night. He had been cooped up in the Keep for the past few nights, unable to take his evening escapes with fellow nocturnal sorts under the moonlight, ever since security had been raised after the visit from The Order of Silver. Since their visit a few of the Castan soldiers had stood guard due to the absence of Oran, Willem, Havander and Adley. Thankfully that morning Adley had returned with Captain Payne and his soldiers after their lengthy pursuit of The Order of Silver. Josef and Adley seemed placated for the moment that they would not see any trouble from The Order of Silver as it seemed they had done what they meant to do, which was to go to the wall to aid Casta in the repelling of the necromancer's undead minions, which plagued that area.

After initially hearing of the visit, Marcus was first pleased and intrigued at the news that two fellow dragonborn had come to Lanos. He was anxious to know more about them. However, he was disappointed, to say the least, when he found out that they were there to cause him harm. Even though Marcus knew he was smarter and more aware of the dangers of the world than other children his age, it did little to placate his anger. It made no sense to him that just because of his heritage others would want to hurt him. Harold and Georgette's explanations were always too vague for him to glean anything out of. He was thankful that Josef had turned to being far more outright in his explanations to him about his heritage and what it all meant. Josef had taken to talking to Marcus, more as a grown up these past few months, unlike anyone else in the Keep. Something Marcus appreciated very much.

It was because of Josef's explanation of the two dragonborn that Marcus was waging a make-believe battle against the pair in a patch of woods far removed from the Keep, to the south. Marcus had come to this patch of woods between neighboring farmlands many times. After trying to make friends with children of his own age and failing over the past couple years, due to the wariness of the other children's parents in Lanos and their own personal distrust of dragonborn and uneasiness they felt around the large seven year old, Marcus preferred to play by himself. That and other children were not as fortunate as him, in his opinion, to be able to wield his very own short sword and dagger, which had been among his gifts during his recent birthday.

"Take that silver!" Marcus yelled as he finished with the final blow landed on his second opponent.

Marcus' ears perked up as he swore, after the silence following the finish of his make-believe battle, that he heard something near his position under the cover of the trees. He scanned the area directly in front of where he thought he heard the silence break. He was not really alarmed at first for he believed it was most likely a deer or raccoon, which were regular inhabitants of these woods. Instead his eyes went wide at seeing the sight of a man approach, and not far from him.

"An interesting battle to watch." Davion Braxton said as he neared Marcus. "Even more so concerning your apparent opponents." He finished after he ended his approach and stood on the edge of the slight clearing of brush and trees that Marcus was centered on.

Marcus was unsure of how to respond. He was far removed from the Keep and was certainly not expecting to see anyone this far out from town. He was very aware of the intent stare that this stranger had on his person though and believed that he was truly in danger.

"Thank you sir." Marcus responded after scrutinizing this human who now stood before him. "If you don't mind it is late and I should return home."

"Oh it's early yet. Why don't you tarry a while?" Davion responded.

Unsure of what tarry meant Marcus stuck to his polite manner and replied, "No sir. I must be going."

"Shame young black. After such a courageous battle against silver dragonborn. You must be proud of yourself." Davion said as he slowly slid his sword from its sheath.

Marcus immediately turned and began running after hearing the change of tone in the stranger's voice and seeing the blade of Davion come forth. His instincts were correct and he was indeed in danger. The worst kind of danger and more than he had ever been in. He ran through familiar game trails and jumped over downed logs and ran in-between trees that marked the clearest path out of the forest hoping he could just make the clearing of the closest farmland so he could run straight on to the Keep.

He didn't make it more than twenty yards though as suddenly the ground came rushing up to meet his face as he was tripped from behind. Marcus rolled over to his back quickly after hitting the ground. Thankfully his sword was still in hand and his dagger was still hanging from his beltline. He scooted his rear across the ground away from the dangerous looking man in front of him as far as he could. He came to rest against a downed log, breathing heavily from the exertion and terrified feelings he was having.

"Come little black. I expected more from your kind." Davion teased as he looked down on the scared child before him.

"What do you want?" Marcus squeaked out.

"You of course. I long to have a black dragonborn under my belt of offerings to Bahamut." Davion exuded as he looked down to the shadowy figure of a boy in front of him.

Marcus didn't clearly understand. He knew of Bahamut of course from his classes at the Keep but he didn't understand what that had to do with him. "What do you mean? Who are you?"

Davion squatted down in front of Marcus, although he was still ten feet or more removed. "Do you not know child? You are the very essence of evil. It is my honor as a member of The Order of Silver to take you from this world."

Many moments passed with no more noise than that of a disturbed forest. Marcus took it all in and centered on Davion's words of being a member of The Order of Silver. What a fool he was to be out here by himself he silently scolded himself, especially this soon after knowing of a threat to his life. Marcus searched his mind for answers but none were forthcoming. Even as young as he was, Marcus was aware of his present state. He was but a child and before him waited a full-grown man with sword in hand wanting to end his life.

Defiantly Marcus stood up and held his sword out in front of him. In his mind it was better to go out fighting, rather than on your back.

With a little laugh Davion stood. "Courage. I like that. It is to be respected."

Marcus did not register the words outright but instead pulled his ruby dagger from its sheath so that he was duel armed. Marcus watched as Davion approached and lifted his sword to strike a blow.

Suddenly everything went black. Marcus could not see anything. It was as though he was struck blind. He twisted and turned trying to get his bearings but nothing was there. Nothing except for sounds of struggle, he noticed after seconds of panicked stricken fear of not being able to see anything. He did not know what to do. He tried to focus his intention and turn his body in the direction of the sounds of the struggle he was hearing.

The sounds went silent and Marcus was once again left alone with the sounds of the forest except, unlike his usual trips to the forest, it was very unnerving to him. He had always been able to see, even in the darkest of cloudy nights. Now he could see nothing. It was as if his eyes were closed. While trying his best to sort through his predicament his eyelids became heavy and the muscles in his body noticeably relaxed. It was all he could do to keep his feet and even that did not last long as he fell to the ground after his blades slipped from his hands, quite asleep.

Davion Braxton awoke after feeling a tremendous blow to his face, as though he had been struck, but there was nothing in front of him as his eyes focused on the room he was in. Unsure of what had happened to him he searched his memory as he tried to recall recent events while looking at the gorgeously adorned room he now found himself in. He struggled to move but found that he was hanging off of the ground by his wrists. He looked up to find he was shackled by both wrists and was hanging at least a foot from the marble floor beneath him.

Davion focused on the room again after releasing the moments of panic that overcame him. The pain from his wrists supporting his weight made it difficult as he hung helplessly above the ground. He could not feel his hands. The blood flow to his hands was obviously gone. It was as though he was experiencing the sensation of a part of your body falling asleep joined with the sensation of pain as the steel shackles that held his wrists so tightly, cut into his skin.

Once again Davion tried to focus on the room. It was well lit with a chandelier hanging in the center of the room with multiple candles. To his right was a fireplace that was well stoked and it burned intensely. Beautifully adorned furniture, ornaments, sculptures, ornately designed throw rugs and plush pillows piled on top of couches along the exterior walls from his present position were numerous. Lying asleep on one couch was something of a surprise to Davion. Marcus, the black dragonborn that had been his prey so recently in his mind lay asleep, hugging the pillow beneath his head with his arms.

"Good evening." Braden Aranor said from behind Davion Braxton, startling him noticeably as he struggled defiantly in his chains in spite of his present situation of hanging and bound in one of his studies.

Braden moved from behind Davion so that he could be seen fully.

When Braden came into full view, Davion asked very loudly, "What am I doing here? Who are you?"

"Shh." Braden answered. "It is my turn for questions Order of Silver."

"How dare you?" Davion yelled.

Davion's outburst earned him two slaps from Braden across the face. One cheek to the next with such force that Davion felt delirious after the blows were meted out.

"Quiet assassin." Braden said when Davion once again registered him standing in front of him. "No need to wake the boy." Braden said as he motioned to Marcus sleeping soundly nearby.

"Why am I here? What do you want?" Davion asked.

"Oh you know the answer to the first. Don't you?" Braden said as he turned his back on Davion and took a couple steps towards Marcus sleeping on the couch. Braden turned back to Davion and continued. "You tried to murder a child."

Davion examined the man in front of him after looking over to Marcus. He stood unflinching and his eyes seemed familiar. It came clear to Davion after noticing the red trim of his black eyes and the paleness of his skin. He had seen his kind before.

"You're a vampire aren't you?' Davion asked.

"Very good assassin. You are not unfamiliar with my kind." Braden answered.

Davion's mine swirled. What would a vampire have to do with this situation? Why was he here?

Braden took him from his contemplations as he asked, "What does The Order of Silver plan with the black dragonborn? Anything further than you?"

Davion breathed heavily as Braden produced a curved flaying knife from his cloak and held it up before his eyes.

After moments of nothing more than heavy breathing from Davion, Braden asked again. When no answer was produced, Braden made the slightest of cuts down the center of Davion's chest eliciting not much more than a growl of defiance from his prisoner. Braden was impressed but not overly so.

A knock on the door to the study took Braden from his contemplations of what he had learned from his prisoner, Davion Braxton of The Order of Silver. Davion hung exhausted and bloody after a couple hours of interrogation. Braden had learned everything he had expected to learn from the righteous follower of Bahamut.

"Enter." Braden said.

The large door to the study swung open and two, seemingly human women entered. Both were well known to Braden. The latter was a newborn vampire. Baylee Kendall was newly turned but she had been a guest at the House of Aranor for over two years. She was previously the blood slave of Wefene Swift, Braden's lover for the past one hundred years, when he was at his castle. Braden's eyes went to her alluring form as she sauntered over, while he leaned against the desk in his study. She was of unusual beauty for a former human living in Drilain for she did not hail from its shores. Her people came from a different continent that was mostly under control of the Yuan-ti, a snake-like race that ruled their continent with the utmost cruelty over other races, especially humans.

Braden could not help but be allured by her presence alone as she approached with Baylee. She was a singular beauty. Her body was curvaceous, her hair long and black, so black it almost appeared to have hints of purple in it. Her dress was most revealing of her form, leaving more skin exposed than white silk that she wore so elegantly as she neared.

"My lord." Wefene said before she grabbed Braden by the back of his head as she neared and embraced him in a passionate kiss.

When their embrace was finished, Wefene continued, "You have been gone too long my love."

"Apologies my love but I come bearing gifts." Braden finished as he pointed to Davion still hanging from his chains.

Curious, Wefene scrutinized the prisoner for a moment then turned back to Braden. "For me? Hardly necessary my love."

Braden gave a brief laugh after another short embrace from Wefene's lips. "For your new charge." Braden said while looking to Baylee who seemed hardly able to control her nervous movements as she stared relentlessly at Davion's bloody body hanging from the chains.

"Oh." Wefene said as she looked from Davion to Baylee. She had turned Baylee only two nights prior after consideration and approval from Braden to turn her weeks before. She turned back to Braden, "You are too kind my love but you know she has already fed."

"Appropriately I hope?" Braden questioned.

Braden, as head of the vampire nation held the strictest of rules for vampires under his charge. Vampires were not to feed indiscriminately. In their lands such things were possible, of course, but new vampires out in the world needed to know how to handle themselves, else be destroyed quickly. It was for this reason that newly made vampires were held to the strictest of standards right from the start of their new lives to help them control their bloodlust, which came with their new life of vampirism. It was their maker's responsibility to see that promising young vampires reached their potential or else face their fate of destruction with failure of them to adapt to vampire society.

"Of course my love." Wefene answered. "She has fed off of blood slaves quite nicely since her turning."

Braden stroked the long black hair of Wefene and smiled wide for his lover. "A treat then. Let your child have her first kill under our watchful eye."

Wefene smiled wide as her fangs shot forth while she looked to Davion hanging from the chains while being in and out of consciousness before she looked to her newborn, Baylee. After, she looked back to Braden. "You honor us my lord."

"No. It is my honor." Braden said as he grabbed Wefene around the waist and pulled her close. "This is your first child of darkness and I would see her well sated to our lifestyle. Best she learns from the best."

If Wefene were capable of blushing her cheeks would have ran red with joy. To have the lord and founder of all vampires first take interest of her and then to keep taking care of her down to her first born vampire child was beyond any honor shown to any other vampire she knew.

"Shall I do the honors?" Wefene asked excitedly.

"Please my love." Braden answered.

Wefene turned to Baylee who absolutely looked ready to burst after hearing the news of her first kill. It was hard indeed for vampires not to kill when first receiving the gift of vampirism. The past couple nights had been the hardest of her life to resist such temptation. She was only able to stop feeding on blood slaves after Wefene pulled her off of her meal, quite brutally, before she was able to drain them to the point of death.

Wefene looked to her beautiful creation. She was almost as rare as she was among the beauties of House Aranor. Baylee was beautiful beyond compare, expect for maybe Wefene. She had dark hair, though not as dark as Wefene's, and a small bone structure, for a human woman. Before her turn she was most desired as a blood slave by other vampires in House Aranor, though Wefene rarely leant her out to fellow vampires, preferring to keep her to herself.

"Please darling. Feed at will." Wefene offered as she pointed to Davion hanging from the chains.

Like a bolt from a crossbow, Baylee was hanging from Davion's neck, seemingly instantly. Her feet were farther off of the ground than Davion's as she clung to his formerly limp body. Now he screamed out in pain as Baylee dug her newly acquired fangs into his flesh.

Braden and Wefene watched on like proud parents as Baylee bit Davion from one part of his body to the next, draining his precious blood to sate her hunger. After a considerable time Wefene looked to the corner and saw a child sleeping on one of the couches.

Wefene pointed in Marcus' direction, "What is that my love?" She asked of Braden.

"Politics for one of my games." Braden answered nonchalantly as he watched Baylee finishing her first full meal.

Marcus woke slowly under the canopy of the forest he had been playing under hours earlier. His head felt fuzzy and it took him a few moments to realize where he was. The last thing he remembered was being chased by some man trying to hurt him.

"Good morning young Marcus." Braden said.

Marcus stood upright with a start. Braden stood to his left looking down on him in the darkness of the morning still bereft of the sunlight.

"What happened?" Marcus asked.

"Trouble I'm afraid." Braden started as he squatted down in front of Marcus who was still rubbing his head trying to clear some dizziness away. "Seems you are prone to trouble young Marcus."

"I don't understand." Marcus stated.

"Well you were being pursued by a most evil man." Braden answered.

Marcus took a few more seconds to recollect the last things he remembered. He saw clearly the man before him pulling a sword and threatening him. He looked around quickly from right to left looking for his attacker.

"Not to worry young Marcus. He is gone." Braden announced.

"How? Why?" Marcus asked.

"Fortunately you called me with the dagger I gave you." Braden lied.

The dagger Braden had previously given Marcus could serve that purpose as Braden had explained before but Marcus was fortunate that Braden was watching him prior to being needed.

"I don't remember that." Marcus declared as he stood.

"Well you took a little knock on the head from that man." Braden lied again.

It came rushing back to Marcus. "He was of The Order of Silver. He meant to kill me."

"Yes. But fortunate I was in the area." Braden explained. "You ought not wander alone so much young man."

"Where is he? What happened?"

"Not to worry." Braden said as he came closer to Marcus and grabbed him by the shoulders helping to steady his erratic movements as he looked around searching for answers that were not there. "He is gone."

"But how? I don't understand!"

"I'm afraid it's not an answer you want Marcus." Braden said while gaining the full attention of Marcus. "He was intent on harming you. I could not allow that."

Marcus looked into the eyes of Braden. They seemed sorrowful. "You mean you killed him."

"I mean I stopped him from harming you."

"What does this mean?" Marcus asked after looking into the eyes of Braden for long moments.

"It means you have more secrets to hide or tell Josef what happened. It's up to you." Braden answered as he looked over his shoulder to the sunlight fast approaching on the horizon.

After thinking it through Marcus had no clear choice on his decision. He looked back up to Braden hoping for answers. "What should I do?"

Braden stood again and began walking away as he answered, "It's up to you young warrior. Whatever you decide it was brave of you to stand against that man and I applaud you for it. Whatever you decide, there is more trouble coming once his friends learn of his fate. Either way you need to run home before your family awakes so you don't get in trouble."

Marcus looked behind him to the direction of the Keep. When he turned back around, Braden was gone, leaving him alone to figure it out.

CHAPTER TWENTY-SIX

Battle in the Talts—Fandril, 1021

DALIN FIREFIST WALKED in front of the line of his soldiers inspecting his men with his son, Denstrom, in tow as they awaited the word for the battle to begin. After hearing of the demise of the creature that was stalking his scouts, Dalin decided to march on the orcs immediately before their numbers grew any larger. With full support of the other clan chiefs for him to act as lead in the upcoming battle, considering his clan was the most affronted and the largest, Dalin was optimistic of the battle that was to ensue shortly.

The orc horde that had brought this battle about stood some hundred yards away. Excellent scouting by Willem Lindsey and Oran Righe had numbered their strength at over three hundred, not including goblins, which dwarves tended to disregard as anything significant. With well over a hundred dwarf warriors in their ranks, Dalin thought the impending battle could not be anymore in favor of them than it was in terms of sheer numbers. Dwarves found themselves outnumbered most of the time when dealing with orc and goblin armies. Their numbers were simply far superior to that of dwarves due to their extensive range and ability to breed much faster than the dwarven race.

Dalin looked up and down at each warrior he passed. He knew his dwarves were far superior in fighting skill to that of the average orc. His warriors were stouter, stronger, more resilient and armed to the teeth. Though they were not one combined and practiced unit like the armies of Iron Hall, he knew the orcs were not either. They were bands of ravenous bandits mostly, with goblin slaves amongst their ranks. Dalin was optimistic and excited to prove his leadership in battle once more.

The dwarves had gathered at the first clearing after exiting the valley amid the high peaks they called home. Though not a large clearing, most of the battle would take place within its boundary. The dwarves waited here so that the battle would not take place among the trees, though many on either side of the line were nestled under the high branches of the trees surrounding the clearing. So too was it for the orcs on the opposite end of the clearing.

Dalin had planned his spot well though. He did not march his force all the way to the orc encampment. He opted for open battle on semi neutral ground or so he would have the orcs believe. This clearing was within range of his catapults that his men had taken along with them and waited now at the end of the road the Firefist Clan had built long ago. Though the catapults were only three in number, the orcs had no idea that even now they were within range. Dalin merely waited for it to get a little darker so that the first missiles fired by his catapults would not be detected until it was too late.

Nighttime fast approached as Havander waited among the ranks of dwarves accompanying him on the left flank of the dwarf line. Well within the cover of the trees they waited, hopefully unbeknownst to the orc enemy waiting for the battle to ensue. Not that the orcs didn't know the dwarf lines extended into the trees but Havander and his men had a specific mission. The orcs had among their ranks a couple dozen of worg riders who had positioned themselves on their own right flank so that when the battle commenced they could quickly travel down out of the hills and hopefully roll up the dwarf lines fighting in the field. Worgs were often used by orcs and goblins as mounts. These large abominations of wolf kind were very large and ferocious in battle. Given the opportunity they could create havoc amidst an opposing army. Something Havander and his cohort of dwarves meant to prevent.

After the last rays of sunlight passed beyond the mountains Dalin gave the order for his men to light their torches. All along the line of his men their torches lit up. The response from the orc line was expected as they roared in defiance to the their dwarf enemy waiting patiently for them on the opposite end of the field.

Many opposing enemies of orcs or goblins would not choose to fight them at night. Humans for example could not see well in the darkness. This was not so for the dwarves. Long centuries of working in deep mines have led to their evolution of night vision. While not as keen as some other races, it did little to damper their spirits, especially with torches lit and the ensuing onslaught which was about to occur on the orc lines.

Cagorn Blackripper cheered wildly amid his ranks of orcs. Finally his time had come. His forces would crush the dwarf clans allied against him and issue in a new era of orc dominance in the Talt Mountains. He was located directly in the center of the field looking across at the torches recently lit by the dwarves. Just as he was about to give the order to charge several orcs directly to his left were suddenly squashed by a massive boulder as if from nowhere.

Screams of the dying rang out amid the orc ranks as other boulders crashed in as well. Cagorn scolded himself for not thinking the dwarves capable of such a ploy. All of their eyes were on the torches in front of him. They had not thought to look to the sky. Dwarves were not known for employing archers, certainly not to the amount necessary to thwart his numbers, and so he had not employed them either. Cagorn hoped for open battle and advantage of number over the dwarf scum.

He certainly did not count on ballistae as being a factor in the battle for he could not have employed them in the battle in either case due to the rough terrain they would have had to traverse in order to get any to the battlefield.

He watched most intently as the next barrage of incoming from the catapults came into view over the tree line. This one clearly visible, unlike the first barrage, as sparks trailed behind the flames accompanying the missiles in their ascent towards his army. No doubt the dwarves now launched flaming pots of oil. He had to think quickly and there was only one real choice. Cagorn ordered his men forward and took off in a charge to get inside the range of the flaming pots that were about to burn many in his ranks.

Oran and Willem watched from a hillside behind the orc lines as the forces of dwarf and orcs met in the middle of the field. Behind the orcs, flaming spots of tall grass had appeared before the two forces had met. In those flaming spheres of burning oil and grass were orcs and goblins thrashing and running about wildly trying to douse the flames that had erupted suddenly in their ranks.

Dalin had thought out the beginning of that battle well. Oran was impressed with the battle tactics of his friend. Although the beginning of the battle went obviously to the dwarves, they were still outnumbered by a large margin. Oran had nothing more to do than hope that their battle prowess would win out as he and Willem took to running down from their location to aid in the battle.

Oran detested being involved in an open battle amid two opposing armies because it left a skilled swordsman such as himself and Willem at a disadvantage to their skillset. While their likelihood of emerging alive was more than others, the variables involved with missiles coming at you from unknown locations and enemies surrounding you at all times, left even the most skilled warrior with weaknesses. No one, not even them, could defend at all angles all the time, so he found a more appropriate mission for himself and his apprentice.

After their defeat of the astral walker it was clear that the orc army, to some extent, was using witchcraft. Its origin was the unknown factor and one that Oran and Willem hoped to exploit in the confusion of the battle. They did not believe they would be facing anymore of the assassins they had already dispatched since such a creature was rare here on the material plane but its master could still inflict great damage from afar. Something Oran and Willem hoped to prevent if they were lucky.

As Oran and Willem reached their descent of the hillside they were on, a large explosion could be heard in the distance along with a glaring light over the top of the trees on the far side of the battlefield. Oran knew Havander was at work on his part of the battle and continued on.

On cue with the dwarf and orc forces clashing in the middle of the field, the worgs could be heard howling as they started their decent on the battle taking shape to Havander's right. Miscellaneous orcs and goblins could also be heard making their way through the trees towards his company's location. Havander held up his hand to halt his dwarf companions from advancing though it was not necessary. More seasoned in battle than the young human apparently commanding them now, they waited for their opportunity to unfold.

Havander waited until he had the first worg rider in sight. Upon seeing him among the shadows of the trees, barely being illuminated from the fires now coming from the field, Havander enacted the power in Etburn and sent forth a stream of lightning, instead of a single ball of lighting energy, into the area of his focus.

Hidden amid the trunks of the trees were numerous clay pots of oil. Normally designed to be thrown from their catapults, Havander had found another purpose for the oil filled pots. The dwarves would only be able to throw no more than one barrage of the oil filled pots without hurting their allies so Havander had taken the majority of the pots with him and positioned them among the trees, with lines of oil running from pot to pot along with potions of oil of impact sitting atop the clay pots. Oil of impact is a very productive product if the purpose is to cause an explosion. They act like a miniature fireball spell once the contents within are mixed with air. Their effect along with the oil strewn upon the ground and the clay pots that they connected to was undeniable.

The lightning cast from Etburn hit numerous locations at once, lighting the oil in several locations just as the majority of the worg riders were in their midst. What followed was an explosion of flames that took Havander and his dwarf companions back a few steps. Out of the turmoil of the explosion and the rolling flames that followed amid the trunks of the trees and surrounding brush was something to behold. A couple trees of considerable girth fell in the process adding to the destruction when they crashed to the ground.

Orcs, goblins and worgs battled for their lives amidst an enemy that would not yield. Those that weren't blown apart scrambled for their lives as the seemingly unyielding flames erupted all over their skin and hair. As if that wasn't enough the dwarves ran past Havander who stood in awe at the humbling devastation he just released upon his enemy. Havander watched for a few awe inspiring moments as the dwarves began cutting down those aflame trying to put themselves out until he noticed orcs not caught up in the explosion and trying to reach their companions and the dwarves finishing them off. Then Havander turned back to Etburn and began releasing bolt after bolt of lightning energy into their ranks to bolster the attack of his dwarf friends.

Dalin ducked from the sound of the explosion coming from his left, after dispatching the most recent goblin to meet its end after being struck by his warhammer. He smiled in recognition of what had just happened. He was dubious of Havander's plan to have his fellow dwarves haul away the majority of the oil he wanted to throw at the orc lines. Apparently he was wrong and his left flank would now be even more secure against his enemies' plots.

Denstrom crashed into his father's backside with his own after dodging the swing of an orc axe. The push took Dalin from his thoughts and he pivoted in a practiced motion, as well did Denstrom so that they took each other's position. Upon turning to his left Dalin swung his warhammer and took the orc who was trying to kill his son directly in its side before it could ready another swing. Dalin's swing blasted the orc to the ground where another dwarf stepped in and crashed down upon his chest with his own warhammer summarily dispatching it.

After, Dalin surveyed the scene while coming in line with his son once again. His dwarves were doing well. They were taking ground and moving across the field as more orc and goblin scum fell than precious dwarf bodies. Even the wounded dwarves fought on. Not so much could be said on the opposing side as orc and goblin started fighting defensively while backing towards their original side of the field. Wounded himself from a glancing blow he took earlier, Dalin waded into the next trio of orcs who came at him and Denstrom. The father and son pair dispatched the trio quickly as neither accepted a hurtful blow. Only a slight ding to Denstrom's armor could be marked as any sort of win for the orcs lying dead at their feet.

"There father!" Denstrom said while pointing ahead of their position.

Dalin looked through the throng of those fighting around them. One particular orc stood out as he dispatched one of Dalin's men with a swing of a greatsword and then began shouting orders to the orcs behind him. The orcs were rallying to this orc's orders. It was obvious to Dalin that this orc was likely the orc commander.

"Let's go son!" Dalin said as he continued forward.

Willem and Oran closed in on the far edge of the battlefield. Through the last few remaining trees they could see the battle waging in the center. The field was full of bodies from both sides and fires had broken out in numerous locations. Bodies of orcs and goblins burned among the tall grass closest to their side of the field. On their right the trees and surrounding area were on fire as well thanks to Havander's plan.

It was near Havander's location that Willem's attention was drawn to as suddenly multiple missiles of some sort of magic shot out from the tree line they were now occupying. Dwarves on that end of the field could be seen toppling backwards after being hit by the strange looking balls of energy. They reminded Willem of the magic missile spell that Havander often used except they didn't shoot straight. Instead they curved and tracked a target hence missing the orcs and goblins all together but struck the dwarves in the vicinity.

Willem sped off in that direction and Oran followed suit close behind him. Even in the darkness among the trees they skirted the edge of the battlefield with ease. Over downed logs and around trees they continued until finally they saw what they hoped to see all along. Twenty feet out from the safety of the trees a pair of women stood, with two orc guards watching their backs, shooting bolts of energy into the left flank of the dwarf line.

"Witches." Willem whispered to Oran standing next to him.

"Havander was right." Oran squinted his eyes trying to focus more clearly on the pair. "One appears to be human. Quickly we must stop them."

Like two predators who had practiced this routine many times, Willem and Oran, emerged from the tree line and encroached on their prey. The orc guards standing vigil over the witches were back a few feet from them leaving no choice but to have to strike them down first else their swords would be at their backs.

Oran went straight for the orc on the right and Willem the left. Worried more with speed than stealth the pair of hunters dispatched the orcs quickly hoping to move onto the witches before they were noticed. Oran stopped in his tracks just briefly as he lopped the head off his orc while Willem slid the back of his blade in his right hand clear through the throat of his target.

The sounds of the battle in front of the witches kept the orc witch focused on her casting and she seemed not to notice or hear the sounds of her guards being slaughtered behind her. Unfortunately for Willem and Oran the human witch was apparently more wary of her surroundings. She turned and emitted a blast of energy from her hands, hitting Willem and Oran before they closed the distance to their intended victims.

The blast shot out from in front of Merill Siske, even clipping Katlika Saurtaker and pushing her to the ground sideways. Willem and Oran took the full force of the blast though. It felt as though they had been blasted by wind thrust forth from the edge of a hurricane. The blast itself did little to damage the pair but it blew them backwards and they toppled and rolled across the field back towards the trees.

"What in the hells was that?" Willem asked after he came to a stop.

Oran spit a blade of grass from his mouth then answered, "An influence push spell I believe. Combination of telepathy and wind."

"Oh is that all." Willem replied as he stood and surveyed the scene. The witches both stood facing them. "What now?"

"Use your blades to deflect or slice through their minor missile spells as you try to get close." Oran explained as he stood.

"What? We've never practiced that." Willem complained.

"No time like the present." Oran said as he advanced past Willem after seeing more of those small bolts of energy get released from the witches and arc in at their location.

Oran and Willem advanced while the witches backed away from them and cast wave after wave of magical bolts of energy. Each time they cast the spell a pair of bolts went towards Oran and a pair at Willem and each time the excellent swordsmen sliced through the bolts. The magic in Willem's blades was strong enough to deflect or slice through the spells like Oran had suggested but Oran's sword destroyed them entirely.

After a little cat and mouse across their end of the field, Willem stopped and admired his blades. "How'd you know I could do that?"

"You'd know too if you ever paid attention to me talking while we practice back home." Oran explained while shaking his head.

The two chiefs of the opposing forces fought furiously in the center of the battlefield. Allies of each stepped back and embraced alternate opponents leaving the two alone as if they would determine the fate of the battle alone.

"Ahhh!" Dalin roared in defiance to the blow he accepted on his shoulder, which sent him sideways until he could once again regain his balance.

Cagorn had landed his first significant blow after accepting and pushing through several glancing blows from the Firefist Chief. He brought his greatsword over his head as he pursued the stumbling dwarf. He brought it down in a powerful swing barely missing Dalin as he rolled away from the heavy blow leaving the blade nothing to find but the soft ground.

The battle between the chiefs reset once more as Dalin stood before Cagorn once more. His left shoulder felt somewhat numb but thankfully his well-crafted armor, bearing the sigil of his clan, a stone fist wreathed in flames on his breastplate, did not give way fully under the blow from the large orc, a testament to dwarf craftsmanship. No doubt his shoulder would still be damaged to some extent when his nerves allowed the pain to fully set in. No time for that now as Cagorn came at him again with another overhead chop of his greatsword. Dalin used both arms to lift his warhammer up to black as you would with a staff and guided the heavy blow past his right shoulder dropping his warhammer in the process and rushing forward immediately following its release. Dalin grabbed Cagorn around the waist and lifted the orc in the air and slammed him to the ground.

Though Cagorn was large for an orc he certainly wasn't the largest that Dalin had ever seen. Despite their differences in height Cagorn probably didn't outweigh Dalin by much in his estimation either. He needed a change in tactics and getting inside the reach of the greatsword was key to victory.

Years of working in the mines had molded Dalin's hands into vice like tools. He gripped onto the armor of Cagorn and pulled himself up the length of the orcs body, ignoring the blows being landed to the top of his head by Cagorn. Cagorn squirmed as best he could trying to extricate himself from under the weight of the heavy dwarf but to no avail. Once

Dalin was in proper position he lifted his body up and landed a solid blow to the jaw of Cagorn, dazing him considerably. After that, blow after blow came reigning down on the orcs' face. In a last ditch effort Cagorn reached for his dagger he knew to be on his belt but it was no use. Dalin's body was blocking the attempt and after a couple more fists to the face Cagorn went limp.

Breathing heavily Dalin finally took in a full breath after sensing that the fight in Cagorn was extinguished. He lifted himself up and walked back to his warhammer lying on the ground. Once in hand, Dalin walked back to the prone orc chief, lifted his hammer over his head with both arms and brought down the massive blow right on top of Cagorn's skull; crushing it in entirely.

Havander and his dwarves exited the tree line they were occupying so they could join the fray in the center. They had dispatched all the opposing forces on their left flank and meant to further disrupt the battle in the middle. Once Havander entered the field he noticed that many of the orcs and goblins were beginning a defensive battle back towards their side of the field. Victory it seemed was close at hand. Soon their enemies would be in full flight.

Out of the corner of his eye Havander recognized spell usage of some kind. He stopped, letting all his dwarf charges run past his position. Not too distant from his location he could make out Willem and Oran dancing this way and that across the field in pursuit of two spellcasters. Havander began racing to their aid.

As he neared, the battle before him was intense to watch. The witches were casting their version of a magic missile spell, he supposed, at Willem and Oran who summarily dispatched the magic with swings of their blades. Before Willem or Oran could get within striking distance the witches would cast again making Willem and Oran stop to defend against the incoming magic. Once, Oran got close enough to strike but the witch dissipated into a grey mist and flew some thirty yards or so away from Oran, where she took form again and launched another wave of missiles.

This battle was more akin to Havander's skills. As he neared the witch facing off against Willem, he enacted a magical barrier spell for protection. Once in place he was well within range of the orc witch who had not seen his approach because her back was to him. Willem was quickly gaining ground on her position as well, which forced her to change tactics. She cast a burning wave spell hoping to engulf her little pursuer. Willem was the quicker though and rolled out of range before the flames engulfed him.

Havander had seen enough. Without slowing he enacted the power within Etburn once more sending a bolt of lighting into the back of Katlika. The blast stopped short of her body for a few brief moments as its energy arced off of her protective shield. She turned in time to see Havander, gaining ground on her position. Katlika barely had time to register the sight she saw before the power of the continuous lighting broke through her shield. What she did see was impressive. Lightning reached out at her from the end of a staff being held by a human cloaked in dark blue. Small arcs of blue and white lightning raced across his body as though he was a living vessel of lightning itself. Her awe was short lived as the lightning broke through her magic protections and blasted her with enough force to send her flying backwards.

Havander reached the body of Katlika at the same time as Willem. Her green skin was scorched and smoking. The smell of burnt hair was heavy in the air and made Willem cover his nose with the back of his hand before turning to Havander.

"You've got to be kidding me! You know how long I was working on that?" Willem complained.

"Your welcome." Havander replied and quickly stepped over the dead witch and took position ahead of Willem as two magic missiles raced in at them from the tree line.

With Willem behind him, Havander let the missiles hit his shield without thought of trying to block the spells or dodge them in any way. His barrier held soundly and for an instant the magical barrier around Havander could be seen with the naked eye as an opaque sphere surrounding his body entirely. Havander was pleased with his newest spell he had learned for his arsenal. The magical barrier spell was stronger and encompassed him fully unlike his magical shield spell he had been using prior to this trip to the Talts.

His moment of elation was brief however as Merrill raced towards his position. Her lower body was in the form of mist and she flew above the field, ten feet off of the ground. Two more of those magic missiles raced ahead of Merill as she advanced. Havander ignored them completely as arcs of lightning energy raced over his skin and clothing once more. Immediately following the collision of the magic missiles on his defense he released bolts of his own at the witch.

Merrill stopped in midair as three bolts of lightning energy approached her. As each neared she cast a smaller version of her influence wave she had used on the other two humans. She cast it sidelong at the approaching blasts, one after the other, batting them aside to fly off harmlessly in the air.

Merrill had to reassess her situation. She now stood alone against the two obviously skilled warriors wielding weapons capable of disrupting her spells and now this wizard had appeared on the scene dispatching her apprentice. These allies of the dwarves no doubt killed her beloved assassin as well. She could not believe that the dwarves were wise enough or strong enough to finish him. No. It had to be these three.

Quickly she looked over the battlefield. The orcs and goblins were now in full retreat. A wave of anger took over her thoughts as she thought of her lost companion. It had taken years to mold that astral walker to her will and now her plots to destroy the dwarves in their homeland was all for not. In a final effort to enact some form of vengeance she began casting again.

Havander watched as the floating mix of mist and human hovered before him. Behind her, Oran emerged from the trees. Havander could not tell but Oran's armor was smoldering in the center of his chest after taking one of the blasts from the magic missiles she was employing earlier. He turned his attention back to the witch as a ball of light left her hand. The seemingly small flame grew larger as it approached.

"Go left!" Havander shouted to Willem as he took off right.

Willem did exactly as Havander had instructed thankfully. Havander recognized the spell for what it was and didn't want to test his defenses against that of a fireball just yet. The ball of fire exploded as it hit the ground where the pair had been previously standing sending dirt and other debris flying outwards from the center of the explosion.

Dirt and rocks bounced off of Havander's magical barrier. He looked back up to the witch and saw another ball of light leave her hands. Acting instinctively, Havander sent a continuous flow of lightning at the small sphere. His aim was true and the lightning collided with the fireball

R. A. HAYDEN

not too distant from the witch's position. The shockwave emanating from the blast was closer to Merrill than Havander and it sent her flying backwards but not completely out of control.

Enough, Merill thought as she regained control of her movements. Still hanging in the air but much closer to the ground, she was about to make her own hasty retreat. Her vengeance would have to wait another day or so she thought.

Oran jumped and stabbed forward with his enchanted sword, shattering the protective enchantments surrounding Merrill and driving through her body at her midsection. The two of them fell from the air with Oran on top. Merrill landed face first in the ground. Oran's blade protruding from her stomach stuck directly into the ground.

Oran stood and watched as the mist reformed around Merrill's lower half taking the form of her legs once more. Her life-blood was flowing fast into the ground beneath her body and Oran knew the fight was over. He stepped back and looked across the field to the dwarves in pursuit of the remaining orcs and goblins taking flight to his left.

Havander and Willem joined Oran at his vantage point as Merrill breathed her last before Oran decided to pull forth his sword. Willem was brushing off dirt from his jacket and muttering complaints under his breath.

"What is it Willem?" Oran asked.

"Havander took my witch from me!" Willem complained.

Oran smiled as he looked to Havander who was wearing a mischievous looking smile. He nodded his approval to the young mage. His skill was now more obvious than ever and he knew that without his help that at least this witch before him may have at least escaped.

"What now Oran? Do we help the dwarves in pursuit?" Havander asked.

Oran looked once more to the dwarves who were actually ending their pursuit at the tree line. Cheers erupted from their ranks marking the end of the battle. The day was theirs.

"No. Now we see to the wounded and then go back to the village." Oran answered.

"It's not always gonna be like this," Willem began complaining again as they walked back towards their dwarf allies, "First you get the final blow on that demon or whatever he was and now you two get the witches. My time is coming mark my words."

CHAPTER TWENTY-SEVEN

Cowardly Proposal—Fandril, 1021

H AROLD ENTERED THE classroom, where Josef was conducting a class with Marcus as his sole student following their midday meal, after rushing through the door without knocking. This was unaccustomed for Harold so Josef knew right away that something was wrong.

"What is it Harold?" Joseph asked concerned.

"This just arrived for you sir." Harold explained as he closed the distance to Josef and held out a small scroll.

Josef took the scroll and examined the seal. It was sealed with wax and stamped into that wax was a small sigil of Bahamut.

"Who gave this to you?" Josef asked Harold after figuring out whom it likely came from.

"A man rode up to our back gate and shouted out to me. When I approached he slid it through and said to give it to you immediately then rode off without another word."

Josef looked to Marcus who looked on intently then walked over to his desk and took a seat laying the rolled parchment onto the desktop. Unsure of exactly what ends The Order of Silver would go to cause harm to him or his family Josef enacted a detect magic spell before cracking the wax seal. He thought it unlikely but better safe than sorry. When he was content it contained no magical trap or curse he unrolled it fully.

Righe,

I would like to take you up on your previous offer and face you and your watchdog in open battle. You need only respond by showing up, with the black dragonborn of course, at the Netley farm a few miles distant to the south of your Keep before sunset. If any Castan soldiers are seen accompanying you, trailing you, or trying to outflank us in any way then this family of blasphemers will be given the opportunity to make their case to our almighty god.

—Ramsay Pinkerton

Josef looked up from the parchment and looked over to Marcus still sitting at the desk with quill in hand twirling it in his fingers. Finally he thought, it took over seven years but at last an outright battle would have to be fought to secure the future of Marcus Alio.

Josef slammed the paper onto his desk and looked to Harold. "Go get Captain Payne and Escott Claridge!"

Harold did an abrupt about face and headed for the door in all haste. Only rarely had he seen such fire behind Josef's eyes. Just as he exited the door he could hear Josef yelling further instructions of not to bring anyone else besides Captain Payne and Escott Claridge and to yell at Adley to come downstairs immediately.

Captain Payne and Escott Claridge followed Harold into the classroom, where Josef and Adley awaited them. Upon seeing them Adley turned his attention to them, leaving Josef alone to look into his scrying pool, now centered in the middle of the classroom instead of its usual spot in the corner.

"What is it?" Captain Payne asked of Adley when the pair neared.

Adley held out the scroll that had been delivered by The Order of Silver. Captain Payne took the scroll, unrolled it and held it aloft so that Escott could read over his shoulder.

"Surely not." Escott said in disbelief when he was finished reading.

Captain Payne turned to him and looked on in shock as well, then the pair turned to Adley.

"Well this can't happen. You two are not going to face them alone." Captain Payne asserted.

"Thank you for that vote of confidence Captain." Josef said without looking up from the seemingly still water contained within the scrying pool he was most intent upon.

"I only mean…"

"I know what you meant Captain." Josef said, interrupting him.

Josef looked up from the scrying pool and motioned for them all to come closer. Escott was anxious to look into the marvelous looking scrying pool and rushed past Captain Payne and Adley. Though this was certainly not the time to give praise to Josef for his excellent looking classroom, Escott was nonetheless impressed. Having never even stepped foot below the ground level of Silver Guard Keep, probably due to the circumstances regarding his initial duties at Lanos Outpost as a spy for Headmaster Usarus. Thankfully those times were long past and the relationships he felt with those at the Keep and his own Captain were now firmly secure.

Long ago Escott ceased reporting on The Silver Guard for Hareth Academy, as there wasn't really much to discern according to him. The Silver Guard did most of everything out in the open and were not the conspirators that others at Hareth Academy had suggested. He cautiously reached out and touched the thick copper edge of the pool. He did not have much experience with scrying as it mostly remained outside his expertise but that did little to diminish the excitement of working directly with Josef Righe in his very own laboratory.

"It's a world pool isn't it?" Escott asked of Josef after closer inspection.

Josef smiled and placed a hand on the shoulder of Escott, which he noticed visibly relaxed the nervous wizard. He was pleased that his relationship with this man had turned for the better after initial disagreements.

"Yes it is." Josef confirmed.

Escott stepped back a step to examine the pool further. The large copper bowl was centered on a three-tier stand of steel, engraved with various magical markings much like the rim of the bowl. Scrying pools and crystal balls were used by wizards for communication across great distances and for the spying on of one's enemies. A world pool however was used more extensively with locations thus aiding in the secrecy of the whole affair. Scrying directly on a person who was capable of sensing the magical intrusion could block the scrying attempt or at the very least alert them. World pools were harder to detect. After his examination, Escott looked over the rim of the bowl to see what exactly Josef was looking at. What he saw was a bird's eye view over a small farm.

"That's the Netley farm isn't it?" Escott reasoned.

"Yes and on the edge of that farm," Josef made a motion with his hand over the still waters directing its focus elsewhere, "We can see our enemy."

Adley and Captain Payne stood extremely close to one another as the bowl of the scrying pool was not overly large and they leaned over sideways to veer into the waters. Harold, standing behind the pair and leaving Josef and Escott ample room to do their work, stood up on his tiptoes to try to catch of glimpse of what they looked at but to no avail.

Now centered in the pool was a gathering of men standing near the edge of a small patch of trees. Not too distant from the edge of the trees was the Netley family: tied, gagged, and tethered to the fence running the perimeter of the field. Though it was hard to ascertain their exact condition they seemed not the worse for ware considering the circumstances they now found themselves under.

"Bastards!" Captain Payne shouted. "The Netley's are a good family. Not to mention the tying up and treatment of two children like that is despicable." Captain Payne pushed past Harold and rubbed his chin while thinking as he paced before the nearby table.

"Indeed Captain and a situation they will not find themselves in for very long." Josef declared.

"Well I'm all for that. What's the plan?" Captain Payne asked.

"Let's state the obvious first." Josef started. "We cannot march in force. Your forces would be seen as they have chose their spot well."

Josef motioned over the pool again and it re-centered itself again on some distance away from the main group.

"Here are two spotters on the nearby hilltop. While not very far away it gives them a vantage point for miles around. Any movement in that area can be seen by them and they will alert their company."

"Fools. They can't possibly get away with this. They are countless miles away from Kodia. I need only alert my men and they would be hunted down like animals." Captain Payne avowed.

"Not like animals. They are indeed skilled. We should have watched them more closely. That fault lies with me I'm afraid." Josef conveyed.

"Still they would not get away." Captain Payne continued.

"They are not far from the Mehm River. They need only cross it and could if alerted to an approaching force." Adley chimed in.

"And enter Cruz. That's ridiculous. Cruz and Kodia are enemies." Captain Payne reasoned.

"Yes but the Cruz are not looking for them. They probably have skill enough to skirt the Mehm River to the coast where they could board a ship and sail for home where they would be forever out of reach." Adley responded.

Captain Payne shook his head but agreed with the assessment. He did however find it hard to believe that they could be that hell bent on killing Marcus, a single child who was no obvious threat. Fanatics were obviously beyond his reasoning.

"I wish Oran and the boys were here." Captain Payne said.

"As do I. Myself and Havander conveyed messages back and forth to each other yesterday and they are at least a week out having just left Firefist Village this morning." Josef explained.

"What of Marcus?" Captain Payne inquired.

Josef looked over to Harold and recognized the worried expression on his face. "He will stay here. I'll not put him in direct danger."

"They may hurt the Netley's if they don't see him with us." Escott said.

"That is a risk we are going to have to take but I believe they will be happy with the apparent odds stacked against them."

"They still won't be happy seeing us four instead of just you two." Captain Payne asserted.

"Ah the crux of the matter." Josef said and once again put a hand to the top of Escott's shoulder. "Tell me. How good exactly are you with your phantasm spells?"

Riston Browning looked into the conjured water in the whole he had dug into the ground. Pleased with what he saw in the makeshift scrying pool he stood up from his seated position.

"Any changes?" Ramsay Pinkerton asked.

"No commander. I have watched their approach and it is still just the two men and the boy." Riston said quite pleased.

"And no one following?"

"No commander."

"Nor have the scouts indicated any movement behind their approach." Ellen Nubula chimed in.

Ramsay Pinkerton was delighted with the news. It seems this famed wizard, Josef Righe, was a bigger fool than he had hoped. This trip, it seemed, would soon be over. Though they would be considered outlaws in Casta from this day forth, they would be hailed as heroes amongst their own in Kodia. Even those who argued for renewed ties with the mages of the world would not be able to deny his altered version of their visit to the lands of Casta. The disappearance and apparent murder, as he would tell it, of his most trusted scout, Davion Braxton, along with the destruction of a black dragonborn and the blasphemers who protected him would raise the praise already given to The Order of Silver.

Ramsay moved over to three of his men and ordered them into position behind them in the woods. These three archers would fire from afar as his clerics poured their divine power over the supposedly formidable wizard followed closely by him and his remaining troops engaging them in melee if necessary. His plan was coming together well.

On a small hill, with a few trees for cover, Captain Payne appeared next to two horses belonging to the scouts posted for The Order of Silver. Having never transported or traveled in any way by means of a spell was an odd sensation and he felt dizzy.

Josef and he had stayed behind as Escott and Adley traveled by horseback to the Netley farm. They watched the world pool waiting the proper moment to thrust themselves upon the scene. Josef had explained the plan in detail before their departure and it seemed a feasible plan and one that would surely take The Order of Silver by surprise.

Continually surprised by the power that Josef held was nothing new for Captain Payne because it happened on regular intervals throughout his long friendship with him, however he never imagined that Josef was able to teleport himself or someone else at such a distance. Josef had explained to him that it was something he preferred not to do but as the Netley farm was not that distant it was certainly within his power though he could only do one person at a time or himself and doing it twice would drain him considerably but not so much that he would be ineffective in the battle. With the illusion set that Josef and Adley were en route to meet The Order of Silver and would be arriving shortly, Captain Payne shook his dizziness off as quickly as he could before setting out.

He moved quietly from tree to tree to the very top of the hill where it leveled out. As he crept around one last tree he spotted the scouts, hidden behind some brush and the low hanging branches of the trees above at the end of the tree line. They appeared completely unaware of his presence and they looked out over the fields below to the pair of horses nearing their position but on a path that would lead past them and down the final descent towards the field below where their companions waited. Even at this distance Escott and Adley would be in range of the long bows they carried with them. Something they were sure to do once the battle began.

Captain Payne crept closer and leveled the crossbow he had taken with him at the pair. He knew he had to be quick and his kills would have to be sure. Any alarm to their friends would ruin the whole plan. Thankfully they were intent on watching the riders approach and scanning behind them for any sign of the Castan forces from Lanos.

Well within striking distance, and actually very few feet away, Captain Payne announced himself, "Hay."

Both turned and reached for their swords. Captain Payne shot the man to his right, in the chest. The blast from the bolt sent him backwards and he would surely not be recovering. Captain Payne immediately dropped the crossbow and pulled his own sword while rushing at his other opponent. Taken by complete surprise the other scout had trouble and fumbled getting his sword out. Captain Payne did not hesitate and sliced right into the crevice where neck met shoulder as the man tried to step backwards away from his attacker.

The second scout went down hard and grabbed at the wound with both hands trying to stem the flow of blood that was spurting out the side of his neck and onto his already dead companion. Captain Payne watched as the man tried futilely to stop the blood flow. He figured he probably should not have warned them of his approach before firing his bolt, as cowards such as these who would harm children were not deserving, but he would not have felt great running them through the back. All in all it went well and the first part of their plan was complete.

Marcus sat on his bed disgusted with himself for not telling Josef, or anyone for that matter, about his recent mishap in the woods which led to the death of one of The Order of Silver. If he had warned them earlier perhaps this wouldn't have happened. Perhaps he thought it was not a good idea to keep so many secrets from everybody. He didn't like it being done to him and Braden had told him it was up to him so its not as though he was betraying anyone.

"Braden." Marcus whispered aloud to himself after finally thinking of a solution of sorts or so he hoped.

Marcus leaped off of the bed and threw open the chest at the foot of his bed. Buried under the extra blankets and secreted away among his toys, the ruby pommel dagger that Braden had given him was wrapped up and secure in its hiding place. After unwrapping it from the multiple layers of cloth concealing it he climbed back into bed and sat staring at the ruby.

"Braden I need your help. I'm in trouble." He said while looking into the large ruby. After many seconds of no response he continued. "Braden please come like you did before. I need your help."

Again there was no response and Marcus had doubts that the dagger actually did anything. Everyone else had lied to him about various things so why should Braden be any different?

Just when he had given up hope a small illumination of red light caught his attention. It emanated from the ruby.

"What is it young Marcus?" Braden's voice sounded in his room as though it was emanating from the walls.

Marcus looked around in disbelief. It actually worked though he couldn't see Braden.

"Where are you?" Marcus asked aloud while looking around his empty bedroom.

"I'm here Marcus. Speaking to you through the ruby."

Marcus looked into the ruby, examining it. For the briefest of time he thought he saw an eyeball appear on its smooth surface area. Shocked, he pushed the dagger back to arms length and heard a laugh following the movement emanating from the dagger itself.

"Hold it closer so that I can hear you. Its use is limited under the protections of your house." Braden announced.

Reluctantly Marcus held the dagger with the ruby pointed towards his mouth. "Is this better?"

"Yes. Now what is it? Surely this isn't an emergency from within the walls of The Silver Guard Keep. You are lucky I answered. I don't often hear things during the middle of the day. I tend to be up at night like you."

"But it is an emergency. Josef and the others are in trouble and could use your help." Marcus explained.

"Trouble from what?"

"The Order of Silver. I didn't tell them about what happened in the woods and now they are all out fighting somewhere."

Again Marcus heard the distinct laughter of Braden emanating from the dagger.

"I assure you Josef will be just fine."

"But he won't. There are too many of them. Josef only has Adley, the Captain, and Escott with him. Surely you can help them like you helped me."

"Calm Marcus. Surely you don't know the true power behind my old friend. If those fools were stupid enough to face Josef than you have little to worry about. Few in this world can match your teacher in sheer power."

Adley and Escott, in the form of Josef and riding along with Marcus in front of him apparently, stopped their horses on the narrow road that lead to the Netley farm at the top of the hillside. Down the small decent to the field below and across the expanse of the field, now thick with grass as it was not farming season, The Order of Silver could be seen waiting their arrival. They walked their horses down and entered the field in a large opening of the surrounding fence line.

As they neared Adley recognized right away that only fourteen of them could be seen. Two scouts, he knew were being reckoned with, hopefully by Captain Payne by now, but three more were not among their ranks. A detail that hopefully Josef had not missed out on all the way back at the Keep.

They edged their horses along the fence line parallel the position of The Order of Silver until they came in line with them and the trees behind their position. Once there they edged their horses forward to about forty yards away from where the Netley family was being held and halted them.

"We are close enough now that they can detect my ruse if they are so inclined." Escott whispered over to Adley.

"Well they don't appear to have done so yet." Adley responded as he surveyed the positioning of their enemy.

Ramsay Pinkerton stepped forward with Riston and Jorah on his left and Ellen to his right. Five of the men flanked out further right slowly while two more did the same to the left leaving three men standing guard over the Netley's.

"Well met Master Righe." Ramsay announced a bit sarcastically. "I have to admit I'm surprised you followed through with your boast of facing us."

Ignoring the tone of Ramsay, Escott, who sounded exactly like Josef, hollered back, "The Netley's. Let them go. They are not part of this."

Ramsay nodded in agreement and waved his right hand in the air briefly. Behind him the three men cut all four of the Netley's free of the ropes tying them to the fence posts but not undoing their hands or their gags. Like the bullies they were the man who cut Dudley Netley, the father of the family, free kicked him to the ground. He recovered quickly and rushed to the side of his wife and girls. The men yelled at them to leave and waved off in the direction of their farmhouse.

"Satisfied?" Ramsay asked after looking back to the hurried departure of the farmers.

"Quite." Escott said and him and Adley both began dismounting.

Ellen Nubula thought it odd that Josef, a man of considerable years, was dismounting while still holding onto the large child that was Marcus Alio without any real effort. That and Marcus seemed not to move as though he was a living coherent boy. Quickly and quietly she cast true seeing, a spell designed to see any illusions or falsehoods cast by magic wielders.

When she was finished the truth was apparent to her eyes. Fully dismounted and standing before her was not Josef Righe but that other wizard they had encountered in Lanos. Now standing before him was not Marcus Alio but merely a burlap sack resting at the wizard's feet.

"It's a lie!" Ellen shouted. "That's not Josef or the boy." She pointed at Escott and screamed to her companions.

Escott dropped the illusions and loosed the reigns of his horse as he threw the sack containing nothing more than a blanket to the side.

Ramsay, Jorah and all of his men drew swords as Ellen and Riston began casting. Before any spells were finished or any of the combatants moved so much as a step a large explosion could be heard and felt as the shockwave from it blasted across the field from behind The Order of Silver's position.

All eyes turned in that direction and the three men who had cut the Netley's loose and were closest to the blast were now laying flat on the ground trying to recover. Ramsay's stare went beyond his downed men to the other three men he had positioned in the woods. Now, two lay just feet away from the edge of the fence and one was draped over a length of fence between posts. All three were on fire, as was much of the trees and brush where his men had been and Ramsay could only guess that all three were dead.

Through the smoke and fire, Josef Righe stepped forth, unhurt by the destruction around him or the flames licking at his clothes and failing to catch fire.

Ramsay, aware that enemies were still behind him, turned back to face Escott and Adley. Behind their fleeing horses another rider, advanced from the position where his scouts had been stationed, and Escott's form suddenly became six. The mirror images of him appeared slightly blurry and the true Escott could not be determined.

All at once everyone began moving and the battle commenced.

Josef centered his next spell beneath the fence line directly in front of him. He knelt down and would have appeared to be talking to the ground if anyone was close enough to hear him. He was doing far more than that though, as he called to an old friend. One he had not asked for aid from in many decades.

The ground beneath the fence posts began ripping apart and then rushing up into the air as if a giant mole was returning to the surface. Fence posts stuck fast into the ground raised with the mound of dirt, rock and grass rising into the air, including the length of fence where one of the bodies of Josef's first victims hung across its length.

All the men who were previously rushing at his position halted as the colossal mound of ground took roughly the form of bipedal creature. Once fully erected the earth elemental, standing close to twenty feet high, turned to Josef, who nodded in appreciation of answering his call.

"You know what to do old friend." Josef said.

The earth elemental turned and roared an earthy growl in response to the small balls of flame now colliding with his massive body. The dead soldier hanging from the fence in the center of his back went flying, returning to the ground. As he turned he saw his accoster. Riston was hurling small balls of flame, one after the other at him. He took his first step towards the not too distant cleric who had just earned his ire.

Escott watched as the rolling Ramsay Pinkerton dodged his magic missile. Escott looked to Adley who was walking with shield raised towards the massive silver dragonborn, who likewise moved closer to Adley. Just before he could launch another spell to aid Adley a wall of flame erupted between him and Adley's position, summarily taking out the last mirror image of himself to his right and separating him from Adley, Ramsay, and Jorah. He looked straight back to his left in time to see Ellen Nubula cast another spell and launch a magical stone into another of his mirror images dissolving it completely. Adley it seemed was on his own as he had his own issue in the form of a female silver dragonborn intent on destroying him.

Escott bowed, or four of Escott bowed to his opponent. Then Escott quickly cast a magic missile at Ellen, which she accepted on her magical defenses, which did not break from the miniscule spell. After, she cast another magical stone hitting Escott, the real Escott, on his magical shield thus ending the mirror image illusion he cast of himself. Now the two faced each other one on one despite the conflicts taking place throughout the field.

Both began casting simultaneously but Escott was the faster. A small flaming sphere erupted from his hands shooting right past the spiritual hammer spell that had taken shape between the two combatants. His fireball spell erupted right where Ellen had been standing but thankfully for her she dodged to her right at the last second. The fireball spell was powerful enough however to break her magical defenses in place, in spite of not hitting her directly.

Escott looked on in satisfaction as the spiritual hammer dissipated. In order for her to use that spell she would have had to keep concentration to some extent and that was taken away from her by his powerful fireball spell.

Ellen picked herself up and began casting once more. A small circle of fire erupted around her feet on the ground and then winked out of existence as though it was never there. Escott recognized the spell work and knew that she had cast a shield protecting her from fire spells. Thankfully his repertoire did not consist of any further fire spells at the moment.

Instead Escott started casting magic missile, one after the other at Ellen as he began walking towards her rapidly. The first couple she dodged completely but they were coming at her fast and prevented her from casting. After taking one of the missiles in the chest she resorted to her mace and began smashing the missiles out of the air, as she too advanced on Escott. Her thoughts were clear. If she could not win the spell battle than she would bludgeon her opponent to death.

Once in the range Escott wanted, he launched one more magic missile knowing it would be deflected but immediately began casting what he hoped would be his trump card. After hitting the latest missile aside Ellen roared in defiance and charged. Unfortunately for her she charged right into the wake of a cloud of vapor erupting and fanning out before Escott.

Ellen stopped running and began choking on the yellowish vapor she was inhaling. She dropped her mace as the acid began reacting within her mouth. Unlike her tough skin and scales, her mouth and throat were as soft as any humans. She fell to her knees as bile began emanating up her esophagus and out her mouth. She looked through the yellowish haze and saw the triumphant looking Escott look on in satisfaction. Furiously she reached within herself for her innate dragon abilities and shot forth a cone of frost from her mouth at Escott. The relief of the frost forcing most of the poisonous gas out of her system was short lived though.

Escott took the full blast of the cone of frost from Ellen and it was powerful enough to break through his shield spell but it went no further.

The extent of the contents clung to the shield spell and only when it was at its zenith did the last of it pile up on the shield and break it leaving a varied array of ice crystals falling to the ground harmlessly at Escott's feet.

After having her hopes fully diminished, Ellen once again felt the acidy burn again take shape. She slumped all of the way to the ground as the acid burned further into her insides and her lungs began bleeding leading to her choking to death on her own sacred blood.

Adley blocked a blow from Ramsay with his shield and ducked under a massive swing of Jorah's morning star. Adley was doing well, even landing a blow on Jorah, but doing little to slow the monstrously sized dragonborn. Although his blow pierced through Jorah's armor, his tough scales underneath accepted the weakened blow and blood was not drawn. At this rate Adley would slow considerably and eventually Jorah would connect with his massive weapon.

Fighting defensively and hoping for an opening Adley continued backing. He couldn't allow the two to be on either side of him so he had to move rapidly to stay ahead of their attempts to do so.

Another block of Ramsay's well aimed sword thrust followed quickly by Jorah left Adley with no option but to attempt to block the morning star with his sword. The blow took his sword out wide and Jorah followed with a kick, hitting Adley in the chest and sending him backwards into the dirt.

Ramsay was quick to follow and was about to swing his blade in on his downed opponent when out of nowhere Ramsay was hit by a collision with a horse, steered by Captain Payne right into Ramsay sending him flying towards Jorah.

The triumphant roar by Captain Payne was short lived though as Jorah swung his massive weapon and connected with the horses' neck before Captain Payne could bring his sword down in a swing at the behemoth.

The horse tried to rear up from the blow but toppled sideways sending Captain Payne from the saddle and into the ground hard and sending his sword from his grasp. Jorah went to follow through but he had to maneuver around the dying horse. Before he could he was hit on his side by Adley's shield, who rushed at his large opponent. The largest of the spikes in Adley's shield pierced through Jorah's armor and scales, digging deep into his side. Before Adley could follow through with a swing of his sword though, Jorah swung with a backhand catching Adley in the side of the head and sent him stumbling away without his shield.

Jorah looked down at the shield on the ground and his blood covering the spike. He then inspected his wound as best he could. It was a good hit but far from life threatening.

"Come on worm." Adley egged Jorah on and waved him forward after shaking off the blow that sent him staggering away.

Jorah looked to Ramsay who was regaining his feet to go after the rider of the horse. Jorah spit in Adley's direction and advanced.

Riston was blasted away by a glancing blow from the enormous earth elemental. He looked up dazed and was fortunate to find that his fellow soldiers had averted its attention from him. They came at the elemental and swung with their weapons furiously trying to chop down the terrible construct. Riston did not believe it would be enough. Neither were his spells as he had tried, unsuccessfully, to blast the elemental apart and when that failed he tried to dispel the connection it had to the material plane but to no avail. He had not planned on fighting dirt and rock.

He lifted himself up searching his mind for a plan as another of his men was crushed under the weight of a stomp from the elemental. The sheer size of the elemental was awe-inspiring and Riston was secure in the knowledge that they had indeed underestimated the reputation of Master Righe.

The ground beneath Riston rose into the air suddenly and with enough force and speed to send him flying through the air once more. He landed with a thud and rolled to his back attempting to regain his breath after having it blasted from his body. When he could again breath again he looked up to see Josef Righe staring at him and waiting patiently for him to regain his feet. Riston looked behind him to the tower of rock and dirt standing sideways up into the air. Apparently Josef had been the cause so now he faced him alone and with no help of allies as he looked around to find nothing more than more bodies of his men lying about, close to Josef.

"You have erred greatly cleric." Josef said when Riston was once again on his feet and facing off against him.

Not clearly resigned to his fate Riston hoped to bargain. "I advised against this action if it is of any consequence. I cared not about the disappearance of Davion Braxton."

"None at all." Josef said, a bit confused for he knew nothing for the name Riston had just said to him and didn't know the meaning behind it. He then looked over to the battle still unfolding in the field. "Soon my elemental will be finished chasing the last of your so-called warriors and you will join them in the afterlife."

"I am at peace with my god. Are you yours?" Riston questioned while readying a barrage of spells to follow the shield he was about to enact.

"Lets find out." Josef announced before beginning his own casting.

To his credit Riston was able to enact another shield spell before Josef enacted his offensive spell but it did little to protect him from the wrath that was Josef Righe.

The first meteor that left Josef's hand was enough to break the shield spell enacted by Riston and the second blasted him to almost nothing. The two flaming spheres of rock that followed hit nothing but air and were not needed. It was not a pleasant thing to attract the anger of Josef Righe.

Captain Payne raised himself up from the ground just in time to push inside the reach of the swing coming at him from Ramsay Pinkerton. He caught Ramsay's wrist with his own and delivered a punch to his jaw with his right hand sending him backwards a few steps. Quickly Captain Payne glanced around looking for his sword but did not see it. Instead he pulled his dagger from his belt when Ramsay came at him again more measured this time.

"Funny it should come to this." Ramsay said as him and Captain Payne circled one another. "Two commanders facing off like knights of old."

"Knights are a thing of the past." Captain Payne responded.

"Not where I come from. Just because your pathetic kingdom has done away with the practice doesn't make you the center of the world."

"You're no knight and even if you were, you sully the title."

Ramsay responded with a sidelong swing of his sword forcing Captain Payne to back a step before following through with a more powerful two handed swing aimed at the shoulder. Captain Payne reversed the grip of his dagger catching the blow with his blade but the force of the blow forced the dagger's sharp edge through his bracer and deep into his forearm. This did not slow the captain down though. Accustomed to receiving blows in battle and the adrenaline of the moment kept him fighting with a clear head as he connected again to the head of Ramsay, this time with a left cross.

Captain Payne did not relent this time either. He stayed on the heels of Ramsay punching out with his free arm and slicing back across with the reverse grip he still held on his dagger. Ramsay retreated defensively barely staying out of reach of the relentless captain. He did however back himself right up to the flaming wall, enacted earlier by Ellen Nubula. Upon sensing his predicament he lashed out with his sword to fend off his attacker but Captain Payne was inside the reach of the long weapon and caught Ramsay's forearm under his arm, letting the blade pass behind his back harmlessly. He followed through with a head-butt to the nose watering Ramsay's eyes and allowing him to break their embrace. Ramsay attempted one final swing with his sword, which flew before the captain missing badly with his impaired vision. Captain Payne was right there behind the swing stabbing his dagger downward into the collarbone of Ramsay and then releasing his grip of it as he pushed him backwards into the flames.

Ramsay fell backwards and his clothing was set on fire in short order. Instinctively he rolled but that only furthered his predicament for he was rolling with the length of the flames and not away from them.

Captain Payne turned around to search for his sword, leaving the commander to burn to death, as he deserved.

Jorah kept Adley backing away and fighting defensively with swings of his morning star. Adley could ill afford to be struck by the massive spiked head at the end of the weapon. His hope was that the heavy dragonborn would soon tire but it didn't seem to be coming to pass anytime soon. The stamina of his opponent was impressive.

Adley reached into his belt and produced a small throwing dagger. After one particular swing that Jorah kept concluding his attack routine on he let fly. The small blade dinged undamagingly off of the formidable armor and Jorah merely bared his teeth in what Adley assumed was a grin.

Adley was not finished though. He produced another as Jorah advanced again. This time he tossed it up to Jorah as though they were playing catch. Jorah's eyes went to the blade for just an instant. Adley timed his swing perfectly with the movement but Jorah was still able to block the blow from Adley's sword but not to the full extent. Near the end of the blade the weapon slipped through a crease in his armor and dug deep into the scales underneath the armor and into his flesh. Adley retracted the blade in a slicing motion further lengthening the slice now on Jorah's triceps.

Anger rose inside Jorah and he pushed forward even faster; the response Adley was hoping to illicit. He was still able to back step away fast enough and Jorah's swings became less measured. Finally openings in his offensive style were beginning to emerge.

Adley jabbed quickly after two consecutive swings from Jorah, both catching Jorah in the stomach, albeit slightly. The blows drew little blood as his armor and scales protected him greatly but at least he was damaging him.

Jorah came forward in a great rush ignoring the opening he left open for Adley and accepting the recent blow without complaint as Adley's blade dug deep into where the spike had previously pierced his armor. It was no matter to Jorah now as he clenched his strong hand around Adley's throat and lifted him from the ground with one arm.

Adley was forced to drop his sword and fight with both hands at the grip squeezing his airway. Strong himself, Adley began making headway but with Jorah's right hand still on his morning star and raising it to strike him, he had to react quickly. Adley launched his feet upwards and caught Jorah in the mouth with his right boot. The blow was hard and unexpected. Jorah dropped Adley as he backed up a step and reached to his mouth, now in pain. He spit once more, this time a tooth came out with the saliva and blood flowed into his mouth from where the tooth had been extracted.

Jorah looked to Adley who seemed to be moving to regain his weapon. He chopped down hoping to catch Adley on back of his helmet but the movement from Adley was a feint. As the heavy swing came at his position he jumped straight up at Jorah and to the left side of his body avoiding the swing, which now became overbalanced trying to follow Adley's movement.

Adley reached behind Jorah's head and pulled hard on the handful of scales he grabbed that acted like hair for the dragonborn, tilting his head back so that he could thrust his signature silver steak into the lower jaw of Jorah. Adley held on and kept pulling Jorah backwards forcing him to the ground. When he finally fell like a stubborn tree finally breaking away after being pounded on by a relentless storm, Adley pushed farther with his left arm and using the sudden stop of Jorah's head against the ground he thrust the stake all the way up into his brain.

"Well played my friend." Braden said under his breath.

Braden took another drink of his wine as he looked into his scrying pool, at the moments following the end of the battle between Josef and his companions and The Order of Silver. Josef had just released his hold on his elemental, sending it back to its own plane and the dirt and rocks that formed its huge body crumpled to the ground leaving a considerably large mound next to the hole it had formed when it crawled into the material plane.

With a wave of his hand Braden released his own spell he had over the scrying pool and extinguished its image before Josef was aware of his spying. After, he moved over to the large lounge chair set in the corner of his private scrying chamber and laid back against the plush red velvet pillows adorning it. There he took another long drink of his wine and relived the battle through memory and fully enjoyed the scene that he had just previously witnessed.

Braden was very pleased that Marcus had awoken him from his slumber even though it was not yet nightfall. Safe from any sunlight deep in his castle and the constant cloud cover that hung over the valley and peaks his home rested in, he had rushed to his scrying chamber after his brief conversation with Marcus.

He was pleased at the devious scene that unfolded before his eyes. In times past Josef was much more straightforward when going into a battle. Perhaps long years of pursuing him in times past had finally changed Josef's tactics to some degree. He remembered fondly the first time he personally encountered the earth elemental that Josef had swayed to his cause in his second encounter with Josef and a spell duel ensued between the pair.

Braden sat in the seclusion of his chamber and ran through his mind both of the recent battles he had witnessed from afar for a considerable amount of time. Of note he was most pleased with the performance of Adley. Previously he had thought of him as no more than an above average warrior. Even after Adley had dispatched the wild newborn that Braden had released upon the farms surrounding Lanos years ago to give the Castan soldiers something to do. Now he had taken down an arguably superior foe in the form of the very large and powerful silver dragonborn. He would have to rethink his feelings further on Adley in the years to follow.

Oran fought well as always as he relived the memory of the fight with the witches, but perhaps Oran was slowing a step, as he had feared. In times past that one blast of magic that took him from the battle temporarily would never have happened. Thankfully the emerging prospect in the form of Havander was there to help out the despicable, yet oddly charming, little thief, Willem.

Of all the members and companions surrounding The Silver Guard, Braden was least impressed with Havander and Willem, though he could not count out their skillsets. They were impressive but the thought of a young mage like Havander wielding Etburn irked Braden as he assumed it would lead to inflating Havander's already large ego. Not only that but Braden knew the real Markus Etburn and had fought against the dangerous elemental on a couple of occasions alongside Josef. It did not seem right to him that Etburn was in the hands of anyone besides Josef. The two of them had formed The Silver Guard and now apparently Josef believed this boy was worthy of being his successor.

All in all he concluded that the newly formed Silver Guard was impressive and with Marcus growing quickly, perhaps they would be stronger than ever, once he met his full potential. In any case Braden looked forward to watching one of his most particularly interesting games for many years to come.

EPILOGUE

S LAVES, BOTH DWARF and human alike, shielded their eyes or turned away entirely as Brosa of Drae and Jhaeros Drae passed by their position en route to have a conversation with their master. No one wanted to earn the wrath of these two dangerous drow especially the three fingered scarred one and his horrible gauntlet hanging from his waist.

As they passed the living quarters being expanded upon for the drow, especially the nobility of House Drae, Brosa was pleased to see them taking shape more everyday. In the last year many of the projects taking shape in their secret underground complex were coming to fruition; including the huge double doors, which lead to the long tunnel that was the exit to the outside world and the horrible sunlight on the surface. Though Brosa had not clearly seen the need for such fortifications, as no one knew where they were located, he was impressed with the craftsmanship of their dwarf slaves.

The pair of drow stopped their advance towards their master's quarters and walked over to the ledge, which doubled as the main walkway outside of their living quarters and an important vantage point to oversee the overall construction efforts going on below. Back to their right the newly finished double doors could be seen and were hanging open as it was still daylight outside and many of the human slaves were outside doing their part for the drow efforts underway. Back directly in front of them the main work floor was bustling with slaves going about their work with drow and orc slave masters wielding their whips over them, ready to punish any not meeting their potential. Beyond the work floor the fires of the distant forges could be seen fully ablaze and to their left the slave quarters and the shaft entrance to the mines further underground seemed to be in order as carts of crushed rock and ore emerged on rail carts being pushed and pulled along their tracks by their numerous slaves.

Satisfied with the scene before them the pair moved on to the meeting with their master. The worked stone on the long path they walked cut back away from the work area directly after a large area that had been worked away to serve as an observation area large enough for their master to stand upon with plenty of room to maneuver when he was in his true form. The path that lead beyond that and through the large, naturally shaped stone under the mountain stopped in its nicely worked stonework and once again turned into a more conventional looking cave with rough edges and stalactites hanging at various locations above them from the high ceiling.

Gone too was the light from the many torches and forges so momentarily Brosa and Jhaeros' vision switched to that of their night vision before once again adjusting when light from other sources ahead of them, emanating from their destination, appeared in the distance.

After passing two drow sentries posted at the edge of their master's chamber and standing in front of huge wards carved into the stone, Brosa and Jhaeros found themselves on worked stone once again. On their left as they continued on their path they passed by the magic workshop carved directly into the rock face, where young drow wizards and priestesses called home mostly due to their endless work and long hours within the confines of its walls. Strange noises emanated from within that workshop coming from magical creatures crammed into cages and spells being cast by their drow brethren.

At last the pair rounded the last large corner and across the vast circular chamber, their master in drow form and Camuzen Drae, were at work. Amid the large desk were various scrolls, tomes, maps and various instruments to aid in the magical inscriptions they worked on.

As they ended their approach, side by side, Deathmar the Black didn't bother looking up from his scroll he was working on but Camuzen stood up to full height and inspected the pair of assassins. Brosa briefly locked stares with Camuzen but it did not do well to show any kind of threat toward the head wizard of House Drae. Camuzen was brother to their matron mother and his skills in arcane magic had earned him the honor of being one of the most feared mages in all of Veszdor.

Brosa turned his gaze to his left and admired the large portal they used for trips back to their home city and remembered a time when they used it for the gathering of slaves throughout the continent of Drilain. He often thought of those times when looking at the portal. Old memories still haunted him as he remembered losing the two smallest digits of his right hand.

For a drow the time that had passed was not so long ago. Feuds between drow lasted for centuries and were a constant form of life for the militaristic and murderous drow societies of the underdark. Brosa longed for a return to the surface to avenge the wounds he suffered against the human swordsman, Oran Righe.

After those encounters with The Silver Guard, Brosa's reputation had been damaged for some time. It took him a couple years to regain the fear and respect of his fellow drow. In order to do that he had to change his fighting style to a large degree, in his estimation, but a change nonetheless that had been most productive in his ascent to greatness once more. Before his encounter with Oran Righe, he fought two handed with scimitars, one in each hand, as many drow did. Now with the loss of two of his fingers he could not secure a hold on a scimitar properly to defend against a seasoned drow warrior.

In order to compensate for this deficiency he had crafted for himself by skilled drow armorers and sword makers a gauntlet of sorts. The excellent weapon was actually a kind of punching dagger with excellent drow steel fully encompassing the grip below the duel blades at its end that protruded from the surrounding armor parallel to one another and curved inward ever so slightly to give the appearance of two overly large talons. When worn the gauntlet fit perfectly and locked into the matching set of armor running down the length of his right arm from shoulder to wrist. Along the bracer were two thick parallel blades that ran all the way to the elbow. Their true purpose was not to be used as blades, though they could serve that function, but rather to be used to block. The entirety of his armor on his right arm was heavily warded and he wielded it as though it were a shield in his improved fighting style.

Other drow competitors of his thought it ridiculous and would surely slow Brosa down, which it did to some extent, but the asset was not truly having to worry about blows from light weapons leaving opportunities for killing blows with his always quick and still dangerous scimitar he wielded in his left hand. A few drow found this out in his ascent to being number one among the assassins of House Drae once more.

Also very different from before was his relationship with Jhaeros Drae. In the past the two had feuded, almost coming to blows on several occasions. Jhaeros' attitude towards him had shifted dramatically after seeing what was done to those who had gotten in Brosa's way and he was a favorite of their master, Deathmar. Brosa too found it advantageous to put aside past differences, as it became a necessity to have an actual family member of House Drae backing him at times. Though they would never truly trust one another, their working relationship had been advantageous to the pair and even lower class females steered clear of the pair; something few females did for any male.

"What is it?" Deathmar finally asked after making his pair of assassins wait a considerable amount of time while he finished his latest scrollwork. He did not look up however and remained fixed on the parchment, examining every letter for perfection.

"My Lord, we have run into a problem with production?" Brosa answered taking lead as he most often did when dealing with their master.

"Explain yourself."

Brosa was direct as possible. He knew Lord Deathmar did not like skirting the root of the matter. *"Veleli Drae is causing an issue with our slave numbers. She is torturing and killing far too many of them. At this rate production times will decrease dramatically."*

"Kill her." Deathmar said quite bluntly and without a seconds worth of thought.

Camuzen looked across the corner of the table to his partner. Veleli was his sister after all and although she was a royal pain, she was the next in line to be named Matron Mother of House Drae if Sedori Drae's daughters did not live long enough to fight for their mother's position.

Sensing the tension in the room Deathmar finally looked up from his work and Camuzen's gaze shifted downward immediately. Though they were partners in their efforts away from the underdark, Deathmar was the true power behind the coveted seat of matron mother. A power that Camuzen, although powerful himself, did not want to test.

"I said kill her." Deathmar repeated. *"Sedori Drae will not lament long the absence of her fat sister or Veleli's efforts to kill her daughters. That is the reason she was sent here in the first place. To slow Veleli's ambitions and so Sedori can think she has some say in what goes on here but she has many spies beyond that of her sister. Kill her immediately. I will not have her alter our plans. It is imperative we do not slow for we are still years away from completion and I do not wish to hinder our efforts with further trips to the surface at this time."*

"My Lord, Matron Mother Sedori will send another true family member female to replace her." Camuzen responded.

"Good. She can send that lowly niece. The daughter of her already dead sister. You know the one I mean. She is far more beautiful and pleasant to look at, unlike Veleli." Deathmar insisted.

"Kerel Drae." Jhaeros responded.

Kerel is Jhaeros' sister and only other surviving direct family member of his after their mother's death at the hands of Veleli Drae. He was pleased with her appointment and even more so that it was he and Brosa who would finally avenge his mother's death. He would have to make it a point to Brosa that the final blow must be struck by him.

"Thank you Jhaeros. Now you two see to it immediately and inform me of any further complications. I want work steady now and always." Deathmar finished and then went back to examining his latest scroll.

Brosa and Jhaeros exited quickly following their meeting. Both had a hitch in their step as having permission to kill a female drow was rare but Jhaeros was pleased with the outcome beyond compare to that of Brosa.

Made in the USA
Middletown, DE
18 January 2016